**When the stakes are this high,
only one man can cover the bet . . .**

Somewhere, amid the tarnished glitter of Las Vegas, is an atomic bomb so powerful that it could level the city in seconds. Billionaire Francis Carrington Shaw is willing to gamble for it. Ruthless international terrorists pursue it. And hard-nosed weapons dealer Sam Goines dies trying to sell it.

No one is strong enough to own it—or even find it. No one, except the man they call Preacher.

But time is running out. And Preacher may be the next to fold with the lethal hand of . . .

Aces & Eights

Don't miss *Preacher*—also by Ted Thackrey, Jr.

Jove Books by Ted Thackrey, Jr.

PREACHER
ACES & EIGHTS

Watch for

KING OF DIAMONDS
Coming in December!

ACES & EIGHTS

TED THACKREY, JR.

JOVE BOOKS, NEW YORK

ACES & EIGHTS

A Jove Book / published by arrangement with
the author

PRINTING HISTORY
Jove edition/July 1989

ISBN: 0-515-10080-3

Jove Books are published by The Berkley Publishing Group,
200 Madison Avenue, New York, New York 10016.
The name ''JOVE'' and the ''J'' logo
are trademarks belonging to Jove Publications, Inc.

PRINTED IN THE UNITED STATES OF AMERICA

10 9 8 7 6 5 4 3 2 1

A SERMON

Dear friends,

Our text this morning comes from the Book of Psalms, thirty-seventh chapter, thirty-fifth and thirty-sixth verses:

"I have seen the wicked in great power, and spreading himself like a Green Bay Tree.

"Yet he passed away, and, lo, he was not: yea, I sought him, but he could not be found."

The Psalmist—King David, according to the tradition—seems to warn us here of the transitory nature of power, of its vanity, especially when held and exercised by those who would misuse it. David was a man who knew about such things. For he was himself a man of great power . . .

1

THE VOICE OF Heaven on Earth uttered a blistering oath and then fell silent, appalled as much at the words as at their cause.

I couldn't really blame him.

He had just dropped $45,000—funds no doubt already consecrated in his heart to propagation of the Word among the heathen—on a poker hand he absolutely knew could not lose. A thing like that can be embarrassing. And expensive.

But that's the trouble with cheating at poker: Every now and then you run into someone who cheats better and quicker than you do. I sat still and let him think it over.

The Voice of Heaven, also known as the Very Reverend Holroyd Josiah Gillespie, D. D., was no smarter than I remembered from the days when he was just plain ''Holy Joe'' Gillespie, a lean and hungry sometime Bible salesman from North Carolina studying for the ministry in the class ahead of me at Sewanee. He had been a smooth, flannel-mouthed, self-hypnotized shitkicker in those days, and he was no better now—except that now he was rich, internationally famous, semi-universally beloved, walking around in elevator cowboy boots built to accentuate the slim height that was now a part of his carefully tended persona . . . and the proud possessor of a dandy bag of second-rate card tricks.

Watching him use them on the table-stakes poker players assembled in the living room of one of the $5,000-a-day suites that crown the Sultan's Turret at the Scheherazade International in Las Vegas, however, left me with a decision to make.

Cheating is always stupid. It can get you killed. Worse, it is the recognized mark of an incompetent player. A chump. No one who can really play that game has need of the Arts Arcane; he can win—handsomely—without them.

2

Handling the cheater, on the other hand, calls for a certain amount of finesse.

You have options:

You can walk away. It's not heroic and it's not profitable, but no one ever got shot by finding a good acceptable reason to leave the game, and I have done it often enough when I've been a stranger in town.

Or you can accuse the cheater. It's the first thing that occurs to most players, and the most natural. But exposing the cheat makes you the bearer of bad tidings—with all the attendant negatives—and can get you killed if the accused player has more friends in the room than you do. Count carefully before opening the mouth.

Or you can cheat back . . . which is what had happened to the Voice of Heaven on Earth, and I think it may have been a novel experience for him, because after letting fly with the single expletive, he sat tongue-tied and awe-struck as I raked in the dove-colored poker chips he knew should have been his own.

His world had tilted.

The Great Zot had belched.

The poor bastard simply could not see what had gone wrong . . .

This game was seven card stud, played without a professional dealer, and the Voice had more or less deftly stacked the deck on the pickup to deal me what was supposed to look like a world-class betting hand—queens over deuces full—in the sure and certain confidence that I would bet the sky against his two exposed eights and single king. Since he had also taken the trouble to give himself another kowboy and another eight in the hole, his hands had already been cupped to rake in the pot when I turned my final card to expose a fourth deuce.

The look on his face was almost worth framing.

And his audible reaction was almost too good to be real. Years had passed and seasons had ripened and the world had moved and altered around him, but poor old Holy Joe still hadn't learned to engage his brain before operating his jawbone. Never an unexpressed thought.

"But . . . you cheated!" he said.

And suddenly the room was totally silent.

I froze with my hands in sight on top of the table and let the words hang there in the filtered air for a moment or two.

The Scheherazade is one of the newer pleasure domes on the

Strip; sound insulation has come a long way in the past few decades and all the forces of art and science had been marshaled to assure its guests of immunity from unwanted auditory stimuli. Not even the air conditioning was permitted a whisper. So there was no competition for the words of accusation, or for what followed.

"Is that a fact, now?" I said, smiling at him when I decided the moment had gone on long enough. "What makes you think so, my friend?"

It was an offer of amnesty.

He could still back off. I hadn't sunk the hook yet, and the rest of the scene didn't have to be played. He hesitated, and for a moment I thought he might have more sense than I'd imagined. But no.

"That last two of spades," he said, his voice rising to a pitch of righteous wrath. "It wasn't in your hand!"

Oh, well, hell . . .

Poker-playing styles are as individual as a personal signature or the shape of a head. Or fingerprints. A working professional learns to recognize each pattern, categorize it, and turn to his own account the insights gained. It takes a little extra time and effort, but these are always well repaid and I had been quietly going about that part of my business when the larcenous quality of the Voice of Heaven's game became too evident to ignore.

He wasn't even very good at it.

Even so, I had taken my time deciding how to approach the problem and then waiting for just the right opportunity.

I had realized from the moment I saw him execute a rather clumsy pull-through—whip one-half of a riffled pack through the other at an angle and then slap them together to nullify the shuffle and the previous cut at the same time—that he wasn't the brightest cheat I'd ever met. But I really had thought he might be smarter than that, so I let the silence hang again for longer than it should have in the hope that he might change his mind and do something intelligent.

But he didn't, and at last I was forced to give him the only response possible under the circumstances.

"Well, now," I said, still smiling at him. "Well, now—and just how would you happen to know what cards I had in my hand, sir . . . ?"

Rational thought finally began to percolate through whatever he was using for brains, and he halted, balanced insecurely at the

verge of whatever he had intended to say next. I had asked a
question to which there was only one possible answer, and the
reply was necessarily damning. He realized that now, and so did
everyone else at the table.

What he didn't know was how to back out.

So I decided to help.

A little.

The deal had passed to me and I did a workmanlike job of
collecting the cards, seemingly at random, aligning them hori-
zontally, and shuffling.

"We live," I said, smiling brightly to center his attention on
my face and on what I was saying while my hands lived lives of
their own, "in a world of wonders . . ."

Sorting the cards to re-create the last hands was no real
problem.

"Mysteries surround us. Miracles abound. We accept them as
our due, never voicing the questions that ought certainly to be
our constant concern . . ."

Individually, or even strung into phrases, the words were
empty of meaning. But their tone and cadence were calculated.
And effective.

Saiminjutsu is a slightly arcane Oriental version of hypnotism,
a method of tuning the mind's own defenses against it. Properly
applied, it can achieve more than any unsupported combination
of kata. But it requires the full power of *shinki kiitsu*, that unity
of soul, mind, and body that is the very essence of the martial
arts.

I invoked that unity now, grounding its power in my own
hara, to hold him thoughtless and pliable.

"Why is this so? How can we bear to live lives of unexamined
context? How dare we sojourn alone and unarmored on the
darkling plain that is the arena of this earthly existence . . . ?"

The Voice of Heaven wanted to speak now, to throw off the
stifling mind-blanket. But it was too late. He sat still, listening in
silence, mouth slightly agape.

Good.

Good . . .

I went on talking, looking at him, letting the moment build
while I ran through two false shuffles, passed the cards to my
left for a cut, and then nulled it on the pickup.

No one seemed to notice.

"We see here the eternal mysteries of life itself," I said.

"Who are we? Where are we? How long will we stay and where will we go?

"And there are the more temporal concerns as well, smaller questions, but no less demanding of answers: What work shall we do in the world and what pay shall we ask . . . and how did that fourth deuce get into the hand of the tinhorn crossroads hustler when we were at such pains to be sure it went to the man across the table . . . ?"

As intended, the final words broke the spell.

It was time.

"The answer," I said, "is in the sight and smell and touch of the world around us, the world of here and now."

Some people are more suggestible than others.

The Voice of Heaven was awake again, no longer lulled by the cadences of my voice, alive to the dangers of the situation surrounding him. But he could not seem to force his eyes away from my face, and I found myself marveling at his apparent lack of personal force. Of *mana*. Without a superabundance of it, how had he ever managed to mesmerize the multitude in those nightly televised prayer meetings?

A contradiction. But it made things easier; I stilled my center and concentrated upon void.

"These," I said, squaring the deck in my left hand and gripping it with the forefinger crooked a bit under the forward edge, "are the memory of wonder and the illusion of reality . . ."

I began to deal, sensing rather than hearing the Voice of Heaven's sharp intake of breath as he saw the cards arrive in front of him—two down, five up—re-creating the hands we had just played, but in reverse.

He had the kings and deuces I had played; I had aces and eights, with a final down-card yet to be dealt into each hand.

"Accept reality," I said.

The Voice looked at me as if he had never heard such a proposition advanced before. He was fully awake again now, but the suggestions he had accepted moments ago had done their work; his eyes and his mind were wide and uncritical.

Open to wonder.

"Accept the world as it is, and your own place in it . . ."

I turned my hole cards to expose the king and eight he had thought would win for him.

"The concealed cards in your hand," I said, "are a queen and a ten . . . which leaves you backing a full house, just as it did me a moment ago. A good hand. But one that will lose to the stronger combination of aces over eights . . .''

I glanced quickly around the table.

No problems.

The Voice of Heaven seemed to be the only one who couldn't see what was about to happen . . . and that was just as it should have been. He was still staring at the cards when I looked back.

"The only card that can beat me," I said, "is the fourth deuce. And it is under your left hand."

He blinked.

His left hand was flat on the table beside the cards I had just dealt, and he knew there was nothing under there. There couldn't be. But things were going wrong for him; the world was tilting at an angle to the accustomed order. He simply couldn't resist the urge to look.

Hesitantly, carefully, he raised the hand.

"Is it there?" I asked.

"No."

"Are you sure?"

"Yes!"

The hand was still in the air, poised but forgotten in the exchange of words.

Cham-Hai, the semi-meditational state of becoming one with the environment, had begun, and the world around me was beginning to slow down as my own perceptions of it increased in speed.

Power was there in the belly, ready and waiting. I had shifted the grip down a finger, and my left hand now concealed the deck from his eyes, allowing the right fore and middle fingers to clamp hard on the top card, awaiting the burst of electric energy that would send them into action.

"It is there," I said.

"No, it isn't!"

"Slap the table with your hand . . . now!"

The last word was the trigger. It brought his eyes back to my face for a single instant, and it was as though the world had suddenly gone into stasis with only my hands left alive.

No magic; no miracle. It takes practice, but an hour or two of effort will make the move quick enough and accurate enough to be effective. Coupled with the personal acceleration that is perceived as a slowing of the world, it can have the quality of true magic. But it is only psychology. And physics.

In the instant that his hand began to descend, the top card from the pack was also in motion, winging flatly across the two feet of space that separated us. And by the time his palm was flat on the table once more, the card was under it. I hadn't breathed or moved anything except the two fingers that held the card. No one else had so much as twitched.

"Accept reality," I said again.

He blinked.

The impact of his hand on the table had slightly and momentarily deadened his sense of touch. He didn't know the card was there yet.

"Accept the world as it is," I said. "And accept the gift of awe and wonder . . ."

Another moment passed before he was ready.

But when he finally raised the hand for another peek, the reaction was all that anyone might have hoped.

And more.

The deuce of spades has no face.

But the grinning countenance of the devil himself could have had no greater impact.

Some people are born to accept the evidence of their senses; others are not. The Reverend Holroyd Josiah Gillespie had lived his life in a world where objects at rest stayed at rest and those in motion stayed in motion, a world where the sound of his voice and the power of his personality produced a pleasant kind of reality that he could accept. A world of his own making, where his card tricks always worked and nobody objected because the Almighty willed it so.

But this world was different. It was a place of wrongness, a universe at odds with all past experience, a threatening place where inanimate objects had minds of their own.

And it was just too much. A single timorous sheep-bleat was the best the Voice of Heaven on Earth could offer in exculpation as he did the only thing a man of his background and persuasions could do in the circumstances.

He rejected the experience.

Eyes uprolled as if to examine the ceiling and mouth slack, the sometime back country Bible-hustler from North Carolina sagged sideways in the chair and then rolled awkwardly out of it to sprawl full-length on the camphor-scented carpet. His jaw clenched and relaxed once or twice and I wondered, fleetingly, if he might be in danger of choking on his own tongue.

Not that I gave a damn.

The spell of silence that had descended upon the other players in the moment after the Voice of Heaven's initial accusation still hung thick and stifling over the room.

They had come to play poker, not to be entertained by a clown act.

Still, it isn't every day you are privileged to see a professional blatherskite wag his jaw without talking, and the unexpected discovery that a media icon—spiritual leader of a television ministry estimated (even by skeptics) at upward of fifteen million souls—was also a sleazy little card cheat might be worth the price of admission.

And there was a bonus.

His trip to the floor had been bumpier than I'd thought—and one of the bumps had dislodged something from the breast pocket of his coat. A small, neat packet of white powder lay forlorn on the carpet beside him, and its mate could be glimpsed peeking out from the space between lapel and shirtfront.

It explained a lot.

Or maybe it didn't. At any rate, Sam Goines was not pleased.

"Preacher . . ." he said.

"That's what they call me."

He did not speak again, but he was still communicating and I heard every word of it. As he knew I would.

Lots of people call me Preacher.

The name fits and it's easy to remember. But not everyone knows that it's not entirely because of the black suit and string tie that are my poker-playing uniform. Sam's silent monologue was a rebuke, not subtle and not accidental, and there were replies I might have offered. But I kept them to myself.

If complaints were in order, he probably had a right to them.

He was a friend, someone who had been to see the elephant. Once upon a time—back before the beginning of recorded history, it seemed now—we had been close, protecting each other's backs in a world made of broken glass and sharp objects. That alliance, and the reasons for it, had passed long since into dim memory. But friendship had not, and this session had been arranged as a kind of ten-year reunion. The boys in autumn. Sam had set up the game, selected the players, and included me among them as an act of amity, an evocation of times long past but well remembered. And now I had flattened one of the guests and perhaps offended the others.

On the whole, though, I can't say he had any real cause for complaint—and the Voice of Heaven might even have glimpsed in it the protecting hand of the Almighty.

Down there on the floor, the larceny-hearted bastard was safe.

And that was a lot more than you could say for the rest of us.

We were all sitting upright, exposed, and taken entirely by surprise a moment later when the double doors to the VIP suite exploded in a ruin of splinters and sound to admit two men wearing dark workmen's jumpers and stocking masks, who opened fire on us with mini–Uzi submachine guns.

A SERMON (Continued)

Power, for this ancient ruler, had been a matter of violence, always. He had come to his throne by violence, and he spread his kingdom by violence, and he remained a violent and wrathful man all the days of his life.

In this respect, he is a man of our time as well as of his own.

For we live in a world of violent events . . .

2

ONLY HEROES ARE required to be heroes; the rest of us are exempt. My first instinct was to hit the dirt and roll toward darkness. Humankind survived its infancy by an inborn tendency to flee from loud noises and unexpected visitors; run now and think later. Its claws may be sharper than yours.

But time means change and change means learning.

The modern world has developed all kinds of situations where instinct must be subdued in aid of staying alive, and I had that in mind as I lunged forward—in the direction of the nearer of the two stutter-gun mechanics—instead of joining the general scramble to the rear.

Fully automatic weapons have a logic all their own.

So do closed rooms.

Escaping from just one Uzi in the hands of just one competent user can pose a real problem when the field of fire is unrestricted and cover virtually nonexistent. Getting away from two of the damn things is a labor that admits of no solution whatever within the realm of sane and considered action—and therefore must be attacked, like any truly impossible project, with total insanity.

Right up my alley.

And I had an extra advantage: The world and I were already moving at different speeds.

The little scene with the Voice of Heaven on Earth had put me in an unusual frame of mind for a man who has been playing poker all night. I was alert, reflexes at peak and primed for intense effort, with senses and perceptions at ultra pitch. Everything around me still seemed to be in slow motion.

The unannounced entrance of two machine gunners, therefore, played itself out almost leisurely from my point of view and gave me far more time for reflection and decision than I might otherwise have had.

12

I used it as well as I could.

First a little distraction: I sent the poker table flying toward the gunner farthest from me. The shower of cards, chips, ashtrays, and drinks, kept him busy for a moment and left me free to deal with his colleague.

Form is much in the martial arts, and for classic performance the move that I made—a forward roll to remain under the general line of fire before ending on my feet with arms crossed to deliver a double kite—should have been accompanied by *kiai*, the deep-chested shout intended to transfix one's opponent and to intensify one's personal force.

But I attacked in silence. The *kata* of the martial arts are intended for close combat, with the exception of those few that may involve evasion or harmless interception of hand-and bow-powered missiles. Firearms at any range outside the reach of an arm are all more or less beyond consideration. A no-no, Hollywood chop-socky notwithstanding. And the kind of firearms that cycle 950 nine-millimeter Parabellum rounds per minute are definitely in that category. Machine gunners, therefore, become accustomed to the standard reactions of flight and interposition when dealing with unarmed prey.

Targets that attack bare-handed are the stuff of dreams. Of nightmares . . .

Faced with such a situation, a gunman can find in himself doubts and hesitations that he thought he had put aside long ago, and the target's best move is to keep him thinking that way as long as possible. This time it worked well enough to bring my hands within range, but not well enough to end the engagement then and there. Both my kites missed. The one intended to crush the intruder's larynx broke his collarbone instead, while the blow I'd hoped might stop his heart did no more than loosen his grip on the Uzi.

But that was sufficient.

A burst of fire that might otherwise have turned my head into pink mist rattled harmlessly into the ceiling and I was able to take the weapon with me, breaking his right forefinger in the process, before beginning a second roll in the direction of the other gunman, who was swiveling in my direction after evading the table.

He was quicker and smarter; instead of firing at the spot where I had been—the reaction I had hoped to see—he swung the metal stock of his Uzi toward my oncoming head and almost connected before I was able to parry with the weapon I had taken from his partner.

That was bad, too.

The metallic clangor of the colliding weapons was something from the known world. Real. It shattered the tenuous fabric of illusion that had slowed and confused the intruders and left me facing the pair of them on even terms. The one who was still armed pivoted like a bullfighter to avoid the rush to which I was now physically committed. I turned a shoulder under to deflect myself to the right and used momentum to lend emphasis to that most ancient and effective Oriental maneuver known vulgarly as a Kick in the Formal Dances.

It was as subtly efficacious as always.

The gunman screamed, folded at the middle, almost dropped his Uzi—and gave me a moment or two for recovery and reflection.

I needed all the moments I could get. The man now clutching his midsection was still armed and therefore still had to be considered the more dangerous of the pair, but it was his un- armed companion who now constituted the true threat. He was not where he was supposed to be. I had left him nursing a ripped and fractured finger when I went for the other Uzi-bearer and had hoped to see him in the same position when I turned with the captured weapon in my hand.

But he was gone.

Where?

The room was now virtually innocent of obstruction, chairs and tables all swept aside in the general confusion. No place to hide.

The shattered double doors, however, were still open and I thought fleetingly of rushing through them in hot pursuit. But not for more than a second.

I'm crazy, not stupid.

Besides, there was still the problem of the remaining gunner. The Uzi dangled, apparently forgotten, as he remained in the classic *September Morn* pose of true visceral distress. But he was still alive, awake—and dangerous—as I discovered when I moved to snatch the Israeli chopper from his grasp.

"Fuck you, asshole!"

They were the first words he had spoken, and I found them almost touching in their earthy familiarity. My kind of folks. My feelings were almost brotherly as I watched him swing the Uzi once again in the direction of my head and force himself—with an effort and control that must have been expensive—to stand erect.

I dodged easily, and wondered if perhaps he had forgotten that the thing in his hand was intended more for shooting than for batting practice. I certainly hadn't, and my own fingers were already curling around the rear pistol grip of the stutter gun I'd stolen from his partner when I understood the reason he hadn't tried to blow me away.

The Uzi is a clip-fed weapon, and he was using the standard thirty-two-cartridge combat box. He hadn't fired because the clip was empty, and now he was trying to release it from the pistol grip and insert another. His movements were cool, controlled, and efficient. Behind the stocking mask, his eyes seemed to widen and bulge, fixing on the center of my face as the mesh-flattened mouth thinned to a hard line. The world began to slow.

Oh, this one was good.

Professional.

Deprived of all other weapons, he was using the *mana* of his own gaze in an all-out effort to hypnotize me—hold me in situ long enough for him to get the fresh clip out of his jumper and into the weapon. And it might have worked. Even filtered through nylon mesh, his eyes were compelling, filled with the power of his persona. It was a good show, worth paying to see. But not worth dying for.

I snapped myself back into the real world.

"Freeze," I said, bringing the ugly little snout of my stolen weapon up into firing position as I released the safety.

The button man's hand stopped moving, but I could sense no attitude of resignation or surrender. He looked at me for a moment and then at the hand-chopper. He was thinking, and if I'd had sense enough to do the same I would have used the time to jam the Uzi into the still-tender area of his midsection, just for luck. But firearms are a snare and a delusion.

They give the impression of power and control, channel thought into a single straight line.

And that's how funeral directors get rich.

"Fuck you," the hitter said again, and threw the Uzi at my head. I ducked, curled my finger around the trigger, aimed for the legs to make sure we would have a chance to talk later . . . and found out why he had seemed so confident. As he had suspected, my ammo clip was as empty as his own.

Well, hell and harpsichords . . .

I made a quick grab in his direction, reflecting darkly on the vanity of all human works and earthly endeavor, and wasn't at all surprised when I missed. He was already in motion, making for the shattered glass double doors that led to the balcony, and I was going to be too late to stop him, though I couldn't see why he wanted to go out there.

The balcony was narrow, surrounded on three sides by Nevada night air, and thirty-two stories above the earth. The tower penthouse suites are built on an aesthetically interesting overhang that would rule out any thought of through-the-window-below movie heroics.

But he hadn't planned to go down.

Our button man was, it seemed, an acrobat of sorts, and it was becoming increasingly clear that preparations for tonight's operation had been both thorough and competent.

The Sultan's Turret of the Scheherazade is designed to look medieval Eastern, pointed and moody-looking, from ground level. But its top is really flat, and the architectural grace note that makes it look otherwise is an overhang that provides partial shade for top-floor balconies.

Disregarding what must have been serious complaint from his battered testicles, the fleeing gunman took two quick steps toward the railing—and leapt into space, catching himself at the last moment on the edge of the overhang. Heels together and toes pointed, he began an easy swing that was intended to use his momentum to skin the cat in a back somersault onto the roof tiles.

I could hear the sound of a helicopter approaching at flank speed.

Their escape vehicle . . .

His partner, I realized, would already have reached the rooftop pickup spot, and I had to admire the thinking that had gone into the evening's program. If all had proceeded according to plan, it should have worked like a watch . . . and even with all that had gone wrong, it almost worked.

But almost isn't even nearly good enough.

What happened wasn't the fault of the planner or of the man who had to carry it out. His groin was still throbbing and the rhythm was wrong, the sense of sureness and power suddenly less reliable. He was plotting each movement now, forced to use the conscious mind in a way that can inhibit a trained athlete by a critical fraction—and can make all the difference.

The upward swing halted, achingly, in mid-turn with the toes not quite ready to complete their arc toward the surface of the overhang . . . and then the right hand slipped, altering balance.

Even in darkness I could appreciate the muscle-tearing effort to hang on, to force the stunt through. But it was no go.

There was a grunt of pain as the right hand slipped, and then a sob that mingled rage and fear in equal parts as the full weight of the body loosened the left hand's grip on the roof edge. An instant later he was in free-fall.

But only for about nine feet.

I had been too late to prevent him from reaching the balcony and beginning the acrobatics that might have left him free on the overhang. But I was just in time for the finale. My foot hooked solidly around one of the railing supports, and my hand shot out to close around his left wrist as he began the windmilling descent to Gehenna.

Hara.

The individual is a whole that can be directed; I seized the moment to center every ounce of power in the fingers of my right hand, and even so the sudden shock of his full weight—doubled and more by the accelerating force of gravity—came scraping and scratching to the very edge of being too great to bear.

But then the fall stopped.

And it was over.

We held that position in tableau for a long moment, my legs and body braced against the anodyzed aluminum of the balcony railing, one arm rigid in space beyond with a mass of human terror and surprise at its end. Ballet by Hitchcock; choreography by Stallone.

A moment to remember.

But too good to last.

"Hi, there!" I said. "In a hurry, or can you hang around for a while?"

Sometimes I'm such a cornball . . .

The face that looked up at me was still distorted by the stocking mask, but the depths of its eyes burned with tiny hell-points.

I let him dangle.

My sense of time had slowed again; the acceleration that had enabled me to move quickly and accurately in the moments just after the initial attack was gone now and I was back to living the minutes and seconds at the same rate as everyone else. The quiet center was spent and exhausted.

But, moment by moment, I was now able to force the world back into a semblance of order, to reestablish control. The noise of the helicopter above us helped; it made reality of what was, essentially, disorder and insanity. I thought of a card from the Greater Arcana—Number 12, the Hanged Man—and brought its image to bear on the man suspended below me.

It helped a little.

The power that had centered momentarily in my right hand was redistributing itself after the near-overload performance, and I was able to use a part of it to reach out, probing for his *wa*, the personal aura and magnetism that surround all living beings. I found it without difficulty. And was immediately sorry.

I had expected the chill of terror; the dream-sweat that accompanies the sudden and unexpected perception of imminent death.

But his *wa* was hot. Marveling, even in recoil, I forced myself to face and evaluate the roiling nova of rage and frustration—and something else—that were the soul and center of his being. Fear was there, yes. But it was a prisoner, caged and impotent before the all-embracing authority of malice, centered and focused.

On me.

That was a surprise . . . and a revelation, because hatred of that intensity is not cheap. It does not come on command, and it cannot be bought or commanded.

It requires time. Effort.

And personal acquaintance: The man whose rage and detestation came hammering up in waves of heat could not be a stranger. He knew me and I knew him, and sometime, somewhere, we had been close enough to touch minds.

Yet even this was not enough. The something-else I had sensed at first contact remained between us, flavoring and warping the rest. A crosscurrent almost of friendliness or fellow-feeling mixed with the angry heat of rejection.

Enough. I closed the way that had opened between us and groped for the unity of mind and body that is the essential condition of clear thought.

He knew me, but I still didn't know him.

All right. Worth a thought, but not immediately useful. The rage, however, was a different matter. Not the best. Not perfect. Not what I might have picked off the shelf and not the kind of thing you want to face every wee-hour morning of your life. But serviceable. Utilitarian.

Hatred can be turned to account.

A worthy workman employs the tools at hand . . .

"Long as we've got nothing else to do right now," I said, showing him a bland and friendly smile that I hoped might expand rage to the exclusion of thought, "let's have a chat."

The fire-points of his eyes blazed up, yearning toward me in a lava-flow of virulence.

"I know you didn't mean to be impolite," I went on, coaxing and encouraging the Furies, "but you interrupted our game. You and your partner. I'm sure it wasn't intentional, and to show you I'm a sport, I'm going to let you have a chance to make it up to me. You'd like that, wouldn't you?"

I felt a hesitation.

The waves of energy radiating from below stuttered for a moment, and when they returned they were changed. Fury and hatred were alloyed, now, with speculation. With doubt.

The man below was wondering if I might be crazy.

"What we'll do," I said, helping him to go with that thought, "we'll play us a different kind of game here. Just you and me."

His immediate reaction, not surprisingly, was an overwhelming negative. But I had expected that. Concentrating again on my hand I relaxed its grip for a bare nanosecond, allowing its burden to slip a terrifying half-inch earthward before clamping firm again, and was instantly rewarded by a single breath of cold air . . . a momentary ice-touch, damping the heat of the *wa* before the hellfire flared up again.

"All comfy?"

No answer. So I let the arm swing a little.

"Rock-a-bye baby . . . ."

"Jesus!"

I widened the idiot smile and clucked reprovingly, shaking my head in time with the metronome of his body. "He hears you, son," I said. "Yea, verily! And marks the books of those who take his name in vain! But about our little game: I like the kind where you ask questions and people have to tell the answers or pay a forfeit. Do you like that kind, too?"

Another ration of silence. So I repeated the earlier lesson, allowing him to slip one more millimeter toward death, and this time the reaction was more than could be accepted. Full appreciation of his situation was finally beginning to seep around the adrenalin-laced edges of perception.

One more jolt, I decided, ought to be enough. But I never got to put it to the test.

Suddenly we were out of time.

The noise from the helicopter had gotten louder as it took off from the roof, but I had dismissed it from thought—and that was a mistake. The pilot had something more than escape on his mind, and I realized what it was as he edged the ship crabwise, away from the tower but not in the expected line of quick retreat.

It was a Huey, and in an instant I found myself back on a hillside in Vietnam . . . not as the rifle-bearing grunt I had been, but as the enemy we had stalked even as he stalked us. I was Charlie, black pajamas and all, and the bird hovering near was the heart of darkness, the symbol-made-real of hatred and death. There was a door gunner, and he was lining up the shot.

I understood at once.

Guerrilla disengagement maneuvers—like machine guns and closed rooms—have their own logic. You take with you those who can come. But you do not leave the rest.

"No!"

The single word-sound, expelled from me in a frantic blast of breath and lung power, was enough to alert the dangling man to his danger. But not enough to allow us to do anything about it.

A decade had passed since the last time I heard the peculiar sound of .50-caliber ammunition at close range, but it is not a sound you forget.

The gunner's aim was excellent.

And the shot was easy.

The man below me was dead—and I knew when it happened; the heat became ice and then was nothing at all—before the second burst tore his body free of my grip to fall, limp and tenantless, to the parking lot three hundred feet below.

I scrambled backwards, moving by instinct rather than intention, quickly enough to be out of the way when the gunner put another burst into the penthouse to keep everyone's head down. It was an effective argument and might have done the work as intended but for the decorative genius of the Scheherazade's lighting engineers who had ringed the entire top floor with spotlights whose beams converged in the sky at the far end of the building, illuminating the sky above the hotel . . . and capturing the Huey for a single instant as it clattered away.

The image was compelling. And indelible: N.A.N.G.

Clear, prosaic markings on the side and bottom of the gunship informed the world that one killer had just escaped and another had been summarily executed under the All-American red-and-white-and-blue auspices of the Nevada Air National Guard.

A SERMON (Continued)

We live, indeed, in a world of wonders where deadly fumes fill the sky and poisons spew into the oceans and murder is become the casual sport of children. A world where inconstancy is the only constant, where chance is the only certainty . . .

3

THE FIRST FEW moments after the helicopter was finally out of sight were only an extension of what had gone before—a waiting, to see who would start shooting next.

And then reaction set in.

My hands were bleeding from contact with broken glass and other unfriendly objects, and when I tried to haul myself erect I discovered that it wasn't as easy as I remembered. Ask anyone who has ever survived a firefight. The shakes begin when the shooting ends. And then come the sweats.

Leaning on the track-sprung jamb of what had recently been a heavy glass door, I found myself fighting a sudden lunatic impulse to laugh.

Tables, chairs, cards, chips, broken glass, weapons, bullet holes, assorted wreckage—and money in every denomination except small—were strewn about what had lately been an elegant penthouse suite with a kind of lunatic precision keyed to the presence of three supine bodies and a few wild-eyed survivors now emerging hesitantly from inadequate cover.

Raw material, perhaps, for the brush of a latter-day Bruegel.

Or Gahan Wilson.

But I had come to Las Vegas in aid of financial enhancement—to play a game of high-stakes poker against people who could afford to win or lose with equal grace. A quiet professional exercise, arranged by an old friend and undertaken in the reasonable hope of profit.

Surveying the result, I had to think it was one hell of a way to run a business . . .

Summer is an easy time in the little Sierra town of Best Licks where I live, and until four days ago I had been enjoying it to the limit. But then the letters came.

Three were from banks, informing me that I was broke.

A fourth was from the Department of the Treasury, explaining why.

Income tax is always a problem for anyone who makes all or part of his living from any activity even loosely definable as gambling. He does not dare tell the truth. List your profession as "gambler" or "betting agent" or even "casino operator" and your tax return gets a bright red "RACKETEER" stamp across its front—open invitation to the unwelcome attentions of every government agency from the Secret Service to the FBI, with carbon copies to the State Department just in case you ever need a passport.

So the gamblers have to lie.

I know one former world poker champion who lists his occupation as professional golfer (God knows he is that; never play that man a round at $100 Nassau!) and another who claims to be a billiards instructor; a world-renowned casino boss who had set up and operated gaming operations throughout the Caribbean and Central America went to his grave insisting that he was an educator (he ran a school for blackjack dealers during the last few years of his life), and the number of Las Vegas hustlers who represent themselves as traveling salesmen (you buy and sell the cards, right?) is almost beyond counting.

I call myself a Minister of the Gospel, and I can prove claim to the title.

Sort of.

The room in my house that serves me as office and citadel has a number of items displayed on the wall, including devil masks from Sri Lanka and Madagascar, a handsome and carefully counterfeited treasure map that I keep to remind me that I am not a genius, and a Malay dagger that had to be pried out of an inconvenient spot in my back in the days before I started learning to pay close attention to my surroundings.

There is also a framed certificate declaring to all and sundry that I am ordained a minister of the Universal Life Church, Inc. (Kirby J. Hensley, D.D., president and presiding bishop), and entitled to all privileges and considerations pertaining thereunto.

It is quite legal.

It costs nothing.

You can get one like it by mailing a simple request to church headquarters in Modesto, California.

And it is prominently displayed in the interest of heading off any inquiry that might arise concerning other certificates, dated a few years earlier and hidden elsewhere in the house, attesting to my ordering as deacon and priest of the Protestant Episcopal church in the United States of America.

Not many people remember that such documents exist, and only two of them live in Best Licks. All the others up there accept me as a hypocritical Bible-thumping humbug, and attend my Sunday services at the town's beat-up little church because they believe it's all a part of an elaborate scam invented by their pastor to pry money out of the bureaucrats at various welfare foundations and government agencies.

Actually, the occasional infusions of money that support the annual deficit of the town of Best Licks—and its oddly assorted population—come not from the long-suffering taxpayers or from charitable groups, but from the pastor's poker fortunes.

A satisfactory arrangement, and a long-standing one.

But now the Internal Revenue Service was having an acute attack of curiosity. Someone in the Fresno office had decided there was something decidedly peculiar about the Church of Best Licks, its pastor, and the whilom ghost town in the Sierra. It wanted to ask some questions, and to make sure it got some answers, all bank accounts and other assets of church, town, and pastor had been impounded.

Margery, the electronic genius and majordomo without whom the whole shooting match would have turned back into a pumpkin long ago, gave me the bad news when I returned from a pebble-catching session with our resident *mahayana* master, who had been showing me a brand-new exercise: Hold a pebble on the back of each hand, raise your hands to shoulder level and as far behind you as possible—then move your hands quickly and accurately enough to catch both pebbles in your palms . . . before they have fallen more than three inches.

Great for the reflexes.

But the glow of accomplishment that comes with even the most meager and halting progress evaporated the moment I got back to the office. Margery is aware of where the money really comes from and has too much sense to be impressed—she knows how easily a poker player can get broke, and how often it happens to me. I'm only a winner over the distance; short term is in the laps of the gods and the laws of probability.

"They get it all?" I asked.

Margery shrugged.

"Most of it," she said. "Weren't any letters from the banks in Modesto or San Rafael; I checked by phone and the balances there are still where they should be."

"Not a hell of a lot."

"Better than nothing."

"If you say so . . ."

Neither of us talked again for a while and I used the silence to consider various ways and means, but we both knew the bottom line without any real need for discussion. I was going to have to find a game.

And soon.

Poker is a phenomenon that flourishes from one end of the nation to the other; no city and no town is complete without a regularly attended and socially (if not always legally) accepted game or two. The developing professional can support himself well enough by working a kind of circuit among them, never staying long enough in one location to wear out his welcome and never neglecting a stop for so long as to become a stranger.

While moderately profitable, however, these locally established games usually have built-in betting and raising limits that keep them within the range of acceptable pain for middle-income losers. An indispensable training ground. But the professional who pays his dues and learns his trade must graduate to the arena of table stakes, no-limit play where it is possible to win or lose a young fortune in an evening or two of friendly action.

Such contests are not rare. But they are harder to find than the middle-level kind, and require a certain amount of discreet probing among friendly contacts in the trade—an inquiry here and a word there—to find out who is holding and who is hurting and who is looking for a chance to play some poker.

It can take time, and I was about to make the first of what I knew would have to be several long-distance calls when my own phone rang.

Margery picked it up, said a word or two, and handed it to me. I clamped my palm across the mouthpiece.

"Who?"

She shook her head. "Male," she said, "maybe mid-forties by the voice—said ask you if you'd tried to kill any hospital orderlies lately . . . ?"

I thought it over, and the first name that came to mind, in view of the inquiry, was that of Mistah Dee Tee Price, the sometime demolitions sergeant turned boardroom takeover pirate who had aided and abetted me in various enterprises over the years since our failed attempt on the life of that obnoxious medical corpsman.

But Margery was well acquainted with Dee Tee's east Texas rumble and would have told him to cut the crap.

Which left only one possibility.

"To hell with you, Goines," I said, lifting the receiver to my ear. "We should have set that trap for you instead of the pill-roller."

Sam Goines laughed, and we spent another minute or two exchanging insults in lieu of small talk to bridge the more than ten years since our last conversation. And then he came to the point.

He was putting together a friendly little game—say $100,000 buy-in—and would I care to take a hand?

Well, sir, then, there now . . .

I make it a point never to question the ways and works of the Omnipotent and All-Seeing. Ask and ye shall receive. Knock and it shall be opened unto you. Your Father knoweth ye have need . . . and all these things shall be added. Them as has, gits. Never look a gift game in the mouth, and behold, O ye of little faith.

Amen, bro.

Packing took five minutes and transportation to the nearest major airport took a little longer. But not much, and floating down on the desert metropolis of Las Vegas the following night I had moments of leisure in which to be struck, as always, by the sheer unlikelihood of the place. A town of its size simply does not belong where it is, and no explanation for its existence—its continued prosperity—has ever seemed entirely adequate.

Everyone has his own theory.

One of the more logical was put forward in a television interview a few years ago by a man of thoughtful years and respected credentials (three times poker champion of the world in the days when that title was anchored in reality, and a legendary hand at the game before he was old enough to vote) who had been a fixture in Las Vegas for longer than most people can remember and had better reason than most for appreciation and understanding of the local scene.

But his view was not the sort to make him a local hero. "Look at the faces out there on the street," he said. "Not the ones over on the straight side of town, where they join the PTA and work for a living. I'm talking about the faces out there on the sidewalk in front of the casinos.

"Just look!

"Those faces are hurt. They are damaged and the people that own them are the ruins. The dregs. Every loser and hustler and thief and (bleeping) son of a (bleep) from every part of the country and every part of the world winds up out there. In Las Vegas. All crowded together in the middle of the desert where they can tear each other up and tear themselves up and throw themselves away any fool way they please and nobody will give a good goddam.

"That's why this town is out here where it is.

"And a damn good thing, too. The only other business that this kind of country is good for is maybe testing atom bombs, and by God if they don't do that now, just a few miles away from here, over at the Flats.

"Think for a minute: If you wanted to build something really dangerous like a germ warfare factory, say, where would you put it? In the middle of New York City? Chicago? Los Angeles, maybe? Hell, no! You'd put the filthy thing out here in the desert where it couldn't hurt anything or anyone who matters a damn . . ."

The interview aired on ABC's *Wide World of Sports,* and the Chamber of Commerce people didn't speak to him for a month.

Not that he noticed.

All the same, the town has continued to thrive amid constant predictions of gloom and doom, and a big part of what has happened and is still happening there is visible to the eye. Especially from the air. Especially at night.

To passengers approaching McCarran International, an airport capable of serving a city six times the size of Las Vegas, the massed lights of the town have a nervous and shimmering quality that gives peculiar emphasis to those dark patches near its center. They suggest unfinished business, and this is accurate because Las Vegas is still busily inventing and reinventing itself and its myth as it stumbles into the final decade of the twentieth century.

Just a year or two ago the place was generally believed to have suffered mortal injury when gambling was made legal in the decayed New Jersey seaside resort of Atlantic City. Existence of the new East Coast competitor was expected to cut deeply into the annual "handle" of the casinos, which is the only true and reliable measure of prosperity in the desert of southern Nevada.

And for a time, that is what happened.

Development came to a screeching halt, some of the older and weaker hotels were driven nearly to the wall. The casino at the Aladdin Hotel actually closed for a time, and many of the more prosperous casinos joined a general rush to throw up clones of their Las Vegas entities on or near the Boardwalk.

But then the trend slowed.

And reversed.

Organizers of gambling tours, lifeblood of the successful hotel-casino operation, discovered that their erstwhile eastern high rollers were gradually drifting back toward Nevada. Proximity and easy access notwithstanding, Atlantic City simply did not have and could not seem to acquire the glitzy ambience to which the game-seeking junketeers had become accustomed.

They wanted to go back to the Strip . . . and there, in ever greater numbers, they went.

Las Vegas showrooms that had been on hold, offering cheaply produced revues and "dinner theater" to avoid having to close up entirely, suddenly found themselves able to afford the likes of Johnny Carson and Bill Cosby and Danny DiMarco again . . . and local real-estate operators took their first deep breath in a year or more.

The place had always been boom-or-bust.

The first real settlers, Mormons sent there by Brigham Young, stayed only a couple of years before they were called north again to help defend Deseret from the U.S. Army. The Nevada legislature legalized gambling in Las Vegas and elsewhere throughout the state in 1931, but this only gave official sanction to a known and notorious situation—gaming casinos had been part of the scene ever since the Mormons departed—and the place went almost unmarked until 1905 when the railroad finally deigned to put in a stop there on its line from Salt Lake to Los Angeles. And even then the town had to wait another quarter-century for its first real boom.

In the early 1930s, construction workers from the nearby Boulder Dam project needed a place where they could raise hell on the weekends, and Las Vegas obligingly transformed the area surrounding the railroad station into a town-sized gambling hall-cum-whorehouse that kept right on growing after the dam was finished.

A highway had been built by then, and Hollywood notables were quick to discover the joys of boozing and gambling in a warm and dry climate where almost anything could be delivered to poolside for a price.

At the end of World War II, eastern hoodlum Benjamin ("Don't call him Bugsy—he goes bughouse!") Siegel used stolen materials and mob money to build the first really plush casino on a part of Highway 91 that would become the Strip. But he had only about six months to enjoy it before his partners got tired of his blatant embezzlement and blew him away. Yet he had set a pattern.

From that time forward—state gaming commissions and federal tax investigators and Chamber of Commerce protestations notwithstanding—the mob was in control, and God help anyone who objected.

Not that many did. When the Blanc family set up the Monte Carlo Casino in 1863, they made a deal with the ruling prince that no citizen of Monaco would be allowed to gamble there. With good reason. Any gaming casino that allows local residents to patronize its tables will eventually absorb so much of the local capital that the town will have to find new sources or be pauperized, and the Blancs had been driven from their former lodgment at Bad Homburg, Bavaria, by an aroused citizenry that regarded them as a race of vampires.

But there was no such protective covenant in Las Vegas, and the need for infusions of outside capital was an accepted and ever increasing factor in all local planning.

Syndicate money flowed.

New hotels—each with its attached casino—sprang up as quickly as occasional death threats to the suppliers of building materials and wholesale bribery of union officers could manage.

No federal or state tax accountant was ever able to penetrate the casino counting rooms, which made Las Vegas a prime source of the kind of funds that leave no paper trail, and public image became so important to those who held real power that for nearly two decades almost no one was actually murdered inside the sacred precincts of Clark County . . . though there were occasional unexplained disappearances among the locally prominent, and the circling of buzzards at remote points in the desert did not always indicate the final resting place of a jackrabbit.

All the same, records of the state gaming commission indicated an era of rare purity.

Applicants for casino licenses and point-owners in the hotels came under microscopic scrutiny; conviction for any crime more serious than reckless driving was grounds for rejection (unless the offense was related to gambling; fun is fun, but let's not get unreal), and major crime figures were even barred from entering the hotel-casinos on pain of license revocation.

It looked good.

Some people—an investigating senator or two over the years, and one incredible director of the Federal Bureau of Investigation—may even have believed it. But casino and hotel points did seem to wind up in the unlikeliest hands at times.

A doctor living in Beverly Hills and a lawyer with offices in San Francisco might not seem too far outside the realm of probability; even a movie star or two could be accepted as genuine. But casino points (each point represents one percent of ownership) are worth millions, and even the veriest country cousin might find it difficult to believe that two or three such shares could really be owned by the proprietor of a dress shop in the hotel's shopping mall or the manager of a semi-prosperous secretarial service on the mezzanine.

The gaming commission professed to believe it, though, and has continued to treat such patent nonsense as gospel to the present day.

Some things are just too too profitable to change.

Reclusive billionaire Howard Hughes stirred the locals up more than a little when he moved to town and acquired a clutch of hotel-casinos in the name of his Summa Corporation during the 1960s. A few people saw it as the beginning of a new and semi-legitimate era in Las Vegas's history. But even the most powerful magnates age and go senile and die, and their holdings are administered by mere mortals. And mortals can be had. The good old game of skim-the-take, with its tolerance for "inside" and "outside" casino points, goes on as before, and the gradual evaporation of the eastern threat has brought back the aura of boomtown.

Hughes's place in the town's mythos, once considered unique, was handily re-filled with the arrival of San Francisco inventor–financier–movie magnate Francis Carrington Shaw. His apparent retirement from the financial wars of California—and subsequent entry into the battle pit of real-estate and hotel manipulations around the world's favorite Sin City—added just the yeast of moneyed mystery and madness needed to keep the losers interested.

Not that I object.

People need to live their own lives and are responsible for themselves. Having a gourmand's gobble of the craziness confined to one spot in the desert is a definite advantage for a man who makes his living by playing money games with hopeful lunatics.

I don't make the rules.

For me, it's enough just to figure out what they are this week . . .

A SERMON (Continued)

Yet the words of the Psalm have meaning for us; they are an echo, not of things past but of things to come. Sudden and violent death was a constant of that long-vanished world, as in our own. And so it was of death that the Psalmist sang . . .

4

BUT THE GREAT ZAP is always waiting.

Rules, games, and mythology all dissolved into their cobweb components as I surveyed the general disaster that had overtaken the Scheherazade's most luxurious accommodation. There is no gainsaying a submachine gun.

The decorator would have wept.

Random bullet patterns are purely hell on plaster-and-flocking walls, and imitation Empire furniture is seldom improved by the kind of massive force that can be exerted by a falling human body. All this, however, seemed almost to take on an air of raffish chic in keeping with the room's new color scheme. A spatter pattern of blood had been added to the puce elegance of upholstery, while larger accents in the same vivid hue now adorned the deep pile carpeting.

Three of the poker players were sprawled nearby. But the blood had come from only two of them.

The Voice of Heaven on Earth was unhurt.

He had missed all the fun. Flat on his back, lids still aflutter over uprolled eyes, he had spent the frantic minutes in shock country, well removed from the line of fire, and I found myself stuck with the depressing thought that he might really have the Personal Relationship with the Almighty that he claimed, after all. Philosophies have been built on far flimsier foundations, and less credulous minds than mine have embraced them. This could be a sign.

If so, then God was either a fool or an impostor.

And the hell with him . . .

The two men lying near him had been less fortunate, however.

And they were going to make headlines.

Closer to me, and to the door where the hit men had entered, was a Face Known to Millions.

Looking at it now, seeing the jaw agape and sightless eyes staring, I felt a small sense of shock to realize what a formidable job of assembly he had represented. It was like seeing a once-beautiful woman without her wig, makeup, and upper plate.

Surveying the remains of the great—and now very late—Danny "Dimples" DiMarco, I realized that the poor bastard had been wearing a full hairpiece, tinted contacts, false teeth, and an elastic jowl lifter, which was glued to his temples. An autopsy attendant, I suspected, would soon find himself struggling with an industrial-strength girdle built into the stylish pleated trousers and a shoulder brace concealed inside the dinner jacket. But none of these deceptions would be visible in the photographs that would fill newspaper pages and we-interrupt-this-program tele-casts for at least a day to come, because the news media are oddly sensitive about publishing pictures of dead bodies. Some-thing about reality being in bad taste, I think. Instead, they would use publicity stills from their libraries—and for once I had to agree with their policy.

Even close friends and associates might have had trouble identifying the husk left behind by the Uzi bullets.

Danny DiMarco had been the bankable King of Comedy for longer than most people could remember, and it was a success that seemed to translate with hardly a lost syllable from the nightclubs where he had started to radio and then to television and finally into musical films that led, amazingly, into a whole new career as a recording artist.

Danny hadn't exactly been a singer; the whiskey-soft voice was too far gone by the time he first tried. But there had been a lilt and a gift of phrasing that seemed to lend a kind of poignancy to the most banal lyric, and the Hollywood youth revolution that had left many another aging luminary dimmed and wandering in the wilderness seemed to touch him lightly—and even then with its customary Midas caress. Paired on film with a nymphet ingenue just under the age of consent, he had turned in a performance that lent believability and even magic to hackneyed nonsense concerning an affair between an adolescent girl and her girlfriend's grandfather . . . and climaxed the wrap party with what turned out, seven months later, to have been a shotgun wedding.

Great for both their careers.

But the mother-nymphet was a widow now, and I wondered what the lawyers and accountants managing her claims on the estate would make of the last thing her randy husband had done in life. Just a dozen or so hours before he sat down for our poker game, the State Gaming Commission had confirmed Danny DiMarco as the new owner and casino licensee of the hotel where he had died.

Now he would never know the joys and sorrows of working the dealer's side of the table.

Just as well, perhaps.

He didn't need the money, and the customers could try the patience of a saint.

One detail caught my eye before I turned away, however; something for the reporters and photographers if they had the nerve—and knowledge—to get it into the record.

Cards and chips had been scattered to every corner of the room when I knocked the green-faced poker table out of the way, but one combination had remained intact. The poker hand that had so impressed the Voice of Heaven appeared to have obeyed Newton's Fourth Law of Motion, remaining at rest for a brief moment after the surface beneath it was swept away, then falling intact, to land on the Dimpled One's chest where the cards waited face up to proclaim the triumph of omen and totem and taboo:

Aces and eights.

Danny DiMarco had checked out lying flat under the dead man's hand.

The other man on the floor was Sam Goines, and at first glance I thought—with a rush of loss and rage and frustration far stronger than expected—that he was dead, too. The idea evoked a well of bitterness that filled the world with mocking laughter. Such a stupid way for Sam to die.

Not exactly unpredictable, perhaps.

But stupid all the same . . .

And then the chest contracted to draw a single convulsive, rattling breath. Sam was still with us, though the condition didn't look at all permanent. I grabbed an absorbent-looking pillow from the couch and dropped to my knees beside him.

One Uzi bullet had torn away part of his left cheek, laying the bone bare and removing enough of the lower lid to keep that eye open while the other was closed. Another slug had taken him in the right shoulder, leaving through-and-through entry and exit wounds that looked both neat and unthreatening.

But a third bullet—perhaps from the other gunner—had caught

him squarely in the ten-ring, clipping the inverted V of the rib cage and hammering on into the moist and vital darkness beyond. Most of the blood on the rug seemed to be his personal property, and I could see that more was welling out of him with each beat of the heart.

That, at least, was encouraging.

Whatever other damage had been done, the pump seemed to be intact. Not much. But far better than whatever was in second place. When the pillow-compress was as tight as I could get it against the trouble spot, I looked up in the hope of finding someone who could call for an ambulance. But there was no need. Our eldest player, tough and stringy old Judge Happy Apodaca, was already talking to the hotel telephone operator, issuing clear and cogent instructions about who was to be called for what . . . and in exactly what order.

No wonder he had lived so many lives.

And prospered in all of them.

The old bastard was one of a kind, a gimlet-eyed survivor of purest ray serene. But the man whose blood I was trying to keep inside him was not your average Rotarian, either.

Samuel Clemens Goines and I had known each other since the day I woke up in the weird ward of an army hospital after my second tour of duty in 'Nam. In semi-criminal conspiracy with a semi-crazed wardmate named Dee Tee Price, we had for a time established what amounted to a reign of terror among the hospital's professional staff—and a wave of prosperity those several corpsmen, aides, and orderlies who could be persuaded, for a price, to obtain certain necessities of life that were flatly forbidden by hospital regulations.

Like everyone else in that ward, Sam was a poor boy in those days. Rich boys did not go to Vietnam as grunts, and there were no officers in the vicinity. But he and Dee Tee were full of plans for world conquest to be undertaken on release, and each had not only attained but far exceeded the goals we discussed during those long days and longer nights of recuperation.

Within a year of his discharge, Dee Tee Price had made his first million in the commodities market, accumulating the bankroll and seeking out the associates he needed to become a feared and respected player in the game of corporate takeover. Nowadays, word that he had become interested in the stock of any company was information of rare worth and salability while it

remained private, and a signal for shark warnings up and down
the Texas oil coast when it came to general public notice.

Sam Goines's ambition had taken a slightly different turn.

Poker had not yet become my steady occupation in those days,
and the penny-ante games on the ward tended to be wild and
wonderful. Sam was a willing and competent player—despite a
strong tendency to bluff really impossible hands—and for a
while I marked him as a possible ally or competitor in my own
post-ward plans. But he needed faster action, and found it.

The mustering-out pay that was probably the most money he'd
had all at once in a lifetime went into a high-rolling crap game
he had located, and I went along to guard his back or lend bus
fare.

As it turned out, neither was needed.

Sam won nearly $50,000 in less than an hour, and the single
effort that was made to take the bankroll from him by force
ended with the would-be bandit flat on his back and unconscious
from a shattered jaw before I could get close enough to take a
hand. Sam's reflexes had always been quick.

The money went temporarily into an account at a discreet and
enterprising bank in the Caribbean, while Sam flew on to Bel-
gium, where he said there was something he wanted to buy. I
drove him to the airport for the first leg of his journey and didn't
see him again for nearly a year—by which time he was a part of
the world's rising phalanx of twilight-legal dealers in military
hardware.

Somehow—Sam had always been wary of identifying his
contacts—he had discovered that the Belgian army was about to
be rearmed with NATO weapons and was trying to find a buyer
for its entire store of semiautomatic rifles.

Using as collateral part of the money he had won (and more, I
suspect, to purchase the cooperation of one or more loan officers), he had obtained the Caribbean bank's backing to purchase
the entire Belgian arsenal. He then resold half the rifles to a
starveling backwater dictatorship in southern Asia, and the re-
mainder in less than a week to an Emerging African Nation with
designs on its neighbors' territory.

Sam never told me how much he made on that first deal, and I
didn't ask—never crowd a known bluffer unless you're ready to
call, and we were playing in different games now—but it must
have been enough to give him a useful reputation, for he became
in the years that followed a steady and well-financed competitor

in the always volatile arena of international arms sales. His off-the-shelf catalog, I was told, might not have the detailed solidity of Interarmco, but he was known for special expertise in high-tech weaponry, a man who was willing and able to satisfy even the most exotic taste in lethal gewgaws.

Ironic to think of him reduced to such straits by a simple and mass-produced weapon like the Uzi. He would probably get a huge laugh out of it. If he lived.

"Ambulance and paramedics on the way," Judge Apodaca said, putting down the phone.

He looked consideringly at the other two men still on their feet in the room, and pointed at them individually to be sure he had their attention. "You and you," he said. "Get the hell out of here."

He paused to let the words sink in, and then went on. "Neither of you was up here last night or this morning," he said. "And neither was that one—" he jerked a contemptuous thumb in the direction of the Voice of Heaven, who was finally beginning to show signs of rejoining the party—"so take him with you."

His tone allowed no room for argument, but there was a moment of hesitation all the same.

The men he was talking to were accustomed to giving orders, not taking them, and I found myself awaiting their reactions with real interest. At least one of them, I knew, hadn't been spoken to in that tone for at least twenty years.

He was an old friend. Or acquaintance. Or contact. Or something.

I had met Manny Temple (né Manfred Tannenfisch), sometime New Jersey mob boss and muscle merchant, on my very first visit to Las Vegas more than a decade ago. Apprenticeship is expensive in the poker trade, and on that occasion it had taken me just four hours and twenty-two minutes to get broke in a $100 buy-in hold 'em game at the Mint casino downtown. Manny had been watching. Friendly, affable, and apparently a bit drunk, he offered to stake me to a second shot at the game and was, I think, shocked almost sober when I turned him down with thanks and the explanation that I was just buying experience.

That called for explanation, and we talked for an hour or so and had been friends—or whatever it was—ever since.

He was, I discovered, a man whose offhand hard-boy manner masked a genuinely warm personality carefully directed by a core of practical intelligence capable of assessing risk, greed, and machismo at their true weight and coming up with a useful balance often enough to remain alive, affluent, and at liberty in a world where just two out of three is considered the measure of true success.

Manny's departure from the East Coast had come in stages, beginning with the issuance of a state grand jury subpoena and progressing step by step through an elaborate "kidnapping" charade, from which he emerged after more than a year with the explanation that the ransom had been difficult to raise. By that time the grand jury had long since lost interest in any questions it might once have wanted to ask him, and most of his numbers, sports-booking, and loan-sharking operations had been quietly but firmly co-opted by minions of the Gihardinelli family who had been given the commission's blessing for a general takeover.

He had departed for the Far West with a smile and, some said, a few odd "sweetener" millions in his pocket to ensure domestic tranquillity.

His reputation in Las Vegas, however, rested less on past laurels than on his covert but generally recognized position as underworld channel and occasional problem-solver for the elusive Francis Carrington Shaw.

How the Temple-Shaw connection had been established and how it had come to endure were questions I would not have cared to ask—and answers I would not have allowed myself to hear. But connected they surely were, and the arrangement appeared to provide long-term satisfaction for both parties.

I was a bit surprised, therefore, to hear Judge Apodaca address him in what was unmistakably a voice of command.

But the judge seemed to take obedience for granted. And so, after a thoughtful moment, did Manny.

The other man, however, took a little longer to make up his mind.

Bearded and bearlike, he stood poised but immobile amid the wreckage of the suite, surveying the damage with a kind of cool self-possession that spoke hard-nosed volumes on the subjects of violence past and violence present.

We were strangers. When I arrived by appointment the night before, I was surprised to discover that I knew all the other players (even the Voice of Heaven on Earth, though he obviously didn't recognize or remember his former schoolmate) with the single exception of the one introduced to me as "Colonel

David Connor. From Florida.'' We had exchanged a sentence or two; the usual guarded and ever-so-slightly-distant pleasantries that nonacquaintances will utter in the moments before they begin an adversarial relationship across a gaming table.

I got the impression of considerable personal force held carefully in reserve—and a feeling that the military title, while perhaps genuine, might not have been one conferred by the armed forces of the United States.

But poker professionals, if they hope to eat regularly, quickly learn to make their character assessments on the basis of a player's approach to the game rather than on anything he might do or say elsewhere. It is a kind of analytical shorthand; instant penetration guaranteed. Just add money and stir . . .

The "Colonel Connor" I encountered during the few hours of our seven card stud confrontation at the Scheherazade, however, was more elusive than most. Knowledgeable but conservative, he had early demonstrated the kind of discipline and patience that are the basic equipment of successful players, and gone on to display both courage and conviction when challenged for pots he thought he could win. Once committed, he was hard to dislodge—but willing to settle for an early call rather than the high-rolling raise that might have tempted a more flamboyant gamester.

Yet there was something missing, something concealed and nurtured in seclusion.

Turning my own center quiet and open, I had gone probing for a sense of his emotional condition and found myself reaching repeatedly and fruitlessly into a carefully tended void that was coupled somehow with a peculiar reluctance, masquerading as inability, to communicate in the silent tongue that is the form and fabric of high-stakes poker.

Yet I was sure he spoke the language.

Time after time, as the hours passed, I saw him deep in the give-and-take of communication with other players. Silence, it appeared, he reserved for me alone.

And that was more than a little strange, for I couldn't shake the sense of having known him somewhere, somehow, in time past . . . but not long past. It was there on the table. Anyone who plays poker more than once or twice a year—anyone with an eye and a memory—knows that every player has his personal tics and quirks; a man's poker style is as distinctive as his taste in clothes or automobiles or women, and I was certain I had come across the colonel's style somewhere before.

His habit of seeing another player's raise on a concealed pair, but straddling—doubling the amount of the bet—on a concealed king-queen or even a queen-jack was familiar; dovetailed with a tendency to stay for the last card on any hand where he'd followed the action to the third round of betting, it added up to someone I knew or ought to know. Or had known.

Someone memorable.

But not named anything like David Connor . . .

Waiting for him to decide whether or not to follow Judge Apodaca's orders, I had a feeling that he might be getting ready to tell the little barrister to go peddle his writs. But then he turned his gaze in my direction.

"How about it?" he said.

That shook me a little—not just because near-strangers seldom ask my advice on whether or not to enter into criminal conspiracies that could send us both to prison, but because there was, once again and more powerfully than before, a sense of the familiar. The phrasing was known to me, the turn of head well recognized . . . but still just outside the perimeter of recall. A taste, but not a swallow.

Exasperating.

But there would be time enough to unravel minor mysteries later; perhaps when the world slowed down again. When Sam Goines was safely in the hospital and the police had come and gone.

"Better do it," I said. "Over the years, the judge has guessed right oftener than he's guessed wrong."

Those seemed to be the right words. I got a grunt of comprehension and acquiescence, and the colonel's mustache dragged one side of the bushy beard up in what was probably intended as a grin.

"Fair enough," he said.

The Voice of Heaven was stirring and trying to sit up now, but Manny and the colonel didn't stand on formalities. Before the Leader of a Million Glory-Bound could get his eyes working together or give voice to what I was willing to bet would be the first of several hundred inane questions, they had him off the floor, on his feet, and stumbling blindly in the direction of the door.

The judge followed, issuing final instructions. "Use the service elevator," he said. "Don't stop till you get to the ground;

then find the Jesus-jammer's limousine if it's still down there and see to it the driver can keep his fool head shut. Or if the damn thing's gone—I think I remember him sending it home last night—get a car, do your own driving, and take him back to that Christforsaken prison camp he lives in, and make sure he gets through the front gate.''

They were in the hall now, and the acoustics there were designed to mute all sound, so the judge had to raise his voice a decibel or two for the parting shot. ''Then each of you go find a hole,'' he said. ''Pull it in after you and stay there till someone tells you different!''

Manny's voice made some reply, but I didn't catch it and the judge gave back a grunt that sounded like assent and then he came back into the room and leaned wearily against the remains of a handsome étagère.

''Christ,'' he said, ''on a crutch.''

It seemed as fair and logical a comment as any. I looked down at Sam Goines again and carefully removed the pillow-compress for a look at the damaged area. Blood was still welling out with each beat of his heart, and his chest was still moving regularly, but it seemed to me that both actions were a little slower than before. Weaker. A bit less sure. I put the pillow back in place and looked down at my friend's torn and battered face. The skin was ashen and shocky-looking under what looked like a sunburn masquerading as a healthy tan. Odd, I thought, for a man who spent most of his days—if you could believe press and news-magazine reports—basking in the expensive rays that fall on the principality of Monaco.

Not that it mattered.

Where the hell was that ambulance . . . ?

''Way we'll tell this,'' Judge Apodaca said, moving across the room to seat himself carefully on one of the undamaged chairs, ''we played us a little game of poker earlier in the night. Four-handed. Just us old friends—you, me, Sam Goines, and Danny DiMarco. No one else.'' He paused to make sure I heard the words and understood them.

I returned his gaze without comment.

''By the time the gunsels busted in,'' he continued, ''the game had stopped and we were just talking. A little business. Nothing important. We got no idea what they wanted or who they were. Any problem with that?''

I thought it over. Except for the subtraction of three people and the addition of the business discussion, what he was asking me to do was tell the truth. Or was it? Item by item, I went back over the events of the night and tried to put them into some order that would punch holes in the story.

But couldn't come up with anything.

I could see why he wanted to tell it without Manny or the Voice of Heaven, but what was it about the colonel that would make it worthwhile to subtract him from the story, too?

I wanted to ask about that. But that question would lead to other questions—a lot of them, maybe—and there just wasn't time for a lot of questions. I gave him a shrug in lieu of an answer and added the silent hope that he knew what he was doing, because I certainly didn't.

"You think anyone'll buy it that way?" I said.

The judge tried to smile, but it was uphill work and the result was a bit wrinkled at the edges.

"Shit-a-mighty boy," he said with sour wisdom, "this is Las Vegas . . ."

A SERMON (Continued)

In his epistle to the Romans, chapter six, verse twenty-three, Paul the Apostle would warn a later world that "The wages of sin is death." And many accepted this as a kind of restatement of King David's observation on misuse of power . . .

5

THE JUDGE WAS right, of course.

For the next hour or two, it was a matter of first things first: Paramedics arrived to take over the job of trying to keep some portion of Sam Goines's blood inside him long enough to move him to an emergency ward, and a whole phalanx of police vehicles were right behind. The city of Las Vegas maintains a special squad for just such situations as the one at the top of the Scheherazade, and they made a quiet and efficient business of taking control, sealing off the VIP floor by blocking access to its single key-operated passenger elevator and stairwell, guarding the hotel switchboard to make sure no unauthorized calls went in or out, and answering no questions whatsoever.

It took them less than three minutes to isolate the trouble spot. And then the investigation began . . . Las Vegas style.

The Clark County medical examiner's office took a little longer putting in an appearance, so all that was mortal of Danny DiMarco lay cooling and stiffening in full view as Judge Apodaca and I delivered our (somewhat edited) accounts of the machine-gun assault. Alternatives were available. We could have been taken into side rooms or into a vacant room elsewhere in the building. But the decision to proceed on the spot didn't surprise me and I was reminded, not irrelevantly, of the time a gambler-hoodlum named Tony Cornero Stralla died of a heart attack during a craps game at the hotel on the strip. Tony was a nice enough little guy—if you didn't cross him—and he had a lot of friends in Las Vegas. But one of the players in the game had been on a hot roll, so the pit boss helped shove Tony's body under the craps table to await later disposal, and the action went on without further interruption.

Tony would have understood.

In the present instance, I was forced to admit to myself that, on balance, the presence of the Dimpled One's remains seemed to have a certain positive effect: It kept things more or less in perspective. Otherwise, I think it might have been all too easy to find the whole day slipping over the edge into never-never land.

Police forces are as diverse as the communities they serve.

It's only natural. The concerns of a community such as Beverly Hills (maximum protection of all kinds for people who live in expensive houses) would have little relationship to those of a city like Miami (preventing newly drug-rich smugglers from murdering one another in such a way as to endanger peaceable citizens). And neither would have much in common with some Indiana railroad town where the worst law-enforcement problem is the care and handling of half-drunk kids who want to cruise around and race their cars on Saturday night.

Police officers are, after all, simply a class of civil service employee hired and armed to execute the perceived will of the body politic. Anything else, while excellent high-protein fodder for movies and television, is really window dressing, and a police chief's true measure of success is the balance he is able to maintain between the prime directive of carrying out public policy and the unspoken demand that he mask it all in a patina of "equal laws, equally applied." Moreover, he must do it at a price. Police budgets rarely reap the benefit of good times in the supporting community, but they inevitably become the first candidates for the administrative paring knife when local economics go awry.

There are social and regional differences, too.

Small-town lawmen tend to be overarmed and undertrained, while those who serve in major cities find themselves confronted more and more frequently by situations in which the best police academy or FBI training is put to naught by the disparity between the .38-caliber revolvers they carry and the M16, Kalishnakov, Uzi, Thompson, and even BAR submachine guns that face them in the street.

Southern cops tend, by and large, to overcompensate—if unintentionally—for the image of big-bellied violence and bigotry they gained via television coverage during the 1950s and 1960s, while their northern cousins fight an ongoing battle against the corruption and multilevel bureaucratic incompetence that have tarnished the image of their profession in such places as New York, Chicago, and Los Angeles.

Even in such company, however, the Las Vegas Police Department is a standout.

One of a kind.

The homicide detectives who interrogated us probably knew their jobs and would have been good at them anywhere else on earth.

But they knew the town they worked for, too, so instead of splitting us up for questioning as would be standard in any legitimate investigation, they elected to conduct the interviews team-style in the living room, where there would be less chance for us to get mixed up and start making mutually contradictory statements. They were determined to get it just right—just the way the management of the hotel and the city's all-year tourist bureau would want it—and I must say I felt a certain left-handed sense of gratitude under the circumstances. The abbreviated story the judge wanted to tell, with three players omitted from the cast, and other little twists in the basic plot line, was just the kind of tale that could generate a wealth of inconvenient detail, leading to later embarrassment. And I always hate to embarrass a police officer.

So I sat quietly, listening and nodding occasional idiot-corroboration while the judge told his version, and then obliged in turn with a slightly less detailed account that went full strength into the detectives' tape recorders and notebooks. Cross-questioning was minimal, and I was just beginning to breathe without difficulty when the dignified susurrus of the passenger elevator door in the hallway announced the arrival of someone with enough authority to get past the police cleanup squad, and I was not much surprised to see that the chief investigator from the Clark County district attorney's office—a cadaverous shamble of surprises known as Corner Pocket—had decided to interest himself in the case.

I had been expecting him.

Corner Pocket and I had known each other for a year or two, and in that time I had found him to be a decent, energetic, competent, and even reasonably intelligent man with a quiet and slightly bizarre sense of humor and some rather clear notions about right and wrong and the responsibilities of the individual in a world that values neither individuals nor responsibility.

An almost-straight arrow.

Which always made me wonder what the hell he was doing in Las Vegas.

Once inside the room, Corner Pocket wasted no time. The remains of the late Danny DiMarco, the general wreckage of the room, and the two police interrogators each rated a single appraising glance en route to the balcony, where he stepped gingerly through and around mounds of shattered glass to the railing and spent a moment or two looking first downward to the spot where the dead machine gunner's body had fallen, and then upward to the overhang.

"One of them was picked up from the roof?"

The question was asked in an almost casual way and hadn't seemed to be directed toward anyone in particular, but he was talking to me and I took care to make my answer as careful and accurate as possible.

"Seems likely," I said. "But I didn't see it happen, and later I was too busy staying alive to take much interest."

He nodded. "Can't say I blame you."

He moved back into the room and came to a stop beside the divan. A floor lamp that taken more than its share of damage lay on its side near the wall, and he bent absently to put it back on its base, but stopped just before his fingers would have made contact. "Forensics lab's been in here already, I suppose?" he said, looking over his shoulder at the detectives.

Momentary hesitation.

"They're on their way," one of them said finally.

Corner Pocket's hand moved away from the fallen lamp and he eased back to his full height. "You've checked out the bedrooms? The rest of the suite?"

The taller and beefier of the detectives, an affable sort who had introduced himself as Bill Bowers, stirred uncomfortably, trying to keep his eyes on the notebook that was still open in his hand but not having much luck. "Gotta be empty," he said in a voice that seemed almost strangled.

Corner Pocket nodded. "Well," he said evenly, "since you're sure of that, don't you think one of them might have been a better place to ask your questions—just to keep the crime scene intact until it can be examined and photographed in situ?"

Even uttered in the mildest of tones, the words were a skin-peeling criticism and professional challenge. But neither of the detectives seemed to want to argue the point, and I couldn't help thinking their silence showed better judgment than I'd have expected. They compromised by sitting still and hating his guts in silence.

"Okay, then," he said when the moment had passed, "I'm going to borrow the preacher, here, for a while."

He turned a cool eye on them, waiting for objections.

There were several. But neither of the homicide detectives seemed to want to put them into words, and after a moment or two he nodded curtly and I stood up to follow him to the door.

That finally got an audible reaction.

"Wait a minute . . ."

Bowers put his notebook down and shifted his bulk into what might or might not have been an attitude of truculence, prepared at last to regurgitate all the words he had swallowed in the past few minutes. But he never got the chance.

Corner Pocket turned his head to look, as though seeing him for the first time. "Why, hello there, Bowers," he said in a friendly tone. "Stolen any good neckties lately?"

The big man froze, lips already formed around the next syllable but unable to force it out of his throat.

His face drained of color, then blushed a bright red and then faded to white again, and I was surprised to feel the white-hot intensity of rage and hatred that he concentrated momentarily on Corner Pocket . . . and then turned on himself. I wondered how he was able to live inside there, and found myself cringing from a sudden close-up view of pounding lungs and tortured digestive organs. As answers go, it was detailed and explicit.

If Bowers couldn't learn to like himself a little better, he was not long for this world.

"Okay, then," Corner Pocket said.

Nobody seemed to have any objections to offer this time as he headed for the door with me in his wake, and he left the room without a backward glance. But I couldn't resist looking back for just a moment.

The two detectives were still frozen like flies in amber, gazing in the direction of the door, hating the world and themselves and Corner Pocket with their eyes and every line of their bodies. But Judge Apodaca was having a fine time.

Visibly diverted, he sat relaxed against the cushions of the ruined divan, savoring the greenish cigar he had just set fire to and tapping the ashes onto the blood-spattered carpet with the cavalier unconcern of a man who knows himself to be on the side of the angels.

And he was right. No doubt of it.

But I couldn't help wondering what the forensics people would make of it all . . .

Corner Pocket—the name came from the time a few years earlier when he had almost become chief of police, but found himself relegated to second place in a typical Las Vegas political squeeze—didn't seem to have much to say until we were in the service elevator watching the floor numbers slip by en route to the basement, and then he seemed to decide that his exchange with Bowers needed some kind of explanation.

"I can be such a son of a bitch," he said.

I favored him with my very blankest country-boy gaze and waited for more. "They speak well of you down at the Elks Club," I said.

That earned me a sour grin and a shake of the head.

"Bill Bowers," he said, "is a total pain in the ass. It isn't that he's dumber than an ox. He's not. But he isn't any smarter than an ox, either, and along with it he's a snotty, opinionated loud-mouth bastard and a bully, and five minutes of his conversation would be enough to put Albert Schweitzer in a mood to punch his lights out."

"I kind of got the idea that he admires you, too."

"All the same," Corner Pocket went on, not hearing me or not giving a damn, "he's a fairly competent thief-catcher when you leave him alone to do the job. Not that he gets a hell of a lot of practice, because no one ever lets cops alone in this town. All part of the Las Vegas mystique, so I hear tell . . ."

His voice trailed off and I tried to think of a remark that would be snotty, loud-mouthed, and bullying enough to make him feel better but couldn't come up with anything.

"That bit about the neckties was below the belt, though," he said a floor or two later. "Now I'm going to have to find some way to apologize to the stupid prick without really apologizing, and . . . God damn, will you tell me why I'm laying all this crap on you?"

I thought it over. "My honest face and sensitive nature?"

That actually got a smile. Junior grade. "Oh, the hell with you, Bible-thumper . . ."

We descended a few more floors in companionable silence.

"Neckties?" I prompted, when I thought he was ready to talk again.

Corner Pocket snorted and shook his head.

"The poor dumb bastard," he said. "It happened more than ten years ago. Ten years! And no one's ever let him forget it. Including me. Five weeks after he joined the force, fresh from the academy, there was a kick-in at a men's store downtown one night and he caught the squeal along with his partner, a drunken, burned-out old hairbag who was supposed to be his field training officer.

"Bowers played it strictly by the book: radioed for backup and then covered the front of the store while the supposedly more experienced and competent man went in through the back door to check out the premises and make sure the burglars weren't still in there. Or, anyway, that's what he told Bowers he was going to do. What he really did was walk in there and select two or three good-looking sports coats he thought would fit him, ditto a few pair of slacks, and some neckties—believe it—and stash them in the trunk of the prowl car.

"Guys in the backup car never twigged and neither did the robbery team when they got there, so the hairbag waited until Bowers had to pee and took off in the prowl car, yelling something about an emergency call. Took him only a minute or two to dump the coats and slacks at his place, of course, and then he went back to pick up Bowers, saying the emergency was a dud. Which still might have been okay. Nothing new in the annals of police science. But the hell of it was the old fart had been nibbling all night long on a flat pint of vodka he had hidden in the car, and he took an extra moment or two to pour himself a big one while he was home, so damn if he didn't forget to unload the neckties . . . and there they were, staring up at him, when Bowers went to unload the trunk at the end of the watch."

I sighed, seeing how the story had to end. "Naturally, Bowers blew the whistle," I said.

"Naturally."

"And naturally his friend and mentor, the hairbag training officer, never saw those neckties before in his life."

"And naturally, Internal Affairs found the coats and slacks at the old son of a bitch's house, but still had no way to go except to kick Bowers's ass all the way around the four hundred block of Stewart Avenue—more for industrial-grade stupidity than for any suspicion that he'd really tried to steal any neckties—and the hairbag went on three months' vacation and then retired, and Bowers got a month's suspension to go into his personnel file where no one would ever forget it or let him forget it, either.''

"Including you."

"Including me." Corner Pocket said. "Jesus, Preacher, sometimes I get so damn sick of being me . . ."

The elevator stopped in the hotel's subbasement and we turned to face the metal door.

"Well, then," I said, "maybe you could go be someone else for a while."

"Yeah? Who'd you have in mind?"

I considered the proposition while the elevator hummed and hitched, easing itself into alignment with the floor.

"Francis Carrington Shaw?" I suggested.

He seemed to think it over, but shook his head. "Too old," he said. "Besides, they say he's sick."

"But rich."

"Who wants to be rich?"

"Both of us!"

The doors rattled open and I followed him out of the cage and along a metal catwalk to a door that I knew opened on the parking lot that was sandwiched between the rear of the hotel and the pool-cabana area.

"I tell you what," he said, fumbling with the security lock. "Suppose you be old, rich, sick Frank Shaw—and I'll be a smart New Jersey hood named Manny Temple, and skim all the money away from you . . ."

He went out the door without waiting for my reaction or even checking to see if there was one, but I had known Corner Pocket too many years to think he had picked Manny's name out of the blue, and I had lived too long to believe in coincidence. He was trying to tell me something.

And maybe he had.

It had been a long night. Clocks are hard to find in Las Vegas—even gift stores rarely stock them—but darkness was fading, and the quiet suburban developments that stretch out across the east side of town were already reflecting morning light as we started around the side of the hotel to the spot where the gunman's body had landed.

Corner Pocket had used the service elevator and the side approach to avoid the news media, but apparently no one had bothered to tell the reporters and photographers about the body outside the building. Their cars and relay vans seemed to be queued up near the Scheherazade's main lobby entrance, at the top of an embankment and nearly a block away from where we were. The cleanup squad had done its usual quiet and effective job, and we had the section of the parking lot nearest the tower pretty much to ourselves except for the technicians of the police forensic detail.

"Meat wagon's on its way," Corner Pocket said. "But I noticed that the guy was wearing a stocking mask, and I wanted you to see him without it."

"Thanks a group," I said.

"Don't mention it."

The trouble with violence is that it is so terribly violent.

Human beings have survived thirty-two-story falls. Movie stuntmen jump from near-comparable heights to earn a few thousand dollars' worth of talent and danger fees; ordinary people who inadvertently do the same thing because of awkwardness or drunken ineptitude—and live to celebrate the experience— are an infrequent but ever popular staple of television news broadcasting.

Stuntmen, however, land on air bags, and nonprofessionals who survive unrehearsed seem always to have found convenient canopies or awnings or haystacks or even flat van roofs to soften the last few inches of descent.

The gunman who had dropped from the penthouse balcony at the Scheherazade had enjoyed no such good fortune. True, he had probably been dead for several seconds before he began his descent, and I had somehow supposed that this might mitigate the more spectacular effects of the sudden stop 300 feet below; total relaxation of the body and noncirculation of blood should, I reasoned, minimize postmortem damage.

But I was wrong.

Trauma center physicians have long been aware that the human body is a complex of contradictions—tough and resilient and self-repairing under many trying circumstances, but infinitely delicate and frangible in others. And the insult that can be inflicted even on lifeless tissue by contact at near terminal velocity with concrete-based asphalt is more intricate and various than even the most clinically detailed report can convey.

None of the bullets fired by the Huey's door gunner seemed to have stayed with their target; the wounds were of the sort associated with armor-piercing ammunition rather than ordinary military ball—neat entry wounds stitched into the back and untidy exit blossoms on the chest. I could see both kinds without having to turn the body over because impact had twisted his torso through a full 180 degrees of arc, rearranging hips and legs in what might have been a running attitude had they not been turned at an angle so impossibly opposed to the rest of him . . . and had the legs not been so misshapen, so much shorter than the legs I remembered.

Unusual position and misproportion were, however, mere details when compared to the color. Collision with the parking lot's surface had turned the dark coverall a grayish pink, and radial streaks and even mounds of brightness were distributed over a radius of several feet surrounding the body. I found myself thinking of strawberry jam, and was immediately forced to beat back a full-scale rebellion in the digestive tract.

"Hit feet first, seems as if," Corner Pocket commented.

The tone was casual, the words dipped in cynicism, and I rounded on him, ready to ease my own guilt and revulsion with a few well-chosen words about humanity and decent respect for all life, but stopped short at the sight of his face. The skin had gone bloodless white, tight and transparent across the cheekbones; it was the face of a man far older and sadder than the one I knew, with all of the emotions, which were usually so well disguised by professional attitude and control, naked and helpless to the self that lives just behind the eyes. Here was simply another human being, shocked and humbled in the presence of the Great Death—and dealing with it in the best way he knew.

"That's why I wanted you to look," he went on after a moment. "See, the face is about the only part of him that came through intact, and it seemed like a good idea for you to have a look, in case it was anyone you might know."

The forensic detail's work was almost finished. A chalk line now detailed the final position of the body and I could see that some brave soul had gone through the dead man's pockets, though there was nothing in their carefully labeled envelopes but arid Nevada climate and a few specks of dark-colored lint. The gunman had carried no identification, money, or other pocket stuffers, and I made a quiet note under "professional" while keeping my mouth firmly shut and adding the silent wager that the labels would also have been cut away from the clothing and any identifiable dental work removed.

Corner Pocket looked a question at the head of the forensic team, got a nod of response, and bent—with visible reluctance—to remove the ripped and laddered remnant of the nylon stocking that had covered the gunman's head.

Poker is a learning experience. It prepares the dedicated player for all manner of life situations, honing and refining such useful skills as freehand psychology, probability mathematics, and manual dexterity, and encouraging the cardinal virtue of patience. Also, it teaches physical control, particularly of the facial muscles.

The term "poker face" is more than a cliché.

My own exterior was, I think, composed in lines of total repose as I gazed for the first time upon the only-slightly-distorted features of the man who had seemed to try so hard to kill me in the moments just before his own death. He was about my age, dusky-skinned and black-browed, the nose and cheekbone and forehead slightly tilted and flattened on one side as though from a long-ago mishap imperfectly repaired. I looked, and was startled to find myself suddenly in conscious control of the cadence of my own breathing, of my balance and stance and position on the face of the earth. The brightening air was electric with ozone and the tips of my fingers were sensitive to its ions as I concentrated on a single object—a pebble on the asphalt—and narrowed my vision until it filled the world.

The state of nothingness consumed me and assumed automatic control of the periphery while I strained to be sure that nothing of my shock and incomprehension was permitted to disturb the surface.

"Nope," I said. "Don't know him."

Corner Pocket sighed and shrugged, handing the ruined stocking to one of the technicians and turning away.

"Worth a try," he said.

I didn't reply, and offered no resistance as he headed back to the hotel, this time by way of a side door that I knew would lead us up a short stairway to the lower lobby level. I hung back a bit, an elementary maneuver intended to discourage conversation while I sorted through the chaos of memory and emotion evoked by the death mask that hung now in the center of enigma.

The flattened cheek and bent nose were unmistakable, the face older than at our last meeting, but recognizable nonetheless beyond all possibility of coincidence or error.

The dead gunman was Jorge Martinez.

We had known each other for just three months, more than a decade ago, but in that brief time we were in many ways closer than brothers.

Sergeant Martinez was at Khe Sanh the day I was hit, and he risked his life to pull me out of the line of fire. He had been my platoon leader.

And my friend.

A SERMON (Continued)

But those who equated the two spoke without thinking—or, at any rate, without careful reading. The wages of sin may, as the apostle says, be death. But . . . are the wages of power death also?

6

SOUND IS THE signature of our times. Millions of dollars are spent daily to drive a mind-battering aggression of music into the workplace and the home and the automobile, invading even the fleeting shelter of public transportation and the elevator. New and expensive sound systems capture the fancy of the consuming public to the tune of billions per annum, and vibrations just above and below the threshold of audibility are commonly used to alter mood, homogenize milk, and cook food.

Meanwhile, still more millions are spent to cancel out ambient amplification.

Earplugs are the secret solace of a with-it generation constrained by peer pressure to attend the more acoustically hazardous rock concerts; scientifically designed ear shields are standard survival gear for those who work amid the jet blast of modern airports; electronics magazines are bright with advertisements for "counter-sound" devices that nullify intrusive noise by generating interdictive resonance; owners of cheaply built and stupidly designed office buildings camouflage the sound-permeable thinness of wall partitions by installing noisy air conditioning that smothers hearing and thought in an all-consuming sea of extraneous sound.

And the body has defenses of its own.

Over the millennia of evolution, human beings have learned to protect themselves by constructing mental filtration systems that reduce familiar and repetitive sound to something like true inaudibility, through selective disregard. We hear these sounds, but we do not heed. This is one of our best and most complex adaptations. But it has its limitations. Sudden changes in the local sound pattern still require conscious adjustment. The damn filter leaks.

Outside the hotel, the omnipresent buzz and rattle and whoosh of highway traffic had been partially blocked by the bulk of the building itself and by certain adroit plantings not selected entirely for their visual aesthetics. Together, they left an impression almost of tranquillity in the zone so adroitly quarantined by the police cleanup detail; someone blessed with vivid imagination might even have thought he heard the distant song of the meadowlark.

Reality, however, was as close as the emergency exit, and I was forcibly reminded of this as I followed Corner Pocket back into the maw of the Scheherazade.

The door we used was not normally a means of ingress; police emergency had required that it be fitted temporarily with a rough wooden shim that kept it slightly ajar, and we were careful to leave it in place when we passed through. But this was mere habit, the unconscious cooperation of the civilized animal. Our minds were not on the door or on the little wedge of plywood or even on the all too mortal remains we had just left to the mercies of the coroner's retrieval unit.

Our minds—and bodies—were for the moment fully occupied with an act of resistance. An insistence of thought and ego, assertion of self in the face of contradiction by a tyranny of sound.

Las Vegas hotels are, in their way, a true flowering of the architectural designer's art; pseudo-elegant and mock-efficient in the hospitality that would be their aim and function anywhere else on earth, they are utterly without peer in the service of their actual mission, which is to make certain that no visitor misses an opportunity to visit the casino to which each overblown hostelry is, after all, a mere adjunct.

The builder assumes that you are in town to gamble. And he means to see that you do it. Right now.

Hotel registration and cashier's desks, bellman desks, lobby accommodations, and vehicle ports all are flow-patterned to make it impossible for you to engage in any activity whatsoever, from the moment of arrival to the final tip-hungry palm of departure, without passing through the main concourse of the casino.

And the sound is part of the come-on.

It is unique, a thing composed equally of the singsong chant of the blackjack dealer, the greed-laced shriek of the craps shooter, the dignified click of the roulette ball, and the raucous summons of the keno player demanding that someone come and take his money away from him—all minced and mingled and mangled and melded in the air-conditioned milieu of the casino, then spread, homogenous and all-pervading, across the jingle-clatter base rhythm supplied by those ranks and banks of slot machinery that are the truest expression of the Las Vegas mystique.

Here it is, folks—a machine!

Just what you need: It doesn't play music and it doesn't show movies and it doesn't pour coffee and it doesn't make change or dispense stamps or even shine your shoes. If you pull its handle often enough, it will swallow every coin you have or can get your hands on, and it doesn't do a single damned thing! You just push your money into the slot for the hell of it.

I halted for a moment, just inside the door, reacting to the sudden impact and allowing my senses to catch up with the rest of me and wondering if the noise sometimes affected Corner Pocket in the way it did me. He had been born here in Las Vegas. Brought up in places just like this one. Perhaps it was different for him, too much a part of the normal and accepted world to be worthy of conscious acknowledgment.

Inhaling deeply to rid my lungs of the clear morning desert air, I risked a covert glance in his direction and found myself obscurely pleased to note that he was no more immune to the overload of sound than I. It was all there in his face.

But with a difference.

For him it was balm. And welcome. The friendly insinuation of a kiss.

"Come on," he said, altering the timbre of his voice to give it an edge that would be clearly audible through the interference. "Let's find a nice noisy place and have a talk."

That brought me to full alert.

Eavesdropping is a cottage industry in Las Vegas. The gaming profession thrives on information—coke-head athletes who may be bribable, horse trainers in financial straits, professional golfers whose doctors have told them to slow down—and bugging devices thrive on quiet spaces.

Truly private conversations, therefore, are usually conducted in places where extraneous noise acts as cloak and buffer against the skulking electronic ear.

Even excessive sound can have its uses.

A private conversation with Corner Pocket, however, was the last thing on earth I wanted just then. The night had been long, the morning even longer, and the identity of the dead machine

gunner was just the kind of extra factor that could turn an already
confusing situation toward the foothills of chaos. I wanted time
and space, an opportunity to examine the various elements and
arrange them, if possible, in something like logical order. I
wanted a chance to figure out what was happening. And why.

But I wasn't going to get it. Corner Pocket led the way to the
stand-up bar at the edge of the casino, and the morning shift
bartender, who knew both of us, brought two bottles of mineral
water without being told and shook his head when we tried to
pay.

"Mr. Goines's orders," he said. "Preacher's money's no
good at the Scheherazade until further notice . . . and I guess
that includes anyone who's with him."

I resisted the impulse to fill him in on recent developments,
and took a pull at the mineral water. It tasted like frozen leaves,
but I swallowed it because it was wet and available and what's
taste anyway and besides I needed something to do with my
hands and face to avoid turning them toward the man who was
about to start a conversation that couldn't possibly make either of
us any happier.

"That," Corner Pocket said, ever true to form, "is one of the
things I wanted to ask you about . . ."

I didn't want to answer, so I just looked at him and waited.

He didn't mind a bit.

"I already know the story the way old Happy Apodaca told
it," he went on, "and he is a good old boy and a hell of a
lawyer and one of the smartest sonsabitches who ever walked
around on two legs in this smartass town. The newspapers and
the television people will eat it up. And that is just fine with me
because the people I work for will like it, and they didn't hire me
to rock any boats that don't have to be rocked."

He paused for a lubricating swallow.

"But the hell of it is," he said, "no matter how I try, I just
can't get the story he told to fit the physical facts."

This time, I think, the pause was to give me an opportunity to
object or express innocence or something of the sort, but I just
stood still and waited for him to go on.

"Your old buddy Sam Goines," he said, consulting a not-too-
expensive wristwatch, "has been in town exactly twenty-seven
hours, give or take a few minutes one way or the other, but you
have to say he didn't waste any of it. By the time you showed
up—about seven o'clock last night, that would be—he had made

eleven long-distance telephone calls all over the world, using a tricky electronic scrambler that was too much for even the local professionals . . ."

That gave me the sorry ghost of a smile and seemed to affect him the same way.

". . . while his wife arrived on a separate airplane from a different point of origin and checked into a separate suite at the Scheherazade."

He gave me a moment to digest that, and I was grateful. I knew, or had heard, that the Sam Goineses had been moving around the world separately for a while, and there were rumors that they might be ready to make the split permanent. But I hadn't known that Moira Goines—Maxey—was in town.

And it made a difference.

"So after he finished making the calls," Corner Pocket said when he decided I was ready to listen again, "various citizens began to get interested in who went into the penthouse suite and who came out. The standard telephone and room bugs weren't working because Goines travels with his own personal debugger, who is very good at his job. But a whole human being is hard to conceal even when it goes up and down in a key-lock elevator that can start at any floor, so there goes the part of the judge's tale about how you and he and Goines and DiMarco spent the evening alone together—playing a little bridge, was it? Or maybe pinochle, four-handed? Even if the number of chairs and the size of the table and the amount of money and the chips and all the rest of the physical evidence I could see without even trying didn't tell it a different way."

He finished the mineral water and put the empty bottle down on the bar and turned to look at me with his sad, pale eyes.

"Lie to the marks and the mooches and poor bastard cops like Bill Bowers all you want, Preacher," he said. "But don't lie to me. This isn't for the record and it isn't for the newspapers and it isn't for your book of golden memories, but I want to hear the whole story again. This time with three more people—whom we will call Holy Joe Gillespie, Manny Temple and, Colonel David Connor, just to pick three names out of the clear blue sky.

"Think you could do that?"

So of course I went right on lying. More or less. I told the story again with Sam and the colonel and the Voice of Heaven in it, sure, and the poker game continuing right up to the moment when two killers came through the door.

But still without Sergeant Jorge Martinez's dead face looking up at me.

And without Holy Joe's card tricks.

Corner Pocket seemed to know it was still partly bullshit. He is a realist and he is the second generation of his family in the law-enforcement business in Las Vegas and I think the only way I could really have surprised him would have been to tell the full, unvarnished truth. So he kept his cool and nodded at all the appropriate places and waited for a moment or two as if to assimilate and take it all in when I was done and then nodded solemnly and thanked me and said he was grateful for my candor, and now would I please fill in a few details and I said I would do that, and wondered what he was going to zap me with next.

I found out in a hurry.

"Now," he said, "what I would like is, I would like it if you would tell it all again, you Bible-banging, poker-hustling Tennessee highbinder."

"I'm from Ohio," I said mildly.

"You were born there, but grew up in Colorado till your folks were killed in that freaky accident and you got sent off to Sewanee, and yes, I did a whole big fancy background check on you when you first turned up out here and don't try to change the subject, old friend of mine . . ."

"Anything you say, Charlie Chan."

". . . only when you tell it this time, I'd take it kindly if you would put in some words on how come I saw the dead man's hand laid out on Dimples DiMarco's chest, and why I had a personal telephone call from Francis Carrington Shaw at six o'clock this morning to make sure I got out of my nice, warm bed and came down here."

"I hear tell he stays up late."

"And when you're done with all that, there is one other little matter I think you might clear up for me."

The cynical, semi-bantering tone had entirely vanished with the last words, and I responded by swallowing any reply I might have had in mind. One thing about doing business with Corner Pocket—he gives you fair warning when playtime is over.

"A week ago," he said, the pale blue eyes suddenly sharp and deadly serious in the sad-lined farmboy face, "the police intelligence bureau got a telephone call from Interpol, the international police agency, and passed it on to me. Seems an American citizen named Samuel Clemens Goines who they had been keeping an eye on for ten years or more, ever since he started buying and selling things for people to kill each other with, had gone and got himself into one hell of a jam.''

He paused to check out my reaction, but it was all news to me and after a while he went on.

"What Goines had done," he said, "was to tell some government in North Africa—one of the less popular ones, that even their neighbors are scared of—that he could get them an important piece of hardware, something every road-company Napoleon asks Santa Claus to bring him, and they must have believed he could do it, because they fronted him the money to grease the deal."

"But he didn't produce, and now they want their money back?''

Corner Pocket shook his head.

"If it was just that," he said, "I don't think Interpol would give a damn. Cheating some goat-stealing strongman in that part of the world ranks as kind of a misdemeanor where they're concerned. No, the hell of it is, while Goines was off stealing the item or buying it or whatever he did, the guy who made the deal with him guessed wrong once too often and there was a little tin-pot revolution and when it was over the winners shipped the former head honcho home in six different boxes.''

I shrugged.

"So . . . no problem. The deal's off and Sam can either negotiate with the new regime or find a new buyer or maybe even keep the toy himself, seeing it's already paid for.''

Corner Pocket just looked sadder.

"Uh-huh," he said. "That's what I guess Goines must have thought, too. But the generals and colonels who are running the show now don't seem to see it that way. They're saying a deal is a deal and the money was paid, and where's the beef?''

It had taken me long enough, but I was finally beginning to understand. And it was starting to look like a long, long morning.

"So what you figure," I said, "is that the attack on the penthouse was a little expression of pique from the generals. And you want to know how much I know about the deal, so you can make some informed guesses about what's going to happen next?''

Corner Pocket's eyes never left my face.

"What I want to know," he said, "and what you are sooner

or later going to tell me, is all about the game and why you were in it and why the others were in it and what kind of deals were made during the night and why Francis Carrington Shaw is so damn interested and why those five cards—the dead man's hand, for christsake—were laid out on DiMarco.

"And then, by God, we are going to get down to business and try to figure out just what the hell Sam Goines thought he was going to do with his own personal atomic bomb!"

A SERMON (Continued)

We know more of power, in our time, than Paul or King David knew in theirs. And not only because we are better educated or because we live in an age when men of power and their doings are shown to us daily in living color in our own living quarters . . .

7

NEITHER OF US said anything for a moment or two after that.

My first reaction, of course, was to dismiss the whole thing as a bad joke. The Sam Goines I remembered might have been odder than a square grape—and a dedicated bluffer besides—but the wildness and the bluffing had always been tempered by a powerful streak of cold, practical realism. He had an eye for the main chance and no use at all for the kind of blue-sky adventure Corner Pocket was describing. Somebody had to be kidding someone.

But Corner Pocket wasn't smiling.

"Nobody could really get an A-bomb," I said. "That's ridiculous."

He nodded.

"That's what I thought. But it turns out your old buddy isn't even the first to bring it off. There was a terrorist group in Germany, one of the Red Squads according to Interpol, that actually made one."

I didn't believe it, and my face must have said so.

"Yeah," he said. "That was my reaction, too. But think of this: Do you remember a few years back a college student—an English major, not someone from Caltech or M.I.T.—made a bet that he could draw up plans for an atomic bomb just by reading nonclassified material available in any library? He won the bet, you know. Won it in just two weeks. Without half trying!"

I remembered.

"But that's not building a bomb," I said. "That's just knowing how. To build one, you'd need fissionable material of a certain grade."

"Right! And that's always been the argument. That no one

could get hold of the stuff. Trouble is, that whole line of reasoning turns out to be absolute, demonstrable bullshit.''

"Who says?''

"Interpol, for one. And the Nuclear Regulatory Commission for another. The NRC's own records show that more than two thousand units of fissionable material—enriched uranium and plutonium, just what your Junior Achievement A-bomb factory ordered—is officially missing. Some of it is just bad bookkeeping, sure. And some of is just pure, ordinary human stupidity and incompetence. But some of it is really gone, stolen and for sale on the open market. And, old friend, it only takes about fifteen units to make an A-bomb.''

I took a deep breath and let it out slowly.

"Okay," I said. "All right, then. So someone could build one. But that doesn't mean it would be portable enough to move around, even in a truck. You could set it up somewhere, maybe, and threaten to touch it off. But it wouldn't be too useful for some tenth-rate Arab army junta. And that isn't what you were talking about anyhow. You didn't say Sam made a bomb or found someone who could make one.''

"I said he got one. And that's what he did. A real honest-to-Einstein military weapon.''

I was ready to shake my head again, but I didn't do it. Corner Pocket and I play word games with each other sometimes; it beats staring at the middle distance. But I was finally beginning to realize that this wasn't one of those times. I sat still and waited for him to go on.

"The French government, back when that big-nosed general was running the show, pulled out of NATO and began testing its own homegrown atomic weapons in the South Pacific. Everybody screamed bloody murder, but the general didn't give a damn. He went right ahead and the governments they've had since then have done the same thing.''

He paused to see if I was with him. I nodded.

"The peace-movement people still try to sail ships into the French test area in the Pacific," I said. "And there was some trouble a while back when a couple of French spooks sank one of the peace-movement ships at a dock in New Zealand or somewhere.''

"Right. But meanwhile the French have been hard at work making a whole arsenal of their very own homegrown bombs, and the intermediate-range systems to deliver them—and now one of those bombs is missing.''

I thought it over, still looking for an out.

''No way,'' I said finally. ''For one thing, if someone actually stole a military atom bomb the various news media would have set up a howl you could hear all the way to the moon.''

It was a feeble effort, and I knew it and so did Corner Pocket.

''When you read the newspaper stories about what happened this morning up there in the penthouse,'' he said, ''how many reporters do you think are going to have been in the room and how many of the other details do you think you are going to recognize?''

I didn't argue the point. It wasn't worthwhile and besides he was right.

''I got all this from Interpol as soon as they found out Sam Goines was going to be in my town,'' he went on. ''And my reaction was enough like yours that I got some State Department people out of bed back in D.C. to confirm the story and flesh it out for me before I could make myself believe it, and I still feel like I'm a couple of minutes into a really bad dream. But I'm not, and what they told me makes sense.''

My mouth was suddenly very dry and I think his was, too, because we both looked around for the bartender. But he was busy answering a phone at the other end of the catwalk. Corner Pocket continued.

''Without going into too many details,'' he said, ''an atom bomb isn't something you can just bolt onto the front end of a missile and let it go at that. The damn things are as delicate as a firefly's fanny. There's a lot of sophisticated circuitry in there to go bad. So you have to set up a maintenance routine, a servicing system like the one for a car or an airplane.

''But you don't just leave the delivery system there without a warhead while the bomb's in the shop. What they do is rotate the damn things the way you do bulbs on a string of Christmas tree lights when one goes bad: The first warhead comes off and is replaced by one that's just been serviced. Then it goes to the shop and when it comes back you put it in place of the next one on the route. And so on.''

I could see where this was going now, and there was suddenly a cold spot in the very middle of by stomach. The same one I remembered being there the first time anyone ever shot at me in earnest. And all the times since.

"So all you'd have to do," I said, "would be to substitute a dummy somewhere along the chain—"

"And it wouldn't be spotted until the next round of servicing, which could be almost a year later. But it was spotted, because the officer who'd been bribed to make the switch was even more gutless than anybody thought, and the day after he handed the package over to Goines or whoever was running the errand for him, he turned right around and went home and swallowed his gun—after writing out a suicide note in neatly phrased schoolboy French."

"But by that time—"

"But by that time, Goines was out of the country and in deep cover in some part of South or Central America where someone owed him a favor, and when he popped up again in Monaco he was as clean as a nun's confession."

I grinned at him.

"Not the happiest choice of simile, old friend," I said.

"You go to hell, Preacher," he said, and we sat for a while listening to the rhythms of the casino while we worried the corners of logic still hanging loose.

"He stole it for the Arabs," I began finally. "But the guy who made the deal with him got turned into lamb patties."

"At just the wrong moment," Corner Pocket agreed. "I never knew Goines. But nothing I've heard of him in the last few hours would make me think he's some kind of idiot, so I'd assume he meant to go through with the deal one way or another and only began after the fact to think about what a dandy little toy he had found."

There was more, I think, but I never got to hear it. The bartender finished his phone conversation and picked the instrument up and brought it to where we were sitting, then handed the receiver to Corner Pocket.

"For you," he said.

Corner Pocket wasn't surprised and neither was I. No one is really hard to find by telephone in Las Vegas.

He put the receiver to his ear, identified himself, and listened for about thirty seconds, nodding absently from time to time.

"Okay," he said when the caller was done speaking his piece. "We'll be there."

He hung up, set the telephone down, and looked at me. "You got wheels?"

"Rented."

"Outside? Now?"

"Unless they've been stolen."

"We'll use them. I came with a guy from my office and he'll still be busy."

I dropped a five dollar toke on the bar and stood up, feeling twice my age.

"Do forgive me," I said, "if I seem to come on all curious, but do I get to know where we're going or does it have to stay secret until we get there?"

The words were snottier than I wanted them to be, but Corner Pocket didn't seem to mind. Or even notice.

"That," he said, "was my man at the hospital. The doctors think your buddy, Goines, is going to be conscious again before long. And maybe able to talk . . ."

It was, indeed, turning into a long time between naps. But suddenly I wasn't as tired as I had been.

Three minutes later, by the mental clock, we were out of the parking lot and into a side-road shortcut that would miss early morning traffic.

A SERMON (Continued)

We know of power because we possess it, because we are the first generation of humankind born with power in hand to destroy not only ourselves but all life. To wipe it forever from the face of the earth . . .

8

EN ROUTE TO the hospital, I did my lying best to convince Corner Pocket that the revised version of events I had told him was the only one I knew.

He listened in silence, but I could see he wasn't buying.

Considered from the standpoint of cold logic—and that was the only angle I could expect—the story had more holes than an ant farm. No one in his right mind would believe that a man who made his living playing poker and who had come to Las Vegas by invitation for the specific purpose of playing seven card stud with six other men, also present by invitation, would be there unless he knew all about them and all about his host. If something more than a poker game was involved, and Corner Pocket seemed convinced that something was, he would be sure to know about that, too. Unless he was a damn fool.

And I had an extra handicap.

While laboring righteously to make Corner Pocket understand that I was, indeed, the damn fool who had done all that, I was also trying to edit everything I said in order to keep from admitting to the single black lie that was mixed in with all the truth.

I had told him I didn't know the man who had fallen from the penthouse balcony after being killed by the door gunner on the Huey. And I intended to go right on telling the story that way until I could get the whole thing straightened out and making sense in my own head.

Uphill work. But poker is a number one school for dissemblers and I thought I might be making some kind of progress until we turned off Paradise Road into the unusually wide side street that leads to Mount Etna Hospital–Medical Center.

Then he sat up and shook his head and grinned at me.

"You're good, Preacher," he said. "Real good. I'll say that

for you. No wonder that flock of yours buys the bullshit you feed them about where the money comes from. Those Sunday sermons of yours must be a pistol. But no, Not this time. No way! The more you rev the engines on this one, the less it wants to fly."

I sighed.

"Well, hell, then," I said, not bothering to argue the point. "I'm doing my best. How about a little help?"

"Okay. Try this . . ."

I pulled the rented car into the hospital parking lot and found an empty slot and filled it and set the brake and turned off the engine and swiveled around to listen.

"For openers," he said, "nothing you said or can say is going to convince me or anyone else that a poker hand composed of three eights and two aces landed on a dead man's chest by accident. I don't mind an occasional coincidence, friend, but give me a little running room. Even Bill Bowers gagged a little, and he is a man who has learned to swallow elephants on demand."

He paused to let me think it over, and I did and I had to admit he was right. Even having seen it at first hand, I was beginning to have a my doubts.

"But the really bad part," he went on, "was the helicopter."

One of the worst insults you can offer any confirmed liar is to doubt him when he is telling the unvarnished truth, and I was on the point of indignant—and, for once, pure-hearted—interjection when he held up a warning hand.

"Let's don't get all hot and bothered here," he said. "I can go along with the part about how the other gunsel got away. You say he went to the roof and was picked up by a chopper there and I believe it because it is just about the only way he could have gone and because if I was planning a hit like that one, it is the escape route I would have picked and because a hell of a lot of other people heard the noise of a whirlybird coming in close at about the same time all the shooting was going down."

"Then, what—"

"I said the others heard the chopper. I didn't say they saw it. Still real dark out, remember, and even the way you were telling the story the chopper was running around up there without lights."

"Of course."

"Of course. So, Preacher, all the other people in the tower

suite with you had their heads down, hoping to stay alive, and
everyone else who had a window that could have showed them
anything seemed to have something else to do and no one in the
parking lot below saw anything until the body in the jumpsuit
came flapping down out of the sky. You are the only one who
claims to have seen the helicopter itself.''

"So? If other people heard it and you say yourself it had to
have been there . . .''

He shook his head. "I said a helicopter had to be there, and I
think one was," he said, "but that doesn't mean I believe what
you told me. Look—I spend a lot of time on the job, but you
know what I do for kicks in my off time?''

I shrugged; the conversation was getting a little weird around
the edges. "Chase girls?" I suggested, just to make noise.

It earned me a sour snort. "In this town," he said, "who
would have to chase?''

Good point.

"No, Preacher, I don't chase girls—though sometimes I think
my wife would take it kindly if I did—and I don't gamble and I
don't play golf or pan for gold or take part in amateur theatricals.
What I do is, I play soldier.''

That was news to me. Somehow, Corner Pocket just didn't
seem the type for peacetime war games. But I still couldn't see
what it had to do with the helicopter.

"I flew Thunderthuds—F-105s—in 'Nam," he said, "and
when I got home and tried flying as a civilian, the kind of
airplanes I could afford just didn't thrill me.''

I could understand that. "So you stayed in the reserve?''

"Sort of. I'm a bird colonel in the Nevada Air National
Guard.''

He let the words sit there in the air between us, as though I
ought to be able to fill in the next sentence or two for myself, but
it was lousy interrogation technique from my point of view
because I still couldn't see the point, unless it was pure resent-
ment at my saying that one of his outfit's choppers was involved
in the hit. And he had never seemed the type.

"What I saw," I said, letting the words out slowly and
distinctly, "was a Huey. A Bell UH-1A. It was painted military
olive drab. With the letters N.A.N.G. on the side and bottom.''

His face didn't change. It was still arranged in lines of disbelief.

"N.A.N.G.," he repeated. "You're sure there were four
letters, not three? Not just N.N.G.?''

Weirder and weirder.

"Four letters," I said, seeing them again in memory. "Big ones on the bottom with a serial number, smaller, below them. The bird went through an amber light, one of the decorative spots on the side of the building, just before it was out of sight. I had a clear view. And I'm not mistaken."

He paused again, as if to let me change my mind. But I didn't and finally he nodded and unlocked the car door and got out.

"Okay," he said, slamming the door behind him and turning toward the visitors' entrance. "We'll leave it there for a while and I will even admit that I believe you—or, anyway, I believe that you think you saw those letters."

"Thanks a group."

"Don't mention it. But I think I also ought to tell you I still don't believe it was an Air Guard copter that made the pickup."

"But—"

"The Nevada National Guard—N.N.G.—has a few Hueys," he said, cutting me off. "And the regular army even loans them a few from time to time, though those would have camouflage paint instead of olive drab. But I can tell you, from personal knowledge, that the Nevada Air National Guard does not have a single Huey—not on active duty or even sitting around being cannibalized for parts.

"The order that got rid of the last of them was issued three whole years ago, Preacher. And the name on the bottom was mine."

Mount Etna Hospital–Medical Center is a pint-sized medical-surgical showcase, built two decades ago with mob money carefully filtered through a couple of union pension funds and dedicated to the proposition that criminals are as much entitled to first-rate medical care as anyone else.

The problem was of long standing. Individuals on the wrong side of the law had always been forced to make do with the questionable efforts of those sundry quacks, alcoholics, misfits, and convicted malpractitioners whose incompetence and/or character defects had brought them at last to the very lowest reaches of the medical hierarchy. In retrospect, it is probably wonderful that anyone survived.

The emergence of Las Vegas as a kind of town-sized neutral zone, a place where any criminal family recognized by the national commission might peacefully establish a hotel and casino fiefdom without regard to territoriality, led to speculation over other possible benefits. A tame legislature and biddable judiciary made the whole state a favored place of quiet and almost extradition-proof exile for those whose activities elsewhere had drawn unwanted attention from various law-enforcement agencies.

Mount Etna Hospital was the next logical step.

Over the years, a shooting gallery of hoodlums ranging in magnitude from a couple of crime syndicate members (suffering, respectively, from prostatic cancer and multiple bullet holes) to a fleeing ward heeler (in desperate need of plastic surgery), have benefited from the farsighted benevolence of those gangster forefathers whose orders brought it into being. Nowadays the goombas can't see how they ever got along without it.

And best of all, the hospital's records are stored in a computer, which makes total secrecy—and instant forgetfulness—a routine part of the service.

Patients check in quietly under whatever names they fancy (so long as proper financial arrangements have been made) with the assurance of such total privacy that neither their presence nor their medical records will ever become a matter of public record—subpoenas and federal grand jury orders notwithstanding. Some of the world's leading investigators and computer experts have, from time to time, attempted to retrieve restricted information from Mount Etna's special security files. All have failed, for the simple reason that those records were entered through a system devised by slightly more skillful, and more expensive, experts who countered every move in advance. Yet those elusive records, complete with true names neatly bracketed and cross-filed with the pseudonym under which the patient was treated at Mount Etna Umanita, pop up at the touch of a computer key for those who know the routine, while the wastelands of southern Nevada are final home to more than one initiate whose loyalty came somehow into question.

Mount Etna has no sense of humor at all.

Corollary to all this, of course, is the quality of medical service provided—total security is cold comfort if the doctors on staff got their diplomas by mail order. The men who endowed Mount Etna could afford to hire the very best. Results were in no way surprising.

Despite its background—indeed, as its direct result—Mount

Etna Hospital–Medical Center is now recognized throughout the
world as one of the miniature gems of medical science.

In size, Mount Etna is classed merely as a regional hospital
with (very) limited teaching facilities and a research program
peculiarly devoted to the allied fields of dental and reconstructive
(plastic) surgery. Yet in these selected fields, its work is always
well beyond the leading edge of the art elsewhere . . . and other
specialties are represented not only by a truly top-notch attending
staff resident in the vicinity, but by commanding names from
other parts of the world who are on call for immediate consulta-
tion or personal services as need may arise.

It is, withal, a fine and thoroughly discreet place to be sick
when you can afford the very best.

And Sam Goines had the price . . .

Walking through the lobby, I glanced around for the tradi-
tional information desk and finally managed to pick out a likely-
looking facility, complete with exquisitely groomed attendant,
partially hidden in a copse of artificial desert vegetation near the
elevators.

But we didn't have to ask directions.

Before my eyeballing of the area was half completed, a beefy
individual had detached himself from one of the couches to
approach Corner Pocket with a few quiet words in which a
number was not quite audible. Mission accomplished, he returned to his assigned duty of guarding the hospital's frontal
access route and we followed what I presumed were his directions to Sam Goines's floor.

Security there was tighter and more evident; hall guards were
uniformed and openly armed. But they knew Corner Pocket and
decided after only a question or two that I might safely be
permitted to accompany him. Goines, they said, was in the
intensive care wing on the far side of the building, and with the
ease of long practice, Corner Pocket traversed the rabbit warren
of corridors leading there. He had been a cop in Las Vegas for
most of his adult life.

Access to the ICU, however, involved a different set of proce-
dures altogether.

Mount Etna Hospital–Medical Center, it seemed, had more
than one intensive care unit and more than one surgical floor.
This was the one set aside for patients whose ''special circumstances'' exposed them to risks other than those common to

medical practice. Somebody had watched the hospital sequence
from *The Godfather* and taken it all as gospel. This was the floor
for hoods.

The nurse in charge knew Corner Pocket by sight, but still
telephoned the main admissions desk for permission to allow him
through the door, and I had to hold still for a careful and
professional body search before being allowed to accompany him
inside.

"Nothing personal," the nurse said, grinning a little as she
groped my crotch for a concealed weapon. "All part of the VIP
service in this part of the building."

It felt pretty personal to me, but I didn't say so and waited
patiently, trying to look nonchalant, until she was finished.

"Okay," she said at last. "You're here for Mr. Goines, and
he should be conscious again in the next hour or so. But no one
is to go into his room, or even near it, until the doctor—and
Mrs. Goines—give permission. Clear?"

We said it was, and waited while she went back behind the
desk-counter and pushed the little electric button that opened the
double door.

The unit's main monitor station was at the far end of the
corridor, but there was a pint-size waiting room just inside the
doors, fitted with predictably expensive carpeting and functional-
plus couches fronted by a bare little coffee table that seemed to
have been dragged into the picture from somewhere else. It
seemed well designed for its purpose, which was to keep the
nearest and dearest in one place and out of the hair of the
working staff until such time as someone was ready to deliver a
progress report or bad news bulletin.

Just beyond, at the edge of the holding pen, two women stood
with heads together in conversation so deep and quiet that they
did not immediately notice our arrival. One of them was a nurse,
starchy and official and clipboard-bearing in hospital whites,
complete with crepe-soled white shoes and what struck me as a
rather oddly shaped cap.

The other was Sam's wife, Mrs. Moira Fonteyn Goines.

Maxey.

I had been expecting to see her, of course. Corner Pocket had
told me she was in town, and the ICU door-guardian nurse had
intimated that she was on the premises, and even if the rumors
about a rift between her and Sam were true, she would certainly
be at the hospital and waiting here, and I had thought I was

prepared. Yet seeing her again was an almost physical shock. As always.

I hadn't thought it would be that way.

Her back was toward me, and it had been more than ten years, and memory is supposed to be a liar. Childhood houses get smaller and meaner when you go back to see them again in adulthood, and old friends are fatter or thinner or smarter or duller. Nothing ever stays the way you left it, and sometimes it is hard to associate old names and places after a while. I had half expected to have trouble recognizing the woman I had known a long time ago in a very different world.

But nothing had changed, and I suppose a small part of what I was feeling must have shown in my face because the nurse suddenly became aware of us and nudged Maxey, who turned her head to give me the full ultra-light power of the blue-violet eyes I had never quite forgotten.

There was a moment of pure paralysis.

But it went on for too long.

''Hello, Maxey,'' I said, responding more to the urge to make a noise in a silent place than from any need for oral communication. Only two words; not at all impressive or original. But the effect was pure disaster.

The eyes widened to full bore, then fluttered an unmistakable distress signal as all color drained from her face. A tiny, almost despairing whimper emerged from her barely parted lips and then the knees turned traitor, refusing to support the elegant torso.

Moving quickly, I was just able to prevent violent contact with the floor, and the last traces of consciousness seemed to have vanished by the time my arms were in position under her legs and back.

It seemed to be my morning for giving people the vapors . . .

A SERMON (Continued)

Other ages have been violent. Others have been perverse. The Nazis were not the inventors of genocide, only its best-advertised practitioners. We have been killing one another by every means at our disposal since the beginning of time . . .

9

I CARRIED MAXEY to the nearer couch and noted that it was, as usual, too short for her. But this time her extra height was an asset, and I used the obstructing couch arm to prop her feet higher than her head.

Some got it, some ain't.

Dealing with me had sent the Voice of Heaven on Earth on an extended trip to never-never land, and now it was Maxey's turn. Perhaps I had stumbled onto a whole new branch of anesthesiology. It was an irrelevant thought and an idiotic one, but no more irrelevant or idiotic than anything else that had happened in the hours since midnight. What with one thing and another, events were beginning to take on a kind of dreamlike quality, a sense of being a half-step removed from the real world. And the illusion was enhanced when I stepped back to let the nurse, who had been standing just behind me, give Maxey the benefit of her professional expertise.

She was gone. Vanished.

What in the hell was going on here?

But I was given no time to wonder about it. Maxey's breathing had deepened and her eyes were beginning rapid movement behind the lids, and I bent close to take her pulse. It was strong and steady. Unthinkingly, I moved my right hand to brush away the curl of hair that seemed ready to crawl into the corner of her mouth, and my hand was on her cheek when the eyes blinked open, focused, closed tightly, and then hammered me again with that peculiarly penetrating shade of blue.

I am not really the strong, silent type. That's just in John Wayne movies. And poker. Confronted with an awkward social situation, my natural tendency is to fill the world with words, and I had been ready to do that until the moment came to say something and then there didn't seem to be anything to say. My

83

hand was still on Maxey's cheek and I took it away in a hurry and then there was another awkward pause and she finally had to start the conversation without me.

"Preacher?" she said.

"That's what they call me."

"Preacher . . ."

There was something more in her voice than the lingering travel lag of the journey back into the world. She blinked again and moistened her lips and swallowed.

"Lying . . . bastards!" she said, with more conviction than had been there before. She shifted on the couch, ready to sit up and rejoin the group, but my hand was still in the right spot to keep her horizontal and I used it. Gently.

She hardly seemed to notice.

"Bastards," she repeated. "Bastards . . . told me you were . . . dead!"

I grinned at her and made a burlesque vampire-face. Childish, but I couldn't resist. Maxey always did bring out the clown in me—which might, I suppose, be one of the reasons she wound up marrying someone else.

"A moment of pain, my dear," I said, doing a very passable Lugosi. "And then . . . eternal life!"

She didn't smile. "Not funny," she said.

I guess it wasn't. But it was better than telling her what had been going through my mind as I carried her to the couch.

"Okay," I said. "But I'm not dead. Honest . . ."

She closed her eyes and took a deep breath and opened them again and then managed the very smallest of smiles. "Nope," she said. "Still there."

I returned the smile with interest. "Who said I wasn't?" I asked.

She frowned a little, trying to remember, but gave up without too much effort. "Some damn doctor, I guess," she said. "This place is full of them."

"Hospitals are like that."

Maxey made a move to sit up and I started to restrain her, but thought better of it and let her follow her own inclination. Unless she had changed a lot in ten years, she would do as she wanted anyway—and touching her was absolutely out until I had myself under better control. The preacher's memories were getting entirely out of hand.

"Said you got shot," she said when she was upright, back

braced into the angle of the couch arm. "Up there in that damn penthouse. With Sam."

The name brought everything back into perspective, and I followed the direction of Maxey's involuntary glance to the nearer of a two-room arrangement on the left side of the corridor.

"We heard he might be conscious soon," Corner Pocket said.

It was the first sound out of him since we entered the ICU, and it seemed to focus Maxey's attention on him. She looked a question in his direction and I moved, belatedly, to make introductions.

"Mrs. Goines," I said, taking the semiformal tack, "the inquisitive gentleman at my elbow is named Gerald Hope Singleton. He's chief investigator for the Clark County district attorney's office, and he never believes anything anyone tells him, so mind what you say when he's around. You're as safe with him as you'd be with Torquemada."

The smile that cut off the rest of the ritual came direct from Corner Pocket's own personal Greenland glacier, but it warmed quickly enough when he turned to point it at Maxey. She had that effect on people.

"Please, call me Corner Pocket," he said in a voice that would have spread nicely on muffins. "Most people do, and I'm out of practice with the other name."

She smiled back. "I know just what you mean," she said. "My name's Moira. But it's been a long time since anyone who knows me called me anything but Maxey."

It was the truth and it was a lie and it was getting to be the kind of scene that causes acne and tooth decay, and it might have gotten even worse but for an interruption provided by the nurse at the monitor desk down the hall.

Even during the introductions, the part of my mind that attends to peripheral vision had noted a sudden increase in activity there. The nurse was standing up, pushing what were probably reset buttons to check one set of monitors. And now she pressed a different kind of switch on her desk and spoke urgently into a microphone that seemed to be attached to the hospital public address system.

"Dr. Elmer," she said with an undercurrent of urgency strong enough to survive a passage through the loudspeakers. "Five-J-one. Stat!"

The words meant nothing to me, but their effect on Corner Pocket was immediate.

He knew the hospital, and would be acquainted with the codes they used to transmit information quickly without frightening the visitors, and now he was looking toward the room I had decided was probably Sam's. I noted the number on the door: J-1. And this was the fifth floor.

"Dr. Elmer?" I inquired.

"Code for the crash cart," he said.

At that instant, the doors to the unit burst open and two men in hospital greens brushed past, pushing what looked like a wheeled telephone switchboard equipped with extra wiring and a pair of metal Ping-Pong paddles.

They went into Sam's room, followed a moment later by a tubby little man wearing a white lab coat over an expensive-looking pin-striped vest and matching trousers.

"That's . . . Dr. Morse," Maxey said in a voice that was suddenly smaller and more apprehensive than it had been a moment before. "He said Sam was better. He said . . ."

She stopped talking in midsentence and I don't think she knew she had been speaking aloud. No more words came, and we sat and stood and knelt in the positions we had occupied for several minutes, watching the doorway.

A lot seemed to be going on inside.

No shouts or alarums, and except for the haste of the crash-cart crew and the doctor as they entered the room, nothing much was visible except for occasional brief and muted flashes of light reflected by the polished surface of the door. But there were occasional peaks in the volume of the vocal exchanges, though no actual words could be distinguished, and at times we could hear the electric hum-and-thump of what I knew from past hospital experience was a heart defibrillator in action.

Corner Pocket finally broke the spell.

"That's why they call it intensive care," he said, making an obvious effort to relieve tension. "Something comes up, you get quick action."

As a social gesture it was only partially successful, but it ended our stasis, and I finally got up from my crouch and Maxey licked her lips and made unnecessary motions to smooth nonexistent wrinkles in her skirt and to pull it below its designed position on her thigh. Such excess motion and the uneasiness it indicated were a measure of the concern we all felt. But the minutes passed and activity in the room seemed to subside a bit and I think we were all beginning to breathe a little easier when the humming finally stopped and the man Maxey had identified as Sam's doctor emerged from the room.

His face told it all, and I'm sure Maxey could read the message as clearly as Corner Pocket or I. But the habit of denial and the impulse of hope are strong, and the age-old scene had to be played out to its miserable end.

The doctor knew Corner Pocket and nodded absently in lieu of greeting.

I got a more thorough going-over, but my presence inside the doors of the ICU and my position, seated beside Maxey, seemed to satisfy him that I was part of the group, and he paid me no further attention.

"Mrs. Goines . . ." he said.

Maxey's expression was tense and tightly controlled. Reaching out with my mind, I could feel the effort it cost her to keep it that way and admire the force of will involved. The earlier faintness seemed to have passed entirely.

"Mr. Goines seemed to be doing all right after we got him stable," the doctor went on. "The vital signs were strong and, as I told Inspector Singleton here, we thought he would be conscious again about now."

He paused to lick his lips, and I think he was hoping someone would say the rest of it for him. But we waited him out and at last he went on.

"But something happened a few minutes ago," he said. "The monitors showed a sudden drop in blood pressure, and the heartbeat became erratic. The nurse reacted promptly and correctly. She called for the crash cart and I was on the floor and came as quickly as possible and everything that could be done was done. But it failed.

"I am very sorry to have to tell you that your husband simply slipped away from us.

"Sam Goines is dead . . ."

Dr. Morse paused for a moment, letting the information sink in. I needed the time. So did Maxey.

Her eyes were wide again and everything important had emptied out of her face, leaving it in its original bone-supported perfection. Like the surface of a statue. And just as reactive.

Not knowing—exactly—what was going on inside her made it nearly impossible for me to offer much help. But I wasn't sure Maxey needed it. Despite her unusual height and the near-arrogant assurance that goes with trained showgirl posture and carriage, one of Maxey's most attractive qualities had always been a hint of vulnerability visible just below the perfectly manicured surface. It was a quality she shared with Monroe and Liz and all the other power ladies of the screen whose acting ability was always dwarfed and denigrated by their sheer visual impact.

But in Maxey's case, I had reason to know that the defense-lessness had always been more apparent than real.

The woman I had known was a stainless-steel spring, resilient and capable, dressed up in a body that she subjected to the kind of professional maintenance and detached control that a banker would give to his investment portfolio or a race-car driver to his Formula-1.

In the case at hand, I had the feeling of being able to see some of the wheels go around despite the flawless surface poise. The *wa* was changed; I could not touch it directly—contact was too tenuous—but its temperature could be measured and it had gone from cold authority to warmth to heat and back to frozen tundra in the few minutes since Corner Pocket and I came through the door.

It was chilled steel again now as we waited for the doctor to go on, and I found myself speculating again about the rumors concerning strained relations between her and the man who had been her husband for more than a decade. And gave myself a sneer of pure contempt. Sam had been my friend.

The sudden discovery that I had been nursing a sick and secret little letch for his wife for all these years was appalling enough without the added complication of knowing that his death might not have been a total emotional disaster for her.

Not that my own reaction had been much stronger. Somehow I couldn't seem to associate the man who had just died in the intensive care unit of Mount Etna Hospital with the Sam Goines I had known.

Perhaps it would have been different if Sam and I had had more than a few hours to become reacquainted after the hiatus of a decade. But I had a peculiar feeling that maybe it wouldn't. Thinking back to the game that had occupied most of the night and morning hours, I realized that I had spent a good part of the time wondering about him, noticing a kind of emptiness, a lassitude that amounted almost to boredom. Sam had never been that way. I remembered him as vital and interested, bluffing far too often, sometimes just to liven up the action, and determined to win all the time. At everything. Something about him had been different last night, and it was more than could be charged to the lapse of ten years.

In a month or two, when I'd had time to remember the man who had been my friend and the things we had laughed at and the times we had backed each other and the reasons we had had to trust each other, maybe then I would be able to make the loss real and begin my own mourning. But for now my emotional reaction was no more powerful than Maxey's.

And she was handling it nicely.

I think the doctor had expected more, and his pause for effect stretched farther than he had intended before he was convinced that he'd seen all there was to see. Even then, he seemed oddly reluctant to continue with whatever it was he had to say.

"You understand," he said, clearing his throat unnecessarily, "that there are some formalities to be gone through, here . . ."

Maxey nodded, never taking her eyes from his face, and he cleared his throat another time.

"I was . . . ah . . . not Mr. Goines's regular physician," he said.

Maxey nodded. "Dr. LeBatt," she said. "In Monaco."

"Yes."

I think he was going to clear his throat yet again, but stopped himself before it happened.

"Yes. Well . . . ah . . . with no regular physician in attendance, I'm afraid the law in Nevada—"

"And just about everywhere else," Corner Pocket broke in brusquely. "The doctor is trying to say that there will have to be an autopsy."

Maxey turned the eyes on Corner Pocket, and I was vaguely amused to note that he was no more proof against them than I—or any other man I had ever seen. They make you blink and shuffle. Find a way to bottle that and you could conquer the earth.

"Just so," Dr. Morse took back the initiative Corner Pocket had suddenly lost and seemed to carry it with more assurance than before. "Just so. An autopsy. And even if I had been the regular attending physician, I would have wanted full postmortem pathology. Because there are two big things about Mr. Goines's death that puzzle me."

He stopped again to let us react, but this time he was ready to move again when we didn't.

"Firstly," he said, "I believe I told you, Mrs. Goines, that your husband was improving and could have been expected to recover. I also told the police. And I said that because to the best of my knowledge and experience I believed it to be true.

"Mr. Goines had been shot twice: once in the lower abdomen and once in the chest. But only the chest wound was immediately life-threatening, and I am absolutely certain that we were able to reduce it and repair the worst of the damage shortly after he arrived here. He had lost a lot of blood, and there was still some work to be done to contain the damage and make sure of preventing infection from the wound in the stomach cavity. But his crit showed that he had responded well to the multiple transfusions, and his vital signs were improving.

"He was going to make it . . . ."

He paused again, but this time there was no sense of hesitancy or embarrassment. The emotion coming off him in waves was a pungent amalgam of indignation, frustration, and rage.

"Samuel Goines should be alive," the doctor said. "He should be awake and talking to us right now. But he's not. He is dead and I don't know why he died, and until I do know, I'm afraid I am going to be very damned difficult to be around. But that's only part of the problem. The other part is, I think, more in your line."

He had turned to face Corner Pocket, and the last words had been addressed directly to him as he reached into the side pocket of his laboratory coat and rummaged around in the recesses for a moment.

"I told you the monitor nurse reacted quickly to the change in Mr. Goines's vital signs," the doctor went on. "But in the time it took her to move from her station to his room, Mr. Goines's breathing and heart action had stopped entirely. So of course her first thought was to begin immediate cardiopulmonary resuscitation. And that is what she did.

"But she is an orderly person and an intelligent one, and even in her haste to get the patient's heart and lungs back in action she was careful to preserve something most peculiar that she found laid out on the sheet covering his chest."

The doctor's hand emerged from his coat pocket with five playing cards clamped between a thumb and forefinger, which moved with the unconscious ease of long practice to fan and display them for us.

The cards were good ones. Worth betting in anybody's game.

But I couldn't help thinking about all the times they had been losers, beginning nearly a century ago in Dakota Territory and running full-tilt through the years to this long morning in Las Vegas, where their myth and legend were reinforced and augmented. Someone, somehow, had managed to make Sam Goines's final hand a full house:

Two aces. And three eights . . .

A SERMON (Continued)

But our age is unique, for we live in a world of make-believe. A false world, dedicated to propositions of fantasy, because reality—the real world—contains corners too dark for close scrutiny. We lie to ourselves because we think that we must lie. Or go mad . . .

10

FOR A LONG moment nobody spoke. But there was a lot of thinking going on, and I wasn't at all surprised to see Corner Pocket looking at me with a combination of puzzlement and fury. He would be sure now that I was lying to him, and the hell of it was that he was right: I was lying. But not about the things he suspected.

I was holding out on the identity of the dead gunman, and nothing that had happened in the past few minutes had changed my mind about that.

Until I could explain it to myself, I sure wasn't going to try explaining it to anyone else.

But about the rest of the morning's events—the killings and the helicopter and the atom bomb and now the dead man's hand—he knew as much as I did. Still, I couldn't fault him for thinking I had to be lying. Looking back on the morning, it seemed to me that I had been behaving like some kind of hockey puck. Yackety Doodle in Wonderland. Someone, somewhere, had set up a series of unlikely events and led me into the center frame on the obvious assumption that there wouldn't be a thing I could do about it. And so far someone, somewhere, was damn well right.

I could feel myself beginning to steam . . . and ran through a series of mental obscenities with the realization that this, too, was probably an expected and programmed reaction.

Jesus on a bicycle . . . !

"Who else went into that room?"

Corner Pocket had been thinking, too, and not just about me.

The doctor shook his head. "I asked the same question," he said. "But the nurse says everything was normal. The only visitor on the floor was Mrs. Goines."

Maxey blinked and came back from whatever far land of consideration she had been visiting. "What?"

"Sam's room," I said, trying to give her a little time. "You were here in the waiting area. Did you see anyone go in or out?"

She blinked again. "No," she said. "No one—but I hadn't been here very long." She turned her head to look at me. "I'd only been here a minute or two before you arrived. The nurse outside had to check with the police before I could get in, and then I didn't know which room he was in or whether I could see him, so I had to ask a nurse—"

And then my brain finally came to life. "The cap!" I said, cutting her off in mid-sentence. "The cap she was wearing— Maxey, where was that nurse the first time you saw her?"

Maxey looked at me as though I'd suddenly started to drool. But she answered.

"Right here," she said. "In the corridor. Outside Sam's room."

"Had she been in the room?"

"I . . . don't know. Maybe."

"And you asked her where Sam was."

"Yes. And she said he was in there. In J-one. But no one was allowed in there without the monitor nurse's permission."

"And then what?"

"And then you came in . . ."

I closed my eyes and tried to bring the picture of the corridor back as it had been at that moment.

"Medium height," I said. "Late thirties, brown eyes, black eyebrows—rather heavy, artificially darkened, maybe—with a rather large, straight nose."

Corner Pocket still didn't know what it was all about, but he had taken a small notebook from his pocket and I could see that he was inscribing hen tracks I recognized as shorthand.

"All right," he said when he was done. "That squares with what I saw. I don't think either of us saw the mouth or chin."

"No. I didn't, anyway."

"But so what? We'll get the nurse back here and question her."

I shook my head.

"No," I said. "You won't."

Corner Pocket transferred the notebook to the hand holding the ballpoint and gave me his full attention. "Go on."

"You won't question that nurse," I said, "because she doesn't exist. The cap she wore. It bothered me as soon as I saw it, but I didn't know why until now.''

"The cap?''

"Nursing schools are tough," I said. "Graduation is a big event, and it ends with something called the capping ceremony. Each school has its own distinctive headgear, and the graduate R.N. wears that cap and no other throughout her career. Which is why this nurse's cap is so important. It's the little round beribboned pillbox granted by the Sisters of Saint Anselm.''

Corner Pocket didn't understand, of course, and neither did Maxey or the doctor. But they hadn't spent a year as student instructor for Sewanee's course in contemporary church history. And I had.

"The Sisters of Saint Anselm," I said, "were a nursing order with just one school. At Limoges, in France. It was wiped out during the Second World War and never reestablished. The last graduating class was in 1940.

"The youngest person legitimately qualified to wear the cap would now be in her mid-sixties.''

Corner Pocket swore and took two quick strides in the direction of the visitors' telephone. But we both knew it was only a gesture and a pretty useless one at that.

Uniforms are anonymous in a hospital.

To leave the building unobserved, the ersatz nurse had only to keep her eyes front and her mouth firmly shut. Stopping to talk to Maxey must have been an annoyance. An unexpected glitch in an otherwise perfect plan. But nothing serious. Nothing that the sudden arrival of two outsiders and Maxey's reaction to seeing me alive couldn't cover.

The security men stationed in the lobby and elsewhere had no memory of seeing any specific nurse—with or without a peculiarly shaped pillbox cap—and even the nurse assigned to the ICU monitor shook her head in blank incomprehension when Corner Pocket got around to questioning her. She knew the kind of cap he was talking about, but her job was to concentrate on the patients' condition as set forth in the gospel according to Medi-Date Systems, Inc., and not to clutter her head with questions about nursing schools and what business a seemingly legitimate nurse with a clipboard might have on the floor.

She did her job and tried to let others do theirs.

Her attitude was prim and self-righteous and superior and altogether irritating, but I didn't find myself in any position to criticize and I don't think Corner Pocket was feeling especially self-satisfied either. His shoulders slumped a little as he turned away from the monitor desk and faced us with what might have been a diffident shrug that never quite came off.

"Gone," he said.

Nobody seemed to have anything to say about that.

"You got a closer look at her than anyone else," he said, turning to Maxey. "Neither Preacher nor I can remember seeing the bottom half of her face. Anything you can help us with there?"

Maxey blinked, and I knew she was either editing what she was about to say or really trying to remember, and I was surprised to discover that I really couldn't be sure which it was.

"Wide mouth," she said. "One tooth a little crooked in front. I remember thinking she would be quite good-looking if it were fixed, and wondering why she hadn't had it done. And a fairly strong chin. No dimple and not too big for the face, but not undersized, either. I could tell you the shade of lipstick, but I don't think the name would mean anything to you—call it a darker red, keyed to the number three pancake she was wearing."

Maxey stopped talking for a moment and I think Corner Pocket was going to ask another question, but she spoke before he could. "You'll never find her with any description that any of us can give," she said.

Now it was Corner Pocket's turn to blink. "Say what?"

"The descriptions. The ones you got from Preacher and from me. They're no good. Everything, starting with height and going on to the color of her hair and the skin tone and the color of her eyes, every single damn thing, even to the shape of the nose and mouth, is something that can be changed."

"But—"

Maxey shook her head impatiently. "Talking to you just now," she said, "it suddenly struck me: Lifts in the shoes or flat heels or high heels and the design of a woman's clothes can make her seem inches taller or shorter. Take it from me—I'm tall enough to have to know about things like that.

"And the makeup. Preacher noticed the nursing cap but didn't know it was important at the time. I noticed the makeup. Hospital nurses rarely wear much, but she was loaded. A number three pan isn't usually worth remembering and I didn't think about it. Then. Talking about it now, I realize that the amount she had on was unusual. More for television or for the kind of society bash where newspaper and magazine photographers will be popping bulbs and you don't want to come off invisible inside your own clothes.

"Even the eye color could have been tinted contacts. I wear contacts myself. Sometimes."

There was a pause, and I caught the tiniest hint of a side glance in my direction. Did I remember?

Yes. I did.

"Give that nurse, whoever she was, fifteen minutes outside the hospital, or inside it if she has a change of clothes with her and a private place to remove the makeup," Maxey said, "and she could walk past any one of us without a chance of being recognized."

I think we all knew Maxey was right. But Corner Pocket had to go through the motions anyway, and I knew better than to do anything more original than relax.

Another team of detectives and forensic technicians arrived to take over the investigation, and of course each of us had to go through the story again. And again. And yet again. Even Corner Pocket wasn't exempt. And I noticed that the questioning was a lot less gentle and circumspect than had been the case with the detectives who came to the penthouse of the Scheherazade. Hotel killings—even when complicated by factors like masked hit men with submachine guns and a helicopter escape—are one thing; murders that happen in a hospital are quite another. This time the interrogators wanted the straight facts, never mind the polite omissions. And then they wanted the stories told over again, starting and working toward both ends with every detail cross-referenced and rechecked. Las Vegas police can be professional enough when they're allowed. Not that it made any difference.

Sam was still dead.

And the person suspected of killing him was still at large without even a good description available.

There was also the matter of the killer's calling cards. Aces and eights. The dead man's hand. The first time, at the hotel, it could have been coincidence. The cards had been together on the table and they could have been on Danny DiMarco's chest by chance.

This time, however, there could be no doubt. No question of coincidence. The cards had to mean something, had to be some-one's idea of delivering a message. And because of the business

I am in the chances were that it was addressed to me. So naturally I had to know what it meant.

And I didn't have a clue . . .

And naturally Corner Pocket thought I did.

All through the police interrogation I could feel his eyes on me, and the questions he was asking were louder than the ones that were spoken by the investigators. Old friends we might be—or at least respectful acquaintances. But three men were dead now, and there was reason to believe that one of them had been playing some kind of game with a stolen atom bomb. Personal emotions and individual concerns were going to run a bad second to professional duty for the duration.

Which was fine with me.

This was his line of work, not mine, and I was more than content to leave him to it. I had come to Las Vegas to play some poker and make some money, and multiple murders were definitely not on the agenda. Yet I couldn't seem to make myself tell him the one fact I was holding back—not until I was sure what it meant. And that might take some time.

I needed to be alone for a while, have leisure to study the various components of the hand I had been dealt so far, see how they might fit together, and weigh the chances of improvement and decide whether it was time to raise, call, or fold.

Meanwhile, there was Maxey. If Corner Pocket's unvoiced questions were noisy, the silent dialogue between Maxey and me was louder. She, too, was wondering whether I knew anything about the aces and eights. But she had something more than question marks to contribute. Reaching out with the back part of my mind while continuing to answer questions with the front, I tried to reach her. But as before, the *wa* was shielded, hidden behind a wall that seemed to have grown higher and stronger with the passage of minutes.

The only impressions I could get were of fear—a chill that seeped through the shield despite a degree of control that was far stronger than I remembered—and of determination.

Something was frightening her, but not badly enough to keep her from going through with whatever errand had brought her to Las Vegas in the first place.

I couldn't help wondering what it was.

"Mrs. Goines . . ."

The face was unfamiliar, but the attitude and the summons

were not, and I turned away from the detective whose questions I had been answering to see if Maxey needed help.

She had stopped talking, too, and turned her head in the direction of the thin, bald man who was leaning out the doorway of Sam Goines's room.

"Mrs. Goines, I'm sorry, but there is something that has to be done for the official record. Could you step in here for a moment?"

Maxey looked at me. "Preacher . . . ?"

She didn't have to say it twice. I think the detective nearest me wanted to put a hand on my arm to keep me where I was, but he didn't do it and that was just as well. I moved across the room to stand beside her and stayed close, with my hand touching her arm, as she went into the room where her husband had died.

A sheet had been pulled over Sam's face and the various tubes and wires of intensive care had been disconnected, but the place still showed signs of the frantic effort that had been made to draw him back from the shadows.

Someone had pushed the nightstand away from the bed with a rough hand. It was angled against the outer wall of the room, and a tray that had been on it had fallen to the floor, spilling various items of hospital bric-a-brac. The crash cart stood forlorn in another corner, its mission a failure. And the sheet covering the body had come loose at its lower end.

Alive, Sam Goines had been vital and determined and full of slightly cynical laughter. A successful man and a tough one. A winner. In all his years, few had ever pitied him—or had reason to.

But death is the card of change.

The loosened sheet had left Sam's feet exposed and somehow their nude and flaccid immobility brought a run of compassion for the man that would have been unthinkable only a few hours earlier. Maxey saw it, too, and I sensed a rush of emotion from her that paralleled my own. And that was a surprise.

I had been an old friend.

She had been his wife.

But there was more. Something besides sorrow or even regret. I stood still, trying to identify the feeling, while the man who had summoned her into the room drew back the top of the sheet to expose Sam's face.

It was relaxed, composed. Almost smiling. And it crossed my mind that he might have had reason to smile. Sam's life had been a texture of money acquired and secrets kept, and he had died in possession of a secret that a lot of people would have paid a lot of money to possess.

All the same, there was something else . . .

Maxey looked for a long moment at the exposed face and then nodded. The coroner's man replaced the sheet and thanked her and then seemed to notice the exposed feet for the first time. He moved at once to cover them—and then I knew what had been disturbing me. I had a final moment in which to check before they were out of sight, and then looked at Maxey to see if she had noticed the same thing.

But her face was closed and quiet.

If she knew what I knew, and I was almost certain that she did, she wasn't about to tell anyone about it.

Together we walked in silence from the room.

A SERMON (Continued)

We tell ourselves that ultimate weapons held not just by both sides but by all sides in a world of diverse aims and conflicting needs and values will never be put to use because they are too terrible. Too totally devastating. Too effective . . .

11

THE QUESTIONING RESUMED as soon as we were back in the corridor, but the edge was gone and it gradually petered out with the standard injunctions: Don't discuss this among yourselves, keep us informed of your whereabouts, let us know if you think of anything else. Written statements will be ready in a day or so, and we will want you to come in and sign them.

And Corner Pocket had a quiet word of his own to add. "You stay in town," he said. "We are going to talk again. Soon."

I allowed as how it did seem likely.

Maxey had come to the hospital in a police car, and Corner Pocket said he was going to be busy at the hospital for a while, so I offered her a ride back to the Scheherazade.

She accepted without comment, and we rode the first few blocks in what amounted to silence, though we continued to exchange small talk that would probably have made sense on playback if any outsider had been listening. But it was tinfoil, sound in an empty room.

There were things I wanted to say.

And ask. And tell . . .

Traffic was heavier now, even on the side streets, and I edged the rented car into a left-turn lane and waited for the light to let me swing onto Paradise Road, but before I could do that Maxey touched my arm and made the first sensible suggestion I'd heard all morning.

"Turn right," she said.

"I thought you were staying at the Scheherazade."

"I am."

"Well, it's to the left."

"But I'm hungry." She turned her head to give me another dose of the armor-piercing eyes. "I thought you might know where we could find some Chinese food . . . ?"

I looked back at her and found myself marveling once again at how few changes ten years had made. A touch more self-assurance, perhaps, though Maxey had never been exactly shy. And the kind of clothes that are so expensive they don't need a maker's name stamped on them. But the face hadn't changed. Flawless, if you discounted the nose she'd always said was just a little bit off-center. And the woman who owned it seemed to be someone I remembered, too.

"I think I might know a place," I said.

She grinned at me. "So turn right, dammit, and let's get out of this desert sun."

My hands moved the steering wheel and my feet made the car go and my eyes kept us from running into solid objects. But they were on autopilot, doing their own thing while the rest of me sat still and reacted to Maxey—as always—with as much cool restraint and poise as one of Pavlov's dogs.

All things considered, I didn't seem to have changed much, either.

One of Las Vegas's worst kept secrets is the Chinese food at the coffee shop just off the casino in the Golden Nugget, downtown.

Been that way for a long time.

Menus on the counter and at the booths are all carefully calculated to proclaim café-American, solid sandwich-and-blue-plate fare, perhaps a cut or two above average for the genre but certainly nothing to paste in the memory book.

The knowledgeable, however, are aware that a quiet request to the waitress for the Chinese menu is the passport to the best oriental cookery east of San Francisco.

The Golden Nugget is located in that part of Las Vegas known to visitors as Casino Center and to regulars as Glitter Gulch, world capital of neon-and-plastic kitsch, where the only way to be sure whether it is midnight or noon is to walk into the middle of the street and look up.

The intersection it shares with Binion's Horseshoe, the Fremont, and the Four Queens is the ground-zero center of town, the place where gaming operations finally came into their own after the early years of trail-town stagnation, and from that crossroads to the Union Plaza a couple of blocks away, the area is zoned, planned, and deliberately decorated to offer a kind of all-casino ambience calculated to attract wonderment and dollars.

And in this milieu the Golden Nugget has flourished.

Even before the hotel was built, it was known as the biggest and most successful of the downtown casinos, occupying a full frontage block along casino row.

It was during those non-hotel years that the tradition of elegant Chinese cuisine in the coffee shop began, and all subsequent managements have been wise enough to keep this intact no matter what other innovations might be under consideration. The Golden Nugget could probably survive without the Chinese food—we live in a world of wonders where human beings are able to live for long periods without lungs or kidneys or even flesh-and-blood hearts, and some few cities have achieved a certain weird zombie-life after the destruction of their downtown commercial centers—but it would have no soul.

On arrival, we turned the car over to a valet parking service outside the early-whorehouse facade, walked through the lobby to the casino, and turned left toward the food.

Maxey was a stranger to the place by now, but I spend enough time in Las Vegas—and like Chinese food well enough—to be considered a regular, and the waitress turned away to fetch the special menu without having to be asked. A pretty meager perk, to be sure. But pleasant, and I settled myself to study the slick-finished trifold with a sense of comfort and familiarity . . . which turned to pure déjà vu when I glanced at my dinner-breakfast companion.

This was the place where it had started.

I had been on terminal leave from the army hospital for three weeks and in Las Vegas for two—long enough to find out that I didn't know as much about the game of poker as I had imagined, but not long enough to be sure whether I would ever be able to learn.

There was a little money. Uncle Sugar is not precisely bountiful when it comes to ex-corporals who have managed to lose an eye in combat, but various politicians over the decades have finally gotten him out of the old-time habit of telling them thanks a lot, now go root hog or die. So for the time being I was receiving regular checks from the Veterans Administration, pending final disposition of any claim I might have for disability.

I had discovered the Golden Nugget's Chinese menu on my fifth day in town and had been a regular ever since. Even in those days, I was savvy enough to keep my eating and drinking to an irreducible minimum while playing poker, so of course I ended every game ravenous and sleepy, a mind-bending combination for a man whose dreams were already less than comfortable. Chinese food, particularly Cantonese cooked by people who knew what they were doing, turned out to be a palatable—if somewhat addictive—answer.

I could eat it with relish and digest it without nightmares, and I was about to do both the night someone seated in the booth opposite my own leaned across the aisle to demand immediate information on the source of my goodies.

The person who had spoken was on my right side, which is to say my blind side. I turned my head to see her before answering . . . and temporarily forgot how to speak the English language.

Maxey always had that effect on me.

Fortunately it was a reaction she had seen before and was used to. She gave me a moment to recover scrambled wits and then repeated the question.

I explained about the menu, but there seemed to be another problem: She had lost one contact lens at work and taken the other one out, and the regular glasses, which she hated anyway, were at home. Could I possibly . . . ?

I could. And since it was awkward for me to twist my head so far around to see her—I wasn't about to look away—it seemed the most natural thing in the world for me to move over into her booth. Which, in turn, led to introductions. And a few minutes later we were splitting a double order of won ton, curried chicken with peppers, Peking braised lamb, and spicy eggplant with more steamed rice than any six people could eat. But we made a valiant attempt.

Maxey affected my speech centers, not my appetite.

And later I found myself talking easily, too. Concealed behind that high-impact exterior and the imposing professional-dancer name of Moira Fonteyn, I discovered, was a twenty-four-year-old registered nurse named Dorothy Maxine Mankowski, whose imposing upper and lower measurements had ruled out all hope of a ballet career by the time she was seventeen.

"Even then," she sighed, "I was five feet eleven, a hundred and plenty. Pivot hard enough and the top of me could knock one of those poor little male dancers into the middle of next week. So I went to work on the line at GM to get enough money for nursing school."

One graduation, one marriage, one divorce, and one elderly

private patient later, she was in Las Vegas. And back to being a dancer.

"Well . . . sort of," she amended. "Most of the show I just stand there wearing about thirty pounds of stuff on my head and six ounces everywhere else. But we all do a kind of time-step for the finale. So I say I'm a dancer, because that's easier and nicer than saying I'm scenery, even though that's what I'm really hired to be."

The words held no bitterness, only calm acceptance of an existing situation, and she snorted at the idea of returning to the nursing profession.

"Not till I'm old and gray and too bent to get into that damn headdress," she vowed. "The hours are long, the work's hard, and even though being an R.N. takes a couple years of college and you're supposed to be a kind of administrator, the doctors treat any nurse like rented furniture—or an off-hours sex toy if they think they can get away with it—and I have sort of got out of the habit of being either one."

I said I could see how that might be.

Las Vegas, she said, wasn't a half-bad place to stop and rest and figure out what to do with the rest of a lifetime.

Which jarred me a bit.

Because I was in town on the same errand.

Even with the garnish of easy conversation, a breakfast of Chinese food isn't much foundation for any kind of lasting relationship, and I was only half-hopeful when I suggested that there were more things to do in town than hang around the casinos and eat curried chicken.

But the gallon or so of spiced tea I had consumed had left me both alert and optimistic, and it turned out to be her day off, too—I hadn't yet told her that it was always my day off if I wanted it that way—and we started with a game of tennis that must have amused anyone who was watching even more than it did us. Which was a lot.

Moira/Maxey, I discovered on the first serve, was by no means as blind as a bat without her glasses, but all the same suffered from a myopia that gave her less than a split second to react to the ball. Her reflexes were good. Excellent, in fact. But seldom good enough to connect.

I, on the other hand, was playing tennis for the first time since becoming monocular, and I hadn't yet had time to achieve the mental compensation that eventually simulates normal three-dimensional sight.

The result, so far as tennis was concerned, was a comedic turn that finally and mercifully ended in mutual hilarity after the second set.

Maxey—she had asked me, as a favor, to call her that after the second time I addressed her by the mouth-filling professional name—said she hadn't noticed the prosthetic eye that I wore, and though I put that down to nearsightedness, her only reaction on closer contact was curiosity. Wearing her glasses, she wanted to see me take the glass eye out and put it back in. Perhaps it was the background in nursing, perhaps simply an open and accepting quality that seemed basic to her nature, but it was the only attitude I could have lived with at the time. I was still a little squeamish about the damn thing myself.

And of course she had to hear how I had come to need it.

But all that happened later.

That first day, we rented a car after leaving the tennis center, stopped by her apartment long enough for her to retrieve the spectacles, and then moved on to the golf course at the hotel where she worked—where she proceeded to beat the living hell out of me hole by hole until the seventeenth green where I demanded that she accept at least the handicap of putting without her glasses and she said she would do that if I would tee off with my left eye closed and I agreed and we actually tried to do it . . . with results roughly comparable to those we had achieved on the tennis court.

The game never really got finished.

We were laughing too hard and the foursome behind us was too impatient and besides, the sun was going down and it was time for the nineteenth hole.

Nowadays I drink only occasionally, when the potation is worth it (the triple-run blockader that enlivens an occasional evening at Best Licks, or a really celebratory dinner wine) or when the occasion seems to demand it. But in those days I was having a sick little love affair with the bottle, feeling sorry for myself and using that as justification on hangover mornings. So the evening got a lot wetter than I had intended and I sort of lost track of events between the golf course and the moment, quite a few hours later, when I woke up in a bed I didn't recognize, staring blearily at the ceiling of a room I had never seen before.

I was alone, but there was ample evidence that the other half of the double bed had been occupied at some recent time, and I lay still for a while trying to remember who it might have been. But it was no good.

A blank.

I did the only thing I could think of to do, which was sit up and look around for my undershorts. And regretted it immediately. Bells were ringing in the far distance, and the room seemed to want to remain on its side.

Maxey walked in a minute or two later and gave me what might or might not have been a smile. A glass of something dark and violent-looking was in her hand. Her I remembered.

Oh, yes.

The morning improved at once.

"Old family recipe," she said, aiming the glass in my direction and waiting for me to take it from her hand. "Passed along from generation to generation for—oh, three or four weeks now. Don't think. Drink."

She waited for me to do it and I thought about saying no, but I didn't say anything like that because she was standing there in glowing good health and fully clothed in a rusty-red practice leotard and therefore in a position of obvious moral ascendancy over a one-eyed man sitting on the edge of an unfamiliar bed in his skivvies. And anyway, it didn't really matter whether the contents of the glass cured me or killed me. Either way would have to be an improvement.

It was chilled and spicy and I drank it all and was about to hand the empty glass back when it exploded.

"That's the cayenne," Maxey said, evidently reading my expression.

Something powerful went to work on the nerve centers at the back of my head, tingling and pummeling as it moved down my spine to the muscles of the shoulder yoke and on to lower regions. There was an itch I couldn't scratch about three inches below the surface in the vicinity of my kidneys and it moved rapidly into my hips and thighs.

"Ginseng," Maxey said. "And other things. Being a nurse has its uses."

She took the glass back without further commentary, showed me which door led to the bathroom and which to the living room, and left me to deal with recovery in my own way.

I did my best.

And it seemed to be good enough.

Toweling on the mat a few minutes later, I was surprised but not displeased to hear myself humming a light and somewhat bawdy song. The day was definitely on an upswing.

I took the prosthetic eye out and cleaned it as well as I could without the special chemical bath I had learned to use, and went through the still unfamiliar routine of plopping it back into the socket. There, now! The stubble-crusted face that looked back at me from the mirror was not handsome. But I recognized it as one I had seen before, and that was a victory of sorts.

I crawled regretfully back into yesterday's shirt, socks, trousers, and shoes and went out to peddle the abject apology I had been manufacturing for the past several minutes.

But I never got to recite it.

Maxey was sitting at a table beside a window that looked out on an apartment courtyard and pool, peering at a newspaper through the owl-eyed glasses I remembered, and the plate across from her was piled with toast, cantaloupe, and orange slices.

She seemed to be interested in something on the financial page, but tore herself away to look up at me when I sat down.

"Better?" she inquired.

"Immeasurably," I said.

That got the first real smile of the morning.

"Hah!" she said. "You're back to speaking English."

Oh, God . . .

"Was I really that bad last night?"

There was coffee in a large glass pot and she turned away to pour it before answering.

"You're Mexican?" she said.

I shook my head, and regretted it at once. Recovery, I decided, was not quite complete.

"German and Irish," I said. "Descended from a long line of drunkards and pig thieves. But as I understand it my parents were busy doing something or other that kept them away from home a lot just after I was born, so they had a live-in Cuban nanny for me and it was easier for her to speak to me in Spanish than in English . . . so that turned out to be my first language."

She put the paper down; the weird story seemed to fascinate her.

Odd. It had always bored the hell out of me.

"How old were you when you finally learned English?" she said.

"Well, Maria—that was her name, Maria Edrosa—died when

I was six, I guess, and my parents came home and found out they weren't exactly on speaking terms with their only child, so they stayed around for a while and I learned English and who they were and all of that. But I never really got over thinking of Maria as *mamacita*."

"Or missing her?"

"Or missing her."

We drank coffee and munched toast and I tried some of the cantaloupe and it was fine and after a few minutes I finally decided I had the guts to try a little exculpatory rhetoric. But Maxey cut it short after the fourth or fifth word.

"Look," she said, "if this is the beginning of an apology or a dutiful declaration of undying affection or something sticky like that, you'd be doing me a real favor by keeping it to yourself. Okay?"

"Well . . ."

"No 'well' about it." She poured herself more coffee, offered some to me, and put the pot back on the automatic heat plate when I made a negative motion.

I think she was almost ready to leave it at that, but there was something else. I could see it was setting off some kind of reaction inside her, but I couldn't get the sense of what it might be, and that worried me a little because if it was compassion—pity—for me, after my tale of woe, I was going to have to tip my hat and slowly ride away into the sunrise, and I had just realized that I didn't want to do that at all.

But it wasn't pity. Or anything connected with what I'd started to say. I realized, eventually, that the turmoil I had noticed was nothing more than the effort to keep a straight face. She was trying not to laugh about something. And having a real struggle.

"The thing is," she said, "I don't think you remember a lot about last night, do you?"

"Uh . . . no."

Some of the laughter broke through for a moment, and she sipped the coffee to cover it, but it wasn't totally effective and finally she went on.

"Well, then," she said, "I'm not going to go through a play-by-play. And what I said about not needing an apology still goes. Nothing happened last night that I didn't expect or want to happen. I'm just sorry only one of us remembers.

"All the same, if we're going to see each other again—and I kind of hope we'll want to, because yesterday was the first real fun I've had since I got to this Christforsaken town—I can't help hoping that booze isn't a big item in your life. Because, lover, I have to tell you that liquor—or anyway, tequila—seems to have a really odd effect on your bedroom manners.''

I groaned inwardly.

"You mean, I—"

She shook her head emphatically. "No," she said. "You're not reading me. I said I enjoyed the evening, and I meant it. But a girl likes a little romance—a touch of tenderness here and there. Macho moves are fine in their place, and God knows I'm not protecting the Star of India in here or anything. I have had my share of propositions and accepted some of them, and one or two have even been worth remembering.

"But there are limits.

"Offhand, I can't remember a single one before last night that consisted of simply picking me up and carrying me into my own bedroom roaring *'.Abajo con tus pantalones!'* at the top of his lungs.''

A SERMON (Continued)

We insist, against all logic and all evidence, that the hands to which we have entrusted these instruments of total annihilation are sane hands. Reasonable hands. Hands that will not kill us all by whim . . .

12

BACK IN THE here-and-now of penthouses and assassins and hospital murders and rampant nostalgia, Maxey laughed and put down the menu.

"You order," she said. "I'm hungry as a bitch wolf, and you always seemed to come up with just the right things."

It wasn't a total answer to the question that had been in my mind, but any lingering doubts were dispelled a moment or two later when I looked up from pretending to concentrate on the text to find her still grinning at me.

"Something?"

"You."

"My friends all seem to laugh a lot lately. I've been wondering about it."

"And you seem to bullshit a lot, lover. Don't tell me you weren't wandering around in our mutual memory book. I was in there myself, and I saw you."

Well, okay, then.

"I may have let an old afternoon or two cross my mind," I said.

"Hah!"

"And maybe even an evening."

She snorted again, but seemed to accept the admission in lieu of further discussion. She wasn't ready to leave the subject, though. And neither, I suppose, was I.

The smile faded and I went back to the menu, gradually narrowing the choices down to a question of rainbow beef in lettuce leaves or the Peking duck with Chinese pancakes. I was considering the relative merits of stir-fried snow peas and water chestnuts as compared to braised cauliflower and oyster sauce when she spoke again, shattering the still fragile texture of the present with a single sentence.

113

"Do you still dream about Sara?" she asked.

The answer was yes. Of course.

Two days after Maxey and I met, I had paid a final visit to the little downtown hole-in-the wall hotel where I'd been staying, and moved my total possessions—which did not quite fill one battered carry-on bag—into the spare closet of Maxey's apartment. She said she'd had a problem recently with half-drunk show patrons following her home and would feel safer if I was around. But I never believed a word of it. Even then, I knew there would be few if any problems that Maxey couldn't find some simple, nonmuscular way of resolving.

And the muscular solutions were no problem, either.

I had begun studying t'ai chi ch'uan—the Oriental art of muscular control, balance, and contemplation—at the hospital, where it was part of the rehabilitation therapy, and thereafter developed a kind of life of its own.

I was surprised and fascinated to discover that many of the ballet exercises that Maxey put herself through every morning were almost exactly translatable to—and from—some of the convoluted positions of t'ai chi, and she seemed as pleased as I to have companionship in the regular hour-long workouts that were followed, usually, by a mutual shower that always seemed to take longer than it had to—and always seemed time well spent.

So I was surprised, and more than a little taken aback, when she sprang the question on me just after our shower on the morning of our fifth day together.

"Who's Sara?" she asked.

I had been drying her back, and I didn't stop. But I chose my words carefully, wanting to use as few of them as possible to tell whatever was going to have to be told.

"Sara was my wife," I said.

She accepted this in silence, and I waited for the next question.

"Was?" she inquired after a moment.

"She died," I said. "A little more than two years ago."

"Oh."

More silence, and I finished with the back—this time without the embellishments that had become almost a part of the routine—and she turned to face me.

"Did you kill her?" she said.

•   •   •

She had asked the right question, but I wasn't sure I knew the right answer. I'm still not.

It was no, in the sense that I hadn't pulled any trigger and had in fact been otherwise occupied several thousand miles away at the time my Sara died.

But it was also yes, in several ways that mattered—and discussing them with shrinks at the hospital hadn't done much to resolve the matter.

"I'm talking in my sleep?"

Maxey nodded solemnly, the deep-colored eyes even more dominant in a face somehow younger and almost defenseless in its total innocence of makeup.

"Sometimes," she said, "it's in Spanish, and I can't get much of it, and sometimes it's in some language I don't recognize at all. Vietnamese, maybe; it sounds sort of Oriental."

"That," I said, "or Chinese. I speak a little Mandarin and some Hakka."

"But when you dream in English," Maxey went on, undiverted, "it's usually about this Sara. And how it's your fault that she's dead."

Well.

Hell.

I nodded and didn't answer at once and we put on our clothes and by that time the coffee was hot again and we sat down and I told as much of the story as I could and I think Maxey's own intelligence filled in whatever blanks were left.

Sara and I were married the day I graduated from Sewanee. She was there three days later when I was ordained, traveled with me to the Midwest, where I was assigned a missionary circuit of four starveling churches, reacted with predictable outrage and incomprehension when I accepted a commission in the Army Chaplain Corps a few months later, stood waving silently and alone as I boarded the plane that would take me to the port of embarkation. And that was all the marriage we ever had.

She was killed about eighteen months later when some half-trained National Guardsmen panicked and opened fire on a group of peace marchers during a demonstration she had helped organize.

Maxey didn't understand at all.

"So how the hell," she demanded, "does this make you a murderer?"

"She was my wife."

"So . . . ?"

"I was her husband, and I was as much against the war as she was, though for different reasons, and if I'd been there she would still be alive. But I wasn't."

Maxey finished her coffee slowly and thoughtfully and put the cup down with exaggerated care and looked at me with a face that said I was the damnedest fool she'd come across, and not an especially likable one, either.

"You know . . . I killed my husband," she said.

It was a subject we had never discussed; she'd told me she had been married once and wasn't anymore and we'd left it at that. Now she sat waiting for me to react, and all I could do was sit still and wait for her to explain.

"He was a second-year medical student," she went on when she was sure I wasn't going to speak. "That gave him an out as far as the draft was concerned. The thing in 'Nam was going strong, but it would have been over by the time he graduated and finished internship. And that's how it would have gone if we hadn't had a fight over whether or not I should start nurse's training."

I thought I could see where the story was going, and drew breath to interrupt. But she paid no attention.

"The way it went down," she said, "I enrolled one day and he went down to the Marine Corps recruiting station the next. Five months later I got the Navy Department's deepest regrets."

"Maxey—"

"Don't Maxey me!"

It was the first time I'd seen her really angry, and it was worth seeing. But I didn't have the leisure to examine the phenomenon.

"I loved Bart Jelannek—that was his goddam name; I don't think I ever mentioned it before and I'm sure not going to again, awake or asleep—as much as any woman could love any man on this earth and maybe more because I hadn't even looked at anyone else from the time he walked into my third grade class the day after his folks moved into the neighborhood. In two or three ways that are pretty important, getting that telegram was the end of my life as much as the end of his. So don't tell me about loving or mourning or who is responsible for who.

"I got word that he was dead on the day before an important exam, and if I'd wanted to build Bart a monument that he'd have recognized I could have given up right there and blown the damn thing and gotten kicked out of nursing school, which I didn't much like anyhow, and that would have been just great, because you could make a pretty good case that my being in that school and not being willing to back out when he wanted me to had gotten him killed.

"But I read the telegram and folded it into the back of a half-empty photo album of the marriage and went back to the books and passed the exam."

She paused for a moment and the fierceness of her expression softened a little.

"I let myself cry after it was over," she said, "and there were probably more tears for having held them back a whole day. But I did it alone in the room where I lived, and you are the first human being who ever heard any of this from me. I wouldn't be saying any of it now, either, except that I like you and I'm glad to know you and I'd like to go on knowing you.

"But I don't build monuments to dead people and I can't afford to be friends with anyone who does.

"You say you used to be a priest. Episcopal. I don't know much about that. I was raised Catholic and turned in my knee pads about three days after I was confirmed, and haven't been to mass or confession or any of the rest of that stuff since. But if an Episcopal priest is anything like a Catholic one, death is something you're supposed to be able to handle, isn't it?"

I started to answer, but she went on without waiting.

"My husband died because he did things that got him killed. Him. Not me. I didn't send him to the damn recruiting office and I didn't ship him to 'Nam. I was sorry when he died, because I loved him and you want people that you love to stay alive, right?

"But I didn't kill him and I'm not going to live the rest of my life paying off on a bum rap.

"He was a man grown, in charge of himself, or I wouldn't have married him in the first place—and I think your Sara was the same. She got killed because she was doing something she wanted to do and thought was important enough to take chances for, and if you can't respect that, then you're a lot less of a man than I took you for."

She stopped talking again. But not to let me talk back.

And when she resumed, all the anger and remembered pain were gone from her voice, replaced by something at once stronger and less imperious.

"The dead are worth tears, lover," she said. "I cried mine and you cried yours. And they're worth remembering because as long as anyone can remember them, a little part of them is still alive. Anyway, that's what my grandma always taught me, and I never saw any reason to doubt her.

"But monuments, no.

"A gravestone or a wreath on the water sometimes. Maybe. If it makes you feel better and you need it. But more than that is not just silly, it's sick and it's disgusting in a way that I don't even want to think about.

"I didn't kill my husband and you didn't kill your wife. The only monument either one of them needs or can ever have is for us to go on living our lives the very best way we can. If you think you can see it that way, then fine and dandy and I am glad I met you and let's go find some breakfast.

"And if you can't, well, I am still glad I met you. But lover, I want you to pack up your spare socks, shirt, and undershorts and find somewhere else to roost."

As therapy, it was direct and rough and I think I was a little bit resentful at the time because Maxey was taking over the role of wise and steady counselor, which I had considered to be my very own turf.

But she was right, of course, and hearing it from her was somehow more effective than saying it to myself.

It did not entirely stop the dreams.

And the sneaky little worm of guilt still crawled around in the background waiting for more food.

But it served as a kind of watershed for me, marking the day I finally began to shrug off the lethargy that had hung so heavy since leaving the hospital: the day I started to seek a direction without relating it directly to my wife's death or to my lingering feelings of guilt.

A beginning. Small, but very, very necessary.

"Yes, sometimes I still dream about Sara," I said, giving Maxey an answer to the question that had triggered my sudden rush of memory. "But not the midnight war-games you may remember. Quieter dreams now. And lately I've had trouble seeing her face."

She nodded with understanding. "Same for me," she said. "Even when I'm awake, the face I see when I think of Bart is from a photograph. The real one's gone. Faded away. I can hear his voice if I try hard—though I almost never do—but the face, no way. And I don't think it's just because of being with Sam."

I waited for her to go on with that, but she didn't, and I certainly wasn't going to get a better opening to ask the question I'd had in mind for the past half-hour.

So I took a deep breath and let fly. "Speaking of Sam," I said, "just who the hell was that we identified as him back there at the hospital?"

A SERMON (Continued)

Yet, what would King David say of this trust of ours?

Or Paul the Apostle?

13

THE ABILITY TO accept reality, no matter how inconvenient, had always been one of Maxey's more outstanding qualities.

And she still had it. Anyone else might have tried to bluff the moment through or walk away in anger without answering, and I think both alternatives crossed her mind.

But we knew each other too well.

"His name," she said with an air of composure that must have been expensive, "was Terrence Lyle McDuff, if that means anything to you. Probably not. He was an actor. I spotted him three years ago, playing second leads in a dinner theater company that was passing through Morocco. He was a ringer for Sam and he'd been around long enough to know he was never going to make it big as an actor."

"Sam hired him?"

"As a double, yes. Someone to confuse the opposition, Sam said, and leave him free to move around without anyone knowing where he really was. The resemblance was almost scary, and it got better with a little work on the hair color and one session of plastic surgery."

She looked at me expectantly.

"It was the feet," I said.

"Oh . . . shit."

"A fluke. It's been a long time, and I didn't spot anything—well, not anything I'd really have picked up on anyway—playing cards with him all night and all morning. Sam must have filled him in pretty well on me?"

The last was a question, and she nodded absently, waiting for me to tell her the rest of it.

"What went wrong," I said, "was when they called us into the room and you were busy telling them yes, it was Sam. I was standing at the other end of the bed, and the sheet had been

121

pulled up too high. I could see the feet, and . . . you remember, I was in the hospital with Sam . . .''

She nodded again, and not at all absently this time. Maxey was annoyed. With herself. ''And so you'd be sure to remember what kind of a wound Sam Goines was being treated for,'' she said.

''Right. He'd been hit in the leg. Two holes in the thigh, one in the calf—and one round that had chopped a couple of toes off his right foot.''

''Christ.''

''Him, maybe. But Sam for sure.''

We sat in silence for a while, thinking our own thoughts. But I had more questions to ask, and they were important. To me, anyway.

''Where's Sam, Maxey?'' I said.

She didn't answer at once and I still couldn't reach her *wa* to see what was really going on inside, but I think she wanted to tell me to go to hell, and if she had, I couldn't have blamed her much. But she didn't.

Instead, I was astonished to see tears forming at the corners of her eyes, as the carefully manicured hands clutched white-fingered at the edge of the table between us.

''I don't know,'' she said. ''I don't know where he is. I wish to God I did, but I don't. I don't! He's sitting out there . . . somewhere . . . playing some kind of game I can't understand, except that it scares me to death.''

One of the tears got too big for its base and rolled unnoticed down her cheek.

''Old lover mine,'' she said, ''I think my smart, rich, powerful, and famous husband is planning to have me killed.''

That took more than a little explaining, and Maxey spent the next few minutes filling me in—with a brief hiatus for the arrival of the meal we had ordered.

Fear didn't seem to have affected her appetite.

But what she told me seemed to indicate that she had real cause for concern.

For openers, she was convinced Sam had been behind the killings at the Scheherazade.

''He rigged it for sure,'' she said. ''Set it up with that mercenary soldier son of a bitch he's had hanging around for the past few months.''

"The one they call Colonel Connor?"

"Him. I don't know if Sam meant to kill Danny DiMarco. Can't think of any reason why he'd want to do that. But Terry McDuff was a different thing. I'm sure as I'm sitting here with you Sam meant him to die—and found some way to get that nurse in there to finish the job when he looked like he could live through it and wake up enough to tell someone what was going on."

"But why should he want to kill his double?"

Maxey's eyes had changed color. The tears were gone, and it was as if they had washed out some of the deeper tones of violet, leaving them a lighter and less unusual shade. It was a phenomenon I remembered, one that had always fascinated me, like so many other things about Maxey.

"Terry was becoming a problem instead of a solution," she said. "He was a good enough actor, lots better than anyone had ever thought. No one ever so much as blinked when he impersonated Sam. But he couldn't live it on a full-time basis. He started drinking a lot, and when Sam called him on that and put the fear of God into him, he seemed to stop and get along without it . . ."

"But," I prompted.

"Yeah—but," she said. "A couple of months ago Sam found out Terry was doing cocaine. The new kind they call crack. Super-addictive, and a head will do anything to get more when he's running short."

I nodded, beginning to see the pattern.

"So you think Sam couldn't just fire him. Let him go?"

"Not with the kind of memories Terry had in his head," Maxey said. "I think he set up the game to kill him. And I think he got me here to Las Vegas for the same reason."

I thought it over but couldn't make it fit.

Not Sam. And not Maxey. Whatever it was between the two of them had been too real and too sudden not to have a downside, of course. That would only be natural. But . . . kill Maxey?

No way.

I remembered the day I had introduced them; Sam had just completed the second or third of the arms deals that established him as a credible factor on the international scene, and he had come to Las Vegas to look me up for a celebration.

Two weeks later they were married.

Maxey had been a bit wary about telling me what had happened; we were still living together, though I had been away on business—a trip to Alaska for a medium-sized game of hold 'em—and she thought I might not understand.

The hell of it was, I did. Too well.

We had never lied to each other, never tried to make what we had together the great and all-consuming passion of a lifetime. We liked each other and valued each other and were happy together and each supplied certain emotional and other qualities the other seemed to need.

I was beginning to come to terms with the man I was rather than the one I had always supposed myself to be. Taking the first steps along a road I've followed ever since. Maxey's world had settled, too; the loneliness and aimlessness that are the most common problem among people who spend their lives in the midst of crowds were at bay. I was there when she needed someone not to talk to.

We supported and comforted and healed each other, and were there for each other in the most basic way as well.

Love?

Well, it sure wasn't hate.

But all the same, there had never been any talk about making things permanent and by the time Sam came to town we had passed the emotional point where such a thing was likely. It would have ended. Sometime.

So while I wasn't exactly overjoyed to discover that I was on my own again, and thought it had all been pretty sudden, and was maybe just a little bit irked with Sam for moving into territory that was clearly occupied—even though not actually staked—by an old friend, I wasn't really too angry. Or surprised.

The three of us even had a kind of impromptu wedding breakfast together at the airport just before they boarded a plane back to Sam's new headquarters in Europe, and the looks and the smiles they gave each other were enough to remove any lingering doubts I might have had. Maxey had never looked at me like that.

I had managed to lay hands on a little sack of rice, and threw a handful or two as they started down the jetway . . . and that was the last I saw of them.

Until now.

So I just couldn't make it fit.

Ten years can make a difference and hate is not really the

opposite of love and men and women really do kill the people they are married to. But . . . Sam and Maxey?

"No way," I said, back in the present and sure of my ground.

The food arrived and we spent the next few minutes portioning out its various parts and applying the hoisin sauce and fiddling around with scallion brushes. But I knew it was only an intermission, a time to show proper respect for something of value. Maxey would explain in her own good time.

And she did, about the time the tea was ready to pour.

"Sam changed," she said, tasting the flower-scented brew and favoring it with a smile of pleasant memory.

"So I noticed," I said with a bit more acid in my voice than I had meant to be there.

"More than that," she said. "You weren't there to see it. I was."

I sipped my tea and waited for her to go on.

"At first, it was just the frantic activity I'd expected, marrying a man in his business. It wasn't nine-to-five and I hadn't thought it was going to be and the truth was that the pace suited us both. Being apart made getting back together that much better, and if it wasn't a whole lot like most other marriages, that was all right, too. Tell me the truth, lover: Can you see me barging around to PTA meetings with a station wagon full of kids? Or Sam in a scoutmaster's uniform?"

Well . . . no.

"So, all right. Things were good between us and with the business, and the people we knew were bright and interesting and fun. And rich. Say it out loud, so we won't have to talk around it: rich!

"That counted with me.

"Oh, sure, I loved Sam all right. There was a strong physical attraction right from the beginning, and that powerful drive and energy that just always seemed to come off him in waves. He's not the type who would ever have to chase women, any more than you are, my one-eyed seducer of stray show girls. And it was more than physical between us; we were right for each other and we both knew it.

"But the money still made a difference. At the risk of shattering any illusions you might still have about me, dear old darling, let's admit right here and now that I don't think for a moment that I'd have married Sam Goines if I hadn't known he was rich and going to get richer.

"Surprised? You shouldn't be. Lover, you knew me pretty well, knew what I came from. And where.

"I may not have known exactly what I wanted. And maybe I still don't; kind of hard to tell sometimes. But from when I was about four years old, I sure knew what I didn't want.

"I didn't want to stay in Detroit.

"Rich or poor, no Detroit.

"And I didn't want to live the kind of life my ma or my aunts or my uncles or any of the rest of my family did, working their tails off for chicken feed and looking like old men and old women at thirty and dying all worn down to nothing at about fifty.

"Not for Maxey.

"The marriage to Bart was really a mistake; one of the things that hurt worst after he was dead was knowing it wouldn't have lasted if he'd lived and feeling kind of relieved at not having to tell him so.

"There—that's something you never heard from me before, and it's true and it's been eating at me for a long time.

"The nurse's training and then, later, working in shows here in Vegas were all part of that same thing. A way out. And Sam was the final step, the guarantee that I would never have to see Detroit again except maybe under the wing of a jet airliner thirty thousand feet overhead . . ."

It was a long speech and Maxey took a moment to catch her breath while I tried to form the words to tell her that very little of what she'd said was really news to me—and that it was neither unusual nor as totally negative as she seemed determined to make it. But she wasn't done.

"So, all right," she said. "Maxey got what she wanted, and a man she might really have been able to love, besides.

"Only things began to change. In a few years, Sam had all the money anyone on earth could want. More than he could spend in ten lifetimes, even with me to help. But he isn't the kind who can just quit and spend it and live happily. He had to find something else to want . . . and he did.

"He wanted power.

"Not just the kind most people are after, the sense of being in control of their own lives and being able to handle most of the jolts and zaps that come along. That's normal. A part of being human.

"But the kind of power Sam Goines was after was something

else, and I think it may have started a long time before I knew him. Back during the war, or maybe even before that . . .''

She paused again, but instead of interrupting I found myself looking into a mirror that I hadn't known was there. I saw my own face, but there was another behind it—someone I barely remembered. He was listening. And thinking.

"Suddenly we were up to our hips in politicians," Maxey said. "Sam had always tried to stay away from them before; whenever he could, he dealt only with the designated buyers— war ministers or defense secretaries or chiefs of staff or whatever the local money-minding hoodlum called himself.

"But now we were traveling around the world hobnobbing with presidents who hadn't been elected and kings who used to be lieutenant colonels and lunatics whose people thought they were God and who had finally got around to believing it themselves.

"What was worse, he was beginning to act like them . . . and think the way they did.

"The power he was after was the kind they had. Only bigger. He knew, he could see, what it had done to them, but either he didn't care or he didn't think that would happen to him and I could never get him to see that it was happening already.

"I couldn't take too much of that. Weak stomach, I guess. So finally Sam was making those trips by himself and I was moving around the world more or less on my own. We saw each other sometimes. By appointment—the way he asked me to meet him here in Vegas. But even when we got together we had less and less to say to each other.

"There was no big scene. No real split. We never talked about divorce.

"But the marriage was over.

"And then I met Harry . . .''

Maxey stopped talking and waited for me to react to that, and at first I didn't think I was going to.

It had been a long time.

But then the feelings came, of course, and I was both surprised and disappointed to discover that quite a few of them were growing out of a sour little patch of emotional turf reserved for jealousy.

There had been a sense of loss, yes, when she married Sam Goines. But it was tempered by the fact that I liked and respected Sam and thought they might be happy together—and,

just possibly, by the unacknowledged sense that whatever had
been between us was slowly but discernibly moving in the
direction of habit and even staleness.

This was something entirely different, and I found myself
forming a mental picture of Harry: large, attentive, and preda-
tory; costumed, perhaps, as a ski instructor or the kind of
military officer who thrives on embassy or guard-of-honor duty.
Or maybe tricked out in Guccis and gold chains as one of the
"film producer" types that Europe seems to crank out by the
oily job-lot lately.

And then I laughed.

It was the wrong thing to do and the wrong time to do it, and I
could see Maxey beginning one of her rare slow burns. But I
couldn't help it. The situation, and my immediate embroidery on
the facts, was just too obvious—and grotesque —to rate anything
else. I was behaving like the kind of injured husband that even
the dumbest romance novelists have retired to the dust heap.
Disgusting. And too comical to ignore.

"What's so damn funny?" Maxey inquired in a voice I knew
was both controlled and dangerous.

"Me," I told her honestly, and explained.

Her expression had softened by the time I was done, and I
thought that the *wa* I still couldn't quite reach was almost back to
room temperature. But there was still the tiniest hint of constraint
as she continued, and I posted it. Warning: a point not to be
passed if I was interested in staying on good terms with her. And
it was becoming more and more apparent to me that I was
interested.

"At first," she said, "it was just something that happened.
We met in Nice, at one of the world's most boring cocktail
parties. Harry had corralled a waiter and asked me if I wanted a
refill and I said I did and we started talking and after a while we
decided to get out of there and go somewhere else."

She took another sip of the scented tea and then poured for
both of us.

"The somewhere else turned out to be Harry's apartment,"
she said. "And I have to tell you that it was no surprise. I'm not
really like that, lover—believe it or don't believe it, suit yourself—I
hadn't strayed in all the time I'd been married to Sam, and that
was quite a record. Especially for the crowd we were in. By the
kind of yardsticks they use, I was practically a nun."

"But Harry changed all that?"

She smiled at me and there was the trace of a glitter in her eyes. But if she was offended, she didn't say so.

"But Harry changed all that," she said. "Or I changed. That first time started something I found out I couldn't stop. And didn't want to. We were careful in public and careful when we saw each other in private, but there was no chance at all that Sam wouldn't find out, and anyway I told him in the first week or so, as soon as I was sure it wasn't something that was going to just fade away."

"He accepted it?"

She started to say yes; you could see the word completely formed, just below the threshold of sound. But it evaporated before it could be said and after a moment of hesitation she shook her head. Not emphatically, but with sure knowledge.

"He told me he did," she said. "And we never mentioned it again. But thinking about it now, I can see that he never really intended to let it pass."

Maxey leaned back in the booth and let her eyes focus on the cup in her hands.

"Sam Goines," she said, "was going to be a king. An emperor. And kings and emperors have harems—wives and mistresses and concubines and whatever else you want to call them—the more the merrier. That's all right. Fits the picture. Adds to the image.

"But let one of the wives or concubines start playing snatch-grab-and-tickle with the majordomo or the master of revels and all bets are off. It's royal executioner time . . . and I should have known it."

"You think he's that jealous?"

"I think he's that much attached to the image of himself as Henry the Eighth or the king of Siam."

She let it sink in, and then voiced my next thought for me.

"I think," she said, "that this town, Las Vegas, is a place where a man with the right amount of money and the right kind of connections and the right kind of muscle can do just about anything he wants, and I think that's why Sam Goines got us here.

"This is his killing ground.

"I think everyone in that penthouse at the Scheherazade was supposed to die—that's why I was so sure they meant you when they said they found three people down on the floor and one of them was a preacher—and I think Harry and I are supposed to die, too.''

"Harry's here?''

"This is Harry's home. Here in Las Vegas. Which might be just one more good reason for Sam to decide to do it all, clean the books, right here in town.''

Thinking it over, I had to admit it made pretty good sense. Except for one detail.

"If that's what you think,'' I said, "why did you go along with the gag—identify the man in the hospital as Sam?''

She blinked, and the tears were near the surface again. But the voice was steady. "I never claimed to be a hero, lover,'' she said. "I want to stay alive and I'll do anything, say anything, that I think might help. That nurse you saw me talking to in the hospital, the one you think maybe killed Terry McDuff? Well, she was giving me a message from my loving husband. She told me he wasn't in that room—up until then, I'd thought he was— and she said he wanted me to identify the man in there as him and if I didn't I wasn't going to walk out of that hospital, or ever off that floor, alive.''

The tears were gone, but even through the defensive curtain that masked the *wa* from me I could feel the fear-chill that lived inside her.

"I'm shook, old buddy,'' she said. "Terrified out of my mind. And if you're anything like as smart as the man I remember, you'll have sense enough to be scared, too.''

A SERMON (Continued)

King David, in his time, had spread himself "like the green bay tree" over the whole land of Israel, smiting his enemies and dancing for joy at the capture of a major city . . .

14

TERRIFIED OR NOT, Maxey didn't seem to have lost her appetite, and we passed the next few minutes in silence, doing a fair execution on the corn soup, duck, pork, and snow peas.

They were worth the effort.

But our minds wandered, and by the time we were down to the black cherries, peaches, and kumquats, I had come up with the only suggestion that seemed logical in the circumstances.

"You could run," I said.

Maxey seemed to think it over.

"Where?" she said.

"Anywhere you like. You say Las Vegas is Sam's killing ground. All right. So if you're really sure he's in that kind of a mood, make him come after you somewhere else. Someplace where screaming matters and murder gets investigated. Or dig a hole and pull it in after you."

She smiled at me.

"Sure," she said. "It makes sense, and don't think I haven't considered it. But I'm not going to do it."

Maxey put back the last cherry she'd chopsticked off the platter and set the bamboo sticks down in the middle of the table.

"I'm tired, lover," she said. "I want to go on living, but not if it means running and looking over my shoulder for the rest of my life."

Her face was quiet and the words were sure, and I could find no reason at all to doubt that she meant every one of them.

"I told you one of the reasons I married Sam was to make sure I never had to go back to Detroit or any place remotely like it, and I have to tell you I still feel that way. Even if I knew it was going to end like this, I wouldn't go back and change anything. Does that seem crazy?"

I shook my head. "No," I said. "Not crazy."

Sad, maybe. But I didn't say that.

"All right, then," she said. "So try this on: I am awfully damned glad to see you. I can't run and I can't hide and I can't even fight—at least not in any way that would matter. But the best luck I've had in years was for you to live through that business at the Scheherazade. Not just because I like you, though that counts. But more than that, because I think with you around I might really stand a chance of living through the next week or, who knows, maybe even a year . . ."

She stopped talking, and she might have been waiting for a reply. But I couldn't think of a thing, so I dropped enough money on the table to cover the price of the meal and a ridiculous overtip and we got out of there and found the rented car and headed back toward the Scheherazade.

It was a nice speech, and all the nicer because it didn't seem to have been rehearsed.

Nice to know someone had such perfect faith in me.

Nice to be trusted.

Especially by Maxey.

Now if I only had some idea of what was going on and what I was supposed to be doing . . .

It was still the shank of the morning, but I hadn't slept in more than twenty-four hours and so it was only a minor letdown when Maxey left me at the door of her suite.

I offered no objection. But all the same I felt a sneaky little lift when she explained that—murder plots or no murder plots—she had a couple of duty calls to make around town, and she wanted to see me later.

"I have a kind of an idea," she said. "Maybe nothing, maybe something. But give me a call when you wake up. Okay?"

Okay.

I went back to the elevator, but punched the lobby button rather than the one for my own floor. As it happened, I had a couple of errands of my own.

Superspy movies have always left me cold, and elaborate countermeasures make me feel like the central character in some such unlikely tale.

But this was Las Vegas.

I walked quietly through the casino, picked up a pocketful of change, chose a public telephone at random, and placed a long-distance call to Best Licks.

Margery answered on the first ring.

"Thank God!" she said when she heard my voice. "Don't you ever check the messages at that damn hotel?"

She was flustered, and that in itself told me a lot. Margery does not fluster easily.

Part of the problem, it developed, was because of early news reports that I had been shot to death. The good people of Best Licks—Preacher's faithful congregation, bless 'em all—had begun packing and arming with a general view to burning the city of Las Vegas to the ground. The plan had been abandoned—with some reluctance, she said—when a corrected report put me back in the land of the living, and I filed the information for future consideration. It's nice to be liked. But I made a mental note to try to die in some nice neutral manner that would not seem to call for reprisal. My friends might not really have been able to wipe Las Vegas entirely off the face of southern Nevada. But considering some of their histories, I decided they could have dented things up quite a bit.

The narrowly averted massacre was not, however, the principal reason for Margery's emotional upset.

"Some of the alarms went off," she said. "Someone's getting curious about us . . . and you."

That made more sense.

The late Nicholas Dandolas, better known as Nick the Greek, was a man acquainted with the whole geography of gaming; one who had made all the stops from top to bottom and back again and then taken time to formulate a philosophy based upon the information so dearly bought.

He said that "fame, for a gambler, is usually followed by poverty. Or prison. Or death."

It was a dictum that I had always taken seriously, and the alarms Margery was talking about were a part of the distant-early-warning system we had set up in places where information seekers would be sure to intrude—beer-can-on-the-barbed wire alarms passed on to her by people who would, for one reason or another, let us know when anyone started asking questions about me or the town or the other people who live there.

We value our privacy.

"We've had alarms go off before," I said.

"Not like this. I got seven calls in one day—from people in Washington, Chicago, New York, Topeka, Houston, Sewanee, and, believe it or not, Ho Chi Minh City."

I believed it. But I didn't like it at all.

"Any of them know who the questions were coming from?"

"No. But two of them said it didn't seem to be an individual. More like an organization. A group."

"Official?"

"No way, José. But one of them used a kind of funny phrase."

"Funny?"

"Funny odd. Not ha-ha. The one who called from Topeka didn't seem in a very good mood. Kept growling about something called the Mormon Mafia. Mean anything to you?"

I told her it didn't, but I was lying and I spent the time it took me to get back to my floor trying to fit the words into the rest of the picture.

Here was the fifty-third card in the deck.

Margery might not have heard of the Mormon Mafia. She almost never gets to Las Vegas. But I knew that it referred to the squeaky-clean-cut corps of Utah-bred musclemen surrounding Francis Carrington Shaw.

Like another billionaire recluse before him, Shaw was said to have a horror of germs and infection equaled only by his aversion to personal publicity. His bodyguard was, therefore, composed of non-smoking, non-drinking youngsters recruited almost from the very steps of the temple at Salt Lake City and highly paid for a kind of straight-arrow loyalty and competence perhaps available from no other source.

They even had a kind of reserve corps of ex-bodyguards who had graduated to various security and investigative jobs in the Shaw empire, all of whom could be counted upon for immediate and totally reliable service.

Offhand, I couldn't think of a single reason why he might have told one of his minions to compile a dossier on me and mine. But someone was certainly putting one together—in a hurry, too; seven calls from widely separated points in a single day couldn't be read any other way—and Shaw, or someone working for him, was the only nonofficial possibility.

I was at my own door and the key was in the lock.

But I hesitated.

Just a day earlier, I would have entered the room without a qualm. Las Vegas has fewer hotel room holdups than most places. Even first-offense stickup men always seem to get badly hurt resisting arrest, and those who have the ill fortune to be identified as habituals are not infrequently shot to death by officers who explain that despite all warnings the suspect made a sudden movement as though attempting to draw a weapon.

On such rumors are low crime-rate statistics founded.

Events of the past few hours, however, had made me superstitious, and I let the door swing back all the way to the wall before sticking my nose through it, and stopped on the other side of the threshold while I listened to the room with a kind of concentration I had learned with great difficulty from a man who had lost both his eyes instead of only one.

No.

Not this time.

The room was empty. I closed the door behind me, feeling childish . . . and changed my mind again in an instant when visual scanning of the premises stopped at the table arranged with two chairs beside the window.

I had arrived the day before to find it adorned by a bowl containing fruit tastefully arranged around a bottle of Tattinger blanc—a champagne I have been known to consume without protest—and it had still been there when I left to join Goines and the others in the tower suite.

Now it had been moved.

The bowl and the fruit were perched on a sideboard. And the bottle stood alone in the middle of the table, acting as a kind of paperweight for an envelope that didn't seem to be addressed to anyone.

Neither was the note inside. But it was intended for me.

"The ticket is for the hotel safe," it said. "You had $87,540 when the game stopped, and I talked the police out of holding it as evidence.

"Ice this champagne.

"And give me a chance to drink some of it when you wake up."

The note was signed with a large and flourishing "A" and I glanced briefly at the safe receipt before putting it and the note back in the envelope and carrying it, along with the bottle, to the pint-sized refrigerator located under the wet bar, where I stored the bottle at the bottom and the envelope at the top, under an ice tray.

Not an ingenious hiding place.

But proof against amateurs, and I found myself grinning a little as I closed the thermal door on the two items, wondering just what kind of leverage Apodaca had used to pry that money loose from the law. Whatever it was, I owed him. Until now, I had resigned myself to losing the loot that had brought me to town in the first place.

His suggestion of a meeting in the near future—with or without bubbly French wine—sounded like a good one, too.

But for the moment, I was still at the end of a day and standing in a hotel room that had already been entered at least once without my knowledge or permission, and I approached the closet with a wariness born more of habit than any real apprehension.

It was empty, but I got a minor shock when I opened the door. A full-length mirror fastened inside flashed back the image of a rather formal scarecrow.

Skinny, this one, and looking as though he had spent the past few hours rolling around in an alley.

I regarded him without sympathy.

The black three-piece suits I favor—coat cut a bit long and old-fashioned, vest tailored to accommodate certain items of personal security, color available nowadays only by maximum exercise of persuasion—are a necessary part of the professional poker image, like Slim Preston's silver-mounted cowboy boots or Treetop Jack's high-crowned hat and beard. But they serve other purposes as well.

The material is selected to resist the wrinkling and conceal the stains that might otherwise act as tattletales to my mental or emotional condition; the uniformity makes it possible for me to change clothes without having seemed to do so. And the fact that nobody expects to see me wearing anything else has, on occasion, enabled me to move about in effective disguise simply by switching to chinos and a T-shirt.

This time, however, the costume had failed in function.

And in tensile strength. Maxey might, I thought, have warned an old buddy that a seam in his coat collar was strained and that the flap over his left coat pocket was dangling by a thread.

All that could be repaired.

But the shirt was a total write-off. The top button was semide-tached, two other buttons were missing, and one of the cuffs had suffered some sort of mishap that had left its edge ripped, raveled, and dirty. The string tie was still knotted, but strenuous activity had twisted it to one side and frayed one of the ends beyond repair.

The suit went on a hangar, marked and noted and left to hand for the hotel tailor shop. Shirt and tie went into the wastebasket.

And the body that had worn them went into the shower.

First cold.

Then hot.

I emerged relaxed and ready for a good day's sleep.

A SERMON (Continued)

David knew the truth, and said it in his psalm: ''He passed away, and, lo, he was not.'' And yet the knowledge did not deter him for an instant . . .

15

BUT THE EYES wouldn't close.

And the mind wouldn't stop.

I could have forced the issue, of course, left the transition in the care of a mantra that would take me to that upland alp where the sun shines on the upper side of passing clouds and blades of grass growing beneath the hand are the fingers of the Enlightened One, clasping earth and eternity in that unity which is the essence of all joy.

A seductive thought. Especially in the circumstances.

Yet I hesitated, and finally decided to let the mind have its own way. The conscious side of human intellect is limited and usually tied to the pace of the spoken word, while the unconscious is—can be—untrammeled by mechanics.

It was this more competent and efficient side that now resisted sleep and would not be put off with promises of future comprehension.

All right, dammit.

So we will think for a while . . .

I took a deep breath and turned myself inward, groping for the various strands. There were an embarrassing number to choose from, and I selected one at random.

Item: Maxey thinks Sam Goines sent the hit team to the penthouse with orders to kill everyone in the room.

But they didn't kill everyone—and I don't believe they wanted to. If that had been the idea, they'd have sanitized the room first with frag grenades and then come in to hose down anyone who was still moving. More efficient, less dangerous.

No.

That was aimed fire, intended to kill just who it did kill. DiMarco and the poor son of a bitch who was pretending to be Sam Goines. Someone else in the room may have been on the list; I don't think Sam—or whoever really sent them—expected anyone in there to jump the gunners.

Item: aces and eights. Do I really believe someone is leaving a crazy calling card like that?

Well . . . maybe. It's happened twice now, and if the first time could have been an accident, the second absolutely could not. So, yes, someone is doing that, but don't ask me why. Because down inside, where I live, I still don't really believe it, and to hell with logic and the evidence of the senses.

Item: one atomic bomb. Of all the utter world-class hoked-up spies-in-the-woodwork nonsense I ever heard, that has got to be the lemon icing on the cake.

But Corner Pocket believes it and Interpol believes it, and if it doesn't fit the Sam Goines I remember, well, neither do a lot of other things I have been finding out about him in the last few hours, so maybe we have got to keep it in mind as a possibility, if nothing else. At least for the time being.

Item: Jorge Martinez. How in hell did he get involved in craziness like this, and did he know I was going to be in the room, and if he did, was that why he was hired—to kill me or not to kill me, but anyway to be able to pick me out of a crowd?

Another name and face floated up to center stage. Jorge de la Torre. The coincidence of those first names, Jorge and Jorge, had led to nicknames that didn't require explanation: Big Jorge and Little Jorge. Easy to remember, because Big Jorge—de la Torre—was the first soldier, in charge of the whole company, while Little Jorge—Martinez—only had to worry about the platoon.

But the nicknames changed a little after the first few weeks of combat.

They became Big Trouble and Little Trouble, and not just because some of the babies from the repple-depple found them a little hard to please. War, even the mean and idiotic kind that we fought up and down the coastline of Southeast Asia, can be addictive to a certain kind of man. Lunatics, sure. But useful, purposeful lunatics who have found their calling in life. And death.

Big Trouble and Little Trouble scared hell out of everyone. Including me.

Because they were home. They had recognized each other the first time the gunfire was for real, and from that moment on they were brothers in a way that is more than blood, assigning themselves to two-man night patrols that were strictly forbidden by regulation and by specific order of the various officers who sometimes arrived to take charge of things.

Officers assigned to our company never seemed to last long. But when they were gone, Big Trouble and Little Trouble were still there, talking in low tones and cleaning their weapons with that middle-distance stare. R and R did not attract them. Rest areas were places to plan new tactics. For use in the immediate future.

I think the final fight—my final one, anyway, the one the history books call the second battle of Khe Sanh, when they remember it at all—was a kind of present from the gods, as far as the two sergeants were concerned. An ultimate challenge.

Yet I owed my life to Jorge Martinez.

And now I was one of the reasons he was dead.

Item: Sam Goines. If he wasn't lying on a coroner's slab somewhere right now—and he certainly wasn't—then just where was he? And what kind of a game were we playing? I only came to play poker, folks . . . deal the preacher out.

But I was in, and no mistake about it. Dealer's choice and the button's at Sam's seat; table stakes, freeze out with a forced opening and burying money to the losers.

(Old friend, just what would it cost me to buy back my introduction to you?)

Item: cocaine. It was getting to be a recurrent theme. Terrence Lyle McDuff had died of it, killed because he was no longer reliable, if Maxey's version of events was to be believed, and so far it was the best explanation that had been offered.

Who else? Well, the Voice of Heaven on Earth, for one. I hadn't seen him snorting and I hadn't seen him smoking and it would be a spectacularly stupid thing for him to do. But Holy Joe Gillespie had never been a mental giant, and his reaction to the card tricks this morning had been pretty extreme, even for a man faced with a totally novel situation. File him under Probable.

And go on to Danny DiMarco. Hadn't there been some kind of problem with him and coke a few years back? Yes: a bust, with a load of Colombian found in the bar compartment of his limousine. He'd been on the skids in those days and everyone thought he'd started dealing because he needed the money. But it turned out to be his chauffeur, not him. Didn't it?

And a month or two later, he was back on top . . . making a new picture and working in Las Vegas and getting married to his jailbait costar . . . who, now that I thought about it, was the chauffeur's daughter.

Okay. Right . . .

Item: Francis Carrington Shaw. Another recurrent theme. Judge Happy Apodaca worked for him. So did Manny Temple. Danny DiMarco had just bought control of the Scheherazade from one of the Shaw companies.

But there was more. Struggling, antlike, with bits of mental debris several times its size, the librarian of memory finally unearthed something I'd seen a few years back on the business page of the *San Francisco Chronicle*. A rumor that FCS—the initials were also the legal name of his main holding company—had provided financing for some complicated kind of international arms deal, other principals not identified by name.

Would one of those names have been Goines?

And would FCS be connected to anyone else in the game? What about Holy Joe?

Item: the colonel. I couldn't seem to think of him any other way, and that in itself was worth knowing, because it meant I didn't know him at all. I had seen the man and I could tell you what kind of poker combinations he liked to back and some of the situations in which he would bluff and even follow a little bit of his betting psychology.

But I didn't know him.

I knew a beard and a voice, and while the gaming pattern might be as good in some ways as a signature or even a fingerprint, it wasn't the man himself, and we were still strangers.

But . . . not quite. Somehow, I couldn't get over the feeling that I had met him before.

Item: Maxey. Meeting her again after all this time could be an accident, but I didn't believe it for a minute, and if Sam Goines was really behind any of this he must have known how I'd react, and maybe even been counting on it.

Well, okay, then, old friend of mine. You were right.

Whatever it was between Maxey and me all those years ago, it was still there. For me, anyway.

And for Maxey?

Hard to say. I'd been unable to make effective contact with the emotional center. The *wa*. She seemed to feel some of what I was feeling, and I'd swear that fainting spell at the hospital was straight goods. For real. Her lights were well and truly out when I carried her to the couch.

Or was I just too busy with my own feelings to monitor hers?
Mark it a possible.

A lot had happened since the last time we saw each other, but
it was Maxey who'd started my ball rolling again, way back
then, when I was ready to give up.

Not that she drew me a diagram and led me through it.
Nothing like that would have occurred to Maxey, then or now.
But being with her had cut the drinking to a minimum and
started me concentrating on the job of learning to play poker like
a professional instead of an amateur.

And the questions she'd asked about my t'ai chi exercises had
pushed me to begin looking into the Oriental philosophies and
martial arts that stem from them . . . which is to say the whole
panorama. They had led me to Yoichi Masuda, the *mahayana*
master who had taught me and led me and been my friend ever
since, and to the life and work that had evolved.

None of which had any bearing on the main question:

Maxey . . .

The headdress was unfamiliar but the face was one I knew,
and there were too many clothes and the landscape was green
and it stretched into infinity and now I was dreaming and I knew
it, but I couldn't shake it off and wake up.

Or didn't want to . . .

Monocular vision is not natural for any animal I have ever
heard of, ancient legends of the Cyclops notwithstanding, and
adaptation to such a condition comes in dribs and drabs over a
period of years.

You learn to estimate distance by relative size; by strains of
focus rather than the two-eyed strains of convergence that you
learned to use without conscious effort as an infant, but it
doesn't happen all at once. Getting used to the distance between
a plate and your mouth is easy and is one of the first steps in the
relearning process. But you will get some food on your face and
on your shirt before you arrive at the point where you don't have
to think about it anymore . . . and the rest of the learning
process is just as uneven.

Some things, in fact, never change.

After all this time, I still dream in 3-D. Still see dreamscapes
and dream people with two eyes. Even if I've never seen them
that way in the world I believe to be the real one.

Maxey was standing far off across a green baize plain, dressed as a queen. But not of hearts; I'm not that banal, even in a dream. No. She was the queen of swords from the tarot deck, and she was smiling and beckoning and I couldn't quite hear her, which was frustrating because, after all, this was my own personal dream and I found myself wondering—not irrelevantly— why I was dreaming her as such a dangerous card.

The queen of swords leaves a trail of doom and terror through the Lesser Arcana of the seventy-two-card tarot deck, from which the modern fifty-two-card pack is derived, and while she is not as totally devastating as the nine of swords (death and destruction, any way you read it), she is no fun either, a questionable ally and a deadly enemy who can be relied upon to guard herself and her own to the exclusion of all other considerations.

I tried to call to her, but there was no sound and the effort turned the whole scene dim at the edges and suddenly I was standing on the campus at Sewanee, the University of the South, facing Shapard Tower. It was night and I strained my eyes—both of them in fine working order, courtesy of my friendly local subconscious—to see and be filled by the white pattern of moonlight on the knobbed spires.

Queen Maxey was gone, but something was going on to my right. I forced my attention away from the tower to see what it was, and found myself facing another survivor from the tarot, this time a member of the Greater Arcana.

The joker smiled back at me.

But not the leering, devilish face of the modern deck. This was his elder counterpart—Card Zero, called the Fool—whose smile was sweet and trustful as he prepared to blunder over the edge of a cliff. Feather in cap and satchel over shoulder, he was wandering toward me now with a heart full of joy and goodwill. But as he came closer, the face changed.

It was Little Trouble.

Sergeant Jorge Martinez seemed as happy as a clam, but the cap feather was really camouflage worked into the cloth cover of his helmet, and the satchel was a sack of ammo bandoliers hanging from the end of an M16.

What was he doing here at Sewanee?

The answer came almost at once. Still smiling, Little Trouble unslung his burden and set it at his feet, working the bolt of the M16 and shouting something at someone behind me and I turned to see a line of what seemed to be children, wearing National

Guard uniforms. Their M1s had ammo clips in place and they were aiming, ready to fire.

"Stop that," I said. "You crazy bastards, stop that before you hurt someone!"

But they didn't hear me, and when I turned back to Little Trouble, he was invisible and it was snowing. Flakes of whiteness filled the sky and then I remembered—Sara.

We had stood here, outside All Saints, with the snow cutting us off from the world and touched and talked to each other and told each other things no one else would ever hear and been warm in the midst of the chilly whiteness.

Where was Sara?

The snow had stopped and I could see again and Little Trouble and his murderous National Guard children were gone.

Sara had been here; I had felt her presence, and while she was with me the world had been right and possible, a world for living, but now she was gone and I was alone and I had not seen her face.

Her face . . .

The snow wasn't melting, and I understood now that it wasn't really snow. This was just white powder, and I didn't need a closer look to know what kind. I was up to my ankles in cocaine, and the dream was getting a little more literal than it needed to be.

And then the bells of the Polk Memorial Carillon began to ring.

I steeled myself against the sound, trying to hang on to the dream, to find Sara. Or Jorge Martinez. Or Maxey. What was Maxey doing among all those dead people? But the world continued to shudder and parts of it crumbled, and when the clamor continued, the fabric came apart, shimmering into nothingness and contracting to a single point that echoed and vibrated to the kind of sound Edgar Allan Poe had understood so well, tolling and pealing and hammering . . .

A SERMON (Continued)

Paul, too, saw his world clearly. He lived daily with the sure knowledge of the wages of sin, comforting himself with the assurance that—as in the second half of the verse—"the gift of God is eternal life."

16

I WOKE WITH a sense of foreboding and frustration. And loss.

The room was dark, but splinter-bits of sunlight that had somehow wormed their way around the edges of the industrial-weight blackout curtains informed me that it was still daytime, albeit late afternoon, of a day that had started at midnight and seemed to want to go on forever.

Fragments of the dream drifted back from wherever it is that such things go, and I closed my eye in a determined effort to recapture as many of them as possible.

Maybe I could even follow them home.

But the sound that had shattered their world and driven me out of it had more staying power than I did.

Some modern telephones attract attention with discreet chimes, some with a well-modulated electronic tone, still others with a silently flashing light. But the instrument in my room was the old-fashioned kind intended for business lunches and wake-up calls, and its inventor would doubtless have taken a certain modest pride in the way it dragged me back from the twilight border of eternity into crisply air-conditioned Las Vegas afternoon.

I picked it up on the third ring and said something intended as a cross between "hello" and "go away," hoping perhaps that the caller would take offense, or take the hint, and hang up in my ear.

But it was Maxey.

She had known me too long and too well to expect anything like civilized conduct from me in the first few moments after being roused from sleep. And she was in no mood for nonsense.

"On your feet, stud," she said.

"No chance!"

"Open your left eye, put in your right one if it's lying around somewhere—"

"Maxey, dammit."

"—do a couple of those limbering-up exercises of yours, and meet me in the coffee shop. You got ten minutes. And I got us an appointment. We're going to Heaven."

"Maxey!"

But she was gone and if I had any options I absolutely couldn't see what they might be.

I kicked off the covers and ordered my legs to lever me upright.

It took three tries.

But I finally made it.

She had already ordered the coffee—a special blend of hot-and-heady with just the hint of chicory that a few years in Tennessee can teach you to favor—but said the rest of the breakfast, if there was going to be one, would have to wait. We were late.

That was all right with me. The meal we had tied into at the Golden Nugget had been enough to march an army from Beijing to Shanghai, and folk myth notwithstanding I was not hungry again a couple of hours later. I could wait.

For a year, maybe.

Pouring good coffee into a couple of Styrofoam cups and drinking it on the fly, however, was another thing entirely, and I was still protesting with as much vigor and dignity as I could summon even while Maxey was herding me into my own rental car and directing us on a serpentine course out of town in the direction of Henderson.

"Maxey!"

She was checking her wristwatch for what seemed to be the tenth time in five minutes, and did not reply.

"Maxey, you're a lovely lady and a smart one and I am prepared to follow you to the very gates of Gehenna—"

"Whatever that is."

"—but if you don't tell me where we're going pretty soon, I am going to take my foot off the gas and put it on the brake and turn off the engine and go back to sleep right here on the highway."

She looked at me with an expression of surprise that could not have been faked. "I told you," she said.

"You said we were going to Heaven."

"So?"

"So . . . ?"

"So we're almost there."

A minute or two later I understood.

The Reverend Holroyd Josiah Gillespie, D.D.—known to his electronic flock as the Voice of Heaven on Earth, and once famous along the back roads of North Carolina as Holy Joe the Bible salesman—lived in panoply and secure splendor five miles outside the city limits of Las Vegas and a good thousand feet below the topmost reaches of the satellite-transmission antenna that telecast his message to a Gospel-hungry world.

He called the compound his Heaven on Earth, and seeing it for the first time I was a little surprised that he hadn't thought to run tours and charge admission.

It would have been worth the price.

Guards at the gate checked our I.D. and made calls to some inner security office before opening the double-steel-bar barrier and directing us to a visitors' parking lot just inside. No outside cars permitted past that point.

But it seemed we were not to wander about at random, either.

By the time the car was parked and the engine turned off, a customized convertible tricked out with a blue and white awning straight from the *Fantasy Island* television set pulled in behind us and a brightly smiling young thing invited us—by name—to climb in for a ride to headquarters.

"Dr. Gillespie is expecting you," she said.

I smiled back and followed Maxey into the back seat, giving her a hand with the tote-bag purse that seemed only slightly smaller than a suitcase. She was wearing a safari getup this afternoon, and it went with that. But I still had to wonder whether the visit she had arranged was for a couple of hours or the rest of the week.

Roads at the compound were laid out on a winding plan—not a straightaway on the premises—and it didn't take long to understand why. Land use had been planned as carefully as at Disneyland or Six Flags, and extensive facilities were camouflaged, separated from the sight and sound of one another by plantings and the artful arrangement of what I took to be fronts—facades with no real buildings behind them—designed to simulate the streets and byways of an America that never was.

We got the full treatment.

With spiel.

"This," our driver-conductor chirruped, "is our main street, the one you've seen so often when Dr. Gillespie brings the people of television land to visit the Streets of Heaven . . .''

I hadn't.

Years earlier, curious about the impact that my old acquaintance seemed to have on the tube, I had watched about twenty minutes of one of his broadcasts. But then I switched the set off and took a long, long walk in the woods to get the taste out of my mouth.

Things like that give me stomach distress.

But it was evident as we went on that our guide considered the Voice of Heaven's words as water upon a parched earth, and I maintained what I hoped was a properly respectful silence as we moved along.

The Main Street building fronts, I learned, were not as totally false as I had believed.

Real people lived in the houses and worked in the offices and ran the one or two small business establishments visible along the spotless brick-surfaced street; necessary, it seemed, for proper support of an enclave that was in most ways a wholly self-sufficient civic entity, subject only to the continued support and provision of the Almighty.

That had a nice ring, but I couldn't help the passing thought that continued support and provision of Lake Mead and Hoover Dam had something to do with it, too, not to mention a nit-picking speculation at the size of the water bill that had to be the price tag of maintaining so much greenery in the middle of a desert. I kept it to myself, though. Some days my manners are almost civilized.

Turning off the main drag, we found ourselves on what appeared to be the grounds of a small but elegant hotel, and our guide informed us that appearances were not, in this case, deceiving.

"Retreat groups come here all the time," she said. "And there are church conferences the year around. We provide a secure and healthy meeting environment, with conference and banquet facilities, for any Christian organization that can meet certain basic standards. They don't have to be a part of Dr. Gillespie's ministry; he loves all who love the Lord."

She paused for a moment, savoring this all-encompassing quality, and when she went on, the voice was better controlled and the words more businesslike.

"Then, too," she said, "we have important visitors from time to time, so we want to be sure that they are happy and well cared for during their stay.''

Her voice trailed away as she negotiated a particularly sharp curve, and she did not take up her litany again, apparently preferring to allow the next exhibit to speak for itself.

And I could see why.

The Church of the Voice was just ahead.

And I was impressed in spite of myself. Television evangelists tend to package themselves professionally, choosing their pulpits to reflect the basic quality of the persona they are attempting to project.

Try to picture Oral without the Prayer Tower.

Or Billy without the stadium.

Or Bob without the Crystal Cathedral.

Holy Joe Gillespie's working space was, the guide said, a faithful copy of Notre-Dame cathedral in Paris. ''Only better,'' she declared, ''because the people who built the one there in France didn't know about reinforced concrete or have to build it to stand up to an earthquake.''

We digested this in appropriate silence.

The old church by the Seine had been copied full-size, in minute detail, and its very presence in the middle of the south-western desert was enough to give one pause, never mind the effect of scale and proximity. The postcard pictures for sale up and down the state of Nevada and the stock three-quarter-face view that preceded all sermons televised by the Voice of Heaven simply could not do justice to its sheer massive presence.

No wonder Holy Joe wanted it.

But then our guide added a codicil that brought things back down to earth-size, and reality set in once more.

''Dr. Gillespie,'' she said, ''really meant to buy the original one and ship it back here. But the people who own it just wouldn't listen. You know how those Catholics are . . .''

We were about halfway through the tour when I realized that none of this was coming as any kind of shock or revelation to Maxey. She had seen it before.

But I didn't have much time to think about that.

The Voice of Heaven, in person, was waiting to greet us as our canopied tour-buggy made the final turn around the grove of pine trees that formed a screening wall to hide the rearmost flying buttress of Notre-Dame, and we found ourselves riding down the carriage path to what seemed to be an enlarged and restored copy of the mansion at Tara from *Gone with the Wind*.

Our guide concluded her spiel with an explanation. "This," she chirruped, "is totally authentic—the house where Dr. Gillespie was born, fully preserved and authenticated, moved here all the way from North Carolina!"

She smiled at us, and I smiled back without comment.

Nothing to say.

This was a side of Holy Joe I hadn't suspected, and one that I knew would come as something of a revelation to anyone who remembered him as a ragged-assed back-road Bible seller. But if presidential candidates and movie starlets and corporate officers can reinvent themselves, why not television evangelists?

None of my business.

I turned the bottom of my face into a smile and left it that way as we pulled up to the fresh-painted portico.

Greetings were effusive and the Voice of Heaven's dismissal of our girl guide had all the quality of formal benediction, and I was glad when we moved inside.

It was getting kind of deep out.

But even when we were inside the plantation mansion, the professional projections of fellowship and good cheer continued. Holy Joe seemed to be working his way through a somewhat overproduced Technicolor greetings-to-the-visitors tape intended for use on prospective contributors, and I wished I knew where the Stop and Pause buttons were located. A little of that goes a long way.

Still, I managed to keep my mouth closed and my expression neutral through the ritual of finding seats in the main salon (air conditioned; I wondered if that, too, was a fully preserved and authenticated part of the original) and waiting while another bright-faced young thing brought in a tray of coffee and assorted bakery goods.

I caught the elusive scent of chicory and had an almost uncontrollable urge to give the Voice of Heaven a fat lip.

Mean-minded of me.

But I still didn't know why Maxey and I were here—except that it had been her idea and she seemed to be at home on the premises—and I just didn't believe that he liked chicory himself or remembered that I did. Smelling it now, I decided that I could guess who had been poking into my past and annoying my secretary.

I couldn't decide whether I was more irritated about the invasion of privacy or the implied manipulation.

I took a deep breath and tried to concentrate on the Seven Attributes of the Virtuous Man, but some of what I had been thinking must have been reflected in my face, because Maxey used the minor movement of reaching out to accept a cup from Holy Joe to grind her spike heel into my instep while favoring me with her sweetest and most distant smile.

"Shut up," she lip-synched when his back was turned, "or I will kill you."

I don't think she really meant it. But I never got a chance to find out, because the serving of food and drink appeared to have ended the formalities and the Voice of Heaven was ready to get down to cases.

"I remember you now," he said without preamble, standing tall and slim and patrician on a part of the carpet where light from the window gave him an aura while leaving his face in partial shadow.

Watching him, I wondered if there was a special mark that he tried to hit in order to be sure of the effect, but decided it would be too complicated; you'd need a different one for every hour of the day. No. This would be freehand. And good solid craftsmanship at that.

"I suppose," he went on, "that I ought to apologize for treating you like a stranger during the poker game last night and this morning, but there were . . . factors . . . that interfered."

Okay. We didn't need to discuss it; I waited for him to go on.

"Also, I think I ought to apologize for my actions during the game itself," he said. "I've been under some considerable stress of late, and just wasn't myself. I'd like to talk to you about that, if I may; it's why I asked Mrs. Goines to bring you here today."

He paused, seeming to search for words, and I waited for him to find them.

"I am not really a card cheat," he said. "Can you find it in your heart to forgive me?"

I didn't reply and if I had, I am not sure the answer would have been an affirmative, but he took it for granted and went on.

"My ministry," he said, "has come to a crisis point. Something I'm sure you'll understand as a brother minister."

"I'm a poker player," I said.

"You are a priest," he said. "I call you brother and claim your aid and counsel in this, my time of trial. Danny DiMarco and Sam Goines were not the targets intended for the two men who came to the penthouse of the hotel this morning. I am told that you fought them and killed one and drove the other away, and that is nothing short of miraculous. But it is not the kind of miracle we can hope to see repeated.

"Those men had come to kill me.

"I was that target.

"Unless you help me, I will be the target again. And this time I will surely die!"

A SERMON (Continued)

If the wages of sin is death, and the wages of power is death also . . . is the possession and exercise of power, then, a sin? Is this the sorry message that these two men, from their very separate times and very different lives, have to offer us . . . ?

17

IT LEFT ME stuck for an answer.

Holy Joe—I just couldn't make myself think of him as the Voice of Heaven—had uttered the words in a flat tone that ruled out any hint of histrionics. He believed it.

But I couldn't imagine why.

He was standing at the very center of a high-security compound, surrounded by aides and potential bodyguards, protected by several layers of pomp and circumstance, not to mention a set of high-tech systems whose sensors I had noted on our scenic-route trip from the gate.

A mouse might get inside.

But a potential assassin would surely run into trouble.

On the other hand, this seemed to be my day for talking to people who thought someone was plotting to kill them, and I risked a quick sidelong glance at Maxey before turning my attention back to our host.

Maxey hadn't missed the point.

And our timing was, for old friends now become semi-strangers, still remarkably similar. She was in profile, but her single visible eye jinked sideways to meet mine at just the right moment. That was all we needed. Most people can talk for an hour and say less. And breaking away was harder than I'd expected.

But necessary.

"I thank you kindly for your confidence," I said, opting for the kind of citified-country-boy manner I hoped might keep the party polite. "But I'm afraid I don't see—"

"Please!" He held up a hand as if physically to avert whatever it was I might have been about to say, and stepped off the rear-lighting position mark, moving deliberately as if with conscious intention to afford me a closer, unshadowed, and unguarded look at his face.

It was a good move.

If he was acting, he had been doing so for a long time and was too far into the role to get out. The Voice of Heaven on Earth was a strong and ebullient television presence, a charismatic whose flock looked to him for driving energy and positive response to any and all tribulation. They would hardly have recognized the man who stood before me.

The features were familiar: high, pale forehead topped by tight-curled pepper-and-salt hair; slightly oversized nose, well compensated by a slightly prognathous jaw; and wide mouth that showed the prolonged effects of a minor underbite.

But the skin was pale, almost transparent in the slanting light of afternoon, and there was just a hint of moisture in the hollows beneath the deep-set eyes—a suggestion of tears shed or about to be shed, that was emphasized by the slightly tremulous quality that seemed to dominate the lower part of the face.

He had cut himself shaving, and the styptic pencil had evidently not been of much help.

I found myself thinking, fleetingly and with some embarrassment, of skid row derelicts and the inmates of terminal charity wards. The Voice of Heaven's hide might be cleaner and his clothes better groomed, but he carried with him that same air of uncomprehending disorder. Of chaos accepted. Of doom and loss.

It occurred to me that his potential assassin—if there was one—could hardly have done more damage with a hand grenade. Destruction was already far advanced.

"We were friends," he said.

And that was truly pitiful.

For we never had been. And he knew it.

But I was a guest in his house and, for all I knew, a self-invited one. Maxey hadn't exactly filled me in on the details. I smiled in what I hoped was a reassuring fashion and was about to say something banal when there was a welcome interruption.

"Joe," a low-pitched but arguably feminine voice said from just outside the archway that seemed to lead into the dining room of the big house. "Joe, I want to talk to you a minute before Maxey and that gambler friend of hers get here . . ."

This time it was Holy Joe's turn to find himself at a loss for words.

But none were needed.

The woman who entered the room and hesitated for a moment just inside the door was not the kind who would ever need introductions or explanations. She carried hers with her, in plain sight, and they were not the kind that would ever be questioned.

Television had made her face at least as well known as her husband's.

Sue Harriet Gillespie, wife and helpmeet of the Voice of Heaven on Earth, was one of those vital and healthy women that Scandinavia seems to turn out as a kind of cottage industry—a national export against which no trade barrier will ever be raised. Or considered.

Born in Sweden but reared in the lake country of Minnesota, she had been a showgirl in Las Vegas and, like Maxey, had made not the slightest effort to disguise her background after marriage. To the contrary. One of the strongest and most compelling elements in the television image projected by the Voice of Heaven on Earth was the smiling presence of his rangy and beautiful wife, their on-camera love affair and occasional—highly visible—tiffs forming a kind of soap opera subplot to the main narrative line of personal salvation.

Even so, I could see now that the television screen had undersold the product.

Holy Joe Gillespie is tall, and I had thought that the elevator shoes were simply an effort to emphasize this part of his public image. Now I realized that there might have been other reasons as well. Camera angles and out-of-sight stage dressing can be manipulated to increase or minimize relative height at the whim of the director. It is part of the craft. But reality is something else again, and standing near her husband now in the semiprivacy of their home, I could see that Mrs. Gillespie did not need artificial aids to bring her head to a level with his, and the spike heels she was wearing placed her at an advantage of two or three inches.

She was the kind of woman for whom the word "formidable" was invented.

And she loved it.

"So sorry," she said, not meaning anything of the kind. "I was on the phone upstairs and didn't realize you had arrived. Hello, Maxey. So good to see you again. And you must be her friend—the one they call Preacher?"

Some people have more teeth than others. Burt Lancaster. Kirk Douglas. Jim Coburn. Donny and Marie. I have talked to dentists about it and they assure me that I'm wrong; thirty-two is the absolute limit for human beings and many individuals have only twenty-eight, because the final four at the back of the jaws had to be extracted or never appeared in the first place.

But what do they know? The smile Sue Harriet Gillespie turned in my direction was salesman-bright and contained at least sixty-four teeth, not counting the ones I couldn't see.

She crossed the room to not-quite-shake my hand, and stood there giving me a close-quarters shot of animal magnetism.

It held the attention.

Especially Maxey's. I had stood up and turned toward Mrs. Gillespie when she entered the room, so Maxey was on my blind side and it would have been rude to turn my face far enough to be able to see her. But I didn't need to. There was a stirring over there, and a sudden impression of heat that increased for every one of the moments until Mrs. Gillespie turned back toward her husband with an inquiry about something called the "dope fiend script" and then moved away in the direction of the coffee tray.

Flattering to me, I suppose.

But childish. And far too prevalent among supposed adults to be much fun. I was a little surprised at Maxey. She'd never been that way before. But ten years is ten years, and a few changes would be inevitable. So why the sense of loss?

". . . show you the new prayer garden we were planning the last time you were here."

I had lost the thread for a moment, but Mrs. Gillespie's words brought me back into the room with a not-imperceptible thump. Social amenities were afoot. The ladies were moving off into the drawing room and in a moment someone would bring out the cigars and brandy for the menfolk. I thought for a moment of offering some kind of protest, telling Holy Joe and his big blond wife that anything he could say to me could be said in front of Maxey, too. But I didn't. Because the point was minor, and probably not worth too much exertion.

Because I still didn't know exactly why we were there.

And because I wanted to find out.

The two women drifted through the archway and out of ear-shot and there was a moment of waiting silence after their voices trailed to nothingness before Holy Joe began his pitch.

But when he did, there were no words wasted.

"I had Maxey bring you here this morning," he said, "because I have an offer to make. I am asking you, here and now, to join me in my ministry. As a full partner . . ."

It was a perfectly astonishing proposition, and it didn't make any sense at all and I said so.

Holy Joe didn't seem to hear.

"We were in trouble," he said, "a long time before the situation actually became life-threatening. Big trouble."

He took a final sip of the coffee, put the cup down, and turned toward the door that led to the hallway.

"Come with me," he said. "I want to show you some things . . ."

He led the way outside and along the neatly tended street. I followed. And was glad I did; this was not the low-budget, visiting-faithful tour. Here was the nitty and the gritty, the kind of thing I had a feeling not even the big-number contributors would ever see.

Entrance to some of the areas was by security pass only—no guards in evidence, but even Holy Joe had to shove a bit of coded plastic into the slot and then explain matters to a remote audiovisual sensor when the door system for one office building decided that two bodies had entered instead of one. And once inside the building, I could understand the precautions.

The telephone sales room in particular, was the kind of revelation not found at the end of the New Testament.

Not that the Voice of Heaven called it a telephone sales room; that would have been crass. This, he informed me in a quiet voice that nonetheless attracted the wandering eye of a supervisor seated on a dais in the corner, was the Personal Communication and Pastoral Attention Center. The young men and women here were "keeping me in contact—personal one-on-one contact— with every man, woman, and child who has ever shown an interest in the Word of the Kingdom."

Neat bit of phrasing. But there was nothing wrong with my hearing, and the telephoner nearest me was making a hardball money-pitch to whoever was on the other end of the line. Holy Joe noticed that my interest was divided, saw why, and explained.

The instruments in use here, it seemed, were not really telephones.

"Not unless telephones have started to cost ten thousand

dollars apiece," he said. "Oh, no! These are truly special . . . originally designed for use by the CIA. Yes, sir. Yes! For the Central Intelligence Agency. And now doing the Lord's work. Fitting, don't you agree?"

I found myself reserving judgment on that, but listening fascinated to the latest wrinkle in evangelical money-hustling.

Two years ago, Holy Joe said, he had spent a whole week preaching and exhorting—selling—to an audience made up of high-priced electronic technicians and engineers. And to one ultrasophisticated computer set up in their midst.

"The electronics people," he said, "were really just there for window-dressing. To give me a real audience and to check from time to time to make sure the computer they had set up liked what it was hearing and ate up every word.

"When it was all done, they took the result and studied it—with the computer itself doing the real work, mind you—and then turned it all into numbers. What they call digitalizing. And then they ran it through the program we'd . . . acquired . . . from the government."

That last phrase was accompanied by a beneficient smile that was supposed to give me the impression of a gracious federal entity bestowing largess upon a favored son. In fact, the image that I got was one of a gang of thieves blowing a safe. But I kept that to myself, and he went on.

"What this CIA program does," he said, "it changes the sound of the voice that is heard on the other end of any call made from this room."

I thought about it, keeping my face in neutral.

"Changes the voices . . . to yours," I said.

He nodded cheerfully.

"That's it." He nodded again with a bright smile. "These young folks here, they each got their own list of people who either contacted us for one of the free blessed items we send out on request—no strings attached—or are already members of the flock who may be just a little bit behind in paying up the pledges they made. They call these people up on the phone—"

"And what the person who picks up the phone hears is a personal, one-on-one call from the Voice of Heaven on Earth," I supplied.

"Himself!" he agreed. "And there's no chicanery about it. No, sir! Wouldn't stand for a thing like that myself, and for sure the Lord wouldn't put up with it, either.

"The voice is mine!

"And there's nothing that gets said, not by anyone on this end of the telephone line, any time or anyhow, that I wouldn't say myself. I personally interview each and every one of the young men and women who work in this room, seek into their minds and their ideas, make sure in my own heart that they are true believers in the work that we do here and in the message that is my ministry. In the Voice of Heaven on Earth.

"Talk about your executive management! The policymakers of the business world who are so proud of the way their carefully trained staffs carry out the decisions they have made—they are only shepherds of finance. Of money! Let them come here and learn what it is to trust another person with the tending of souls!

"Oh, I know: You could make a fair case against us. Yes, we do ask for money while we are ministering to the spirit and, yes, we do conceal some of the electronic means that we employ to this end. That's why we have the kind of security system that we do. But I'm sure in my own mind: certain that this is acceptable to the Lord. That it's his work we're doing with the tools he has made ready to our hands."

His voice had risen, distracting one or two laborers in the electronic vineyard, and the Voice of Heaven's smile was slightly apologetic as he nodded toward the supervisor before leading me back outside.

"But that is only a sample," he said, when the door to the office building had closed and locked itself behind us. "Only a sample of the marvels that the Almighty has put at the disposal of this ministry."

We were standing on a cobbled footpath between the office building we had just left and a barnlike structure that I mentally (and correctly) identified as a television or film sound stage, and we stopped there for a moment.

"All this," the Voice of Heaven said with a grandiloquent gesture that seemed to take in the entire world but was evidently meant to encompass only the near vicinity of the compound he called Heaven, "all this is His work. The gift of the Almighty."

He nodded back toward the building we had just left.

"You saw only the ground floor," he said. "Perhaps I should also have shown you the floors above and below. Not as impressive, perhaps, as the Personal Communication Center, but every bit as necessary to the work we do here.

"The second floor of that building is the main office, the Correspondence Center, a kind of cerebral cortex where men and women deal with the hundreds upon hundreds of letters and contributions and requests for advice and intercession that come to this ministry daily from all around the world.

"Every single blessed one of those letters is answered—by me!

"Oh, yes, once again we come into an area where there could be argument. Where there could be doubt. No one man, no individual, could deal with one percent of the mail that comes here. Yet the answers are mine. Words and ideas and beliefs and faith. Mine.

"How so?

"Because each comes not from an individual there in the office, but from the mainframe state-of-the-art computer located in the subbasement and proof against all outside tampering from anything up to and including atomic attack!"

He paused to let me digest that, and then went on, apparently taking my silence for agreement.

"The two systems, Personal Communication and Correspondence centers, attend to the pastoral needs of our flock. But the very heart and soul of our ministry, the true Voice of Heaven on Earth, is there."

He was looking in the direction of the sound stage and there was more than a trace of real affection, of what might even have been called love, in his face. I wondered if his wife knew where his true allegiance lay. I suspected that she might. And I wondered what kind of peace she had been able to make with the knowledge.

"Our studios are small, by commercial standards," he said. "Just one real stage, and support units. The warehouse behind there is where we keep scenery and stage properties. And wardrobe. More than five hundred costumes, all fresh and ready for use. You've seen our programs?"

I drew breath to phrase a denial that would be as kind as possible, but no such effort was needed. Self-assurance is a wondrous thing and needs no validation but its own.

"Then you know," he said, "that my wife, Sue Harriet, was an actress before our marriage—before the beginning of this ministry, in fact—and we utilize her gifts in our work. Problems and needs and their solutions are dramatized for the daily installment of an ongoing dramatic serial that follows each of my own telecasts.

"Some people have criticized this, saying we are giving people soap opera in place of true service.

"But these are the words of envy!

"My purpose is to spread the Word of the Kingdom. Did they criticize the Christophers for their dramatizations? Call them charlatans? No! No more than the Catholic church called Fulton Sheen a demagogue for the lectures that gave him the highest Nielsen rating of any minister in early television. Demagogue? They made the man a bishop!"

He paused, for breath and perhaps to deplore the unfairness of the world, and then went on without seeming to notice the break.

"Our writers and producers do their work under my eye and within the policies set for them by this ministry. This so-called soap opera is a morality play, a daily journey into the heart of Christian life and living. Yes, we pay attention to the Nielsen ratings! Yes, they have meaning to us! But not just to sell some product.

"There was a day when the best pulpit God had offered to his ministers was a high altar or the top of a hill where he could preach to those within sound of his voice.

"Then writing came.

"And Gutenberg.

"These gifts from above were intended to the propagation of the faith, for the further enrichment and salvation of men's souls through the Word. Now there is a new dispensation; the Almighty has granted to us a new miracle—television, which has the potential of reaching all humankind in a single instant. Truly the Voice of Heaven on Earth.

"I would be a poor steward if I permitted such a miracle to go unrealized, or if I allowed it to reach only a portion of its potential . . ."

He had continued to gaze raptly at the sound stage and the facilities connected with it, but now he turned to face me and his voice hushed with a subtext of what might almost have been desperation.

"God spoke to me," he said. "God spoke, and I knew that it was his voice, and commanded that I use these tools as he had intended. He guided me each step of the way, and I knew he was beside me and was sure . . ."

This time the pause went on long enough to be real, and I knew it was time to respond. With whatever tact I could summon.

"In that case," I said, "there is no problem. You don't need me. Surely a man who speaks to God and knows his will needs little else . . ."

But he was shaking his head.

"You don't comprehend," he said. "You don't know! You don't understand what has happened: God . . . my God . . . no longer speaks to me!

"And neither does Francis Carrington Shaw . . ."

A SERMON (Continued)

Perhaps. But if so, their argument is as seed cast upon barren soil. For all know the truth: That death is not so much the wages of power or of sin, but merely of life itself . . .

18

THAT NEEDED A lot of explaining, but Holy Joe seemed to think I already knew all about it.

"Shaw started it all," he said. "Gave me the opportunity to obey God's plan. Gave me the money to begin this ministry. Here."

I must have looked blank.

"Everyone's heard the story," he said. "Surely you. . . ?"

My negative seemed to shake him.

Holy Joe Gillespie had been the Voice of Heaven on Earth for a long time. More than a decade. Too long to be able to remember that there were people who didn't think of him in exactly that way or have any detailed knowledge of his personal life.

After all, he had set it all forth in three separate and distinct autobiographies.

"Francis Carrington Shaw," he said, in what seemed more an attempt to jog reluctant memory than to provide fresh information, "bought the land we are standing on when he first moved to Nevada. Bought it and handed it over to me for the building of the Kingdom."

It was news to me and he went on, gathering momentum, as we drifted along the path that led to the sound stage.

"That was his first great gift, but by no means his last. My ministry was just beginning here in Las Vegas, and I had never seen him before, but he said he had heard of the work I was doing out of the little storefront church we'd been able to set up a few blocks from Casino Center.

"We called that place Heaven on Earth, too, and a lot of people in those days thought we were just another kind of skid row mission, a way station for derelicts on their way to prison or the madhouse or the grave. But we changed their minds soon enough . . .''

Las Vegas street people, he explained, are different from those encountered anywhere else on earth. The police see to that. Grimy winos and lunatic bag ladies get short shrift from the law; the route is a quick one from sidewalk to patrol car to courtroom to desert work-gang, and most find means to drift on before being sentenced to a second excursion.

''The men and women who came to that storefront,'' he said, ''were usually sober and pretty well dressed, considering. Their problem was gambling—an addiction that was, for them, more terrible than liquor or drugs. They came to us not merely in distress or in search of a free meal. Not at all. They came to the place called Heaven on Earth because they had hit rock bottom. Because they were destroyed—family gone, career in ruins. And we gave them . . . hope?

''No, brother!

''Hope is a broken reed, an illusion that fades with digestion and the cold light of dawn. Hope had brought them to our door. But they entered and found . . . Heaven. As advertised.''

Early in this dissertation, Holy Joe's voice had started to rise to sermon pitch. But a peculiar thing happened when he spoke of the results he'd obtained in his little downtown mission. The words seemed to calm him, and the voice softened as memory took over, and I felt an unexpected jolt of sadness, watching and listening. I wondered if I might be hearing him describe the last—perhaps the only—hours of real happiness and security he had ever known.

The poor son of a bitch.

But he was speaking again, and the moment passed.

''We couldn't help everyone who came to us, of course,'' he said. ''Some were beyond help, and others needed only a place to stop long enough to get their bearings. Eighty percent, ninety percent, perhaps more, left our little mission no better than they had arrived.

''But the others!

''God talked to me in those days. I heard him. He talked to me every day and he told me what they needed. They were addicts, and if they had been addicted to heroin the medical profession would have treated them with methadone. Why? Because it would end their addiction? No, indeed! Methadone only ends addiction to heroin by substituting the stronger addiction to methadone. But methadone is legal and heroin is not. Do you see the parallel?

"I gave the gambling addicts who came to me a greater addiction—a greater rush of excitement and a stronger sense of power than the dice or the cards or the clanking machines ever could.

"I gave them the world.

"Showed them the men and women they might be if they would only accept the real gamble . . . of life!

"God gave me the words and I gave them the understanding of God's own personal plan for them. Took the thrill and the false, transitory sense of power that lies at the heart of the will to gamble and bent them to the work of the Almighty. Showed them the exaltation and the terror—and the real power—that it could bring."

We had reached the door to the sound stage, but a red light was flashing and we waited for it to stop before going in.

"And Francis Carrington Shaw heard of this. Of your successes?" I said.

Gillespie turned to face me and I was astonished to notice a trace of moisture at the corners of his eyes. He nodded mutely and swallowed twice before he was able to go on.

"Yes," he said finally. "He did. Better still, he came to see for himself."

"In person. Actually appeared at the mission?"

"Yes. This was before he got so sick. So afraid of germs that he wouldn't go out of this room or let anyone in to see him. He had just moved to Las Vegas at the time. Very few people knew him by sight, and he was able to move around without attracting attention. Besides, this time he was in a kind of disguise. Francis Carrington Shaw came to our door as a supplicant, pretending to be a gambling degenerate himself—to see what we had to offer. And he was convinced.

"The next day he sent word that he wanted to talk to me, and I went to where he was living. In a suite he had at the Flamingo, before he bought the other hotels and built the Scheherazade. He sat me down in a chair and offered me . . . all that I had ever wanted."

Specifically, Shaw had proposed an expansion of the Rev. Holroyd J. Gillespie's field of operations and an amplification of his voice. The mission was all very well in its place, but the techniques that had proven so effective there could be applied elsewhere. To a wider array of problems. And to a nationwide—perhaps even worldwide—audience.

By the time Holy Joe arrived for the interview, Shaw had already purchased the two little ranches outside town whose combined acreage he thought might be suitable for their purposes—he seemed to take his new protégé's assent as an accomplished fact—and an architect had presumably worked through the night to produce a basic plan and perspective rendering of the buildings and satellite transmission tower that were to rise there.

"He said my voice—and my message—would be heard wherever there were ears to hear.

"Wherever there was need . . ."

The Voice of Heaven's eyes were focused on the middle distance, on the spot where remembrance of things past always seems to dwell, and the words came softly as if telling the landmarks of a vanished Beulah Land.

"But . . . why?"

It was rude of me, and unfeeling, to call him back from the happy place where he had gone. But my curiosity has always been stronger than my sense of decency. Besides, I thought the answer might be important.

But Holy Joe didn't seem to understand the question.

"Why . . . what?" he said.

"Francis Carrington Shaw," I said, "is an international businessman who inherited a paltry five or six million dollars from his father and turned it into nearly two billion. When he was sixty years old, perhaps because Nevada has no inheritance tax—though that doesn't really make sense, since he has no known family left on earth—he moved here and bought six hotel-casinos and an airport and a couple of high-tech laboratories and a spread of desert land that's said to be the largest parcel of privately owned acreage in the world.

"So far, you've got a reprise of the Howard Hughes theme—and just to complete the picture, the man is now in semi-hermetic seclusion surrounded by a Mormon bodyguard.

"But Hughes's only major philanthropy was a medical foundation that was set up when he got tired of one of his companies. Otherwise, he was so tight in the fist that he outfumbled people for restaurant tabs, never mind charitable contributions over and above the ones he had to make to keep the income tax accountants happy. And you'll forgive me if I say I haven't heard that your friendly benefactor was notably different.''

The smile he gave me was all of sweet accord.

"Yes," he said. "But this time God had spoken to both of us, and told us what we must do . . .''

The red light stopped flashing, and we went through the door to the sound stage.

Inside, it was tear-down time.

Holy Joe's ''soap opera'' television serial was apparently taped with three cameras—one for master scene and the other two for coverage—to cut time and movement to a minimum. But there were three complete sets, unusual for all but the highest-budget shows, and the crew appeared now to be moving equipment from one set to another.

A tall woman with dark hair and eyebrows approached us and I was startled to hear Mrs. Gillespie's voice.

"Has he got your name on a contract yet?" she inquired with a smile that was not quite cynical.

I must have looked blank.

And she laughed. "I keep forgetting," she said. "Yes, it's me in here. I play two roles in this thing—good girl, bad girl, you know? And this is my bad girl getup.''

It was effective.

I made a mental note to have a look at the show sometime. There might be more to it than I'd thought.

"But I still want to know," she went on. "Are you going to join us? Has he signed you up?"

Holy Joe was smiling, too, but he shook his head.

"Not yet," he said.

"But you must! Maxey said—''

I caught the warning look from Holy Joe that told her she'd gone too far, too fast, and her instant reaction came through the makeup intact.

"We thought," the Voice of Heaven said, choosing words with obvious care, "that Maxey—Mrs. Goines, I just can't think of her as a widow, much less imagine Sam Goines being dead— that Maxey might have filled you in on the problems we have encountered of late.''

This was getting complicated.

Maxey appeared to be on closer terms than I'd thought with the Gillespies. But all the same, she hadn't clued them in on the fact that Sam was alive. Or if she had, they hadn't been told that I knew it, too. And the idea that she'd been aware of the pitch Holy Joe was going to make, and might even have considered it a good idea, was less a surprise than a distinct and depressing shock.

Could a few years have changed us both that much . . . ?

"Problems?" I said.

The Voice of Heaven nodded.

"Time, for one thing," he said. "Electronic miracles like the ones in the communication center are all very well, and we can pretty well make our own schedules here to take maximum advantage of our time. But even so, there are just not enough hours in the day for all that we hope to do. All we wish to accomplish."

I could understand, and almost sympathize. But the solution seemed obvious. "Cut back," I said. "Take it a little easier. Surely the Almighty doesn't mean you to shorten your life by overwork."

His reaction was unhesitating and definite. "I cannot do that," he said. "The Lord's plan for H. J. Gillespie has no room in it for sloth. For idleness. The vineyard in which he labors is not his own, and he fears the wrath of a hard master!"

I had a momentary urge to ask him how he could be sure of that when he and the Lord were no longer on speaking terms. But I managed to restrain it, and before things could get any deeper he excused himself, muttering something about wanting to talk to the production manager.

"What we need," Sue Harriet Gillespie said, taking up the slack with a smoothness that spoke of long practice, "is a second minister. Someone with a message of his own that does not conflict with ours. Someone with the charisma to command the same size and kind of audience."

I shook my head. "Wouldn't work," I said. "Look what happened when Jerry tried to take over for Jim and Tammy Faye. Disaster!"

"Jerry was wrong for the job."

"Plenty of experience . . ."

"But no force. No fireworks. No personal aura of love and strength. No *mana*!"

The final word surprised me. I wondered just where she'd heard it and what it might mean to her. Before I could put my curiosity into words, however, she gave me something else to think about.

"Right now," she said, "you have a ministry limited to the sound of your voice and the reach of your arm. Less than one hundred souls—and all of them gathered in a single spot, a miserable little mountain town in California."

I bridled a bit at the word "miserable." Best Licks was, and is, a pleasant and comfortable place in a landscape of surpassing beauty. But the flow of words gave me no chance to object.

"The work you do is good work. Worthwhile. You have something to offer the men and women whose lives were interrupted and deformed by fighting an unsuccessful war under the direction of leaders who can only with charity be thought of as merely incompetent . . ."

Again, I felt the urge to edit and object, and again found myself unable to break through the seamless fabric of words.

". . . and uncaring. But think how much more you could do, how many more you could reach and sustain and nurture if your voice could be amplified and the reach of your arm extended through the power of modern technology."

It was an echo. Her husband had used much the same words to explain his reasons for accepting Francis Carrington Shaw's original proposal, and the questions this raised in my own mind finally forced me to interrupt.

"Tempting," I lied. "But it still doesn't add up. Help's easy to find and there are plenty of ministers who'd jump at the chance to join you—as partners or employees or any deal you'd care to make. You don't need me."

"But we do!"

The reply was too immediate and vehement to be mere persuasion. She meant it.

"Why?"

I let the single word hang there.

It was the most obvious question in the world, but for a moment I didn't think I was going to hear an answer. Sue Harriet Gillespie looked at me with something savage and carnivorous prowling just behind the mirror of her eyes, and there was a moment when I was sure that she was going to tell me to go to hell. But the moment passed and the answer came in the flat tones of verity, edged with ice.

"We've slipped," she said.

She wanted to stop there, and I almost wanted to let her. But I kept my mouth shut and waited it out.

"Joe thinks it's our own fault," she said. "But I don't agree. It started when everyone else went crazy—when Pat started running for President and Oral said God wanted protection money and the Bakkers got into their pissing match with Falwell and Swaggart. Suddenly everyone else in the world was without sin and started throwing stones.

"That was it.

"The donations dried up and the Nielsens went into the dumper and, worst of all, Francis Carrington Shaw stopped returning our telephone calls."

She paused again, as if waiting for me to supply a final line that I already knew. But I had no idea what it might be.

"And then, last week, he sent a message," she said when it was obvious that I wasn't going to jump in. "Didn't you wonder why Joe was in that poker game at the Scheherazade?"

Now that she mentioned it, I had. But Sam Goines had set it up, and I had assumed he knew what he was doing.

"Joe was there," Sue Harriet Gillespie said, "because I got a call from someone who said Francis Carrington Shaw wanted him to use that game to get to know you and try to bring you into this ministry. Surely you're not going to try to tell me you knew nothing about it . . . that Shaw hadn't talked to you about it in advance?"

Well, Jesus out of the boat.

"Mrs. Gillespie," I said, "I have never seen, spoken to, or in any way communicated with Francis Carrington Shaw in all my life. I do not know the man. He does not know me."

She didn't want to believe it and her eyes called me a liar and I think her voice might have said it, too, but we were interrupted by the return of her husband—with Maxey in tow.

"Some hostess you are," he said, only half joking. "I found poor Maxey wandering around all alone outside, looking for us with an armful of mail."

His wife seemed not at all abashed.

"If I know poor Maxey," she said, "a mail clerk was passing and she grabbed the load from him just to keep from getting bored."

Maxey made a face and the two women smiled at each other in the ease of old friendship.

"Well"—the Voice of Heaven handed a sheaf of letters to his wife, glanced briefly at others he had kept in his own hand, and then aimed both eyes in my direction—"has Sue Harriet succeeded in convincing you that your future lies here? With us?"

His eyes were bright and his manner was brisk, all traces of moisture and fatigue I had noticed earlier erased as if they had never been, and I surprised myself with a sudden and vivid recollection of the little packets of white powder I had noticed spilling from under his coat after the machine-gun attack.

No wonder he was in trouble.

"Not exactly," I said. "But Mrs. Gillespie is a powerful persuader."

She smiled at me with all those sixty-four teeth.

"Flatterer," she said. "Just for that, you get one of my specialties tonight—not that I will fix it myself, but it's my recipe: rôti de coq à l'orange. Maxey says you are a man of good appetite. Hope she was right!"

She slipped the letters under her arm with a businesslike air. "Meanwhile," she said, "I am off for the house to get out of this darn makeup. Stick with them, Maxey—make sure he says yes, or we'll have to keep up the sales talk through dinner!"

She slipped the letters under her arm and fumbled a ring of keys out of the tote bag she was carrying.

"Brought one of the tour cars over, thank the Lord," she said. "Otherwise someone'd have to carry me."

"Well, Mrs. Gillespie, if you're looking for volunteers . . ." I said.

"You shopping for a fat lip?" Maxey inquired in mock-earnest.

Holy Joe laughed. It almost sounded real. And his wife grinned at us from the doorway.

"All compliments gratefully accepted," she said. "And please, let's not be so formal. Call me Harry . . . everyone does."

The sound-stage door closed on that pleasantry, and I was beginning to roll it around in my mind—trying to connect it with something only half remembered—when the Voice of Heaven began to make strangling sounds.

Maxey and I turned to see him standing transfixed, a flap-torn envelope still in his hand, gazing in mute horror at the five playing cards it had contained.

Two aces.

And three eights.

"No!" The power of speech, returning, concentrated itself in a single terror-laden word as the moment of paralysis ended and he flung himself upon the stage door, heaving at its sound-devouring weight with the strength of desperation. I moved to stop him, to seize the cards, to ask what he knew about them—and how. But we were both too slow.

The door had moved only an inch or two when the shock wave arrived and the world outside erupted in a cataclysm of light and sound and fire-breathing ruin.

A SERMON (Continued)

Life begins and life ends and the beginning is called birth and the ending is called death and neither can exist without the other. The end awaits the helpless as surely as the powerful, the virtuous no less than the wicked . . .

19

THE EXPLOSION DIDN'T leave much.

One of the experts from the Las Vegas police bomb detail speculated later that it was probably three or four sticks of high-grade dynamite wrapped around an electric blasting cap and wired across the ignition system of the pint-sized runabout Sue Harriet Gillespie had been using.

"The minute she turned the key, that was Katie-bar-the-gate!" he said.

No one seemed ready to argue.

The Voice of Heaven on Earth had been knocked unconscious by the blast that filtered through the partially opened doorway to the sound stage, and it was just as well. That gave me a chance to get him back inside and into the hands of people who liked him and would keep him from going out to look at what had happened to his wife.

Maxey sat with him to make sure he stayed put.

But I had to look at it, the police saw to that, and I was glad when Corner Pocket, who had arrived with the first wave, suggested that they take all of us somewhere else for the inevitable questioning. The bomb squad's guess at the amount of explosive used to produce such results surprised me a little. I'd have thought it was more.

The coroner's cleanup detail arrived just as we were leaving for the main house—I was getting so I could recognize a couple of them on sight—and stood around holding body bags, looking helpless.

They had my sympathy.

But I was only a passing thought, and the interrogation that began as soon as we were gathered again in the living room drove everything else out of mind.

Clark County central homicide meant business this time. Maxey and I sat still and moved our jaws on command. We were almost used to it by now.

But they left Joe Gillespie pretty much alone.

He was conscious by the time paramedics arrived, and he passed their physical examination without difficulty. Not a scratch. But he didn't seem to want to let go of the five playing cards that had remained clamped between the thumb and fingers of his left hand through the blast and its aftermath, and he didn't seem to hear much of anything that was said to him—though he was not entirely speechless.

''They meant it for me,' he said as we arrived at the house.

Everyone paused, waiting for him to go on. But that was all, and he repeated it once more after we were all seated in the living room. And then stopped talking entirely. The compound's staff doctor looked him over and summoned a specialist from Las Vegas, who arrived while the primary interrogations were still in progress. He recommended immediate hospitalization, and there were no objections when he administered a sedative on the spot. But he still couldn't pry Holy Joe's fingers loose from the dead man's hand.

Corner Pocket took it all without comment.

He hadn't spoken again after we left the sound stage. But I could see him slouched in the corner, hands in pockets, apparently oblivious. And I could feel the banked fire of anger that brightened each time he glanced in my direction. He could afford to wait. His turn was coming.

And he had my sympathy.

The answers he was going to get from me were not going to satisfy him one little bit, and no amount of pressure was going to make them any better, because I didn't have any clearer idea of what was going on than he did.

But I did have more information . . .

Carefully measuring the words, I set the front part of my mind to work giving logical and—mostly—accurate responses to whatever the homicide investigators said or did, and wandered into the back room to take inventory.

It was a real mess back there.

Keeping my mouth closed when Maxey identified the dead man in the hospital bed as her husband had seemed like the best thing to do at the time; I had assumed that she would have a good reason, and if the one she had wasn't the best in the world, it was at least good enough to keep me from walking over to the nearest phone and dropping a dime on her. The craziness with the aces and eights that had turned up there and in the Voice of Heaven's mail just before his wife's car blew up connected the two killings, of course. But it hadn't changed my mind about letting Maxey keep her secret as long as she thought she had to. She was scared. She had a right to be. And I couldn't see enough of the cards yet to do anything but check.

And then there was the part that not even Maxey knew about yet. My own hole card.

Jorge Martinez.

Little Trouble.

Try as I might, I could think of no reasonable way to connect him with anything that had happened. It made no sense at all. Danny DiMarco was dead, and Jorge had helped to make him that way, but I just couldn't believe he had ever met the man. Poor dumb Terrence Lyle McDuff was dead, and Little Trouble had helped make him that way, too. But he hadn't quite got it done and someone else—presumably a phoney nurse in an outdated uniform—had finished the job for him.

Now there had been still another killing, one he'd had nothing to do with because he was already dead, but the letter containing the aces and eights made it part of the same pattern. And turned it all into nonsense.

So why hadn't I told Corner Pocket that I knew him?

Don't ask me, brother. I'm a stranger in these parts myself.

"Preacher . . ."

The homicide team had gone away and Corner Pocket was standing in front of me. His face was blank and his hands were hanging loose at his sides, but he was tense as a coiled spring and I could feel the heat rising in him. His turn had finally come.

"Let's take a walk," he said.

It seemed as good an idea as any. I stood up and waited for him to lead off, and he did that without further comment. One of the detectives from Las Vegas made a vague move in our direction as we went out the door, but seemed to think better of it when he got a close look at Corner Pocket's face. Smart cop.

Corner Pocket didn't seem to be in any hurry, and I made a mental note that he was no stranger to the byways of Holy Joe's tightly guarded Heaven on Earth compound for he took a series of shortcuts that brought us almost immediately to a semi-secluded grove of trees in the ersatz woodland screening Notre-Dame of the Desert.

"Now, then," he said, leaning comfortably against the trunk of a well-tended pine tree.

That didn't seem to call for a reply.

"I hear tell," he said, "that you are some kind of expert at Oriental martial arts. T'ai chi for exercise, plus some training in kung fu, karate, t'ai kwon do . . . ?"

"I try to keep in shape," I said. He wasn't making sense. But he wasn't required to.

"Uh-huh."

He looked away for a moment, seeming to find something of interest along the pathway we'd followed to get into the grove, but as a gesture of dissimulation it was a total failure. His *wa* was fire-hot now, feeding on the anger in him and ready to do something about it

"Never went into any of that myself," he said with a continued effort at casual control that must have been expensive. "But I tell you right here and now, Preacher man, I have taken all the shit off you that I am going to. So believe this: In the next five minutes, you are going to tell me every goddam thing you know or think or can remember about your old Vietnam buddy, Sergeant Jorge Martinez . . . or I am going to do my very best to break both of your legs."

So much for my hole card.

Identifying an individual through fingerprints alone can take weeks. I knew Little Trouble's set would be on file in Washington because of his army service, but I'd counted on at least the time it would take to check them out there. And I had been wrong.

Jorge Martinez, it seemed, had spent some time working as a security guard at one of the Glitter Gulch casinos after he got out of the army, and his prints were still on file with the Las Vegas police. Their computer confirmed his identity a few hours after his death, a routine teletype query brought his service record into their hands, and the decoration he'd won in the second battle of Khe Sanh had rung bells for Corner Pocket.

Checking Little Trouble's record against my own, he said, was no more than a formality.

"You son of a bitch," he added conversationally.

Some days it just doesn't pay to get out of bed.

Step by step, I walked him again through my reasons—the real ones; I'd told him the truth about them from the first—for coming to Las Vegas, and how Sam Goines's invitation to a table-stakes game with people who could afford to lose seemed to come at just the right moment.

Explaining why I hadn't told him that I knew the dead machine gunner was a little more complicated, but a slight cooling of the hot-rage aura he had been projecting told me that my reasons at least made sense to him, even if he didn't agree with the logic. He wasn't ready to break my legs anymore. But he still wasn't exactly ready to pronounce absolution, either.

And that was all right, too. It balanced some of the guilt I was feeling for not telling him Sam Goines was still alive.

"I ought to lock you up," he said.

"On what charge?"

"Try obstructing justice," he said. "Or maybe second-degree murder. You were fighting with Martinez when he died."

"He was shot by someone in the helicopter."

"So you say. Christ on a crutch, Preacher, you think I need to be choosy about the kind of charges I throw around in a town like this? I'll slap you in a cell for barratry on the high seas and keep you for a month if I take the notion, and that's no joke!"

It wasn't, of course, and I decided to shut up.

"The trouble with keeping a thing like that to yourself," he said, cooling down a little more, "is that you don't have the whole picture, so you have no way to know whether it fits with something else or not."

"Does it?"

He thought for a moment before he answered, and I think it was in his mind to say it was none of my business or maybe tell me to go and attempt a physical impossibility. No one ever had a better reason. But in the end he shook his head and relaxed a little.

"Not that I can see," he admitted. "But all the same, this is something you ought to leave to the professionals. Do I tell you how to trim a rich poker chump?"

I felt myself bridle a bit at his choice of words. There are nicer ways to describe my chosen profession. Still, it was at least technically accurate, and the point well taken.

"Okay," I said. "But you didn't bring me here—away from the homicide dicks and out of range of the security cameras— just to cuss me out or even to bust me up a little for holding out on you. There is something else on your mind, old friend, and you are looking to play a little holdout game of your own."

He snorted. "Smartass," he said.

"You said it, I didn't."

He took a deep breath and didn't look at me while he spoke his piece, and I had sense enough for once to keep still and let him do it. Despite all he'd said about keeping my nose out of his business and leaving investigation to the professionals, he was having to ask for help. And it burned his butt to do it.

"Of the seven people who were at that poker table last night and this morning," he said, "at least four—Danny DiMarco, Happy Apodaca, Joe Gillespie, and Manny Temple—all had connections to Francis Carrington Shaw."

I nodded. The same thing had occurred to me.

"Danny DiMarco," he went on, "had just bought a hotel from Shaw, and my spies around town tell me that it was Shaw who put out the word to get the old guy bookings and keep the publicity ball rolling when it looked like he might be going down the tube a year or two back."

I'd known about the hotel deal, but not about the other—though it didn't really surprise me much. Shaw might not be a philanthropist, but it wouldn't be the first time he'd taken a quiet interest in one falling star or another. Rumors like that had been around for years.

"Judge Apodaca's another example," Corner Pocket continued. "Maybe even a bigger one, in his day. People tend to have short memories hereabouts, it's the kind of town where that can be a real advantage, but there was a time when old Happy Apodaca really rated the title 'Judge.' He was a distinguished member of the federal judiciary. A U.S. district judge. And when he resigned it wasn't exactly by choice."

He was right this time. And wrong.

I did remember. But I hadn't known that Francis Carrington Shaw figured in the story.

"A few years later," Corner Pocket said, "another federal judge who was in a jam got stubborn when it came time to resign. Wound up having to be impeached while he was actually doing time in a federal slammer.

"Happy Apodaca was smarter than that. Or luckier. Feds had him on a bribery case that was airtight, but he was allowed to resign and go into private practice because Shaw wanted it that way and he owned the senator who had put the federal prosecutor in his job. Turned out the private practice Apodaca went into had just one client—Francis Carrington Shaw."

I thought it over. "Seems like it's worked out pretty well for both of them," I said.

"Doesn't it?"

He stuck his hands in the hip pockets of his trousers and looked at the sky, and for a moment I thought he'd run dry.

"Everyone knows the story about Shaw and Manny Temple," I prodded, hoping he wouldn't let it pass.

And he didn't.

"Uh-huh," he said. "They know half the story is what they know—and not the best half. They know Manny was supposed to be retired when he came here. Retired: That's what you call it when people who are bigger and tougher than you are crowd you out of your home territory but let you live through it. And they know that Francis Carrington Shaw set Manny up as front man for the Shaw hotel and casino operations here in town. Set a thief to catch a thief, right?"

I didn't have to nod. Just standing still was enough.

"Wrong," he said. "The part people don't know is that Manny Temple had a son who was strung out on speed and coke—methamphetamine and cocaine, mixed and injected in seven percent solution—a guaranteed mind-warper. Manny couldn't do anything with the kid. So it was Shaw who looked up the best clinic in the country and got the boy in there and paid the freight and sent him back to his old man all clean and shiny."

I shook my head as if hearing it all for the first time. "Kid still around?" I inquired.

Corner Pocket shrugged. "In a manner of speaking," he said. "The clinic Shaw sent him to turned out to have connections to the Hare Krishnas. About a month after he got back, the kid disappeared again and floated to the surface a little later in one of their temples. You can see him most days just outside the entrance to the main terminal at McCarran, walking around in a yellow sheet with his head shaved, banging on a gong and hustling the incoming and outgoing chumps for change."

"Manny must love that."

"He doesn't talk about it. But about the time the kid turned up there for the first time was when he stopped using commercial airlines . . . always charters a plane nowadays, or has someone drive him in and out of town in that air-conditioned limo."

I had known about the boy's addiction; I hadn't known about the Krishna angle.

Well.

It could have been a lot worse. But maybe not from Manny's point of view.

"Okay," I said, hoping to keep the ball rolling a little longer. "But what about the Voice of Heaven on Earth?"

Corner Pocket's *wa* was down to room temperature now, and the eyes he turned in my direction were positively chilly.

"Never kid a kidder," he said.

"Right! I know Shaw set Holy Joe up out here," I said. "But I thought there might be more to the story—and that you might know the rest."

That was as close to a compliment as you wanted to come with Corner Pocket. Suspicious soul. But the words were honest, even though the intention might have left a lot to be desired.

"Nothing much," he said evenly, "except the word is that things have been pretty cool there lately. Don't know why. Thought you might."

The game works two ways.

Fair enough.

"I don't," I said. "But if I find out—"

That heated things up again.

"If you find out anything," he said, never taking his eyes from my face, "about the Reverend Holroyd Josiah Gillespie or his deceased wife, no matter what, I want to hear about it. You owe me one, Preacher."

He was right. But I wanted him to spell it out, and he did.

"I told you I could land your skinny butt on a jail cot and I can do it. And I will, too, if I find out you've been holding out on me again.

"So far, all I got is four dead people and three poker hands and a little information that may or may not make sense.

"That leaves you loose on the street. For now.

"But I don't believe in coincidences and I don't believe anyone was in that game by chance. So until further notice, I want to hear anything that you hear and anything that you think, and I want to hear it before anyone else does—especially if it's about the bearded guy. The hot-goddamn-shot mercenary."

"Colonel Connor?"

"Him."

I must have looked as surprised as I felt.

"Missing," Corner Pocket said. "The colonel hasn't been seen since he helped move the Voice of Heaven out of that shot-up penthouse suite."

A SERMON (Continued)

And in any case, who among us is wicked? Don't answer too quickly! We all think we can define the word "wicked," and perhaps even nominate someone as an exemplar. But how valid is our definition? How did you pick your nominee . . . ?

20

MAXEY WAS WHITE-faced and preoccupied on the way back to town, and I thought I knew why.

Losing a friend is never easy. And this has been especially sudden. Especially devastating.

But I was wrong, and I found out about it just as we were turning off Paradise Road toward the Scheherazade.

"You must be crazy," she said.

That left me stumped for a moment, and when we had to stop for a red light I filled the time trying to relate the words to what had happened back at the Heaven on Earth compound. But I couldn't, and the next thing she said was no big help.

"He's going down the tube," she said, "and this will just make the slide faster. He was just barely able to hold it together with her there to steer. No way he can survive without her. Dammit, you're the only chance he's got!"

Still lost.

But she wasn't done.

"You came to Las Vegas because you were broke. Income tax collector breathing down your neck; embargoed your bank accounts and left you high and dry. Then you get an offer, a legitimate one that could turn the whole thing around, and do you grab it like any sane man would do? Like hell you do!"

She was really angry and working herself up to be more so, but at last I knew what we were talking about.

"You set it up," I said as we turned into the hotel's unwalled VIP garage and started looking for my assigned parking space instead of turning the car over to the valet service. "You and Sue Harriet Gillespie. That's why we went out there this morning."

"Hoo-ray! You have your choice of a new refrigerator or a trip to—"

"Maxey."

188

"—beautiful Tahiti, all expenses paid. Or would you rather try for our sweepstakes?"

"Maxey, dammit!"

She stopped talking but still didn't look in my direction, and I let it stay that way until I had the car in its own slot with the engine off and the brake set.

"Why?" I said then.

No response.

"What have I ever done that would make anyone—you, of all people—imagine that I'd ever consider joining Holy Joe Gillespie's television circus?"

That finally got the ball rolling. She turned toward me with an expression of combined anger and frustration that should have fried the fillings in my teeth.

"Liar," she said.

"No doubt about it," I said. "But on what subject this time?"

She shook her head, and I couldn't help noticing once again the way her eyes seemed to change color with her emotions. They were purple now. Almost black.

"Holy Joe's a con man and a slimy little bastard," she said. "So what? That wasn't marriage he was proposing back there. The man's got a high-hat cocaine habit he can't kick and if someone doesn't take over for him—I mean take over the whole shebang, get him off the air, at least for the time being—he is going to blow it."

She paused, and I had a minor urge to butt in with an explanation or two. But the emotion spilling off her was so heavy that I was glad I didn't smoke. Lighting a match around there could have been dangerous.

"And don't tell me it's not something you could do," she went on. "You're doing all of it and more right now. For peanuts! I've heard tape recordings . . ."

That jolted a memory.

Services at the Church of Best Licks are open; visitors to town are few and strange faces on a Sunday morning are rare enough to be remembered. But we have yet to turn anyone away.

Five or six months earlier there had been a visitor who fitted no known category. He was dressed for the mountains, but everything he wore was new and he had the hands of a city dweller. He entered late and left early and offered no explanations and none were asked. Best Licks is that kind of place. He turned up again three Sundays in a row and I was beginning to wonder if we had a potential recruit who couldn't get up the courage to say so. By the fourth week I was seriously considering ways and means. But he didn't come back.

"Sermons," I said. "Three of them? From a few months back?"

"And interviews," she nodded. "Sam sent a private detective up there to the Sierra, to find out what you were doing and what people there thought of you. And when he was done we called Sue Harriet and she read the reports and listened to the tapes with us and no one had any doubts that you were just the one they'd been looking for."

"They?" I said. "Holy Joe, too?"

She glanced away from me, waffling. "He knew he was in trouble," she said. "And lately he had got into the habit of doing what she—Sue Harriet—told him. He didn't hear all the tapes, no. But he heard the sermons. And he could see how they would be on television . . . and that's why I called you a liar, lover. Because you thought about it. Joe Gillespie made you an offer, and you turned it down. Sure. But like you used to say, 'Let's not kid the troops, okay?' "

And I was stuck for an answer.

She was right. It's nice to be able to think pleasant thoughts about yourself, and I enjoy it as much as anyone. More, maybe. But honesty has to come in somewhere, and I had taken a moment or two longer than was strictly necessary before turning down Holy Joe's offer. I had thought about it. And been tempted.

"He put it well," I said. "A louder voice. A chance to do the same things I'm doing now . . . but on a much larger scale."

"So why turn it down?"

"Because it's bullshit. The Voice of Heaven on Earth didn't originate that 'louder voice' line, you know. He told me where he'd heard it: The words came from Francis Carrington Shaw, when Shaw wanted to set him up in the television preaching business all those years ago."

"Does that make it wrong?"

"Not necessarily. I wasn't there at the time, and I don't know what Joe Gillespie was doing then or how he was doing it. The work he described sounded reasonable. Effective. A storefront mission to people who couldn't stay away from a craps table. Worth something, especially in this town, if it worked at all. And he said it seemed to."

"Well, then. . . . ?"

"But that's the point, Maxey. A little storefront mission is one thing. That Heaven on Earth compound out there is something else entirely. Nothing in common."

"They both help people."

"Do they?"

"You said yourself—"

"I said the mission was worth something because it helped people. Save souls? Don't ask me. I knew all about that once—back before 'Nam and a lot of other things—but I've been losing ground ever since, and now what I know is about people if it's about anything at all, and more and more I wonder if I even know about that."

It was more than I had intended to say, but Maxey was still listening and I didn't seem to be able to stop.

"Holy Joe was helping people there in that storefront. The work had its own logic and its own demands—personal contact and personal attention to individual needs. Personal caring. Personal advice.

"Amplify that voice, and how personal can it be?

"Oh, sure, the message may be the same. But the logic and the demands of television are not those of a storefront church. Television is show business. Entertainment. No reason, of course, that it can't do good work and be a help to people. None at all. But it is different. The storefront pastor knows he's won a real battle with real stakes when he sees one—just one—more human being standing tall and living a life instead of pissing it away.

"The television minister, no matter what his denomination and regardless of orientation, can only read his mail. Or have it read for him. And check the Nielsen ratings. And audit the books for the incoming donations. And that's the battle he's supposed to tell himself he won. Still nothing really wrong. But for someone else, Maxey . . . not for me."

"Television evangelists do good work."

"Do they?"

"Of course they do, and you know it! They bring a whole church to people who wouldn't otherwise get out of their houses, maybe even out of bed, to go on their own. Their sermons—"

"Maxey, for God's sake!"

"You said it, I didn't."

"And I'll say it again. For God's sake, what do you think a church is—four walls where you sing a couple of hymns and listen to someone lecture once or twice a week, and then hand him your money after he's spent half an hour telling you that money is a snare and a delusion? Nice work if you have the stomach for it. A good living, no pain and no strain. No carrying heavy stuff up and down stairs and you get invited out to dinner a lot. Is that it?''

"Well . . ."

"Well, hell! It's part of the deal, sure. About two percent. Maybe. And it's important. It counts. But a couple of hours on a Sunday morning is no occupation, not even if you add in the time spent writing the sermon and hearing confessions and hustling the really big sinners for the really big bucks that keep the whole thing afloat. That's the icing, not the cake. The real work begins when that's all done and forgotten.''

Maxey was honestly puzzled. It showed in her face—in her eyes, which had turned violet again—and in her voice. "What are you talking about?" she said.

"I'm talking about what the real ministers of this world really do to justify drawing breath and occupying space," I said. "I'm talking about sitting in a hospital room with a man whose wife is dying and she can handle it but he can't and maybe the best thing you can do is just be there to talk to, or maybe there's something more, but either way, you sit there and you do your best and maybe once in a while it helps.

"I'm talking about going down into the toughest part of the toughest town you ever saw to pull your stupidest and most self-destructive parishioner out of whatever kind of cesspool he's landed in this time, when your every human instinct is to leave him there because, what the hell, you don't even like him much in the first place and you'd much rather punch his lights out for getting you up in the middle of the night.

"I'm talking about trying to get a word of sane counsel through to a couple of kids who just want you to shut up and get on with the wedding rehearsal, and I'm talking about watching it go sour for them and then standing firm and trying to heal and patch and back and fill when love doesn't really conquer all and he doesn't make enough money and her breath's bad in the middle of the night.

"I'm talking about fighting for the life of some poor bastard who's just lost the job he held for twenty-eight years and he thinks it's the end of the world and now he's sitting out in the garage of his house sucking on the barrel of a forty-five automatic he never really learned to use while he was in the army but brought home for a souvenir.

"I'm talking about talking to some pregnant teenager who just tried to kill herself because she can't face her parents, and somehow—some damn how, it's different every single time, believe it—getting her to see that the life she's throwing away is worth living and isn't hers to keep or reject, and maybe even taking her the tiniest first step along a road that might just possibly make her a grown-up.

"And I'm talking about failing.

"I'm talking, by God, about losing every one of those fights and maybe all the others, too, because you're only a human being, not Jesus Christ or God Almighty or the Enlightened One or any of the others, but just a poor dumb son of a bitch like anyone else. I'm talking about losing those fights and accepting the loss . . . and going right out there the next day and busting your butt the same way all over again because that's what you signed on to do and you keep your promises, if nothing else."

It was a long speech and a pretty self-righteous one for a man whose congregation—if that's what it is—fits none of the above categories and never will. But Maxey listened and spent a second or two thinking it over before she spoke.

"So the television preachers are dog shit?" she said.

"No. At least, not just because they appear on the tube. A part of what they do is legitimate, and there are plenty of people who bless the invention of television because it brings them the only kind of church service they can possibly attend.

"And you can make a pretty good case that many, many others find something on the tube that they never found in the churches they attended once or twice a year for most of their lives."

"So . . . ?"

"So if the story could stop there it would be wonderful and the lion would lie down with the lamb, but this is the real world and that's not how things really go.

"Television is power.

"Say it slowly. With reverence.

"It sells cars and soap and presidential candidates, and it changes minds and mores, and if you shake it just right, it is a money machine—and that, dear friends, is power of a kind Alexander and Caesar and Napoleon only dreamed about. The television evangelist, with his audience of millions watching and listening with open minds and uncritical hearts, can move mountains. Literally! You don't have to run for President and you don't have to turn your believers into a pack of book burners and film censors in order to make that power felt. All you really have to do is show them the mountain that stands in the way and they will take it apart for you with kitchen spoons.

"That's power!

"And that's where it can all go wrong in a hurry, because if enough people nod you 'yes' enough times over enough years it's only natural to get the idea that 'yes' is the only possible answer to anything you might say or do and that you have some kind of special dispensation that sets you apart from the rest of humanity and exempts you from the rules that apply to the common herd.

"That's when you start buying Rolls-Royces and paying blackmail and going on international shopping sprees and building air-conditioned doghouses with the money those poor damn fools did without clothes or decent medical care or maybe even food to send to you, and when you get caught, the best you can offer is 'Well, those good friends of ours wanted us to have these nice things.' "

Maxey was sitting perfectly still, looking astonished, and when I paused for breath I found that I was more than a bit surprised, too. I hadn't realized all of that was inside me, or how badly it needed to get out.

And there was still more to come.

"The real crunch, though, comes when the donations slack off a little," I said. "When the mail is lighter than usual and the high-powered CPA who handles your books says you might not be able to buy the new DC-nine you had your heart set on. That's when the nitty gets pretty gritty.

"That's when the faithful start getting telephone calls from a voice that sounds like yours but is really an electronic gimmick. That's when you start with the sermons about how we must all trust in God to provide the funds to save this ministry and keep it on the air.

"That's when God turns out to be an extortionist who will kill you if you don't raise a few more million.

"And that's when you suddenly remember how you've been raising people from the dead for all these years but just never thought to tell anyone about it until now."

The car was getting hot, and I was done.

Empty.

And feeling better than I had since the first moment we had entered the simulated pearly gates of Heaven on Earth. I rolled out of the car and stretched my legs and looked—the garage, like most others in the southwest, had no outer walls—at the first red and yellow streamers of what seemed likely to be a long desert sunset.

Maxey got out and locked her door and slammed it and glanced at the sky and turned toward the hotel without a word.

I followed.

We entered by the VIP garage elevator, moving in a bell jar of silence that followed us to Maxey's floor.

But at the door to her room she turned and grinned at me.

"God damn you," she said.

"I suspect that may already have been attended to."

She stood still, looking at me out of those color-changing eyes, still smiling with the corners of her mouth.

"Gillespie needs you," she said. "Sue Harriet was his last hold on the world. He'll drift right over the edge now, if someone doesn't take hold."

"Not me."

"You could turn it around. Do anything you want. Move mountains, like you said."

"No."

She stopped talking, but the ghost of the smile persisted and the eyes faded slowly through violet to deep blue. She handed me her key and I turned it in the door and opened it and she moved inside.

"Impossible bastard," she said. "No wonder I've stayed in love with you for all these years."

The eyes shifted back to violet as she closed the door firmly in my face.

We had a date for dinner, and I used the elevator time on the way to my room for thinking, but it didn't get me anywhere and by the time I reached my own door I was already telling myself to give up.

Lots of questions.

No satisfactory answers.

And not enough information to make a decent guess. But of course I had to make a few, and that is what was going on while I opened the door to my own room and moved inside.

Which is how people get hurt.

The door was closed and latched behind me before the watchdog senses could break through the wall of foolishness to let me know I had visitors.

One in the chair across the room.

The other just inside the entryway, with a hand that clamped onto my upper arm in what might have been friendly contact but wasn't.

Dinner with Maxey seemed likely to be postponed.

A SERMON (Continued)

Years ago, in what we now think of as the infancy of motion pictures, it was easy to tell the bad guys from the good guys. Especially in westerns. The bad guys wore black hats; the good guys wore white ones. But then the movies began to grow up . . .

21

THEY WERE DRESSED like twins in pastel slacks, polo shirts, and blazers, and the one in the chair was smiling. But the one attached to my arm wore no expression at all in a pair of hazel eyes that looked like polished glass.

I stood still and waited.

"Manny Temple's upstairs," the one in the chair said, still smiling. "He's real anxious to talk to you and he'll be getting impatient. We been waiting nearly three hours."

It was semi-polite speech and a reasonable request, and I tried to answer in kind.

"Give Manny my regards," I said. "And tell him I'll be along soon as I dust the century plant and wind the cat."

The grip on my arm got tighter, but its owner seemed to leave oral communication to his partner.

"Manny, he'll be waiting," the talker said, lumbering out of the chair and stretching himself. There was a lot to stretch. I'm not short, but he and his silent companion had two or three inches on me in height and perhaps a fifty percent advantage in weight. Size and body control left a clear impression of athletics on a professional level, and scar tissue just below the brow ridge named the sport.

"We'll go now," he said.

The silent one took two steps, turning me in the direction of the door, and I went along with the motion while gathering hara in the belly and bringing my reflexes to speed.

Screw them.

And Manny, too . . .

Fun is fun and you shouldn't play cards for a living if you can't take a joke, but the whole thing was starting to get out of hand. Ridiculous. I had been in Las Vegas a little more than a day, and in that time there hadn't been a single moment when someone or other wasn't manipulating, shoving, hauling, or generally jerking me around, and it was getting to be a crashing bore and besides, Manny—of all people—should have known better.

My nontalking handler completed the semicircular maneuver that brought him abreast of me facing the door, but seemed to stumble over my left foot as he started to move me through the entryway. The foot he brought forward to save himself got tangled, too, and the hand that could have saved him was still clamped to my arm. I was holding it there, bracing my legs and back to accelerate the motion and turn it into a descending curve as he lost his balance and fell forward.

I caught a fleeting impression of puzzled incomprehension as he went down, but the contact was fleeting and disappeared entirely as his head made contact with the doorknob.

Lights out.

The world had slowed down for me again, and there was a feeling almost of leisure as I turned to deal with the talker. But he was quicker than I had expected and coming in on my blind side and I sensed the punch he had aimed at my neck only in time to intercept it with my shoulder instead of evading it entirely and then wasted another moment lecturing myself on the vanity of overconfidence.

Stupid . . .

I decided I had been right about him being a former pro boxer. Light-heavy, maybe, though he was carrying enough weight now for the big-money division. His feet moved naturally into the ninety-degree stance they teach you around the training gyms, and the way he planted the heel of his right foot gave me plenty of warning this time about the combination he was going to throw. I lifted my hands in what he must have thought was a familiar stance and kept my eye on his face as his left flicked toward me, and moved a little to counter it in the way he expected . . . but kicked his right knee out from under him instead.

He was game. And still quick. Going down, he made a right-handed grab for my crotch that could have turned the afternoon into a long one, but it missed by several inches and left him wide open for the knee I bent into the path of his face. That connected solidly, and I felt the gray mist that flooded suddenly into the space where he lived.

Doctrine and standard procedure both dictated that I follow

with a kite to the back of the head, overloading the *tanden* reflex center, to ensure sweet dreams for at least half an hour.

But the exercise had been a tonic for the spirits and I had no real desire to sit around waiting for him to wake up.

So I switched instead to basic judo, clamping both thumbs on the back of his right hand and turning it quickly while my foot came down on the back of his armpit. I waited for the first struggle of returning awareness and then applied the extra pressure that would turn the restraining grip into momentary white pain.

"Let us reason together," I said.

The words may have meant nothing, but the tone and the pain did and he relaxed, drawing a deep breath and checking the action to me.

Good.

This one had sense.

"The way it is," I said, keeping the voice low-key and neutral, "I say that one kick will put your head outside in the parking lot. Do we agree on that?"

He nodded almost at once.

Better and better . . .

"You carrying?" I asked.

More hesitation this time, but his answer was the right one: He nodded.

"I'm going to let you go," I said. "When I do, I want you to move very slowly. With me so far?"

Another nod.

"I want you to take the piece and hold it by the barrel so I can see . . ."

I let go of the hand and stepped back just out of range of his arm, but not too far for an effective kick. He rolled over and sat up, facing me, and nursed the shoulder for a moment of silent agony and then moved—with a slowness that was almost exaggerated—to retrieve the little Airweight from its ankle holster.

Holding its barrel carefully between thumb and forefinger, he pulled it free and then looked back at me for further instructions.

"The ammunition," I said.

No nod this time. But the cartridges fell, one by one, on the carpet.

"Put the piece back in the holster," I said.

He did it.

"And now do the same for your friend."

The look he turned to me was surprised and almost reproachful.

"Lancelot don't carry a gun," he said. "We wouldn't give him anything dangerous like that. Manny'd never stand for it."

I sighed and looked at the sleeping Lancelot.

Now, wouldn't you know the poor bastard would have to have a name like that?

Manny Temple's suite at the Scheherazade occupied an entire floor of the Sultan's Turret, and he needed the space.

Manny liked company.

We went there as soon as Lancelot's head stopped bleeding and he was as conscious as he was ever going to get. He still needed a little help with things like remembering where he was and how to get through doors. But his companion, whose name turned out to be Chick, said not to worry. Lancelot had always been like that after a bout.

I thought that might explain a lot, and might have said so. But by the time it occurred to me, there were other things to think about. We had arrived.

The front door of Manny's suite was unlocked—step right in and make yourself at home—but the invitation was qualified as soon as we were inside. A lock clicked behind us, and we were momentarily trapped in a vestibule innocent of all decoration and furnished only with a carefully positioned television camera. Smile!

The idea, I decided, was to hold unexpected and/or hostile visitors at arm's length while considering ways and means.

Well thought out.

But not especially hospitable, and so there was a moment of shock when the inner door opened on what seemed at first to be a party in full swing. The living room of the suite, or what I took to be the living room—I later discovered that it was merely one of several—was full of men and women standing and sitting in various attitudes of bored relaxation. The bar appeared to be open, and there was the ghost of a scent that told of organic substances in use. Background music, pouring from some unguessable source, was set at a volume too low to be obtrusive but too high to allow eavesdropping.

The beginning of a pleasant evening in Las Vegas.

But it rang false.

Counting the house a second time, I found what had seemed a random assortment of guests developed several noticable similar-

ities. All of the men, for instance, seemed to be in the twenty-
five-to-forty age group, somewhat above average in height and
weight, and wearing sport coat–polo shirt–blazer combinations
from the same store that provided wardrobe for Chick and Lancelot.
The women were younger—late teens to late twenties—but all
seemed fresh from the attentions of the same professional makeup
artist, and all had been dressed by the same show biz–opulent
couturier.

"Atmosphere," Chick said, noticing my interest. "We all
work for Manny. But he don't like for it to look that way, you
know?"

Manny himself was three doors down the hall and access was
through another security trap, but we were passed through swiftly
and without any words that I could hear.

Inside, a table was laid for breakfast—Manny's hours were
unusual, even for Las Vegas—but the fresh orange juice and
coffee had to wait while he listened to an explanation of the fresh
lump and cut on Lancelot's head, and when Chick was done,
Manny's only comment was to tell them to call the house doctor
for a full checkout. At once.

They left to do it, and he shook his head sadly as the door
closed on their retreating forms.

"Sometime later on today," he said, "I am gonna kick ol'
Chick's fat fanny three times around this room."

He poured coffee, leaving mine plain but dosing his own with
three lumps of sugar from a bowl in the center of the table. I
noticed that he was choosy about which lumps he took, and
filed the information for possible cross-reference.

"Or on second thought," he said after the first sip, "maybe
not. I guess it was my fault, right?"

I grinned at him, and he returned it. Almost sheepishly.

"Yeah, I guess it was at that. All I told the assholes was 'I
wanna see the Preacher.' I should've said be polite. Or, anyhow,
warned them about you."

I went on grinning.

"Gentle as a lamb," I said. "Hope of peace in my heart,
brother; the meek shall inherit the earth."

He snorted. "Oh, hell yes," he said. "Six feet of it—with
luck, and nobody decides to blow you up like that poor bitch out
there at Holy Joe's Heaven. I saw it on the television, what little
they let them show. Shit, Preacher, I met that broad a couple

times before she got married and she was okay. Regular, you know? Blowing someone up's bad enough. But getting the wrong person . . . Jesus!''

Manny sighed, slurping another mouthful of coffee and considering the unfairness of the world and its works. But he had raised a point that interested me.

"What makes you think she was the wrong one?" I said.

That seemed to surprise him.

"Chrissake, Preacher," he said. "Straight broad like that, who'd have anything against her? Enough to want to kill her, I mean. No way, you know? They were after him—the goddam jerked-to-Jesus Bible-pounder. No offense, Preacher. I keep forgetting you're in that line of work yourself. Or used to be.''

I shook my head. "I've heard worse," I said, "and said some of it myself. But all the same, why Joe Gillespie? Who'd want him dead?''

More surprise.

"Shaw, of course," he said. "Who the hell else? Francis Carrington Shaw. He made Holy Joe Gillespie and now he's out to unmake him. Have him killed, just like he wants to kill me . . .''

That called for an explanation, but Manny didn't seem to feel like offering one. He changed the subject. "New game," he said. "You ready for this?''

I wasn't. I wanted to talk some more about murder and Francis Carrington Shaw and Joe Gillespie and related matters. But it was his room and his play, and besides this was something that had been going on between us for a long time.

Manny was crazy about proposition bets.

But only if they were gaffed.

"This game," he said, selecting two more sugar cubes from the bowl, "is called Mosca, and it's a old one, from Italy, the goombahs tell me. To play it, you got to have a fly.''

With the flourish of a stage musician uncovering a hatful of rabbits, he swept away the napkin that had been covering an inverted waterglass centered on the breakfast table. It contained a single housefly. I put down the coffee I had been about to sip and looked at it.

Flies are one of the few pests that Las Vegas doesn't seem to attract in great numbers. I wondered if he'd had to import this one. And if so, how he had phrased the request.

"Get the balcony door, hey," he said.

It seemed a logical enough request if he wanted to keep the fly in the room and I moved to comply, but the door was already closing. A hairy arm belonging to someone standing, not seated, on the balcony was doing the necessary. Security around Manny Temple was even tighter than I'd supposed.

"What we do is," he said, putting one of the sugar cubes on my side of the table and the other on his own, "we let the fly go and bet on whether he'll light on my cube first or yours. Okay? For a honeybee?"

With Manny, that was always the amount of the first bet. A honeybee. One hundred dollars. Then bump the action when the chump wants to get even.

Okay.

I nodded, and he lifted the glass.

For a moment, nothing happened. The fly didn't seem to know it was free, and I wondered if it might have been inside there for too long. But Manny waved a hand toward it, and the motion or the air current seemed to wake the insect up. The fly took off and began to move around in search-circles.

"Takes a minute or two," Manny said, his eyes on the living game-piece. "He's gotta spot the sugar and think it over. Don't make no sudden moves, okay?"

I sat still and wondered what a neutral observer would have said about us. Two grown men sitting in a high-tech room in a high-tech building fitted with several million dollars' worth of high-tech gaming equipment . . . betting on a fly.

Only in Las Vegas.

"Hah!"

The fly had found the sugar cubes, circled mine twice, but then landed on Manny's.

"Way to go, ya little bastard!"

Manny grinned widely and shooed the fly away. "Go again for double?" he said. "Nobody could gaff a fly, right?"

"Right," I said. "But this time, how about we change cubes—I get yours, you get mine. Just to keep us honest, like the fly."

Manny tried to register injured innocence, but he was enjoying himself too much. The grin stayed put as he reached out to switch the cubes.

"Aw, hell, Preacher," he said, doing his best to sound wounded. "Would I cheat an old friend?"

"Not if he's careful," I said.

I spotted the gimmick when he switched position of the cubes.

He hadn't practiced enough, and the move turning both of them upside down was still a bit awkward.

"Double?" he said hands still on the cubes.

I shrugged. "Why be cheap?" I said. "Make it five—or a thousand, if you're game."

The grin widened, but then dimmed for a moment. This was too easy. And I had stolen his line. Nothing could go wrong, of course, but still . . .

"The guy on the balcony," I said, derailing his thought train. "You can trust him?"

The grin evaporated and the eyes turned sharp. Questions like that are not casual in Manny's world. They are life and death, and mine had exactly the effect I had intended. Manny couldn't resist turning away for a long, hard look at the closed door.

Which gave me plenty of time.

"Yeah, sure," he said, looking back at me. "Of course I can. Why?"

"Just wondering," I lied. "Still touchy, I guess, after all that's been happening. Forget it. Okay, then—for a dime?"

There was a moment of blankness while he shifted gears; Manny never liked to mix business with pleasure. But the fly gimmick was too good to forget for long, and a remnant of the grin returned when he settled back into scamming an old friend.

"For a dime." He nodded. "A thousand."

The fly was already in the air again, and this time it took nearly a minute for the little dipteron to get interested in the sugar cubes. Manny's concentration was total as it went through the routine inspection runs, and the grin was showing teeth again as the fly finally returned for a close pass at the cube on his side of the table.

But I had a hard time keeping my own face in neutral when the fly turned away and landed on the cube in front of me.

Manny was snakebit.

Words failed, and his mouth opened three times soundlessly before he was able to put his emotions into words.

"Why, that little motherfucker!" he roared.

I shook my head.

"Perfectly good fly," I said. "Just doing his own thing. Trying to stay alive. The insecticide's on the top of your cube this time; I turned them both over again while you were looking at the door. What'd you use, DDT?"

More speech failure.

And then a huge laugh—which is, I suppose, why we had been able to stay friends for so long. This was the only hood I'd ever met with a real sense of humor, even when the joke was on him.

"Nah," he said, waving the fly away and sweeping up the sugar cubes to drop them into the wastebasket. "Something new; not a poison, it just works kinda like insect repellent."

"And you put one drop on each of the cubes," I said, "and then made sure that the smelly side was up on my cube and down on yours."

"And switched sides when you wanted to trade cubes. Yeah . . ."

The telephone on the breakfast table rang, and Manny stopped talking but didn't answer it at once. I had a feeling it wasn't supposed to do that. Manny had people around to answer phones for him.

But it rang again, and on the third ring he picked it up and listened for a long moment without apparent reaction. Or reply.

And then he handed the receiver to me, covering the mouthpiece with his palm.

"Francis Carrington Shaw," he said in a voice made out of high-altitude ice crystals. "For you . . ."

A SERMON (Continued)

Identification of the heroes and the villains had become more complicated. Or at least people thought it had. Sometimes you had to deal with a complicated, almost human, character—a good bad guy or a bad good guy. Movies like that were called "adult westerns."

22

At first I thought it might be a joke.

Manny doesn't always have a glass head, and it occurred to me that the Mosca game with the gaffed sugar cubes might be just a cover for something more subtle. Something involving somebody who could imitate Francis Carrington Shaw's voice.

But the first few words—and the temperature of Manny's eyes—told me I was wrong.

"You are the one they call Preacher?"

The sentence was inflected as a question, but it wasn't one and the paper-thin voice on the line didn't wait for an answer.

"I believe that we should meet," it said. "And I believe that it should be as soon as possible. Do you agree?"

This time an answer was required, but I wasn't sure what it should be. Especially in present company.

"I understand that's not so easy," I said. "Something about big healthy-looking guys in white T-shirts who don't talk much or open doors."

The voice made a whispery sound, like moths wrestling, and I decided it was intended as a polite laugh.

"They talk," it said, "and open doors when they are told to do so. You will oblige me, sir?"

"Yes," I said.

"When?"

I looked at Manny and tried to guess how long it would take to calm him down and then find my way to the Shaw suite.

"Half an hour," I said. "If you clear the way. I understand you're here in the Scheherazade . . ."

The dry laugh repeated.

"Another misconception," it said. "But one that I have encouraged. For good reason. There is, to be sure, a suite reserved

208

in my name at the Scheherazade, but I am not in it. Never mind. I will send a car.''

Immediate suspicion. We live in interesting times.

"To meet me where?" I said.

No laugh this time, but a pause for thought.

"You are asking more than a location," the whisperlike voice said after a moment. "And I hardly blame you. Would it be of any help for me to say that the car will pick you up beside the spot where your own rented vehicle is parked in the VIP garage . . . and that I, too, feel both regret and responsibility for the death of Little Trouble?"

Well, yes. Knowing where I parked my car and the nickname of the gunman who had died in the attack on the penthouse didn't necessarily identify my caller as Francis Carrington Shaw. But it certainly made him worth meeting, whoever he was.

"Thirty minutes," I said. "In the garage."

"Thirty minutes. Beginning now."

The connection was broken, and I glanced at my watch.

"Good idea," Manny said. "Shaw, he likes things to run on time."

The voice was emotionless, but the eyes were still subarctic.

I relaxed in the chair and tried to get a sense of what was bothering him. The *wa* was running up and down the scale from hot to cold to hot again, and I couldn't see why. A telephone call, even from a man you think is trying to kill you, shouldn't be that important. But the next words gave me a clue.

"You're going to meet him—Shaw? In person?"

Oh.

"He seemed to think it was a good idea," I said. "Come along if you like. He's sending a car."

And that got a laugh.

Manny's central aura was still confused, alternative between fury and anxiety. But my suggestion seemed to have answered some kind of question for him, and the anger no longer seemed to be aimed at me.

"Come along," he said. "Beautiful! Come along and we'll make it a party, the three of us—you, me, and Francis Carrington Shaw. Maybe bring some beer and hot dogs. Go for a picnic out in the desert. Have a couple of laughs."

He sprang up from the chair and began to pace, talking but not looking at me, nervous energy forcing the words out at a rate that seemed more for his own ears than for mine. Part of a

monologue that I thought might have been going on internally
for some time.

"Nobody," he said, "but no body sees Francis Carrington
Shaw without an invitation. Take me along? Preacher, you crazy
son of a bitch, I been working for Francis Carrington Shaw ever
since I moved to this goddam town, and I never met him yet!"

I sat still and listened.

Manny had a lot to say and I had a feeling I might be the first
one who'd heard it. Not exactly True Confessions time; he had
done what he thought was the best thing, and he wasn't the type
to have regrets. But now things were happening that he couldn't
understand. Or control.

"The whole thing," he said, "was going to work for a guy I
only knew on the phone. That was dumb. All right?"

I kept still, and that seemed to suit him.

"I was out, back east. On my ass. A little money, yeah. But
out, and I wasn't used to being out, you know?

"I came out here and I got drunk and I stayed that way for
maybe three weeks and the boys who'd come with me were
starting to wonder if I was really washed up like everyone said
and by the time I sobered up and looked around and smelled the
coffee, you know, it was, like, endsville. Another day or two,
I'd've been alone."

And then, he said, the telephone rang.

"And everything turned around. One call. Shaw sounded
different back then. Like the way he used to in those television
news things where he'd just set a new speed record for airplanes
or bought or sold a movie studio or testified in front of the
Senate and told them politicians to go fuck theirselfs. A *mensch*!

"He had just started buying hotels here in Vegas and he said
he'd heard I was at liberty. At liberty! How about that! Class,
you know? Everything with a kiss. Said he needed someone with
local savvy—what bullshit; he knew I was as new in town as he
was. But I knew what he meant. He wanted me to . . . handle
things for him. Understand, he didn't mean be the front man.
That was Judge Apodaca, old Happy-the-Hand, even back then.
He was already in Shaw's pocket and the word was anything
Judge Happy Apodaca said, it was like Shaw himself saying it.

"But there were other things . . ."

Manny came back to the table and poured himself another cup
of coffee, and I barely managed to keep him from putting the
fly-repellent sugar cubes into it, but he didn't seem to notice and

went back to pacing and talking as though there had been no interruption.

"You fill in the blanks. And then double whatever you thought. Not just muscle stuff, either: For a guy who's sailed as close as he has all his life, there's still a hell of a lot of things that old Happy don't like to mess with."

"For instance?"

It was the wrong thing to ask. Any question at all would have been wrong. But Manny hardly seemed to notice, and he answered without hesitation.

"For instance," he said, "the counting rooms. At the casinos . . ."

One of the running battles between the federal government and the state of Nevada is the counting rooms of the gambling casinos, and the laws that govern them. They are the last bastion of truly free enterprise. Casinos pay federal income tax like any other business, and the Internal Revenue Service always insists on the right of audit—whch means the right to see everything, right down to the contents of the cash registers at any given time of the day or night. How else, they ask, can they be sure of just how much profit the casino is making?

The state of Nevada is sympathetic.

Big problem. Yes.

But all the same, the legislature has never really considered repealing or even amending the law that makes it illegal for anyone except certain casino employees to be in the room where the cash boxes from the various games are counted. And if that seems to exclude snoops from the IRS, well, those are the breaks.

Big problem. Yes . . .

"You got to understand," Manny said, "when Shaw moved in here and took over the hotels and casinos like he did, that didn't mean the people who sold them were really going to let go of their money machine. Hell—how could they?

"A big cash-flow business like that, it's one of the few places left inside the country where you can move dough around without attracting attention."

"You mean the skim?"

He shrugged. "That," he said. "Yeah. The skim is part of it. Understand—there's nobody robbing anybody here. Francis Carrington Shaw, he's an investor, right? Right. He puts money into something, it turns him a good profit, he's happy, okay?

"Ten percent, maybe eleven. Even twelve, you got a good year. That's an okay profit, right? Not as good as drilling an oil well for a hundred grand and find a billion-dollar pool down there, or making a three million dollar movie that grosses back fifty. But how often does that happen, and how often do you drill the same hole and it's dry or make the movie and it's a dog?

"Ten's okay. He's satisfied. So he don't give a shit that the guys who used to own the casino still run it. Call it a kind of, like they say, lease-back deal. Nothing new in Vegas. Every casino on the Strip, there was always inside points and outside points, with the outsides just fronting for the insides and not even getting paid much for it, usually. Something you give a brother-in-law you can't find nothing else for him, okay?

"So after he bought in and got the gaming licenses in his name, he made sure he never looked too close at what was going on, because he knew he would've kissed his own ass before he'd've had a chance to buy into anything otherwise. The skim went on and the laundry went on just like before—and he got his profit just like if he'd bought a steel mill or a car-making company or something. Only surer . . ."

More coffee, but this time I just sat still and waited for him to go on.

"So where does Manny Temple come in?" He grinned, but there was no warmth in it. And no joy.

"I was the handler. The trouble-mechanic. Every operation needs one, baby, and his setup in Vegas was sure as hell no exception. You got different families—mobs—in charge of different casinos, you got a different problem in every single case. Someone gets too greedy, I handle it. Someone gets too sloppy, I handle it. Someone comes to town needs the kid-glove treatment and the sweet, happy ride, I handle it. Make sure they go home with a big smile . . . and who knows, maybe a couple of stills or even a videotape to look at now and then and remember that one hand washes the other. Right?

"So what's wrong with that?

"Believe me, Preacher, a guy can't operate very long in a town like Vegas without a hard boy somewhere in the neighborhood, handling. Shaw and me, we had a good even deal.

"And that's the way it stayed, until late last year. That's when it started going wrong—last year. In August. That's when he started talking in that funny whispery voice you heard on the phone, and that's when I started hearing about how he was getting other people to handle things for him. Without even telling me.

"And then he quit calling at all."

He stopped pacing and looked at me with an expression that I suddenly realized was far too close to supplication to be anything but genuine. The man was actually suffering.

"Preacher," he said, "that call just now—the one for you— that was the first time I've spoken to Francis Carrington Shaw, even over a phone, this year. I don't know what went wrong. I don't know shit.

"All I know, I know what happened up in the penthouse this morning was something he set up. To put me out, along with all the others."

There might have been more.

I think there was; Manny's face didn't have that "I'm done, now tell me what you think" look. But if so I never got to hear any of it, because we were interrupted by a knock at the door to the hallway.

Manny started to ignore it; his mouth had formed itself around the beginning of a new sentence and his eyes said the only sound he wanted to hear was his own voice. But the knock came again and the breath he had taken whooshed out in a nonsound that might have been a dirty word.

He yanked the door open and gave the beefy man standing there a stare that said he had better have a damn good reason for pounding on the wood.

"This come for you . . ."

There was an envelope in the door-pounder's hand, and for a moment I thought Manny was going to make him eat it. The door-pounder thought so, too, and looked ready to cry. But at the last moment something on the face of the envelope seemed to catch Manny's interest. He snatched it and took a closer look.

"How'd it come?" he demanded.

The letter-bearer didn't understand and seemed even nearer to tears than before, but Manny took pity on him and spelled it out. "In the mail?" he said. "By messenger? Carrier pigeon . . . ?"

That seemed to get through at last, and the caller's face brightened with understanding. "I dunno," he said. "Vince took it from some guy who come to the door and give it to me and he said for me to—"

"Yeah, yeah," Manny said, cutting off the explanation with a wave of his hand. "Okay, awready. You done fine, baby. Just fine. Go back and tell Vinnie I said give you a drink and for him to run his own errands from now on. Okay?"

The words seeped in slowly.

But they arrived. The door closed on a smiling and almost worshipful face. No wonder Manny had survived for so long.

He came back to the table holding the envelope by its lower edge and looking at it with a mixture of curiosity and disbelief.

"Maybe," he said, sitting down across from me again, "I ought to call the *Guinness Book of World Records* or something. What we have got here is a real first . . ."

I didn't understand and waited for whatever explanation he might decide to offer. Instead, he showed me the face of the envelope itself.

The words "M. Temple," "Personal," and "Hand Deliver" were typed and centered on the white rectangle. The only other adornment was a set of three italic initials, embossed on the upper left corner: *F.C.S.*

"Yeah," Manny went on when he was sure I'd seen all there was to see and understood whatever there was to understand. "The *Guinness Book*. All these years—all these years—I been working for that old son of a bitch. Never met him once; just his voice on the phone and not even that lately. And now this."

He flapped the envelope and slapped it down on the table between us.

"Everybody knows these damn things," he said. "Everyone knows the raised-up initials at the corner. Knows they get first-cabin treatment: F.C.S.—Francis Carrington Shaw. The mother don't even need to use his whole name. Just the initials and everyone snaps shit. But in all this time, Preacher baby, in all this time, you know I never got one? Never!"

He drew a breath, looking at the envelope.

"It was one of the few good things, you know? All this time and nothing on paper, ever, between us. It worked. I never got one of these goddam envelopes and I was proud of that because it showed we could trust each other—even without we ever, like, met face to face, right?

"Yeah. Well, then, fuck it. Just fuck it! We going to do business through the mail from now on, fuck it and fuck him and let's see what the mother has to say . . ."

He snatched the envelope up and used a table knife to slit it open at the top, and suddenly I wanted to stop him; tell him to forget it and throw it away. Suddenly the envelope didn't matter

nymore and it was as though I could see through it and I knew
vhat was inside.

But it was too late.

The single trifold sheet of paper was blank; no message, not
ven a visible watermark. It served merely as a secondary wrap-
er, concealing the real message contained in a set of five
laying cards from one of the Scheherazade's own decks.

Aces and eights.

Manny looked at the cards for a long moment. And then at
ae. And then back at the cards.

"Look," I said, trying to interrupt a sequence of thought that
as plainly visible behind what he probably thought was a blank
ace, "let's don't ride off into the heat of the day. The cards
on't have to mean—"

"Bullshit."

The word that cut me off was quiet and the voice under
ontrol, but a fire of panic was growing in the place where he
ved and he was feeding it personally and it wasn't something
hat could be contained with such puny tools as logic and com-
non sense.

"You think I don't know what this is?" he said. "Hey, baby,
was there. Remember? The dead man's hand. You dealt it out
 Holy Joe, but it was over there lying on Danny Dimples's
hest when the shooting stopped, and he was the one who was
aken suddenly dead.

"And then, later, I hear things.

"Like how Goines died. What do you think, I got to wait for
he television or the newspapers to tell me things? Sam went out
vith the same cards fanned out on his chest, and then out there at
Ioly Joe's place later, the same thing like we got here. An
nvelope. With the cards in it. No, baby! No way—fuck it.
Ianny's mama didn't raise no stupid kids."

The cards dropped from his fingers as he picked up the
elephone and snapped out a series of orders to whoever was on
he other end. The one about getting new tires on the car and
aving it filled with gas and having fifteen minutes to get it done
eemed to draw some kind of protest, but Manny wasn't listening.

He slammed the receiver down and took a deep, shuddering
reath.

"Okay," he said. "Okay! That's the way the old bastard
vants it—okay, awready!"

"It doesn't have to have come from him," I said. "The envelope—"

But he was already shaking his head, and the look that went with it was full of pity.

"Preacher," he said, "I don't care. You know? It's him okay. If not, still okay. Manny is out. He's going. Now. Mexico, Canada, somewhere—who gives a fuck?

"And if you got as much sense as I always thought, you'll come with me."

A SERMON (Continued)

The confusion also spilled over into real life. We discovered—as countless generations have done, century after century, in all the ages before our own—that human beings are never entirely one thing or entirely another. That we are all an amalgam of positive and negative qualities . . .

23

NOT ALL TRAPPERS wear fur hats.

The only real flaw in Manny's poker game, one that I'd spotted at our first meeting years ago, was an expensive tendency to accept a well-constructed bluff at face value, to fold a potential winner without seeing the other hand. And now he was doing it again.

But there seemed to be nothing I could say to make him see it that way, no words I could use to make him understand that sudden flight might be just the reaction someone wanted, and by the time I left the suite, the door behind me closed on the uproar of imminent departure. Play your own cards; let the other guy play his. Am I my brother's keeper? (And why does my brother need a keeper, anyway . . . ?)

No use at all, of course.

I was still picking at the problem, worrying it to death, when I went off to keep my appointment in the VIP parking garage.

Here, at least, there was no room for argument or error.

Most visitors to the Scheherazade, VIP or otherwise, hand their wheels over to the ultra-efficient valet parking service at the front entrance; elegance is elegance and nobody is immune to the subtle flattery of conspicuous consumption. Even when it has to be accompanied by a five dollar tip.

So my rented chariot was alone on this floor of the VIP garage.

Or had been when I parked it there.

No more.

Beside it, now, was an ominous-looking item that I could see had gone through more than a few changes since the day it rolled off the assembly line at Cadillac.

Limousines are nothing to stare at in Las Vegas. The ambience of the town supports several prosperous auto livery services, and private ownership of luxury vehicles is merely one of the perks of the average casino-manager—like the sticker that confers special street-parking privileges on those with local political clout.

But even in such company, a discerning eye might linger on the car Francis Carrington Shaw had sent for me.

It was black and long, and the dark-tinted glass in the windows was standard-issue. But the car's suspension system was not; chrome was understated, almost stinted, serving to deemphasize the fact that the vehicle it adorned was closer to the ground than most. Not chopped or underslung like some street racer's candy-apple baby, but simply an inch or so nearer the ground than most . . . and making a real effort to disguise the difference that could only be the result of armor plating in the doors, ceilings, and other sides of the passenger compartment. And probably around the engine as well.

Black paint and restraint in ornamentation also failed to disguise the air scoops faired into the front fenders; air scoops that were not for show. I wondered if the engineers back in Detroit would have recognized any part of the power plant—or admitted it if they had.

Moving closer, I noticed that not even the tires of the limousine were standard issue. No flash-white sidewalls, and I would have given odds that these were not only self-sealing but actually proof against anything less powerful than an antitank missile. Nice wheels.

Drag ya for pink slips. . . ?

I was ten feet away when the right front door opened and something just as expensive—and customized—got out to open the back door; six feet two inches tall, complete with white shoes, slacks, T-shirt, and clear blue-white eye coloring. Everything but a "Product of Salt Lake City" stamp on the forehead, and I decided I didn't want to bet on that, either.

It did not smile as it waited for me to get in.

It did not frown.

And I discovered that it did not talk, either, as we ghosted out of the garage and turned north on Paradise. All right, then. Go with the flow. I leaned back against the cushions and looked out at people who couldn't look back at me.

Las Vegas does not turn its electric signs off in the daytime, so they don't have to be turned on again at nightfall. Half a mile away, blue and red and white and green and gold light named and trumpeted the glories of Caesar's and the Dunes and the Sahara and the Sands and the Flamingo, setting forth their attractions in a shriek of candlepower.

They slipped by in march formation as we glided toward the center of town, passing the less ostentatious marquee of the Convention Center, which offered only the names of the evening's heavyweight gladiators (no price around the legal betting shops, and I speculated idly on how many people elsewhere would know that the bout was a fix, and how much money changed hands over the ignorance).

Farther, past the lonely top-heaviness of the Landmark and then left across the Strip and into the darkness beyond.

I wondered, fleetingly, if Francis Carrington Shaw had taken his act on the road and was about to pick up the driver-deck phone and give oral communications yet another try when another turn, this time to the right, gave me an answer that I should have suspected as soon as I knew that he was not really staying at the Scheherazade.

More than a quarter-century ago there had been a fire.

The casino and main building of the oldest and least opulent hotel on the Strip, a rambling Wild West–style establishment called El Cholo Loco, had burned to the ground, leaving only the individual ranch house–villas on the grounds that had surrounded it. The fire was no accident. The owner, an arrogant richboy whose father and uncle had built the place, had publicly humiliated a powerful visiting hoodlum, underboss of a family well connected among the Friends of the Friends. So local representatives agreed that an example must be made, in aid of discipline. The best torch in Cleveland was imported for the job, and before the embers of El Cholo had cooled, the richboy was quietly informed that he was a fortunate man. He had been permitted to leave the building before it was consumed by flames. But—who knows?—another time he might not be so lucky. The place was not to be rebuilt. Or sold. And he was not to return to Las Vegas during his lifetime.

No one was surprised at this. But the richboy turned out to be smarter than anyone had thought. Arrogance at least temporarily cleansed from his soul, he moved forthwith to one of the better-kept sections of Beverly Hills and turned his attention to motion

picture production and the Beautiful People it seems to attract.
Las Vegas saw him no more, and a neighboring hotel was
assigned the task of managing such of the surviving villas on the
grounds as might be rentable.

The owner's death, a few years ago, had caused hardly a
ripple in the local scene. Nor had the sale of his erstwhile
property to the Shaw interest. That transaction had been announced at the same time as two others involving well-known
and active hotel-casinos, and had been relegated to the bottom
half of the resulting news stories. Television accounts did not
even mention the deal.

But of course, it did not pass entirely without comment.

Wise and knowledgeable eyes scanned all real-estate dealings
in southern Nevada, large and small, and they did not miss the
significance of this one. Shaw had a reputation for doing things
in a hurry; for wanting immediate and visible results. No doubt a
new hotel tower—taller and more commodious than all the rest—
would rise forthwith on the long-fallow site. Speculation centered on the Big Man's probable selection of architect and/or
builder. Del Webb seemed the most likely choice; that firm had
built half of the other hotels in the neighborhood and had a
history of meeting its completion dates.

In fact nothing happened at all.

The burned-out foundation of the original casino remained as
it had been, a rotten and neglected tooth in the otherwise spectacular dentistry of the Strip, and with the passage of time,
general interest had become occasional speculation. And then a
sometime random thought. And finally nothing at all.

Newcomers to Las Vegas were the only ones who even noticed the eyesore nowadays.

The rest simply knew it was there and ignored it with eyes
long trained to selective astigmatism.

But Francis Carrington Shaw was a man who played his own
games according to his own rules, and moving through the
semidarkened byways of what had once been the grounds of El
Cholo Loco Hotel and Casino, I decided the one he had played
here was called "total security" and that he had, as usual,
played it well.

The very barrenness of the surroundings made stealth difficult
to impossible by night or day, and surveillance would involve
electronic eyes that made nothing of concealment. Meanwhile,

the closely guarded suite at the Scheherazade would be an effective bit of misdirection, well worth the quiet presence of the squad of tight-lipped youngsters assigned to guard an empty space.

Nice work.

But there was no time to admire it. A final easy turn brought us to the front door of a mock-adobe villa apparently no different from any of its fellows. But the car stopped and my door was opened and I can take a hint as well as the next.

Outside, the air had cooled almost to the temperature maintained inside Shaw's limousine, and the last rays of desert sunset had faded from the sky. I inhaled and was astonished to catch the distant hint of yucca. Nature is not mocked; give her the least opening and she claims her own. Usually with interest.

"Pretty night, isn't it?"

A man stood framed in the open door of the villa, his face obscured by the light that shone behind him.

"Draw up a chair—make a long arm."

Something familiar about the voice.

"Always room for one more."

Corner Pocket.

He was grinning a little as he ushered me inside and closed the door behind us.

"For once," he said, "I think I have surprised the Preacher."

I couldn't deny it.

Or understand. Las Vegas is built on cozy arrangements between local authorities and those who command power and money. But Corner Pocket had missed being chief of police because he refused to play the game ("They told me to scratch a shot, and I sank it in the corner pocket instead") and moved over to the D.A.'s office in protest. What was he doing on Francis Carrington Shaw's elaborately concealed doorstep? And what was it going to cost me to find out?

"Proud of this setup," he said, as we moved into the center of the room. "Designed it myself, right down to the last little thing. Take your shoes off."

He was wearing what looked like paper hospital slippers and there was another pair in his hand. I looked at him and waited for him to explain.

"Oxygen," he said. "Not much real danger of sparks around

here. But the air's dry and these things make sure you don't get static electricity to blow us both to hell."

It made *sense* and I took the slippers and began shucking out of my own shoes, but I didn't stop looking at him and he couldn't help knowing what kind of thoughts were going through my mind.

"Ten years now," he said. "Since before he moved here. The Man's people came to see me just after I bombed out at the department, and made me an offer I could refuse—but only if I was an idiot."

"The district attorneyship?" I said.

His grin widened.

"What a campaign," he said. "Skyrockets and pinwheels! One guy a shoo-in for reelection, suddenly he gets an offer to go to Washington in a corner-office job at the Department of Justice, and wonder of wonders along comes a young lawyer here in town that no one ever paid attention to before, turns out to have some big-bucks backing to run for the vacant office . . . and the only person who runs against him backs out at the last moment."

"Pure coincidence," I said.

"Up yours," he said. "With a boat hook. But don't decide things are one way or the other before you talk to the Man—and don't be too surprised at anything you see when you meet him. You're here on my say-so. I'd hate like hell for it to turn out to be a mistake."

He opened the door and led the way into the next room.

It was about the same size as the room we had left, but there the resemblance ended.

My first impression was of light. And absence of color.

Walls and ceilings had been cleared of decoration and painted a uniform high-gloss white. The floor beneath my feet was the same shade, not painted but impregnated in the vinyl covering that stretched from wall to wall. It gave the place an eerie lack of perspective, making it seem both larger and smaller than it was—an impression in no way reduced or softened by the intensity of light that poured from massive industrial-type lamps, aimed at the ceiling to give an overall indirect brightness to all corners.

But all that paled by comparison to the central artifact.

It was an iron lung, and the head protruding from it—looking at me in the overhead mirror now, with an expression that might have been sardonic amusement—was unmistakably that of Francis Carrington Shaw.

He was older than the pictures I remembered, and the cheekbones stood out more prominently.

"But, yes," the whispery voice I remembered from the telephone broke into my thoughts. "Yes. Oh, yes. It is me. Come a little closer, please. There's a chair in here somewhere . . ."

There were two of them. But Corner Pocket seemed to want to go on standing by the door, so I hefted one to what seemed a likely spot and sat down in it.

The eyes, black and depthless—always Shaw's most memorable feature—followed my movements with interest.

"You are a trained athlete," he said when I had settled myself.

"Not really," I said. "A little t'ai chi each morning. Some training in others of the martial arts."

"Under Yoichi Masuda." The head nodded, startling me by knowing the true name of the man who lived among us at Best Licks as *mahayana* master. "A good man, and a worthy champion in his time—always among the clearest of thinkers. I have read two of his books. And some of the poetry."

More and more surprises.

The books did not bear his name, and the poetry had always been carefully anonymous.

"Master Masuda will be pleased to know of your regard," I replied formally.

"If you live to tell him," the head said, nodding on its pillow. "And that is, I must say, still very much in doubt at this moment. Tell me, sir, have you really so little regard for your own life as recent events would appear to indicate?"

I started to form an answer, but the trace of a smile at the corners of his mouth told me he didn't really want or expect one. It was his idea of a pleasantry.

"We are all in the palm of the Almighty," I said, deciding to play a game of my own as long as he was in a party mood.

But the smile faded.

"I spoke in jest," he said, "and perhaps it was impolite. Your reply, however, was not in kind, coming as it does from an ordained minister."

"I'm a poker player," I said.

"You are a priest. Would you like me to recite the dates of

your postulancy and ordination, and name the bishops present for the latter? Or the names of the missionary churches to which you were assigned before you went to Vietnam?''

His voice had strengthened with the last few sentences, and I took a moment to fill in a blank space or two. Now I would be able to tell Margery who had been nosing into the closed places.

But I still couldn't imagine why.

''Your wife's death—what was her name, Sara? Yes, Sara. Her death was tragic and unnecessary. Shattering. But your reaction was, if you will forgive the observation, juvenile.''

''No,'' I said. ''I won't.''

The smile returned. ''Excellent,'' the head said. ''Excellent! True emotion. Anger without editing. Better than I'd hoped to see and the equal of anything your friend—Corner Pocket, I think you call him—the equal of anything Corner Pocket had led me to believe.''

I stood up and moved to put the chair back where I'd found it.

''If that's all, then,'' I said, ''I'll be on my way. Do I get a ride home or do I walk?''

The smile stayed put. ''Better and better. My apologies, sir. They are sincere, I assure you. But I had to know if my . . . researchers, let us say . . . had been led astray. Their work was hurried; I needed answers at once, and I had been badly deceived in the past by another man of the cloth. A sometime colleague of yours, I think. From the University of the South . . . Sewanee?''

I hesitated, remembering what Holy Joe had told me of his dealings with Francis Carrington Shaw, and wondering how much of it had been true.

If this was another move in Maxey's master plan to edge me into the television evangelism hustle, we were both wasting our time and I had a better use for mine. On the other hand, the man in the iron lung didn't impress me as the type to have any real interest in such matters, and he seemed to have gone to a lot of trouble to get me here.

I put the chair back down and sat in it, looking at his reflection.

''Thank you,'' he said. ''And now to business . . .''

Corner Pocket had been standing just inside the door, watching and listening, and now a signal seemed to pass between him and his employer. He nodded and stepped back into the living room, closing the white door behind him.

''What follows,'' the face in the slanted mirror said, ''is for you to know and others only to guess at. Your friend knows most of it. But the parts he does not know will never harm him. And I can imagine circumstances where knowledge could be awkward.''

I was lost, and made no effort to conceal it, but he continued as though I had nodded in full comprehension.

"This machine," he said, using his chin to indicate the gleaming steel chamber that surrounded his body, "is not absolutely necessary to my survival. At least not all the time. My lungs and the muscles that control them are in excellent shape, considering the years they have been in service, and my physical condition is far better than most people have been given reason to believe.

"In point of fact, my only real impairment—if you discount the rumors of Alzheimer's or worse, and the theory that I have always been a lunatic—is a combination of sleep disorders. Tell me, sir, have you ever heard of Ondine's curse?''

I thought it over and shook my head. "Not really," I said. "There is the mythical tale, of course. Something about a nymph condemned to eternal sleeplessness—''

"Because she would stop breathing while asleep, and die." The head nodded, cutting me off. "Yes. That is the myth and that is the origin of the name. But it is no mere fairy tale, let me tell you. The medical profession's name for the condition is 'sleep apnea,' and it is real enough to have dominated my life for the past two years.''

The head's mouth quirked in self-mockery.

"Remember when this country had a President who wasn't supposed to be able to chew gum and walk at the same time? Funny! Yes. Well, I can't seem to sleep and breathe at the same time, and I assure you I have yet to get a single laugh out of the situation—because my waking and sleeping periods are and always have been somewhat unusual.

"Many people vary from the norm in that respect. And profit from it. Edison, for instance, did not spend his nights sleeping. He took catnaps now and then, day and night, but no long periods of uninterrupted sleep. Gave him more time to work and achieve. A major asset!

"But I don't—didn't—sleep fewer hours than anyone else, or more hours, either.

"Like Edison, I was content with a series of thirty- or sixty-minute naps well spaced through the day. Not a matter of choice. I could not and cannot sleep for more than an hour at a time.

Many people, over the years, remarked on the long hours I seemed to work. Such dedication. Admirable! After a while, I stopped trying to disabuse them of that notion for the same reason that I stopped explaining everything else. It simply wasn't worth the effort.

"I think, however, that you can appreciate the implications when I tell you that of late the catnaps, while not increasing in duration or frequency, have become totally unpredictable.

"Combine narcolepsy with a total inability to breathe while sleeping . . ."

The voice, which had seemed to strengthen and deepen earlier, had faded now to the parched whisper I remembered from the telephone, and if what he said about his condition was true it seemed possible that he was about to fall asleep again.

But the black eyes were still wide and alert, watching me with interest. I had the sudden impression of immense personal force and determination. Imprisoned, but still potent.

"I tell you this," he said after a moment, "because I require your help. An alliance, if you will. And no sane man allies himself with a weakling—or with the moribund. My condition is inconvenient and it forces me to spend much of my time as you see. In a mechanical coffin. Nonetheless, I can be as useful to you as you to me. And I am prepared to show my usefulness first.

"You came here, to Las Vegas, because you need money.

"I can remedy that by placing funds at your disposal. Not unlimited funds; that would be destructive. But more than enough for the purposes of the little town of Best Licks and its resident pastor . . ."

I started to reply. To explain. But the face in the angled mirror had expected the refusal and headed it off without losing a step.

". . . or, if that is not satisfactory, I can assist you with your tax problems. You see, I know their origin."

I shut my mouth and expelled the breath I had taken. Silently.

"The IRS," Shaw said, "is a great bureaucratic beast, and its movements are too ponderous to be really effective. But it can be manipulated. In this case, it responded to what appeared to be legitimate information from a source who outlined a series of irregularities that would, if substantiated, lead to cancellation of the tax-free status of your town and church.

"The charges are nonsense, of course. But disproving them

could take months—perhaps even years. And your assets would be tied up for all that time, while you would be forced to do ongoing business on a strictly cash basis lest any bank account be confiscated.''

He stopped talking, and this time a response seemed to be required. I had one ready.

"Who?" I said. "And why?"

The head nodded.

"Proper questions," he said. "And in proper order. Excellent. The tip came—by a route I could trace only because I began at the other end—from your old friend and fellow Vietnam veteran, Samuel Clemens Goines. And his objective was to bring you here. To Las Vegas. For the poker game he had arranged.''

I thought it over and shook my head.

"Not logical," I said. "Sam didn't have to be devious. And he wasn't. He picked up a telephone and called me and I came. The tax problem wasn't necessary. We were old friends; I'd have come to see him and he knew it.''

"But not to play poker."

"Well . . ."

"You are a professional." The whisper-voice was strengthening again. "You enjoy the game, and it is good to enjoy your work. But all the same it is a business, your chosen craft and livelihood, and you approach it therefore with a certain respect and appreciation. And with a standard of ethics.

"You do not, for instance, play against those who cannot afford high stakes . . .''

"No profit in it," I interjected.

". . . and you do not play against compulsives—degenerates whose secret intention is to lose their money in order to punish themselves.''

"I also don't play with Friday night friends who get half bombed and want to argue about whether a straight beats a flush," I said. "So what? Neither does any real professional."

"Precisely. So Goines could hardly invite you to a 'friendly little game.' Yet he had to have you sitting in on that one.''

"But . . . why?"

"Precisely what I have been wondering." The eyes seemed darker and more compelling than ever. "You see, that game was arranged at my behest, the players selected by me. And your name was not on the list.''

He gave me a moment to digest that, but the time was wasted because it didn't make sense to me, either.

"I set it up," he said, "to pay a ransom—but not for an individual. The ransom was for the city of Las Vegas itself. The whole city.

"It was being held hostage.

"Your friend Corner Pocket tells me you know that Sam Goines had obtained an atomic bomb and was offering it to the highest bidder. What he has not told you, because he does not know it himself as yet, is that Goines had found a buyer. He had sold the device to me.

"But before it could be delivered it was stolen . . . by someone who threatened to set it off in the vicinity of Casino Center."

A SERMON (Continued)

Adolf Hitler was a bloodthirsty lunatic—and a rather passable artist. Albert Schweitzer was a gentle saint—and a thoroughly incompetent physician. We accept these contradictions and make peace with them . . . but we cannot seem to apply the lesson to the person we see in the mirror . . .

24

My FIRST IMPULSE was to ask him what he had wanted with an atom bomb in the first place.

But I stifled it. Beside the point now, and I wanted to hear the rest of the story. It still didn't make sense. But it began to as he went on.

Collecting the ransom, he explained, is always a problem for the kidnapper, as retrieval of the hostage is for those who do the paying. The game seemed a sensible solution. Two items would change hands: the ransom, disguised as a poker pot grown beyond normal proportions between two players with good fighting hands; and the bomb itself, in the form of a key to the house or apartment or room where it was hidden.

"First the money—then the key," Shaw said. "The two principal players to remain at the table until both items had been verified and made secure."

"And the other players?" I asked.

"The Reverend Mr. Gillespie, sad to say, is a card cheat. He was there to manipulate the cards. Make sure the hands went as planned. The others were merely witnesses, not personally involved in the transaction."

"Did they know what was going on?"

"No. They were simply to be my nominees, men who could be counted upon to keep the evening orderly . . . or tell me the truth about what happened if things went wrong."

"But it got out of hand anyway?"

"More than that. Violence, I think, might have been expected. We were, after all, dealing with someone who was prepared to threaten the life an entire city. Yet this was, at least on its own terms, a rational threat intended to produce a rational result."

"Rational?"

"Rational in the sense that we both wanted something and were prepared to take logical steps to obtain it: He wanted money; I wanted my bomb."

I didn't even bother to reply. But he caught my reaction and responded in a way that I found oddly touching.

The head blushed.

"I am not a machine, sir," the dry voice said as color rose and then faded, "present indications to the contrary notwithstanding. And not a madman, either. But think what you like. And be damned to you . . ."

I considered the offer, and nodded. "Fair enough," I said.

The eyes swore at me silently for a moment. But finally he went on.

"In the event," he said, "the attack on the penthouse was not rational, because it came before the ransom had been paid or the location of the bomb disclosed."

That made sense. Pots had run high in the game—higher even than I had expected—but certainly not the ransom for an atomic weapon. And nothing but chips had changed hands.

"All right," I said. "It wasn't rational. But what has that to do with me?"

The black eyes sharpened.

"You," the reflected head said, "are a wild card. The only player in that game not handpicked and approved by me, and the only one with any known connection to the gunmen. Yes, I know that Jorge Martinez was your sergeant in Vietnam. More, you dealt the poker hand—aces and eights—that was found on Danny DiMarco's body and that seems to keep turning up in connection with all the subsequent murders.

"And that is particularly intriguing, since it is the factor that causes other people to believe the killings were planned or ordered by me . . ."

He had lost me again. So he explained.

"James Butler Hickok," he said, explaining, "was the true name of a U.S. marshal and gunfighter known in legend as Wild Bill. He was a sharpshooter, scout, and spy for the Union army during the Civil War and later worked as a lawman in Hays City, Abilene, and other places. Aces and eights are known as the dead man's hand because that was the combination of poker cards he was holding when he was shot to death in a saloon at Deadwood, Dakota Territory, on August 2, 1876."

Still lost.

"Western lore," he said, "is my hobby, and I am considered something of an expert in the field. Especially on the subject of Wild Bill Hickok, whose life has always been a particular interest. Memorabilia: I have handwritten accounts of that last encounter, the reported words of the man who killed him, and the statements of witnesses, not to mention the boots Hickok was wearing when he died, the guns said to have been cocked and in his hands. His badge. A photograph, taken with his friend Calamity Jane, who bore what is believed to be his only child."

"But . . . aces and eights?" I prompted.

The head colored again.

"I call it a hobby," Shaw said. "But obsession would be a better word. And more accurate. I raised the subject only in order to make my point—that the recurrent appearance of aces and eights would tend to implicate me in all the killings."

"And it did that," I said, remembering Manny's reaction, and what the Voice of Heaven had said about his erstwhile backer a few minutes before his wife was killed.

"Yes," he said. "But now we come to the heart of the matter. You were there by invitation. Sam Goines had telephoned you. Personally. And taken certain measures to make sure you would accept. Can you think of any reason why he might do that?"

I couldn't.

Or at least, only one . . .

"No," I said. "Not really. Unless you count the chance that he was behind the machine-gun attack and wanted me dead along with the rest."

"Unlikely. In view of the fact that he himself was one of the victims."

"Yes . . ."

It was an opportunity to tell him that Sam hadn't really been killed at the penthouse or anywhere else. But it wouldn't have made anything any clearer—and besides, I was just beginning to notice the first stirring of what might be an idea in the back of my mind, and wanted a chance to nurture the puny little thing in private before telling the world.

"Nothing else?"

"No," I said. "Nothing but some questions. If you want to answer them."

The ghost of a smile. "And if I don't?"

"Your privilege. I buy myself a ticket back to the Sierra just as soon as I can get to the hotel and check out."

The smile widened.

"In your words, sir, Fair enough."

"All right, then. First question: Who was your player in the game? The one you trusted to get the bomb back in return for your money?"

"Goines. Of course."

"Why 'of course'?"

"Because I had bought it from him in the first place, and because we had been doing business for years. That first arms deal of his, when he bought the Belgian rifles and sold them to two other governments? The Caribbean bank where he deposited the money he had won just after getting out of the army, the one that then financed the whole transaction . . . that bank belonged to me, and still does. Didn't you know?"

I shook my head.

Wheels within wheels. I wondered how many other people—how many governments, for that matter—would have been surprised to hear of that particular connection. But Francis Carrington Shaw seemed to treat it as no secret at all. I filed it as one more piece from the puzzle box with his name on it.

"Second question," I said. "Who was the player on the other side? The one representing the kidnapper?"

The eyes blinked. "Colonel Connor."

I think I was supposed to get some sort of reaction from me. But it didn't, and after a moment he went on.

"David Patrick Connor, if that's his real name—and it could be—claims to be Irish-born. From county Tyrone. And to have gained his initial military experience and American citizenship from service in the early stages of Vietnam."

"Green Berets?"

"Marines, I believe. There is a record of a man by that name. A sergeant."

"But not a colonel."

"The military title appears, however, to be at least semi-legitimate. From a time when he was an instructor–tactical officer in Biafra."

"Professional merc?"

The invisible shoulders seemed to shrug.

"Whatever that may mean. The term has come upon hard times."

"Yes."

No need for discussion on that point, and there was a silence while I waited for him to go on. But the eyes were closed and I thought for a moment that I was witnessing one of the impromptu sleep sessions he had warned me about.

"Forgive me," he said, the eyes snapping open again. "I was searching for more information concerning the colonel, but all I can find is the fact that he is wanted in one or two places around the African continent."

"Nigeria, for one?"

"For one. And elsewhere—among the Arab states."

That surprised me a little, but for the moment I was less interested in the colonel's background than in his more recent activities.

"He is the one who stole the bomb?" I asked.

Shaw seemed surprised.

"Certainly not," he said. "As Sam Goines was my nominee in the game, the colonel was put forward as surrogate for those holding the stolen weapon. And has been nominated again, in the same role."

"Again?"

"Oh, yes. You see, it seems that I am back in contact with the extortionists, and they want to try the exchange again. Another game. That's why you're here. This time I want you to play my hand."

Ask and ye shall receive . . .

For the second time in less than a week, I found myself freely invited into a game I'd thought I would have to arrange for myself or even elbow my way into. And it was a little unnerving.

The last serendipitous invitation had turned out to be a booby trap I still didn't fully understand, and the man staring at me in the mirror now was an even chancier proposition. Byzantine to the core. Absolutely no credentials as an altruist.

A schemer.

A user.

A main-chance, self-aggrandizing son of a bitch that nobody in his right mind would trust for a moment.

"Sounds good," I said. "Where do they want to play this time, and how soon do they want to do it . . . ?"

Corner pocket drove me back to the Scheherazade in his own car and he didn't have much to say on the way. Which was just

as well. I was busy with my own thoughts. They were mostly
interrogatives, and one or two of them centered on him. I
wondered how much he knew of what had gone on in the
white-painted room.

Surely the Mormon Mafia had been able to plant a bug in
there.

And if not, Corner Pocket would have supplied the need.

Yet Francis Carrington Shaw seemed to inspire a peculiar
devotion and compliancy in those who worked closely with him,
and thinking about it in retrospect I had to admit the bare
possibility that my conversation with the man in the iron lung
had been as private as he had seemed to think it would be.

"Don't want the front entrance," Corner Pocket said, turning
off the main highway toward the Paradise Road entrance to the
Scheherazade's grounds.

"No," I said.

We angled through the sunken rear parking lot and I thought
for a moment he was going to take the ramp to the VIP garage,
but instead we drifted around to the side entrance near the place
where Jorge Martinez's body had landed. A lifetime ago.

"None of my business," he said, when we had come to a
stop, "but you want to be kind of careful where you put your
feet, dealing with the Man."

I looked at him and waited. There had to be more.

"He's always been straight with me," Corner Pocket said.
"And that's one of several reasons why I still run his errands and
answer his questions. Aside from everything else, it's an experience just to watch him decide how to handle a problem. That is
one double-tough, brilliant old mother . . . and being sick the
way he is hasn't damaged his brains one little bit."

Still nothing to say.

"But he can only be smart for himself. You got to play your
own hand, Preacher. And don't you ever forget it."

I waited again, but he didn't seem to have anything else to say
so I got out and he drove away without a word and I went inside
and took an elevator to my room.

No one was waiting inside this time—experience had made me
doubly wary, and I took time to sense the surroundings after opening the door—but the red light on the telephone was blinking away
in the darkness, and I went over to pick it up without turning on
the lights.

It was the desk.

Several calls for me in the box, the clerk said, but all of them from just two numbers. Both of them inside numbers at the hotel.

The first I recognized as Maxey's.

I'd canceled our dinner date by phone before leaving the room with Chick and Lancelot. But I hadn't told her where I was going or why, and unless she'd changed a lot over the years she was going to want to know a lot of answers. I turned a few of them over in my mind, trying to decide which information was safe for both of us, but her phone didn't answer and I gave up after ten rings and flashed the hotel operator to leave a message that I'd tried to return her call. Maxey would be furious.

The other number was a stranger to me.

I punched its digits into the hotel telephone-computer system and waited. It rang five times without result, and I was about to hang up and leave a second message with the operator when the other instrument was picked up and someone with a flat western accent said, "Yes?"

Happy Apodaca.

"Operator says you wanted to talk to me."

A snort. "And she said right." The judge's voice contained an asperity that he didn't trouble to conceal. "Thought we had a kind of an appointment, like, to talk things over. In private."

I thought about it and he was right and had an apology coming. Not that he would be interested.

"Sounds good to me," I said. "Where and when?"

"Now, goddammit!" No doubt about the peevishness this time. The judge was not the type to bide his time willingly. "I been waiting half the day, you Bible-thumping bastid!"

I couldn't help grinning. It was just about the first totally honest reaction I'd heard since I hit town.

"You got it," I said. "Where? My room? Yours? On the phone, right now?"

"Don't be a damn fool."

The words were still acidulous, but the tone was back to the outer limits of civility.

"You name the place."

He thought it over. But only for a moment.

"Garage," he said.

"Which one?"

"Which one you think, you crossroading son of a bitch! My car'll be parked next to yours."

The receiver banged and went dead and I put it back in its cradle.

One way and another, the VIP garage of the Scheherazade was getting to be popular in a way the architects had never intended. I wondered how long it would be before the management decided to put up a grandstand for spectators and start selling tickets.

Thinking about it en route to the garage, I realized that the judge had good reason for being upset.

Of all the people I'd been talking to since the shoot-up in the penthouse—and it suddenly occurred to me that there had been a remarkable number, all things considered—the top name on the list should have been Judge Happy Apodaca's.

Why hadn't it been?

Corner Pocket and the hospital and Maxey and all the rest of the distractions had kept me busy, and it would be easy enough to plead *force majeure*. A case could be made. But both of us would know it was nonsense, and suddenly I was as eager to talk to the testy little pirate as he seemed to be to talk to me. Maybe together we could make sense out of what was happening.

The corridor leading to my floor in the VIP garage was empty and silent, but I had been surprised more than once on this trip to southern Nevada, and I opened the door to the garage with more than the usual amount of caution.

Which was immediately justified.

My rented car was sitting where I had left it, nosed into its assigned stall on the opposite wall, and the only other automobile in sight was a black BMW backed into the space beside it, with the driver's door ajar.

Like Francis Carrington Shaw's limousine, the windows of the BMW seemed to have been fitted with concealing shadow glass, and I waited with the corridor door still open beside me to see just who was behind the wheel while the watchdogs of my peripheral senses came suddenly to full alert.

The picture before me was wrong.

Judge Happy Apodaca's head and shoulders emerged from the BMW and he nodded toward the passenger side of the car. But we weren't alone in the garage . . . and the third person wasn't in his car.

Someone—a sentient and malevolent presence—was on the other side of the wall that made a right-angle curve around the angular side of the hotel, about fifteen feet to my right.

"Down!"

I shouted a warning to the judge and took two steps in his direction before ducking into a running forward roll that would take me to cover behind his car's engine compartment. But the words and the action were both too late.

Happy Apodaca's move, ducking back toward the safety of the driver's seat was all too predictable. And fatal.

Coming out of the roll, I had a single flash-vision of a knife—medium weight, balanced, double-honed—in the air less than a foot from the old man's unprotected chest. Something extraneous centered on the hilt guard.

I heard the dull solidity of impact.

And a single grunt from the judge.

I moved, wriggling under my car and out on the other side in an effort to be in the wrong place for the next attack. But a moment later another car's engine roared to life near the spot where the knife-thrower had been hidden and a customized Trans Am burned rubber, taking the corner at full bore and continuing on course for the downstairs exit without pause or further aggression. Mission accomplished.

Swearing at myself and the world, I heaved erect and covered the distance to where the judge had collapsed.

He was dead.

The blade had taken him high on the left side of the chest, near the breastbone, making full entry and covering the wound with the foreign object I'd seen on the guard. Playing cards.

Five of them.

I didn't need a closer look to know which ones.

A SERMON (Continued)

Mirrors show the world in reverse . . . and this is the way we perceive the image of ourselves. We recognize it. But no one else would. Evil? Wicked? These are terms we apply to others . . . never to ourselves.

25

HOPE SPRINGS ETERNAL. Blood was welling, not spurting, from the wound in Happy Apodaca's chest and I spent nearly a minute checking for vital signs—pulse, breathing, heartbeat.

Nothing.

More to the point, when I opened my mind to try to find his aura, feel for the *wa* that could tell me his true state of being, there was nothing to find. Nothing at all. I was alone in the concrete confines of the VIP garage.

All right, then, God damn you . . .

I left him staring wide-eyed and sightless at the ceiling and flung myself into the driver's seat of his car. Keys in the ignition. Good. The engine caught on the first grind and the fuel gauge climbed swiftly toward "full" while other needles showed me a car ready for work.

Better and better.

I slammed the door and said a mental good-bye and godspeed to whatever was left of the little man who had been so tough and shrewd and corruptible. Death is a part of life—a necessary part—and its timing and cause are always less important than they seem. But there is also a fitness to such things. And an unfitness.

Men like the judge, if they die by violence, should not be denied an honor guard.

I gunned the overpriced little sedan out of its stall and down the first ramp toward street level.

National hubris and personal reservation notwithstanding, the Bavarians turn out an almost first rate automobile, and the one the judge had been driving seemed typical of the breed: overpowered and, at least in its custom sedan version, more than a little mushy around the suspension.

241

But you can't have everything. The car I had rented on arrival
at McCarran was a bright-painted little dog stamped out with a
Detroit cookie cutter, and with any luck I hoped shortly to find
myself in a race with a carefully remachined item intended for
long-range road competition. Given my druthers and a week or
two for test-drive evaluation, I might have made some other
selection. But as it was, the judge's taste in motor transport was
probably the best luck I'd had all week.

Not that that was much of an endorsement.

Downshifting and controlling the oversprung four-door without reference to the brake, I learned a little about its likes and
dislikes as we negotiated the dozen or so ninety-degree corners
between my parking level and the main exit. I have survived a
couple of well-considered courses in competition and pursuit
driving, and BMWs are not entirely strange to me. But I had
never driven the late-1980s sedan before and found that it has a
personality all its own. Powerful, and not entirely tame. Like a
grizzly bear trained to perform circus stunts.

The Trans Am was out of sight by the time I reached ground
level, but the back end of my mind had been at work on the way
down and now it was time to bet the bankroll. Everything
depended on whether the fleeing driver was brilliant or merely
smart.

One of the reasons Las Vegas has fewer robberies than you'd
expect with all that free cash floating around is the problem of
getting the loot out of town. Unless you fancy your chances of
getting past security at McCarran International, the only exit
routes are the main highways. And there are only two of those:
one north, one south.

The southern route used to sprout from the nether end of the
Strip. No more. The Interstate supplanted it and now leads
directly into the heart of the city (let's hear it for the Casino
Center Political Action Committee!) and joins the old federal
highway a mile or so after the very last hotel-casino appears in
your rearview.

No matter.

Access is access, and the highway patrol has no more trouble
pinching shut the escape routes now than in the old days. North
or south, it's still a dead end.

In the case to hand, however, I had decided that a brilliant
driver would turn left from the parking lot and try to lose his
overpriced hot rod among the others of its ilk that would be

crowding and elbowing along the Strip at this time of night. The dinner show crowd would be arriving now—dedicated losers prowling for a casino where the tables look hot, plus a small army of local kids cruising just to get a close look at the weirdos.

If he had gone there, he was home free.

I would never find him.

But there seemed a good chance that he was merely smart—in which case he would have turned right, toward Paradise Road, with the idea of getting the Trans Am into the network of back routes skirting the residential side of Las Vegas and then into the desert where the car could develop its full horsepower rating without let or hindrance from other traffic.

Roll the dice!

I swung the wheel hard right, kicked the little sedan square on the pavement, and let it have some gasoline.

Ahead, the way was blocked by someone in a primer-coated rust bucket moving at about thirty miles per hour in a cloud of smoke. I jinked left to go around, emerged from the smoke screen just in time to avoid an oncoming truck, and got back into my own lane in the middle of a self-administered lecture about smartass Bible-thumpers who get to thinking they are immortal.

The intersection with Paradise Road required another decision. Assuming the driver of the Trans Am was only smart instead of brilliant, was he really smart or only half smart?

A man with good sense and a moment or two to think would turn left, toward heavier traffic and the anonymity that two or three quick turns into the residential district could give. His car was distinctive, yes, but not unique, even with that custom blower-snout on the hood. Wheels are a hobby item in Las Vegas; something to do in the desert if you don't want to gamble. He would be among friends.

But again, I had to bet against the odds. I turned right, following Paradise and then turning east at a likely-looking route into the desert.

Southwestern access roads around Las Vegas are not many and are not marked at all. The Chamber of Commerce doesn't really want you to go into the desert if you're from out of town. It's for locals only.

I gunned the little sedan, touched its brakes, gunned again, downshifted, double-shifted, and generally did my best to get acquainted on short notice while following a paved track that an occasional reference to the stars told me was curving gradually away to the south. Booting the BMW into the 90–100 mile range with the engine indicating a steady 4,500 rpm, I did my best to bring a road map of the vicinity up on my memory screen, but was only partially successful. I hadn't really looked at one for years. There were holes, and I was in one now.

The last time I'd seen a map, the road I was on had been indicated as an unpaved track wandering off to a dead end at what I assumed—knowing Nevada politics—was the ranch of a big-bucks party contributor.

Now it was paved. And there were occasional side roads, any one of which could have been a perfect cutoff for the car I was hoping to follow. Land in the immediate vicinity of Las Vegas is flat, but there are enough wadis and other indentations to keep the scenery moderately interesting, and any one of these would have made an excellent hiding place in the stygian velvet that is moonless desert night.

I was driving on faith, chasing the remote possibility that I had guessed right several times in succession, like a crapshooter riding a roll.

And that worried me.

Poker has always been my game, the only one where the individual is not bucking the house but only the other individuals around the table. Blackjack, shimmy-baccarat, and the rest of the casino games all suffer from that drawback, emphasized by the legitimate house percentage that makes long-run triumph impossible. But craps, perhaps because the house edge can be whittled to less than half a percentage point, has always left me especially cold. Chance is a factor in any form of gambling; it must always be taken into account. But the crapshooter—even when he plays the back line and rides the free odds and knows the breakage and manages his money adroitly and comes away from the table a winner—is still just an accident looking for somewhere to happen. He will give the money back soon enough. The excitement of the action, with chip mountains building or melting in seconds, guarantees that he won't stay away for long. It is an addiction stronger than liquor or heroin or even cigarettes.

So here I was, coming out on a point. And an eight at that.

Okay, then: Shoot the whole roll!

I was already going far too fast, outdriving the little krautwagen's headlights, but it was no time to drag the bet. I floored the accelerator, and the tachometer needle climbed toward the red zone and the bucket seat pressed into my back. Guts. The car had plenty, and if mine were about to be spread over the near countryside it would at least be a quick end. Watching the speed climb through 110, I found myself entertaining the semi-consoling thought that at this speed a man might easily be killed. But he was not likely to be hurt.

Where the hell was that Trans Am . . . ?

Miles passed in a blur, and I forced the considering part of my mind to slow. To walk. Halt and wait. *Nariyuki no matsu.* Have patience. Await the turn of events.

Where *was* he?

The road curved right and then left and my hands moved quickly in aid of staying alive, holding the car on the pavement by a combination of luck and good Bavarian engineering. Many more of those and the road crews would be scraping the preacher up with a stick and a spoon. The hand was getting to be a long one; I was rolling numbers, but not my point.

Monocular vision is no big help for driving of any kind, much less for high-speed night pursuit. Two-eyed people judge distance by a largely unconscious ranging system known as strains of convergence. Those who become single-eyed have to learn that part of living all over again, attacking the problem with a combination of perspective judgment and the minor strains involved in focus. Should the single remaining eye chance to be near- or farsighted, compensation can come slowly, if at all. And even the best-adjusted monoculars find night driving a chore.

I stilled my center and concentrated on processing what little information came in from the single visual sensor, now locked firmly on the obscurity of the road ahead.

And suddenly there it was . . .

Dim and far. Disappearing from time to time with the vagaries of the desert road. But unmistakably a pair of taillights. Moving fast.

Eight, the point!
Coming out again . . .

No way to be sure that the lights ahead were those of the Trans Am, of course. Kids trying to scare themselves, maybe. Or a drunk pushing his luck. But I had that come-seven feeling and found myself inching forward in the seat. Trying to give the car an extra boot.

Gaining swiftly, I thought for a moment of dimming my headlights or shutting them off altogether, but decided against it. The position of the lights ahead did seem to indicate a straight stretch of pavement, but even though he still seemed to be in a hurry he would be back to half or three-quarter throttle by now, not expecting pursuit. Headlights on the road behind would not necessarily seem a threat, unless they did something to indicate a desire for concealment.

No. I tried to concentrate on keeping the car steady and left the headlights alone.

Closer now and closing fast. I eased off a little, dropping the speedometer needle back below 100 while maintaining just enough pressure to keep the red twins ahead growing a little. And I tried to get inside the other driver's mind.

He thought he had just gotten away with murder. Was he exultant, savoring the sense of omnipotence and power that such an act can produce? Repentant—a killer-with-a-conscience? Or was there no feeling at all? Men who deal death because the fire at their core needs fuel have been a fact of existence since the beginning of time. Familiar, though on no account to be trusted or tolerated. But if the car ahead was indeed a custom Trans Am with a knife-throwing murderer at the wheel, was its driver one of the breed—once rare, but increasingly common in these final years of the twentieth century—who kill because no fire burns?

Pointless speculation. And it almost got me killed.

The driver of the other car had spotted me and decided to have a look. My foot hit the brake only a second later than his did, but by that time the distance between us had closed to a matter of feet.

I had rolled another point. But the hand was still in doubt.

The car ahead was a Trans Am, and I was close enough to see that there were two heads in the front seat instead of one. The head on the passenger side was turned toward me and my headlights picked out the whiteness of a face that moved quickly toward its window and leaned out to open fire with what looked like the job-lot brother of the mini-Uzis that had been such a problem in the penthouse at the Scheherazade.

He got off two bursts of three before I could edge the BMW out of the way.

My luck seemed to be in.

The dice were still rolling, but it had been a near thing and I hit the accelerator in an effort to turn necessity into advantage. The sedan was game; revolutions climbed toward the red line again and speed came up in a rush. I had pulled to the left and my front fender was opposite the Trans Am's back wheels.

Before the other driver could respond, I yanked my steering wheel to the right and had the satisfaction of feeling hard and effective contact. The Trans Am yawed wildly, skittering on the edge of disaster, and I nosed toward it in an effort to help things along.

But it was no go.

This was a desert road; not much shoulder and no drainage ditch at all. The Trans Am pulled wide to the right as the driver regained control and shot back onto the blacktop in a spurt of gravel and exhaust gases. I could hear his blower cut in, and knew it was time to run.

Skew turns are not a good maneuver for passenger sedans, even when they are made for autobahn speed freaks in Germany. The BMW protested, swayed, and spooked the very edge of the envelope coming through the last few degrees of arc, but I kept my mind on the downshifting and then the racing changes bringing it back to speed, and by the time the world had steadied we were climbing past 100 again, headed back toward town.

But it was a forlorn hope and I knew it.

Some people think well and clearly when they are angry, and sometimes I am one of them, but here was an example of just how far a really potent shot of adrenaline can distort the thought processes. Coming out of the garage and speeding across the desert, I had managed to concentrate on pursuit to the exclusion of all else. Two obvious considerations—the off chance that the killer of Happy Apodaca might not be alone in the car, and the question of what I was going to do with or about him even if he was—simply had not crossed my mind. And this was the payoff.

Craps.

Pass the dice . . .

The Trans Am's headlights appeared in my rearview. The driver had completed his own turn and would be gaining on me . . . with his passenger primed to put a well-aimed burst through the rear window.

Suddenly the loom of the city seemed impossibly distant.

I put the hammer down and let the little sedan have its head. Nothing could forestall what was coming, but there was a chance I could make it happen in an inhabited area—someplace where there would be people to see, and know and remember. Not much consolation. But all I could reasonably ask for now.

Twisting the wheel in time to stay with a minor curve I remembered, I checked the rearview again to see how fast the

Trans Am was gaining, and got a tiny bit of encouragement. The headlights weren't coming up as fast as I'd expected. Maybe the other car's supercharger had packed up.

Maybe it had swallowed a valve or thrown a rod.

Suddenly the city wasn't so far away, and suddenly I was thinking again in terms of minutes instead of only seconds. But it was a mirage. Like chasing an inside straight. The last card is never the one you paid for.

A new sound explained everything: High above and to the rear I heard the unmistakable clatter of a helicopter approaching at high speed and I had a sudden clear flash-memory of a radio antenna spiked on the rear deck of the Trans Am. No wonder they hadn't been in a hurry to catch up. All they had to do was keep me in sight.

Bright light flooded down, illuminating the road behind me and picking out the Trans Am and then moving swiftly forward to center on the BMW. I bled off a little speed to give myself a maneuvering edge, but it couldn't be much; the pursuing car was still there.

The initial burst missed. I braked at the first eruption in the surface of the road ahead and then hit the power to cause the door gunner to bracket the car instead of cutting dead center. Not much of a ploy, but it worked. Once.

The whirlybird noises got louder and the light circle narrowed, beginning to throw slant-shadows as the pilot tried to give the door gunner a better shot.

Screw you, Jack! I braked, feinted left, and then turned off the road into the desert, making a wide circle to the right that would bring me directly under the bird, smothering the gun and giving me a chance to swing back when the pilot corrected.

But this time he was ready.

The helicopter followed my movement perfectly, and I had a moment to see the markings I had expected—the N.A.N.G. that Corner Pocket was so sure couldn't be there—before the BMW's windshield blew away and the tires on the right side came apart and the world bounced once, turned over twice, and collapsed in a wildness of light shards shimmering to zero.

A SERMON (Continued)

Nobody ever really believes that he, personally, wears the black hat. There are extenuations; our motives have been misunderstood. If others knew us better, they would see the basic rightness of our actions . . .

26

RETURNING CONSCIOUSNESS CAME as a real surprise.

And an awful smell. I had been sitting on an Alpine hillside touching blades of grass that were the fingertips of the Enlightened One and contemplating the infinite variety of experience that could be mine now that mortal concerns were put away.

Clouds drifted below, closing off the valley, and the Rebbe from Nazareth said it was time to move higher—perhaps to the timberline of Nirvana—and his friend the Mecca merchant laughed and wanted to know what time was and the Rebbe had just started what sounded as though it might turn into a solipsist's rhapsody when I noticed that something had gone wrong with the air.

Yellow mist had formed around us, and the odor it brought was not of the rose.

I tried to move a hand to hold my nose rather than interrupt the flow of syllogism, but found that I could not. The hand that had touched the digits of Siddhartha seemed somehow to be imprisoned now, and my efforts to deal with the problem only brought the yellow mists closer and I opened my mouth to warn the others but they were gone and sound had ceased and so was the meadow and my eye opened an inch or two from the wet surface of a concrete floor.

Focus took a bit of effort.

But scent identification was immediate. My nostrils were filled with a reek of human waste, only partially masked by the smell of the harsh chemicals employed to neutralize it.

I was back at Sewanee, on the floor of the men's room at Saint Luke's Hall. No. Try again. That floor would have been clean. Maybe this was one of the roadhouses off campus. Or a bus stop in Colorado. Near Fort Carson. What the hell kind of a party was this, anyway?

And what were they putting in the drinks . . . ?

I stirred, still not sure where I might be, but certain that no good could come of lying on a dirty floor next to a dirty toilet stool. And discovered that my hands were still back in the meadow mist. Tied and useless.

My mouth opened to voice an indignant protest, but I caught myself in time and closed it without a sound.

Time enough for that later, if it still seemed like a good idea.

Twisting my shoulders against the concrete and using my elbow, I finally managed at least to sit up. Better. Or worse, depending on one's criteria of judgment. The world was still a bit unreal, filled with the mistiness that follows even the most minor concussion. But having it back on a level plane again seemed a step in the right direction.

The view, however, did not improve. My first impression had been correct. This was someone's idea of a comfort station: Toilet, washstand, and mirror, stained and dirty, were ranged against two walls. A cardboard wastebasket completed the decor. Nothing else.

Except me. I was propped up against the third wall of the room—call its floor space six by five, with charity—and the fourth wall was mostly door. Walls and door were painted the same institutional green, scarred and pitted with the dirt of long abuse, and a minor tap with my head assured me that looks were not deceiving: They were of metal.

I looked up, and it was a mistake. Pain lanced through my skull and I added a wrenched neck to the growing statement of charges that included the hemp rope that had been used to bind my wrists. The knots were beginning to bite.

Still, the single glance at the ceiling had given me the first positive impression of my surroundings. Lighting for the room was not good because it came indirectly, from a far place not immediately visible, filtered through a heavy but widely spaced mesh of wire. The lid on my cage was strong enough. But not solid.

I struggled to bring my feet under me—my ankles were tied with the same kind of rope as my hands—and finally succeeded to the extent of being able to roll forward to my knees and then back on the heels of the boots the bondage freak had foolishly left on my feet when he tied the ankles together. Sloppy work, but I could understand it well enough. Removing close-fitted boots requires a certain cooperation from the wearer: I had been in no condition to give him any. And be damned to him.

The first attempt at vertical posture was a washout.

I overbalanced. Almost fell.

Careful . . . !

Don't want to make a noise; might spoil all the fun.

After thinking the maneuver through in advance, I made a better job of the second attempt, disregarding the urge to move the feet once they were beneath me and holding myself erect by leaning against the wall. A mirror above the washbasin gave back the image of a wreck.

My right eye was gone. Not that it had really been there in the first place, of course, but the prosthesis that usually filled the position seemed to have taken leave when the judge's BMW came to grief, and the lid was down over the vacant socket in the great-grandfather of all dark winks.

Further inspection showed that the rest of the ensemble had fared no better.

Violence had been done the shirt, the second such casualty in less than two days. And there were also pulled seams and buttons missing and one great rent evidently inflicted by something sharp that had penetrated both coat and vest. The trousers were not visible in the mirror, but a downward glance assured me that one knee was open to the world and the opposite cuff had suffered some misfortune that caused it to sag. So much for custom tailoring. They just don't make things the way they used to.

Quietly, carefully, I hop-stepped across the eighteen or so inches that separated my stomach from the washbasin and then turned to look over my shoulder at the bindings on my hands. Competent, yes. But not perfect. Whoever had done the tying had not been accustomed to such chores. An expert would have tied the elbows even if the hands had to be left free. Okay, then, friends: I looked closely at the mirror, but appearances had not been deceiving. It was of metal, not glass. No chance for a knife-shard to cut the ropes there.

Just as well, perhaps. Offhand, I couldn't think of any good way to break glass without making a lot of noise.

Still taking it slow and careful, I seated myself on the closed top of the stool and went to work.

T'ai chi ch'uan, the art and science of balance and muscular control developed for self-defense of wayfaring monks a few centuries ago, places most of its emphasis on whole-body control. The idea is to exercise and create beauty simultaneously.

But the small muscles, including those of the hands and feet, are not entirely neglected. And muscular control can do more things in heaven and earth, Horatio . . .

Pain is the enemy. Intended by nature as a warning device, a signal to take corrective action before damage increases, it can kill a world and become its ruler if not trained and channeled to its proper place in the rightness of things. Sweat started from my forehead and control slipped for a moment, the nothingness of *saika tanden* giving way to mere stoicism, and I almost made it worse by reacting with self-disgust.

Stop that.

Just cut it out!

No superhuman powers here. No Jit Suryoko. No Jaho. Just plain old folks with a little extra training from people who know what they are doing and don't expect miracles from the nonmiraculous. Take it slow. Take it easy. Take the nothingness. Accept reality . . .

A moment later, or so it seemed, the first loop of rope moved free over the end of my right forefinger and I waited a moment, savoring the immediate looseness before going to work on the second.

That went faster.

And the third was nothing at all. Quickly I slipped my hands free of the flaccid coils and exercised the fingers to restore full circulation and sensation before going to work on the ropes around my ankles. They gave a little trouble. But not much.

I stood, with the two lengths of rope in my hand and looked with a kindlier and more considering eye at the room around me.

Big problems call for big solutions, and big solutions call for big tool-kits. But all I had was a couple of pieces of rope.

The door proved to be firmly locked; no response whatever to my stealthy two-way experiment with the inside knob. No surprise there. I stood on the stool to inspect the grille overhead.

Just what it had seemed: rippled eight-inch lengths of steel wire, interwoven and strongly fixed in a steel frame, screwed or bolted—screwed, I decided, taking a closer look—into the steel framing of the four walls. Unpromising. But not impossible. Think about it. Plenty of time.

Turning, I started to ease myself down to floor level again but thought better of it and reached out an arm to touch the wall over the door. The fit might once have been perfect, but time and ill-usage had done their work. Metal fatigue had allowed the

outer edge of the door to sag. More than half an inch of ligh
showed between its top and the upper sill and I used my position
to make a visual survey of the world outside.

Once again, no surprises. The little bit of the ceiling visibl
through the rest room grille had told me I was in some kind o
large metal structure and my door-top peephole confirmed th
impression, identifying the building as an airplane hangar. O
what had once been one. Doors at the far end, almost out o
sight in the general gloom of poor lighting, were of the rollin
type intended to open the entire front for wide-wing ingress an
egress. No airplanes in line of sight right now, and temporary
looking plywood structures along the wall leading to my priso
showed that the place had seen other uses in the recent past.

Yet aerial interests had not been entirely neglected.

Sharp-edged and metallic, an object of peculiar shape hun
suspended from an unseen fulcrum twenty feet to one side an
barely within my restricted field of vision, moving up and dow
an inch or two from time to time with the minor currents of a
circulating inside the building. But I had no difficulty recogniz
ing it as the main blade of a helicopter, or in imagining the oliv
drab color of the fuselage and the letters painted on the tail an
under the fuselage.

I scanned the far corner of the hangar. It was almost lost i
dimness, but even so I could make out an orderly stack of boxes
Rectangular, about the size of coffins. Some kind of markings o
the side, but nothing I could read from across the room. All th
same, I would have given long odds on my chance of being able t
describe their contents. And the smell of the Cosmoline they wer
packed in. If I'd had any doubt that this was Sam Goines's—o
someone's—hideaway arsenal, it was gone now. The ugly nose of
desert half-track was just visible on the other side of the spac
that must have been occupied by the Huey, and the temporar
enclosures nearer my washroom-cell would contain various kinds o
ammunition and/or explosive devices. All very orderly and efficien
And illegal. No permits had ever been issued for any of this.

I looked around for signs of life.

Nothing in sight.

But there was a lot of the room that I couldn't see, and a lot o
information I didn't have. Leaving me alive after I'd survive
the strafing by the helicopter didn't make a lot of sense. Bu
leaving me alone—even tied, unconscious, and locked in th
john—would be an act of outright stupidity.

Suddenly I had to get down.

And sit down. At once.

The soft fuzziness that had filled the world when I first tried to sit up was back at the corners and spreading. I sat down on the stool and lowered my head and waited for it to pass. One step at a time, Preacher. Easy does it . . .

One of the funniest things about prime-time television is the ease with which he-man heroes are able to absorb repeated hammerings on the head. Wallops that would kill or paralyze anything else on two feet—gorillas and orangutans included—seem to do little more than slow them down. Whiplash, vertebral compression, spinal damage, and hospital recovery time never seem to get a mention. A nice comfortable world for a nice comfortable life.

Seated in the dirty little lockup at the hangar-armory, I decided to apply for assignment to one of those lives next time around. Lousy dialogue, maybe, and repetitious situations involving dull people. But the absence of headaches and dizziness might make up for a lot.

As soon as the world was sharp and steady again, I took steps to enlarge my part of it.

The ropes that had been on my wrists and ankles were strong enough but far too short for what I had in mind. More cordage was needed. I took off everything but my boots and underwear.

After tying one of the ropes to the damaged cuff of the trousers, I stood on the toilet stool again to pass the other end of the rope through the center portion of the wire mesh, and then gave it a second loop to reduce spot chafing before bringing it back down into the room and tying it to the sleeve of the ruined coat.

Vest and shirt came next, and I risked turning on the cold water tap—very slowly and very quietly—to wet the garments before tying them together and then tying them to the free end of the ceiling rope.

That left the other rope.

I attached it to the free leg of the trousers and twisted them as tightly as I dared before passing the rope around the nexus of toilet stool and flush box. The coat, vest, and shirt also came in for some solid twisting before I slacked off a bit and tied the final knot that turned the whole mess into a tight but lumpy circle of rope and clothing connecting the dirty solidity of the plumbing to the roof mesh.

Then I removed the bottom of the wastepaper basket, flattene the cylinder, folded it twice, thrust it between the two rope-and clothing cables, and began to twist.

As turnbuckles go, it wasn't perfect, and I tried not to gues what its actual breaking-strain rating might be.

But it took hold of the steel-wire roof of my little prison an made a notable downward dent after the first few turns, and settled down to the work of making sure the cardboard lever kep turning in just one direction.

Each turn was a little harder, and a glance in the steel mirrc didn't help much.

The skinny one-eyed wreck laboring in there was nearly nake and he looked like something out of a Charles Addams dungeon Dirty, bloody, bruised, and comically earnest about what he wa trying to do. I didn't know him and I didn't think I wanted to But he was good for a laugh and I almost gave him one before remembered his vow of silence. No, no! The dungeon maste will get you! I leaned on the turnbuckle and struggled to contrc hysteria.

Cham-Hai, the Chinese meditational state of sinking into one' surroundings seemed indicated.

But out of reach.

Saika tanden, then. I marshaled remnants of intelligence an concentrated on the state that admits all eventualities. On noth ingness. Success was not total. But it was enough.

And the respite had not been a total loss.

Before manhandling the lever through its next turn I glance at the mesh top of the cage and realized that success—and th moment of greatest danger—were both close at hand.

Either my improvised turnbuckle was stronger than I'd though or the metal holding the edges of the grille was weaker. Th whole facing had come loose on one side, and I could see sign of weakening in two more places. Excellent! Amazing! But s lence remained a prime imperative; no E for effort here. Get right and get it quietly the first time, or no trip to Hawaii . . .

Carefully, my attention focused on the grille's edges, I force the lever through another turn. And another.

The corner screw on the left tilted and I held my breath climbing onto the stool to steady it with my free hand befor making the next turn that tore it free from its moorings. A fe flakes of rust followed. All right! Now for the screws nearest it.

I moved my hand to brace the second screw as I had the first, but was a split second too late. No more twisting was required. Those screws were done. Before my hand could make contact, two of them parted company with the wall . . . to the accompaniment of an E-flat screech clearly audible in the next county.

I froze in position, my eye riveted to the crack of light at the top of the door.

Outside, something stirred.

Holding my breath and offering eternal homage to whatever archangels have charge of sound and movement, I awaited developments.

A full minute of nothing.

And then movement, a disturbance of light patterns outside. Sound of footsteps. Shod. Breathing noises. A yawn. The screech had interrupted someone's sleep. But would the someone guess its origin?

More waiting and then another series of footsteps—this time receding in the direction of the hangar doors. A slow march there, checking them out. Another halt at the far corner; something heavy tapping on wood and then on metal. The butt of a rifle, I theorized. A long wait. And then more steps.

Coming in my direction.

He would be armed and semi-alert; not really expecting trouble, but ready all the same. If he opened the door, my best chance would be a quick kick to the head. I clenched the fingers of my right hand inside the grille mesh to steady my base, and waited. But the opportunity never came.

Halting just outside the door, the guard spent a moment audibly shifting whatever weapon he was carrying—I could imagine him settling it on its sling with the snout aimed at the door jamb—and rattled the outer knob. It was secure, and that seemed to be all he wanted to know.

The footsteps marched away.

And I allowed myself to draw another breath.

My wristwatch was gone, as were my wallet and money and keys, but I stood still on the toilet lid and counted out 1,800 seconds before allowing myself to make the next move.

Time enough for a sleepy man to find his way back to dreamland.

And time enough to think up a nice silent way of getting that grille out of the way.

When the time was up, I began slowly to unwind the turnbuckle, handling the lever through each turn instead of letting it do its own thing, while keeping an eye on the grille to see that it didn't spring noisily back into place.

It stayed put, and a minute or two later I was picking at the various knots to take the turnbuckle apart and cursing the inspiration that had made me soak the clothes in water.

But finally it was done.

The shirt and vest had suffered worst. No hope of salvage. Not that there had been much in the first place.

Struggling back into the trousers and trying not to notice the additional damage inflicted by recent abuse, I picked up the rest of my clothing and climbed back on the stool.

Most of the noise had come from the one rusted screw, and I stuffed the remnants of my shirt into the space between the grille and its mooring, smothering the surrounding area as well as possible and stuffing tag ends into the wire mesh to hold it in place. The left side of the grille frame got the same treatment, this time with the vest. And the rear edge, directly over the toilet tank, got the coat.

I took hold of the free side of the grille and began to bend it. Inch by inch, pausing to assess damage and to remove loose— potentially noisy—bits of dirt and rust as well as freed screws and miscellaneous hardware, I was able to pull the free edge down into the little room. I stepped off the toilet seat when the edge was low enough and put my whole weight into the effort of forcing it through the last few inches of arc. And finally it was done.

Sometimes the luck is bad. But sometimes it is good, too. The pulling and hauling and bending produced only one more sound that might have been dangerous; a reluctant screw toward the back of the frame gave way with a sharp snap. But the sound was muffled by the folds of the shirt and brought no footsteps in my direction.

I recovered the clothing I had used as sound dampers and tried not to look too closely as I stacked it on the toilet lid, adding socks and boots as soon as I could get out of them.

Then I put a bare foot on the doorknob. Sprang upward to grasp the top sill of the metal wall.

And climbed into the ceiling.

A SERMON (Continued)

This is the knowledge that we hug to ourselves, the fire of the soul at which we warm our hands in the long winter of self-doubt: "I am one of the good guys . . . and if I had the power, I would use it well."

27

THE LEGENDARY NINJA of medieval Japan are said to have been the originators of *tsuchigumo*—literally, "bat in the rafters"—the technique of hanging undetected from the ceiling of a room.

It's an interesting exercise and I had a little training in it, early on.

But I didn't need that kind of expertise to move around the upper reaches of the hangar, and that was good, because my last practice session was years behind me and I was in no shape to give it much of a shot.

Climbing through the steel girders to the curved side of the roof was a chore in itself, and once there I found that the altered perspective seemed to emphasize the dizziness carried over from recent rude handling. I clung to my perch and offered the only available argument. No hurry, Preacher. No schedule to meet. Don't have to move at all until you want to. We could stay up here for a week, have meals brought in . . .

Slowly, handhold by handhold, I moved down again to the spot where stringers joined the main roof girders and followed one of those laterally toward the sliding doors.

Along the way, I found something useful.

Someone—perhaps one of the steelworkers who built this part of the hangar—had left three steel bolts cradled in a pocket formed by the juncture of two T-bars. I put one of them in my pocket and moved on until I was above the plywood shack nearest the doors.

That was far enough.

Almost too far, in fact. The roof of the shack, like the roof of the steel-walled room I had just left, was made of wide-spaced steel-wire mesh. A guard shack, I decided. With a guard asleep inside.

The man was wearing dark coveralls and there was something

dd about one of his arms. It appeared to be strapped to his
chest. But the important thing was that his eyes were closed.

I eased slowly back out of sight.

And took the bolt out of my pocket.

Surveying the area outside the guard shack, I decided that a
man coming to investigate a noise would be likely to halt about
two feet outside the single door, looking and listening. Especially if he had been asleep.

Guesswork, sure. A best-case scenario in a world of worst-
case events. But I wasn't going to do any better, and besides, I
was getting dizzy again. I waited for the scenery to settle down
and then moved carefully into the perch I had selected, above the
door and just out of sight from inside the room.

I threw the bolt as hard as I could against the far wall and was
rewarded with a metal-on-metal note that would have roused a
statue.

Results were all that could have been hoped.

A muffled oath floated up from the direction of the guard
shack and a moment later the ex-sleeper emerged, mini-Uzi
slung in firing position under his left arm, and halted with almost
uncanny precision on the precise spot I had selected.

I released my hold on the steel rafter and fell on him.

Like a tree.

Weight alone would have put us both on the floor and I landed
rolling, using the guard's torso as a pad and whirling to foil any
possible countermove.

But it was waste motion.

The guard lay still where he had fallen, face down and jaw
slack. I approached with caution—his hand was still on the butt
of the Uzi—and removed the weapon before checking for signs
of life, but there were none, and I wasn't surprised. I had felt the
neck go when my bare foot connected with the head.

No regrets. He was dead and I was alive and that was just the
way I wanted it to be.

All the same . . .

I took a deep breath and rolled him over. And gave myself a
long minute, squatting there, to assimilate and otherwise deal
with what I saw there.

Children live in a world they never made.

But adults have no such excuse; the world they live in is a
world they made and if it isn't one they like very much, well,
tough. With very few exceptions, indeed, the choices are your

own and the consequences of each decision are entirely predictable. Credit and blame alike are the earned portion of the man in
the mirror. But you don't have to like it.

The season of death was upon me.

I had come to Las Vegas for a game of high-stakes poker, but
seemed instead to spend most of my time looking upon the dead
faces of old acquaintances.

The man whose neck I had broken was Jorge de la Torre,
Little Trouble Martinez's sometime drinking and sparring partner
from Khe Sanh.

First Sergeant Big Trouble.

I left him where he had fallen and picked up the Uzi. Habit.
We were alone; if anyone else had been on the premises he
would have seized the moment to blow my fool head off long
ago.

But that didn't make sense.

At least four more people—the driver of the Trans Am, the
knife-thrower who had killed Happy Apodaca, the pilot of the
helicopter, and the door gunner—were in the play. Had to be.
Big Trouble couldn't have filled any of the slots because he had
the use of only one arm.

The other one was, as I had noticed while he was sleeping,
strapped to his chest with adhesive tape and I thought I knew
why. Ex-sergeant de la Torre would have been the killer who got
away after I broke his collarbone during the fight in the penthouse of the Scheherazade; escaped to the rooftop, leaving Little
Trouble to be picked off by the helicopter gunner.

But what the hell had he been doing there in the first place?

And why was I still alive . . . ?

Arranging the Uzi's sling over my right shoulder, I began a
systematic tour of the premises. Know the land, know the equipment, see what is available. Maybe even find a few answers.

Or maybe not. The first door I came to was locked. It was of
wood, like the space it guarded, and I decided a hard kick or two
might be in order. But later, perhaps. When I was wearing boots
again.

For the moment, curiosity was partially appeased by the view
through a mesh-covered window. This was the ammunition locker,
the old-fashioned powder magazine. Boxes of wood and crates
of steel were plainly labeled, .50-caliber armor piercing, .25
caliber small arms, .30 caliber military ball, 9 mm Parabellum,
frag grenades—British, American, and French types, no German

ones for some reason—ranged below a bin of concussion types and some police flash-bangs.

Shelves seemed to be stacked with larger items, self-propelled antitank missiles and similar nasties.

I moved on.

The Huey with the phony N.A.N.G. markings was at the back of the hangar, as I had surmised. I put my hand against the main engine compartment and was surprised to feel a little heat. That meant it had been running less than two hours ago. Odd. I'd expected it to be cold.

Time passes fast when you're having fun.

I checked the side door. It wasn't locked, but the machine gun and ammunition had been removed. Nothing sloppy about these troops. Someone competent in charge. I looked back to where Big Trouble was lying and remembered him and spent a moment or two wishing that I had the past couple of days to live over again, and that was depressing because, thinking about it, I realized that even if I did I would probably do most of the same things again, and the two Jorges would still be dead.

Knowing yourself is supposed to be an asset. And it is.

But no one ever said it would make you happy.

The rest of the hangar was probably about par for the course as small-scale private arsenals go. I'm no expert on the breed. But there was one little room—the only metal compartment in the building except for my late prison—that I couldn't get into, so of course I had to have a look. That's how we primates are put together. Check your local zoo.

On the way back to the guardroom, I stopped off at the john and used the key hanging outside that door to retrieve my clothing.

The coat and vest hardly seemed worth the effort, and I almost left the shirt behind as a matter of sanitary engineering. But the socks and boots were still in good shape and they were first priority if I was going to do any walking in the immediate future. And I hoped I would.

Big Jorge's pockets were empty.

As Little Jorge's had been.

But there was a key rack in the guardroom and I checked it out. Most of the items were clearly marked, and I pocketed the keys to the half-track's ignition system (what lunatic had installed locks on military hardware intended for irregulars?) and a couple of others I thought might be useful, but had to scan the labels a second time before finding the one I was really after. Or what I decided had to be it—the last key on the bottom of the rack and the only one without a label.

Crossing the hangar again, I spared another glance for the remains of Jorge de la Torre and decided we still had unfinished business.

Later, man . . .

The half-track was in good condition and only groaned a couple of times before starting; I let it warm up for a minute or two and then shut off the engine after making sure the fuel indicator was well toward the top. At least I wouldn't have to walk.

And then I went back to the mystery room.

The key slid easily into the lock, which I noticed was new, and turned what felt like a dead bolt without difficulty. But the knob below was original equipment, old and rusted and slightly out of alignment, and it gave me a moment or two of argument before giving way with a rush that sent me staggering off balance a full step into the space the door had been guarding. I muttered something that might have cost me an hour or two of vigil back in seminary and pulled the key loose and turned to give the room a quick once-over. And stopped breathing.

Two boxes sat on the table before me. One large, painted red. One small, painted yellow. Both labeled in French, but I didn't need an interpreter to recognize the stylized trefoils stenciled on their sides. Or to know what they implied.

The big box red would be the electronic half of the system. The detonator.

The little yellow one was the fissionable material. Enriched plutonium, if the label was to be believed.

Corner Pocket—and Interpol—had been right, after all. Sam Goines really did have an atomic bomb.

Past tense.

Now it was mine.

The boxes were heavy and I needed a hand truck to get the larger one over to the half-track, and then the problem of loading it into the bed was simply out of sight. No skip loader, no chain hoist. They must have humped it around by multiple manpower, but I was alone. And in a hurry.

So . . .

The red box came open easily enough. Just two clips at the top and two more on the sides. The device inside made no sense to me, but I hadn't thought it would. Dials, switches, and a shiny globe with wires running into it. Work of genius, most likely. Marvel of the age.

I tipped it out and smashed it to pieces with an emergency ax from the side of the half-track.

Some people like being a one-man atomic power.

Some don't.

When I was done, I picked up the pieces and tossed them into the vehicle, closed up the box and hefted it in, too—still heavy enough, even without its late contents—and put the heavy little yellow box in beside it. Then I went back to the guardroom.

Someone there had been a heavy smoker. Not Jorge, evidently; no matches or lighter or cigarette droppings in his pockets. But the ashtray was full of half-smoked butts, and beside it were the two items I'd hoped to find: a full pack of Marlboros and a book of matches. All right!

I removed the magazine key from its hook and went in there and made the arrangements I'd been planning while I was trying to deal with Sam Goines's private-enterprise nuclear capability. Then I went to the back of the hangar and began the easy but time-consuming work of tipping high-octane fuel drums on their sides and rolling them into positions where I thought they might do the most good.

And then it was time to finish my business with Big Trouble.

A lot of time had passed and a lot of changes might have taken place, but back in Vietnam Sergeant Jorge de la Torre had been a devout and believing Roman Catholic. I had resigned from the Episcopal priesthood before rejoining the army, and we had never discussed religious matters. But resignation does not cancel a priest's orders. Or relieve him of certain responsibilities.

I went back into the rest room and washed out a plastic tumbler I found there and then put a little more water in it and set it aside and went through the ritual of cleansing my hands and then said a few words over the water and took it and went back to kneel beside Big Trouble and began: "O God the Father, have mercy upon the soul of thy servant . . ."

It seemed to take no time at all . . .

And then it was time to go.

The big roller-doors were blocked from inside, and I pushed one out of the way and started up the half-track and drove it outside and left it grumbling there while I went back to attend to the final chores.

In the magazine, I checked the loose powder I had piled in the nearest ammo bin and made sure the paper towels covering it had no stray grains to foul things up and shorten my getaway time.

The place reeked of gasoline, but that was a deception. The stuff I had poured over the explosives was really kerosene—jet fuel for the Huey's engine—with a lower volatility that I was counting on to do the work on command rather than by accident.

I opened the cigarette pack and tapped one out and lighted it and choked on the first drag. But I took two more, to make sure it was burning well, and then used the cover of the matchbook to clamp the cigarette in position under the matches, with the burning end a millimeter or two away from the heads. I figured I had about ninety seconds, give or take a few one way or the other, before ignition.

Carefully, cautiously I set my improvised fuse in the middle of the paper towels. And ran for the half-track.

Its engine had stopped, and I had a moment of real panic wondering if the whole plan was going to backfire on me. But it started again as soon as I turned the key, and I hit the throttle and got away from there.

I had no idea where I was. But the helicopter hadn't needed much time to find us when I was having my little race with the Trans Am, so I guessed that we couldn't be too far from Las Vegas, and it didn't really matter for the moment. Everything in its season. Now was the time to run.

A road led off to the left and I took it, urging the old desert buggy to as much speed as it could manage and finding the headlight switch in the dark after only a couple of tries.

The speedometer was calibrated in kilometers (who had owned this thing last?) and I did the mental arithmetic that told me 70 km was something like 45 mph and tried to urge a little more speed, but the pedal was to the metal. Any way you sliced it, I wasn't going to be quite a mile away when things began to happen. I wished, irrelevantly, for my vanished wristwatch and its night-glowing dial and then wondered why. Knowing how much time had passed wouldn't change anything.

Still . . .

I began to count off the seconds, but that made no sense either and I was ready to have a real argument with myself when I heard the first explosion, and braked the half-track and ducked into the armor plating.

Which was just as well. The first blast hadn't been much, but the second was a head-rattler and touched off another wave of dizziness and disorientation even while it was triggering the other explosions I'd hoped for back in the hangar.

Something hit the side of the vehicle with a loud clang and went whining off into the night and I heard several other things hitting the ground nearby and then the night blossomed briefly into full daylight and I stuffed my fingers into my ears but it still wasn't enough to make the sound bearable, and the following blast-wave tilted the half track and probably moved its front wheels half a foot or so.

After that, the night quieted a little.

But I was in no hurry to make myself vertical and vulnerable again, and I lay still for a while, waiting for the light to die and thinking about what else had to be done before dawn and feeling very, very tired indeed.

At last, however, I forced myself to sit up and look around for the light-loom of the city. There it was—easily distinguished now from the still-bright flickering of the flames consuming what little was left of the hangar-aresnal—and I started up the half-track again and moved off toward Las Vegas, amusing myself a little with the thought of what kind of reaction I would get if I tried to park the thing in the VIP garage and then realizing that I was not only debarred from doing that but would need to find some likely hiding place for the old crock if I was going to use it in the way I was beginning to think I might.

Little by little, the lights ahead got brighter and the one behind continued to fade.

I took deep lungfuls of the night air and tried to get the taste of the cigarette out of my mouth and the scent of gasoline and gunpowder out of my nose, but it was no use.

They were facts of life. Reality.

Like so many other things I couldn't change, I was just going to have to live with them.

A SERMON (Continued)

Power? How odd that so many should pursue it so avidly. For each of us is powerful; the mind and the soul that distinguish us from other members of the animal kingdom are a source of power limited only by the scope of our dreams . . . and the prison of our fears.

28

GETTING INSIDE THE hotel promised to present problems of its
own.

Las Vegas innkeeping personnel are virtually shockproof. They
have seen it all. Twice. And coped.

But they are also trained to head off disaster before it can
occur, and in my present state of disrepair I would look like the
advance man for an earthquake. Security guards would pounce
on me at the door, and access to the premises would be granted
only at the price of a thorough identity check. Which would
mean questions. And I still didn't have a single answer that
would satisfy anyone, including me.

So I came in the back way, avoiding people in the rear parking
lot and heading for the subbasement door that Corner Pocket had
used when he brought me out to see Jorge Martinez's body
earlier in the day. Amazingly, it was still unlocked, and I ducked
through into cool darkness and stood still for a moment or two,
listening to the sound of my own pulse.

Waves of dizziness were still coming at fairly regular inter-
vals, and the distance I had walked since finding a likely place to
ditch the half-track hadn't helped much.

The wonder was that a cruising police car hadn't locked onto
the skinny one-eyed wreck wandering along the quiet sidewalks
in the wee hours of a moonless desert morning. Their questions
would have been as searching as those of the hotel personnel—
and just as unanswerable. I leaned against the doorjamb and
waited for the basement to stop playing games.

Key.

The key to my room had vanished along with everything else
I'd had in my pockets. All right, then. Get a spare from the room
clerk. Sure. And wait while he dials the emergency numbers for

269

hotel security, the police, the FBI, and a straitjacket. Thank you, no.

Well, then . . . ?

The dizziness gradually subsided, and I let myself have another lungful of conditioned air and put my full weight back on my feet and commanded my legs to move them forward. Toward someone who could help. And would.

Toward Maxey.

Luck is for losers. Marks and mooches talk about how their luck was good or how it was bad; they complain about it and hope for it and make jokes about it and build their lives around it and wonder why nothing ever seems to work for them. So depressing.

But not entirely unfounded.

The elevator that took me upstairs was unoccupied when its door opened in the subbasement, and there were no stops before Maxey's floor, and no one was walking around the corridor to see me and remember, either. Which was pure luck. As was the response when I hammered my knuckles under her room number.

The chance of her being in the room was not a good one. The odds on her being awake to hear the commotion were even worse.

But the door opened before I could knock a second time, and Maxey was smiling as she opened her mouth to greet whomever she had been expecting—and stopped short at the sight of me.

We played living statues for a moment.

"Hi, there," I said. "I was in the neighborhood and I wondered if you might need any Avon products . . ."

But Maxey had stopped smiling.

Snake-swift and accurate, her right hand reached out to grasp the remains of my coat and pull me inside. She slammed and locked the door as soon as I was out of the way and then turned to look me up and down with eyes that were pure violet wonder. I was out of words and out of ideas and if she wanted explanations we were both in for a big disappointment. But one of the best things about Maxey had always been her sense of priorities. First things first. I was hoping the passing years hadn't changed things too much, and from that angle her eventual vocal reaction was all that I could have hoped.

"Holy . . . *shit*!" she said.

Couldn't have put it better myself.

Priorities continued to hold the questions at bay for the next few minutes, while Maxey aimed me at a chair and let me collapse into it instead of holding still for the walkaround inspection that was clearly in prospect.

But it didn't keep her from forcing me to sit up while she removed what little was left of the coat, vest, and shirt—and it didn't keep her from muttering under her breath over assorted bruises, cuts, and scrapes as they were uncovered.

She was still shaking her head when there was another knock at the door, and I came to instant alert.

But she waved a restraining hand and jerked a thumb in the direction of the suite's mini-kitchen.

"Room service," she said in a quiet voice. "I was expecting them when you turned up. Just stay out of sight."

I did as I was told.

Door opening and word exchanges and tendering of tip took less than a minute and then the door closed again and I heard her throw the dead bolt.

"Talk about serendipity!"

I moved back into the living room to find Maxey carrying a tray decorated with a bucket of ice and a bottle of Raynal Napoleon. Now it was my turn to smile.

"Same ol' Maxey," I said. She had never been a heavy drinker, but I had a vivid memory of the Raynal bottle that was always on the sideboard in her apartment. No wine with meals, but once in a while an ounce of brandy afterward—or poured into the coffee. And, on widely spaced occasions, a nerve-calming sip at the end of a particularly improbable day.

"And a damn good thing, too," she said, moving the tray to the top of the handout bar between living room and kitchen and snapping the seal from the bottle with the ease of long practice.

"No," she said, heading me off as I moved back toward the chair. "Stand still a minute. I'm going to use some of this to disinfect you."

I shook my head.

"Wasted effort," I said. "And wasted brandy, too. That stuff's strictly for internal use, and anyway what I really need to do is get back into my room."

Maxey halted in mid-stride, bottle in hand, and regarded me with undisguised astonishment that turned almost instantly to real anger.

"You know," she said in a voice that would have frozen a

salamander, ''with just a little effort, you dumb son of a bitch
you could get to be a perfect stranger!''

Listening to what else she had to say, I could understand wh
she felt as she did. And what a good thing it had been that
hadn't risked coming in the front door.

Quite a bit had happened while I was away.

''First,'' she said, ''there was the judge. Little Happy Apodaca
They found his body with a knife in the chest—and those sam
five cards, too—down in the VIP garage. Right beside tha
rented car of yours. Which, of course, meant they came lookin
for you. And couldn't find you. So naturally you are now
suspect number one on their list.''

''Terrific,'' I said.

''There's more: About an hour after they took the judge away
the highway patrol found two big cars—limousines—turned ove
and on fire about ten miles south of town. No witnesses to wha
happened, of course. Nobody dumb enough to admit a thing lik
that. But when they got the fire put out and got inside there, the
found bodies. Seven of them. Cremated. But the license plate
on the cars and some stuff that didn't burn told them who
was.''

''Manny,'' I said, realizing that it wasn't a guess and that
might be the only one who still knew about the aces and eight
that had been in the envelope he got just before he tried to ge
out of town. ''Manny Temple and six of his buddies.''

The violet eyes never wavered. But the message I got was no
a happy one.

''Your friend, Singleton,'' she said. ''Corner Pocket. He'
going to want to hear what you know about this.''

I nodded.

''But later,'' I said.

She thought it over for a moment and went on without comment

''I heard all of that,'' she said, ''sitting here watching televi
sion, waiting for you to show up or call me about putting u
bail. Just waiting. And then, an hour ago, there was more. A
explosion, the news said. Out on the desert away from town, bu
a big one that got all kinds of people calling up the police to fin
out what was going on and making noises about another ato
bomb test or maybe an accident there at the test center.''

''That was me,'' I said.

She nodded solemnly.

''It figures,'' she said. ''But the hell of it is, then you turn u at my door and make like it's all some kind of a joke. Funny! Christ, I just wish you would kind of give me a little warning when you are going to do things like that.''

"Warning?''

"Yes, warning. You stupid bastard, I heard about the explosion and you were still missing and hadn't called me or let me know anything, so I put two and two together and I sent for that bottle of brandy to drink myself drunk.

"This morning—yesterday morning—was bad enough. When I thought you'd been shot, there in the penthouse. But twice in one day is too much. Just entirely too damn much.

"Why do you think I married Sam Goines instead of you all those years ago—just because he was going to be rich and you weren't? Idiot! It was a good enough reason, sure. But not the main one. I married Sam because if I stayed with you, I knew damn well there would come a day just like this one, when I'd get a phone call or hear some news or read a paper and there would be your name and all the details of how you'd finally found a really neat way to get killed.

"So now it's happened to me anyway. Twice over!

"God damn you, lover. God damn you to hell—I don't know whether to cry or swear or kiss you or kick your ass, but one thing for sure: I was right in the first place. You're not just stupid. And you're not just careless. And you're not just suicidal, either.

"What you are, you're just plain crazy!''

It's nice to know people care. By the time all the words were out, Maxey had managed to work herself into a fine Polish rage, and remembering a couple of those from years long past, I wondered if I might be safer taking my chances with a mob of contract killers.

But the moment passed and so did the anger, and Maxey's curiosity took control.

"So,'' she said when her breathing had slowed down again. "Aside from that, General Lee, how was your trip to Gettysburg?''

I grinned. And she grinned. And there was no more talk about trying to get back into my room. And as the first rays of light began to sprout around the silhouette of the hotel tower across the Strip, I gave her a thumbnail account of the evening, beginning with our missed dinner date and going on to Happy Apodaca's death and the chase out into the desert.

I edited the part about the hangar. Jorge de la Torre wasn't in it. I was alone out there, and there was no atom bomb and no half-track either. Just a car that I stole and drove back to town after arranging the explosion. It left gaps in the fabric, but if she noticed them she didn't mention it and I played the whole thing as straight as I could and finally we got back to the immediate problem of what to do with Preacher's beat-up carcass.

It was tired. And dirty. And getting kind of crumpled around the edges. Turn it in for a newer model, soon as the dealerships are open for the day. Trade up. Next time, a Schwarzenegger sedan.

Meanwhile: "Open," Maxey said, holding a two-finger dose of brandy in front of my nose.

"Maxey, I don't—"

"Open!"

I opened, and she poured.

"Now close," she said. "And swallow."

I did, happy to get the fiery lake off my tongue, and felt the lining of my esophagus dissolve as the liquid made its way down into the abdominal holding area, and exploded.

I took a deep breath. And another.

"God," I said. "In . . . heaven!"

Maxey nodded approvingly. "He's an applejack fancier, so I hear tell," she said. "Now walk—that way. Into the bedroom. Strip. And shower. All things considered, I don't think this would be a good time for me to ask room service for bandages and antiseptic, but unless there's some kind of internal damage or one of those is deeper than it looks, soap and hot water ought to do almost as well."

"But I don't—" I began.

"Lover," she said, settling her feet into a stubborn, hipshot posture I remembered well, "don't argue with me. You're a nice fella and plenty smart about a lot of things, but I'm the one with the nurse training. Remember?"

"Well—"

"Just do it."

She moved out of the way and I put one foot in front of the other in the direction of the door to her left and went through it and stopped cold on the other side.

The bedroom was a real specialty number.

Pink and peach, with an oversized round bed draped in water-fall tulle and the coverlet turned back to display silk sheets. There was a mirror on the ceiling, and through the doorway opposite I could glimpse a baronial-sized bathroom complete with a sunken heart-shaped tub.

I started to laugh and couldn't seem to stop.

Maxey's head angled inquiringly round the door frame. "If you're having hysterics in here," she said, "I am going to send for the house doctor, and that's for sure."

I tried to explain, but had to settle for shaking my head and waving a hand.

Maxey didn't get it.

She was looking more and more suspicious, and I supposed hysteria did have some part of the action, so I made a major effort and finally managed enough control to be able to speak again.

"The . . . room," I said.

"What the hell about it?"

"The room," I repeated, controlling another wave of mirth. "Do you think the hotel's own decorator did all this? Or did he have to call in a sex maniac?"

Kinky decor or no, the master bedroom of Maxey's suite was a soft and forgiving place—conspicuously short on hard edges and pointed corners—and I was grateful for that as I eased out of boots, socks, and trousers.

Of the lot, only the boots looked salvageable and I considered stuffing the rest into the wastebasket, but settled for dragging the pants onto one of the hangers and hanging them behind the mirrored door of the walk-in closet.

The man I saw when the door was closed again was not a bundle of charm.

He was a chiropractor's fantasy—an offhand collection of bones, more or less supporting a layer of sinew and skin. Living proof that humankind is close cousin to the other primates. Bend the knees, support the weight on the second knuckle of the fingers, and pick at the head lice. Do not feed the animals . . .

Cut it out, Preacher.

Go admire yourself on your own time.

Maxey seemed to be right. None of the visible damage looked especially serious, with the possible exception of a bruise I hadn't noticed before on the sole of my right foot. The final worldly legacy of Big Jorge de la Torre's neck, most likely. That would be the foot that had done the damage . . .

Suddenly the dizziness was back.

And my stomach came to an adverse decision about the brandy.
I got the toilet lid open just in time.

After that, things could only get better.

Splashing my face with cold water and rinsing my mouth and
wiping it all away, I found that I was able to think clearly and
coldly about things to be done during the next few hours.

First and foremost, there was the game.

Moving away from the lavatory, I reached into the shower and
pulled the central knob and turned the indicator all the way over
to hot and left it there while I shucked out of my undershorts and
hung them on a towel rack, wondering irrelevantly if it might not
be a good idea to wear them into the stall and wash them along
with everything else.

But that was a logical thought, and the thought of logic
brought me back to focus on the game.

Still first and foremost.

Decency, propriety, sanity—and logic—all demanded that it
be demoted, relegated to a far lesser priority. But the back part
of the mind, the division that does the best and most important
work with the least expenditure of time and effort, was hammering on the table and stamping its feet and making threats. So all
right, already! Leave it there. At the top.

The shower was hot now, and I reached in and turned the
knob the other way and gave it a three count to turn stinging cold
and then forced myself to step inside.

It was like an electric shock.

But it cleared away the last of the cobwebs and the dizzies and
settled the world firmly back on its base and made the transition
even sweeter when I finally allowed myself to inch the pointer
back toward warm. And then warmer.

The game tonight would tell all.

Never mind logic.

Never mind correlation of all the factors and touching all the
bases. Poker is an obsession and a weapon and an art and a tool
of matchless potency and precision. A tool to my hand. Tonight . . .

Movement. Behind me.

Standing flat-footed and relaxed in the shower, allowing the
balm of water and steam and warmth to do their work, I was
deaf to any small sounds that might have given early warning.
As it was, the only perception was of a minor disturbance in the

air as the shower door opened and closed behind me. I tensed
. . . and then relaxed again.

Bare arms, deeply tanned and strong, surrounded my chest
and pinned my upper arms, pressing twin circles of warmth
against my back.

"Abajo con tus pantalones," Maxey said.

"Already attended to," I said.

"Well, now, is that a fact?"

A SERMON (Continued)

The only obstacle—the only encumbrance in our path—is the one we have put there ourselves. We must reject the lie, must break through the prison wall of fantasy, put away the dream world that our fears have made.

29

WE SLEPT THROUGH the morning and woke just after noon and made love again and slept again, and when I woke a second time was alone between the peach-pink sheets.

There had been no dreams.

And there had been no strangeness between us; time had taken a vacation. Whatever had been seemed still to be. Older, perhaps. Warmer. More accepting. But recognizable still, and compelling in a way that was familiar yet very new.

No doubts. And no reservations.

I sat up, wincing a bit as my feet touched the carpeting but not prepared to make an issue of it. What can't be cured must be endured—and days like this one make the trip worthwhile.

Blackout curtains kept the bedroom in a state of semidarkness, but the door was open and through it I could see the slanting benediction of a setting sun.

Time for breakfast.

I stood up and stretched and yawned jaw-breakingly and noticed several bruises I hadn't before and decided to treat them as the ancient Greeks had. With contempt. I strode from the bedroom, looking for Maxey to complain about the service—fire that blighter, Jeeves; never around when you want him—but discovered I was on my own.

Not even a note.

Very well, then, a grown man ought to be able to fend for himself even in the wilds of a luxury hotel. I went into the little kitchen and began to forage.

But the full-size refrigerator set the tone: six bottles of Perrier, unopened jar of cocktail olives, ditto cocktail onions, two small bottles of cologne, and something called Facial Toning Rinse.

I closed it and turned to the upper cabinets.

One contained party glasses—virtually unlimited quantities of

cellophane-wrapped plastic highball, lowball, wine, and hollow
stem champagne glasses all bearing the ersatz crest of the
Scheherazade. Its next-door neighbor was more elegant: dinner
plates, cups, and saucers for eight, Scheherazade crest on the
upper surfaces and a startling Haviland imprint on the bottoms.
Touch of class there. Or a working agreement with the Union
Corse.

Silverware and cooking utensils were where they should have
been, crowding the drawers just under the countertop, and the
cabinets below were filled with the various pots, pans, colan-
ders, and kettles of gourmet technique.

But no food.

Not even instant coffee.

The remedy was, of course, ready to hand. Just dial room
service. They deliver.

But they also talk. And ask questions.

No . . .

Desperate, I went back to the refrigerator for a second
look. The cocktail olives were beginning to seem almost palatable, but I resisted the urge and opened the freezer door
instead.

And stood gazing at its contents for a long, long time.

No frozen food. Not even ice cubes. But the space was
occupied nonetheless. Maxey had always been a meticulous
housekeeper—no dishes left in the sink, no undusted corners.

The six sticks of dynamite were carefully wrapped in a cello-
phane bag, with silica gel desiccant.

And so were the electric blasting caps.

I was wearing the remains of my clothing when Corner Pocket
arrived with the key to my room.

He had returned my call to his office within minutes and
retrieved the key without questions and I should have offered at
least a word or two of thanks, but we rode the elevator to my
floor in a silence doubly enforced by the presence of an elderly
couple who had evidently just returned from the hotel's golf
course.

His approach shots had been sloppy and she was being properly supportive. And I was grateful.

I hadn't shown Corner Pocket what was in the freezer compartment because I didn't want to discuss the matter with him

until I was able to sort it out in my own mind, and I had been in a hurry to get out of there because I didn't want to discuss it with Maxey yet, either.

Sufficient unto the day . . .

Once inside my own room, of course, all bets were off as far as Corner Pocket was concerned.

"What the hell?" he demanded.

So I told him. Part of it, anyway: the aces and eights that had been delivered to Manny Temple, the murder of Happy Apodaca, the hangar-arsenal in the desert. But, as with Maxey, I edited, omitting the part about Jorge de la Torre.

And the atom bomb.

"Nice people," he said when I was done. "And I don't suppose I have to tell you that you're luckier than a seven-roll chump."

"No," I said. "You don't."

We stood looking at each other in silence for a moment, and I couldn't help wondering how lucky he'd think I was if he knew the rest of the story.

Maxey.

Oh, Christ . . . Maxey!

But talking about it wasn't going to help anyone or anything, and before the moment could get too long or the silence too heavy I turned away and stripped, checking to make sure my other suit had been cleaned and returned to its rack—it had—and that everything else I would need was in readiness.

All right, then.

First the eye: I took the spare from its case and, noticing Corner Pocket's reaction, went into the bathroom to go through the routine of putting it into place. Everyone has his limits.

Then another shower. Alone this time. To wash away the last trace of the scent that seemed to linger and cling. And clear my mind for the night's work.

Corner Pocket had hitched a ride to the hotel in a police car—as usual—and so we went to the game in my rented wheels. Which was just as well. He knew where it was and I didn't.

Francis Carrington Shaw had made the arrangements; this time we would be playing in one of the individual villas near his own on the grounds of El Cholo Loco. And this time we would be taking no chances.

Cars bearing the seal of something called Beehive Security, Inc., were parked, not unobtrusively, in position to form quick roadblocks on all access roadways, and a discerning eye could pick out various parts of the landscape that had been cleared for what a combat infantryman would recognize in a moment as textbook-quality fields of fire, each with its own guardian, alert and ready.

I looked around for antiaircraft guns and couldn't spot them, but decided that was only because of effective camouflage.

Francis Carrington Shaw did not do things by halves.

We were not the last to arrive, but we were not the first, either.

The Voice of Heaven—gray faced and sweat-shaky, but evidently still obedient to his Master's voice—was seated in one of the chairs arranged around a kidney-shaped casino poker table, staring at the array of chips racked in its center. He looked up when we walked in, but didn't speak, and I turned my attention to the blank-faced youngster seated in the dealer's chair.

Close-cropped hair and pink-scrubbed cheeks and blinding-white T-shirt all proclaimed him a member of Shaw's Mormon Mafia.

I looked a question at Corner Pocket and he shrugged.

"Last time, playing without a dealer," he said, "things didn't seem to go so well, what I hear. So the Man thought it might go better if one of his own troops did the shuffling and dealing for us. Just to keep the party polite."

We both glanced at the Voice of Heaven to see if he had anything to add. But he didn't.

I'm not even sure he heard.

But Corner Pocket's choice of words raised another question.

"You're in the game this time?" I said.

"On a pass. Yes."

I nodded thoughtfully. Some game. I would be playing Shaw's hand with Shaw's money. Corner Pocket the same. And probably the Voice of Heaven, too. Four chairs. The colonel would have to be crazy to walk into a setup like this.

But of course he might not show.

The atom bomb he was supposedly selling us tonight was no longer available. Would he know that and stay away?

I turned the idea over in my mind for a moment or two, trying to see it from his angle, but there were still too many unknowns.

Francis Carrington Shaw had spoken of Colonel David Connor as though he believed the bearded man was acting as agent for the actual possessor of the stolen weapon. But Shaw must also have considered the possibility that the colonel was representing no one but himself.

And if he was—and the more I thought about it the more likely it seemed—then he would be out of the country, or at any rate out of sight, by now.

If Shaw's assumption was correct, though, and the colonel was acting for someone else, then there was always a chance that poor communication or some other factor might cause him to walk back into the steel-lined spiderweb that had been woven around us. And if he did that, there might even be a game. Of sorts. Though certainly not the one that had been proposed.

I sat down in one of the chairs and stared first at my hands and then at the chips and then into the middle distance, awaiting the turn of events.

It was a short wait.

Outside the door, a walkie-talkie buzzed in the hand of a guard I hadn't known was there and he answered in a low voice and a moment later we heard the sound of a car approaching. Stopping. A door opened and closed, and footsteps approached.

"Got to hand it to you yobbos," Colonel David Connor said, striding through the door with a wide smile half concealed in his beard. "Security around here's tighter than a cow's butt in fly time . . ."

Reactions to that were not much.

The Mormon dealer glanced up momentarily from the card deck he had been shuffling and reshuffling, gave the late arrival a good eyeful of bright-cheeked nothing, and returned his attention to his hands. The Voice of Heaven blinked. And neither Corner Pocket nor I seemed to be able to think of anything to say.

But the colonel was all smiles.

"Well, then," he said, "I guess we're ready to play some cards, are we? Let's see . . . everyone understand the stakes?"

He looked brightly at Corner Pocket and then at me, but spoke again before either of us could answer.

"Oh, by the bye, Preacher," he said. "Speaking of stakes, I have something that might interest you. A kind of added premium for the game, as it were. What do you think?"

He reached into his pocket and handed me a color photograph.

It was a Polaroid, slightly out of focus, but recognizable. Someone had taken a picture of Maxey. Quite recently.

She was in a room I didn't recognize. Tied to a chair. Gagged. Blue-violet eyes terrified and blazing an appeal for help that was far louder than a scream.

A SERMON (Continued)

Reality, and the determination to accept it, is the key: To see the world as it is, and to find our own place in it—dealing with that which is real. This is power. Seize it!

30

I WAS THE only one who saw the picture, and I handed it back to the colonel without comment and we sat down at the table and handed our money to the fresh-faced dealer and waited for him to count out the chips and after a few minutes we were ready to play.

By general agreement the game, as before, was seven card stud. Ante $100, with a forced opening and straddle.

A single red chip—the button, used to indicate the theoretical dealer position for purposes of the game—began its rounds to the left of the actual dealer, and we began to play. Or, anyway, the colonel and I did.

Corner Pocket and the Voice of Heaven might as well have been in Peoria. They were only playing for money.

But for the first hour or so nothing much seemed to be happening.

Corner Pocket lost what he probably thought of as a big one—nearly $100,000, a chance he'd never have taken with his own money—to the colonel, who showed real finesse in running what turned out to be a cold bluff.

Not that anyone else at the table knew it. And the only reason I did was that he was showing four cards of a closed-end straight and two of the cards he'd needed to fill were already visible in someone else's hand, while the others were the concealed low pair that I'd folded after the second round of betting.

Nice technique.

But once again I found myself struggling with that peculiar sense of familiarity, of having met the colonel—or someone whose poker game was similar—somewhere before. But I couldn't put a face with the memory. And the beard he was wearing was as effective as an old-fashioned bandanna mask. Jesse James in a bush jacket . . .

Half an hour later, we finally came head-to-head.

I was in the trapping position, to the left of the dealer button, with queen-jack concealed and ten-nine showing. I stayed with it through a deuce and a seven and by that time my only company was the colonel, with three deuces and a king. One other king was gone, which left a good chance that both of us were chasing the same card.

He bet like a man with at least one more kowboy, and I hesitated for a moment before buying my final card, which was an eight.

Well, okay, then. Not exactly what I'd hoped for, and there were still three kings roaming around the countryside somewhere, one or more of them perhaps in the colonel's hand.

But you just don't fold a queen-high straight.

Not when the pot is already up to $26,000. The trips he was showing were best, so he bet first: $5,000.

I wanted to raise.

And if he'd pushed in another $26,000, or even $10,000, I might have done it. That kind of betting would have indicated a probable desire to buy me out of the pot, make it too rich for whatever kind of fighting hand I thought I had.

A mere $5,000, on the other hand, gave the opposite message. It could signal a desire to milk the hand, bring the Preacher along step by step into the trap instead of edging him out. And both could be mere artistry.

That's poker . . .

I counted a $10,000 raise out of the stake on the table before me and got no response of any kind from the colonel and counted the chips again. Still nothing. So I picked up half of the $10,000 and pushed it in, to call.

But I never found out what cards he had concealed. The three deuces were all he wanted to show. Fair enough. I flipped my concealed queen-jack and eight face up and raked in the $36,000. The colonel smiled a little and pushed the remainder of his hand toward the dealer.

"You could have had more," he said. "I was willing to go the distance."

"Maybe," I said.

"It's not even your money."

"While it's on the table, it's nobody's money," I said. "While it's on the table, it's just a way of keeping score."

"If you say so," he said.

And the button moved and we anted again and the game went on.

Twice more in the next hour, the colonel and I found ourselves alone in sizable pots. And twice more we bet into each other—with mixed results.

He was holding an unexpected fifth club the first time, and finding out about it cost me $30,000.

The second time, he had three kings with one concealed and I had two low pair in the open and we bumped the action to about $70,000, with Corner Pocket and the Voice of Heaven standing doggo on the sidelines, and finally it came to showdown and his trips were high and good, but not as good as the third card to one of my pair, which gave me a full boat and the pot.

Call it almost even.

The game had been going on for more than two hours. But it still hadn't gotten serious.

Both of us seemed to be waiting.

Not that the other two players were just sitting around in their chairs. Corner Pocket played a good conservative game with cool and knowledgeable appraisal of the chances, and if his pile of chips seemed slowly to dwindle, it was because the cards just weren't running for him yet. Given a full night or more of play, that condition would rectify itself and he seemed to have the good sense to wait it out with the patience that is the recognized First Commandment of Poker.

Meanwhile the Voice of Heaven on Earth was actually having a pretty good night.

The first few hands had seemed to draw him back from whatever nightmare he had been living through when we first arrived, and as time passed he seemed almost able to submerge himself in the game. Three or four times he was able to milk moderate hands for respectable sums, and for almost an hour—until the colonel trapped him into a betting match he couldn't win and nearly couldn't get out of, either—buying three out of four pots on the second round by moving in heavily before the other players' hands were fully developed.

The colonel's move broke him of that habit, and immediately afterward he made the first of what turned out to be a series of visits to the bathroom, and when he came back, the shine in his eyes told me everything I needed to know about what had happened in there.

But the twin demons of bereavement and guilt were temporarily blocked and held at a distance, and that was probably all to the good. Or as good as he was ever going to let it be.

Time passed.

The dealer changed to a new deck and dumped the old one into the basket beside his foot, and play resumed.

I waited for the colonel to make his move.

And he waited for me to make mine.

The gloves finally came off an hour or so after midnight.

The colonel and I were alone in the third round of a pot that had grown to more than $200,000 before the Voice of Heaven finally dropped out, and now we were bidding for the fourth exposed card.

He had paired fours and an ace.

I had three clubs exposed, not in sequence, and another concealed.

His pair had bet $50,000 and I had bumped it $10,000 to see what he wanted to do, and he came back with my $10,000 plus $40,000 more and I needed only a moment or two to decide my hand was worth the money. So I pushed in the chips and the dealer gave him an ace, for two pair showing.

My $100,000 had bought a useless jack of hearts.

I took it without comment and waited for him to lead off. But he took his time, and that was all right with me because I had two bits of information he didn't: My hole cards were a four of clubs and the ace of diamonds, and the fourth ace was already gone.

Unless he had the last four in the hole, his only chance was to catch it on the final card . . . which is pretty long odds. But the pot was big enough, and he was in deep enough, to make it worth thinking about. The wait went on for a minute. And then two. And then three. He still had a good stake in front of him and could buy more chips after the hand was done if he had to. But money wasn't the object here, and we both knew it. Somehow he had to get a piece of information from me—get me to put it in the pot against the picture he had shown me before we started to play. And in the end I think that was the deciding factor.

He pushed $50,000 into the center of the table and looked at me. I matched it, and the dealer gave us our final cards.

His got a single glance, and then nothing. His face was still unreadable, and I had to admire the control.

My own seventh card hadn't been the club I needed. But it had paired one of my hole cards . . . and left the colonel with a tactical decision to bend the mind. I had caught the four of hearts.

His hand was still best.

But he didn't know it.

I sat still and wondered how he would handle the problem: The next few minutes would tell me more about him than I could have found out reading a private detective's report. He riffled the chips, back-rolled one of them a couple of times, counted his total stake, looked suddenly at me and then away. And opened with $50,000.

My turn.

The bet he'd made was good technique. Excellent, in fact. Too high to indicate lack of confidence, but low enough to look a lot like a man trying to milk a winner. All things being equal, it should have worked—convinced me that he had a full house, and driven me out of the pot.

But all things weren't equal.

I drummed my fingers, looking at his cards and at the pot and then at him again—and pushed my whole stake into the center of the table.

Still no message from the colonel's *wa*. But his hands relaxed for a moment of inner exultation and then tightened once more— ready for the big moment of the game. Ready to win.

He had been dropping occasional hands for the past hour or so, and the pile of chips in front of him was too small to cover my bet. He counted it and looked at the pot and waited, but I wanted the words to come from him.

"Table stakes, Preacher," he said. "I'm forty thousand short. You'll have to pull some back if you want to call."

I shook my head.

"You're still holding," I said. "The picture you showed me. It's there on the table."

He almost licked his lips, but now was the time to find out how I wanted to handle the bet we had come there to make. So he asked.

"The picture's worth more than forty," he said. "To me, anyway."

"Maybe."

"You're holding, too."

All right. The only thing left on my side of the table except for the seven cards was an envelope, blank faced and sealed, that I had taken from my inside coat pocket and placed there when we sat down to play. He knew what had to be in it. But he wanted to hear it from me.

"Nothing in the envelope but a note," I said. "With an address on it. Your picture doesn't have that."

His eyes thought it over, and his hand went into the side pocket of his jacket and brought out another blank envelope, and he wrote something on the back of the picture, shielding the writing with his hand, and put it in the envelope and sealed it.

"Now there's an address," he said.

"Then let's do it," I said.

And he almost did.

The sealed envelope went down beside the chips and the hands moved in behind the whole mass to push it into the center and there was no way I was going to raise or call that bet. The bluff he thought he was running was really no bluff at all, whether he knew it or not. His two pair really were best. But at the last moment he hesitated. And thought it over. And backed off.

"On second thought," he said, relaxing and taking his hands away from the chips, "maybe not. Maybe you've really got some cards over there . . ."

He shook his head. "You're a good player, Preacher. Better than I remembered. Better than they told me. And lucky. Thanks, but no thanks. I think that's as far as I want to go this time."

He favored me with a broad smile and leaned back, stretching and clasping his hands behind his head.

And suddenly I could see him.

Clearly.

The way a man plays poker is individual, unique to him alone, and does not change with time. It can grow and it can be honed and refined and sharpened. But, like handwriting or fingerprints, the basic pattern remains.

In that instant, the elements of the cards and the betting and the intelligence behind them had finally merged and showed me the face that had been hidden behind the beard across the table.

Told me what kind of game I had been playing ever since I got to Las Vegas.

And who had been playing the other hand.

The Voice of Heaven had made another of his regular visits to the bathroom and returned bright-eyed, but his grasp of ongoing events was getting closer and closer to zero. I could understand—dimly—why Francis Carrington Shaw had wanted him in the first game. But why had he put him in this one?

Corner Pocket, however, was something else again.

As a poker player he was about amateur-average, just right for Friday nights in the neighborhood. But he knew exactly what was going on around him and I was sure he had heard and understood most of what had passed between the colonel and me. Except for the most important part . . . and that was still mine alone.

I hugged the knowledge to me and tried to keep my face composed and my emotions under control, playing cards with the front of my mind while fitting all the pieces together in the back room.

Full understanding is a luxury, though. It could wait. The chance to use what I knew—at once and with real effect—came just a few hands later.

Corner Pocket's luck had seemed to be changing and he was still in the pot after the third round, showing three sevens against the colonel's five-six-nine of hearts and the paired kings and lone queen that had kept me in the pot. He offered $5,000 for a look at the sixth card, caught the eight of hearts. And folded.

I winced, and the colonel favored me with what might have been a wry smile.

"Takes all kinds," he said.

I didn't reply. My pair was next and I paid to find out if I could improve; worth the money, since one of my hole cards was another queen and I hadn't seen either of the others fall as yet. I pushed my checks in and the card I had bought was a trey, which was just dandy because I had another one in the hole beside the concealed queen. But all it did was give me three pair. No improvement.

The colonel paid and caught a deuce. Of hearts.

That's why they call it gambling.

My kings were still technically best, no matter what the realities of the situation, which left me facing an immediate

unch. The chances of improvement were excellent. No doubt
out that. Any one of three cards would give me a winning
nd; Corner Pocket's eight of hearts had removed any chance
at the colonel could pick up a straight flush. But the colonel's
ance of improvement was still just as good as mine. Several
arts were gone, to be sure. But several were left, too.

I counted $50,000 and pushed it into the center of the table.

The colonel looked at it.

And at me.

And grinned.

"All right, then," he said. "Let's boogie!"

He counted a hundred of the dove-gray $500 chips, pushed
em into the pot, and waited for the dealer to do his thing. The
al cards arrived before us, face down.

Mine was another trey.

I concentrated on breathing, taking over manual control for a
oment or two until *saika* was in control of the *tanden* reflex
nter.

His face told me nothing and his *wa* was, as before, too
eply layered to touch. But for the moment it didn't matter.

For now, the problem was to see how far the hand could be
ilked. Perfect cards rarely present perfect opportunities, even
 draw poker; I have caught the occasional royal flush in my
ne but never yet made any real money on one. In fact, the
ghest single score I ever racked—in the millions, believe it—
as on a stingy little two pair that wouldn't ordinarily have been
orth a first-round bet. Hell of a game.

I stacked up another $50,000 and pushed it forward.

The colonel's face didn't change.

But his hands were ready, and I could see that he had made all
e decisions he needed to make. He didn't believe the cards and
 didn't believe my bet, and he wanted to take full advantage.
he only question was whether I was more likely to bite on a
w bet or a high one—raise me enough to keep me coming, or
 for broke and take a chance on scaring me off?

He went for a $50,000 raise.

My turn.

Poker table dramatics are an art in their own right. Less is
ually best, and interpretation depends more on small gestures
an on spoken lines or facial expression. In this case, I was
ing an impression of a man caught bluffing and trying to
uster his way out of it. So I spent nearly a minute studying a

pot I had already counted, and taking another peek at hole ca
I could have recited in my sleep. And fiddled with a button
my coat. And riffled a double stack of chips and merged the
with one hand.

And bumped the action another $50,000.

He looked at the money and at me. He was still short. Meeti
my raise would cost the rest of his chips—and bring us back
the point we'd almost reached the last time we'd bumped hea
But this time he had the cards. He grinned at me and pushed t
whole pile into the pot, dropping the envelope that contained t
picture on top.

"Guts, Preacher?" he said.

I looked at him for a long minute and tried to feel somethi
and was surprised to discover that I couldn't. Too much h
happened. Too many years and too many decisions and too mu
money and too much power. And too many deaths.

There was nothing to say as I picked up my own envelope a
placed it on top of his. And waited for him to turn the only o
of his hole cards that mattered.

His seventh card was the king of hearts, which filled up
flush, and he favored me with the widest smile he'd allow
himself all night.

"No bluff this time, Preacher," he said.

I didn't smile back.

"You're still not out of here," I said. "And the place
crawling with security types who look like a SWAT team. H
do you figure to get past them?"

His smile never wavered.

"No problem," he said. "You'll walk me out. That's wh
told the Man I wanted you to play his hand in this game
because I could trust you not to welsh. You're a man of hon
Preacher."

It was a nice speech, and it might even have been true. Bu
shook my head.

"You take a lot for granted," I said. "Too much . . ."

I turned my own seventh card to show the full house—ki
and treys—that it had built for me and let him look at it fo
minute. His face froze and so did the hand he had moved i
position to rake in the pot.

"And you're still a bluffer," I said when I was sure he w
listening again. "You were bluffing when you came here, beca
you and I both know you didn't have an atom bomb to bet wi

omeone stole it last night. And you were bluffing about Maxey,
o, weren't you?''

Corner Pocket suddenly came to life and started to ask a
uestion of his own, but what he saw in my face seemed to stop
im.

The colonel shrugged. ''She's safe,'' he said, ''in her suite at
e Scheherazade.''

I nodded.

''Always bet into a known bluffer,'' I said. ''Nick the Greek
alled that the Third Commandment of Poker. But until a few
inutes ago, I thought I was playing against someone called
olonel Connor, so I guess I can be forgiven for taking so long
 obey it. And in a way I'm kind of grateful.

''It's not every day a man gets to be present for an honest-to-
od resurrection. Maybe we ought to have a moment of prayer.

''Or maybe not.

''Gentlemen, won't you all say hello to our old friend, Samuel
lemens Goines . . . back from the dead, and still bluffing.''

A SERMON (Concluded)

Accept reality! And . . . have a nice eternity.

31

HERE WAS A moment of silence. And then everyone tried to talk at once. And then more silence.

And then the colonel laughed.

"Sam Goines is dead," he said. "You saw him, and so did Corner Pocket, here. Both of you were at the hospital when he—"

"Terry McDuff is dead," I said, cutting him off in mid-lie. "Terrence Lyle McDuff, a poor little road-company actor who never had any luck in his whole life."

Corner Pocket was boiling over, ready to explode in my face, and I turned to him with the first real apology of the day.

"I played cards against McDuff all night and all morning and never knew he wasn't really Sam until he was dead," I said. "And even then I didn't know who he really was or what was going on. Saying I'm sorry isn't much—"

"No, it's not," Corner Pocket said.

"—but it's all I have to offer."

The colonel wasn't done. "No apologies needed on either side," he said. "I'll lay it out for you again, and I want you to know I can prove every word I say: Sam Goines is dead. And he is going to stay that way."

I turned back to face him and waited for him to go on.

"Identity, in the part of the world where we live," he said, "is vestigial. You carry it with you, in your wallet. Or get it out of a file somewhere. Documents and forms, tenuous enough back in the days when it was all on paper. But at least the paper was real. Now even that much reality is gone, and the bits of data that say who is who are all on magnetic tape or disks, waiting for the program user to make them real again."

Corner Pocket shook his head emphatically.

"It won't fly, Colonel," he said. "Somewhere there's a record still on paper. Something . . ."

The colonel nodded, no longer smiling but still confident. "(
course some of it's still on paper," he said. "The original bir
certificate. Some school records. Pictures in an old high scho
annual. Things like that. But they don't count."

"They—"

"They show faces and achievements," the colonel went on
"But not identity. Those records are different—fingerprints ar
dental X rays. All on microfiche. And therefore vulnerable."

"Your foot," I said. "The toes you lost in Vietnam. That
how I knew the man who died in the hospital wasn't Sa
Goines."

The colonel smiled again.

"Sure it was," he said. "Check those records today, an
they'll show Sam Goines was in that hospital for an appended
tomy. And you'll find the scar to prove it on his body."

"While David Connor—"

"—was in a naval hospital at San Diego recovering fro
several bullet wounds, one of which resulted in the loss of
couple of toes. No, Preacher. No, no. Sam Goines is dead, jus
as he was intended to be."

I looked at the man who had been my friend and wondere
how he had gone so far. Had it always been there inside him
hidden and waiting? Or had it come later? Seven people, seve
human beings with lives and friends and hopes and memories
had died in two days and if he hadn't pulled their chains person
ally, he had given the orders. And it was nothing to him, just a
plan carried out. A matter of efficiency.

So maybe he was right after all.

Sam Goines—the man I had known—was well and truly dead.

Requiescat in pace.

Good-bye . . .

Maxey had spoken of Las Vegas as Sam's killing ground.
Recalling the phrase now, I found myself wondering.

"The game," I said. "That first one, at the Scheherazade.
It wasn't just to get rid of Sam Goines. Those aces and
eights . . ."

The bearded man's mouth quirked in the half-promise of a
smirk.

"Stage dressing," he said. "Pure stage dressing. You were
out there on the balcony playing hero. I was inside staying alive.
And I saw the last hand you showed Holy Joe, here, and
remembered Francis Shaw's love affair with Wild Bill Hickok.

The thing there in the penthouse had gone wrong; I grabbed the cards and put them on DiMarco's chest as a distraction . . . and the cops ate it up so well that I made sure they never went hungry again.''

I'd wondered if it might have happened that way, but there was more I wanted to know.

"That was the play, then? Everyone in that penthouse suite was supposed to die—except you?''

The colonel's answer was immediate and indignant.

"Don't be a fool," he said. "Of course not! Remember who the gunners were?''

I remembered.

And understood. And realized what I would have to live with for the rest of my life.

"God damn you, Goines!" I said. "God damn you—and God forgive you, too. Because I never will!''

The colonel seemed genuinely taken aback.

"Without admitting anything at all," he said, "Martinez and the other one were only two out of several hundred men who could have been picked for the job. My contacts are more extensive than Sam Goines's ever were.''

"But you picked Big Trouble and Little Trouble," I said.

His face turned bland.

"Someone picked them," he replied. "Someone who had your best interests at heart. Someone who went to the trouble of finding a couple of mercs who knew you personally. Who could be trusted to see that you survived.''

"But . . . why?''

The colonel shrugged. "You were there on a pass," he said. "Francis Carrington Shaw had set the game up to get back the atom bomb that had been stolen from Goines. All the other people at the table belonged to him. Who knows? Maybe Sam Goines just thought he ought to have a friend of his own on the premises.''

But now I could see the whole outline, and it was no go.

"More bluff," I said. "And more lies. I was there as a convincer, someone to tell people—like Corner Pocket—that the man who got killed was Sam Goines. No matter what Shaw thought, no one was ever going to give him the bomb he wanted. Not then. And not now.''

The colonel opened his mouth, ready to give back as good as he was getting. But I think he saw the answer in my face. And kept quiet.

"There never was a bomb," I said.

Corner Pocket started to object. "Interpol—" he began.

"Interpol only knows what it's told," I said. "Television hype notwithstanding, it's just a kind of information network. Doesn't do its own investigations. So when the French government said it had lost an atomic weapon and offered the thief's suicide note as evidence, Interpol accepted the story at face value. They hadn't played poker against Sam Goines.

"What were you going to do with the dud, Sam—set up in business as an independent nuclear power, or just go in for a little quiet terrorism?"

The colonel stirred. "I keep telling you," he said, "Sam Goines is dead. Kaput. Finished."

"And so's his nuclear potential," I said, letting it pass. "But how'd he wind up with an ersatz bomb in the first place?"

You could see him decide not to answer and then change his mind. What had happened still seemed to rankle. Nobody more righteous than the hustler who's been hustled.

"The French," he said, with an audible edge in his voice, "couldn't organize a piss-up in a brewery. And that goes double for their army. It's an open secret—in some circles, anyway— that half their so-called independent nuclear force is bullshit because they don't have and can't seem to make enough weapons-grade cores. For what it's worth, the little bastard who stole the thing for me was as big a con man as anyone. The warhead he came up with was one of their phonies—all the electronics in place and in good working order, but a core made of pure industrial-quality lead."

Corner Pocket looked incredulous, but I nodded, still looking at the bearded man.

"I can testify to that," I agreed. "I took an ax to the electronic components before I left that neat little hangar-arsenal out there in the desert. Just for luck. But driving the old half-track around the boonies, maybe it was the night air finally got my brain working and I noticed I hadn't seen any radiation dosimeters or other safety items around. And it got me to wondering . . ."

The colonel actually smiled again. "So you used the scintillometer from the half-track's prospecting kit—"

"And it told me that the stuff in that little yellow box was slightly less radioactive than the desert sand. All that trouble. For nothing."

The colonel shook his head. "Not for nothing," he said.

But before he could go on he was interrupted by another voice; one that did not come from any source in the room.

"No, indeed," it said, in a paper-dry husk I recognized. "Not for nothing. To the contrary, sir!"

This was Francis Carrington Shaw's home turf. Naturally he would want to come to the party.

"The objective was power," Shaw's voice went on. "Power of a kind beyond even the dreams of most men."

I did a visual area-search of the room and located the sound source without too much trouble. Furnishings in the room were Spartan but elegant. The Empire breakfront against the far wall had seemed solid at first glance, but now I could see that a part of its scrollwork was pierced in the pattern of a medium-sized speaker . . . and what had seemed to be a keyhole in the face of the third drawer was actually the opening for a television camera lens.

Nothing is private in Las Vegas.

"A dud bomb's no power," I said, turning to face the camera.

The dry voice snorted something that might have been a cynical laugh.

"If you believe that," it said, "then I wonder that you are able to make a living at poker. In my day, the ability to bluff was as much a part of the poker player's armament as his ability to estimate odds."

"And it still is," I agreed. "But like any powerful weapon, it is best used with discretion. And sparingly. That's where Sam Goines always went wrong. He was basically a crapshooter; playing poker, he bluffed so often that no one would let him get away with it. That won't work with an atom bomb."

"Won't it?"

"No. Because sooner or later someone will call your hand, and you'll have to show openers or fold."

Another desiccated laugh. "Nicely put, sir," he said. "Nicely put. But inaccurate. Don't you read the newspapers?"

"I read them."

"Every major power on earth," Shaw's voice said, "now poses a nuclear threat of one kind or another. Even without a rocket delivery system, it is potent because components can be smuggled to a sensitive point—the center of New York City, for instance, or London or Paris or even Moscow—and reassembled there to hold the city and its people hostage.

"Yet in the more than four decades since the Nagasaki detona-
tion, no atomic weapon has been exploded in anger. No one, a
you say, has had to show openers."

I thought it over and thought I saw the hole in his argument.

"Governments don't use the weapons," I said, "because
they're afraid of retaliation. Mutual devastation, a no-win situation. But a private operator, one with no territory to defen
. . ."

And there I stopped short, appalled by the abyss that had
opened beneath my feet.

Shaw let me look into it for a while.

"As you perceive," he continued when he was sure I'd seen
enough, "the threat of retaliation keeps governments reasonable
But put such a weapon in private hands and the potential fo
nuclear blackmail is virtually unlimited."

"And the risk of calling the private party's bluff—"

"—would be totally unacceptable, especially if the demand
made were reasonable and the threat credible."

I nodded in the direction of the breakfront, as though talking
to a visible presence. "Which it would be, because of the
Interpol report. But that wouldn't stand up for long: Interpol ma
not know that the bomb was a phony, but the French governmen
certainly does. They'd be sure to blow the whistle."

"Not in this world." The voice was edged with contempt
"The British might and the Russians might and even the Unite
States might. But not the French. Their politicians have th
minds of children, their civil servants are arrogant incompetents
and the national capacity for hubris is absolutely beyond belief
No, sir. No! They would die, literally die, rather than confess
the hollowness of their *force de frappe*."

"And so, you—"

"He wanted the power, yes." The colonel broke into th
exchange. "Like anyone, he wanted the power and he though
Sam Goines would sell it to him."

I turned to look at him.

The bearded man's face was composed now, and he seemed t
feel himself on solid ground, directing his words to no one i
particular, but making sure everyone—especially the one no
physically present—could hear.

"Most people think money and power are pretty much th
same thing. Interchangeable. And to an extent that's true. Bu
Francis Carrington Shaw wanted more, and he thought an ator

bomb, real or not, would give it to him. He was going to run the United States from behind the scenes.''

''And why not?'' the dry voice demanded. ''Why not? Who would be the loser? Could anything be worse, more muddled and incompetent, than the kind of government we've had for the past twenty years?''

No one said anything.

''This country was once the greatest and most powerful on earth,'' Shaw's voice went on. ''And it could be again. All it lacks is determination. You doubt it? Think of what happened in Vietnam. In your own war—all of you.

''It could have been won at any time.

''Lyndon Johnson had committed the troops, and he had even sold himself on bombing Hanoi, because the air force told him they could promise results if the attack was heavy, sudden, and unrestrained. And they could have proved it. But they never got the chance, because Lyndon just wasn't the hard-nose he liked to impersonate.

''The gutless, flannel-mouthed bastard hesitated! And temporized.

''After the Tet offensive, when the North Vietnamese and the Cong had shot their wad and had nothing left and we could have walked over them and taken the whole country, he backed off. When a determined and ruthless bombing effort could have succeeded, he moved slowly and let them build their shelters and bring in their Russian defensive missiles. He threw away his war and he threw away men like you—like you, Preacher. And you, Singleton, and you, Goines. You came home from your war to a nation that spit on you, not because of the stories the news media had been bleating out, but because you had done the one thing Americans will never stand for, will never accept: You had failed to win a war . . . and that damned all of you in the eyes of your countrymen.

''But you had not lost!

''Johnson had lost the war by not being tough enough, while the leaders of North Vietnam had not wavered, never lost sight for a moment of their determination to secure their basic aim, which was nothing short of the total domination of the entire country. At any cost.

''Never were they influenced in the smallest degree by casualties their people suffered . . . or inflicted. The bitterest irony of all was the accusation of genocide made against the Americans. Not one single charge offered at the so-called Stockholm War

Crimes Tribunal of the late 1960s had even the smallest basis in fact. To the contrary, it was the American leaders' squeamishness in using their full potential for destruction that led to their eventual defeat.

"Francis Carrington Shaw wants power?

"You're damned right he wants it! He wants the power to stiffen his government's backbone, to force it to take those actions that are needed if this nation is to survive into the next century. For that power I will take any risk, dare any contumacy. I want it. I need it. I will use it to save us all. Now . . . tell me that this is unworthy. Or that I am wrong."

The voice from the loudspeaker had strengthened as the words went on, rising by degrees to the force and timbre it must have possessed in youth, and the final sentence left a thunder of silence.

I looked at Corner Pocket, whose eyes had gone empty, and he looked away. Some things are too painful for speech. This was a man he'd respected.

But the Voice of Heaven didn't see it that way.

"God!" he said. "God has spoken!"

He fell to his knees beside the poker table and held out his arms toward the breakfront camera, real tears streaming from his eyes.

"This was the one who guided me," he said. "The one whose guidance I have so sorely missed. He speaks now and I hear. Kneel, all of you! We are in the presence of the Almighty!"

Corner Pocket took a deep breath and finally managed to look at me.

"You feel that way, too?" he inquired.

"Not exactly," I said. "But then, I've heard it all before. Or read it, anyway."

His face said he didn't understand.

"History," I said. "It's in there, almost word for word if you change a couple of dates and the names of a battle or two. These are the same arguments—the stab-in-the-back ploy—that Adolf Hitler used to take over Germany in 1932."

A BENEDICTION

May Almighty God, the Father, the Son, and the Holy Ghost, bless you and keep you, now and forevermore . . .

32

FRANCIS CARRINGTON SHAW was done with us. No more words came from the speaker.

But Holy Joe Gillespie couldn't seem to take silence for an answer and remained on his knees beside the table, begging the god of his choice to bless him with divine guidance and promising to be a good and worthy servant—yea, even unto the gates of Sheol. It went on and on, and finally the Mormon youngster who had been dealing took charge, raising the Voice of Heaven to his feet and escorting him out the door to one of the waiting automobiles. He was still babbling when the car door closed.

In marked contrast, Colonel Connor—or Sam Goines, or whoever it was now—had nothing to say at all when two of the security guards who had been hovering outside the villa came inside and made an efficient business of cuffing his hands behind his back. He paused for a moment to look at me just before they went out the door and I looked back but neither of us spoke and the look said nothing at all. We were strangers.

"Think you can zap him on any of this?" I asked when Corner Pocket and I were alone in the room.

He shook his head. "Not even going to try," he said.

I didn't understand.

"We could maybe make a case on Sam Goines," he explained, "but if what he told us is true—and I suspect that it is—we'd play hell proving that he and Colonel Connor are the same man. No. There's an easier way. I'd already given it some thought before we knew who we were really dealing with, and I think it still works. Colonel Connor is going to leave the country the same way he came. In Francis Carrington Shaw's personal Boeing 767, with nothing on his passport to show that he was ever here."

"But—"

"Sam Goines is wanted in lots of places," Corner Pocket went on, paying no attention to my interruption. "Hotter than a pistol. That's why he had to 'die' up at the Penthouse and then switch into the role of a bearded mercenary named David Connor. But he didn't think it all the way through. David Connor was a real live human being—died about a year ago training troops in Chad—and he had a life of his own. Real friends. And real enemies. They still want him in Nigeria and in the United Emirates and in Saudi Arabia and Libya. Take your pick. The 767 will make a fuel stop in one of those places, en route to somewhere else."

I nodded. Slowly. "They'll hang him?"

Corner Pocket shook his head. "No way," he said. "All those governments abolished hanging when the colonial powers pulled out. Uncivilized. Gone back to good old-fashioned public decapitation."

He needed a ride again, and I said it wouldn't be out of my way to take him back to his office—which we both knew was a lie.

But we still had things to talk about.

"Shaw's dying," Corner Pocket said when we were back in my rented car and threading our way through the grounds of El Cholo Loco. "Goines must have known it and thought he could use the atom bomb scam to take over. Getting rid of the Man's closest associates would have been the first step. It's the only way the killings make sense . . . if they're going to make sense at all."

I shrugged.

Nothing to add.

"Jorge Martinez," he said, moving to a new subject when I didn't reply. "Turns out he had more of a local record than we knew about at first. Glitch in the police computer."

I kept my eye front and concentrated on maneuvering the car through a left turn to the inbound lanes of the Strip.

"When they got the kink ironed out," he went on, "the files told us Martinez had lost the security guard job here in town for some reason not stated—and a couple months later he and another guy were picked up for peddling toot."

"Other guy name of de la Torre?" I inquired, still not looking at him.

"Uh-huh. Cross check showed they were in 'Nam together.

Along with someone else we know. So we thought we might ask their mutual friend if he thought it would be worth our while to go looking for de la Torre. For the penthouse shoot-up."

I shook my head. "Forget it," I said.

He didn't reply, and we made the rest of the trip in silence. Thinking our own thoughts.

At the curb outside his office, though, Corner Pocket seemed to have trouble leaving the car.

I waited him out.

"One other thing," he said.

I thought I knew what it was, and I didn't want to hear it, but it was his play and would have to be by his rules.

"Found the phony nurse's uniform," he said finally. "Funny little pillbox cap and all. It was in the wardrobe room out at Holy Joe's place."

He waited to see if I had anything to say. I didn't.

"What we think," he said, "is that Sue Harriet Gillespie was the nurse who killed Sam Goines—or rather McDuff, the actor who was pretending to be him—there at the hospital."

I nodded. "That's how it looks," I agreed.

"Yeah . . ."

He toyed with the door handle and I wanted him to push down on it and get the hell out of there, but he wasn't done talking yet.

"Autopsy didn't turn up much," he went on. "Doc says whoever did McDuff probably used insulin. Leaves no trace, you know? So we figure we're looking for someone who would know about that stuff. A diabetic, maybe . . . or a nurse."

"Yeah," I said. "I kind of figured it that way, too."

He sighed and finally managed to open the door. "You'll tend to it, then?"

"Yes."

He got out and stood up and closed the door behind him.

"My heart's in my mouth doing this," he said, bending down to look back in at me. "The law enforcement in this town is something fierce."

I tried to think of something to say to that, but there wasn't anything, and after a moment or two he stood up again and I drove away.

My floor of the VIP garage was deserted again when I pulled into my slot and shut the engine off.

The door that would take me inside the hotel was directly

opposite and my mind was already up on Maxey's suite. But it
came back to where I was before I had locked the car door.
Easing back into the seat for a moment, I fished the key out of
my pocket and put it back in the ignition and turned the car's
electrical system on, and then pulled the key back out of the slot
and got out again and closed the door and locked it.

And wished I were someone else.

Anyone.

Maxey was waiting with smiles and champagne.

I recognized the clothes. They were the ones she had been
wearing in the Polaroid picture the colonel had shown me before
we started playing poker. But I didn't say anything about that as
she poured champagne into two fluted glasses and handed one to
me and proposed the first toast of the day.

"To us, lover," she said. "And to all the good things of the
world."

I held the glass but didn't drink.

"Come on, come on!" she said. "It's celebration time. Ten
years late, maybe. But we'll make up for that."

My face must have told her she was wrong, and I could feel
the chill that touched her center as she read what was there. She
froze, with the champagne forgotten in her hand.

"What about Sam?" I said when the silence went on too long.

"What about him?" she said. "He's dead—or you wouldn't
be here."

"And Colonel Connor?"

A little hesitation this time.

"Same answer," she said.

"And Harry . . . ?"

This time the pause was a long one, and the *wa* scurried up the
thermometer from cold to hot and back down to cold again and
she took a long, deep breath and put the champagne glass down
on the table.

"Harry?" she said.

"Harry," I said. "You remember Harry—the lover you told
me about? The one you found after Sam got too busy. Harry's
dead, too. And we both know how she got that way."

For a moment, she was going to deny everything and I could
see it building up behind her eyes. Those damned violet eyes.
But the pronoun I'd used in the last sentence told her it was no

use, and her face emptied and she took a long, cold look
reality and accepted it for what it was.

"How long?" she said quietly.

"How long have I known who Harry was? Not long. I shoul
have twigged back at the Gillespie compound, when Sue Harri
told me to call her Harry. The name rang a bell. But th
explosion came right afterward, and I didn't think about it aga
until this morning."

She nodded slowly, seeing how it had been, and then gave m
her very best shot.

"You could forget it," she said. "I could make you forget."

And she could.

It would be easy, because I would be helping, and I coul
probably even have found a way to straighten things out wi
Corner Pocket—or at least keep him quiet until we could b
somewhere else. Sitting there and looking at her and remembe
ing how it had been for us and how it still was, I wanted her in
way I'd thought was over for me, ended long before we met, an
the knowledge came as a shock of recognition. A realization
what I was about to lose, and the certainty that it didn't have
be that way. That all I had to do to change the future was no
my head. And overlook a couple of murders.

It would be easy.

So easy.

"No," I said, forcing myself to look directly at her as
said the words. "No, Maxey. I would if I could. God knows
would . . ."

"God."

The single word said it all, a paragraph passing between ol
friends and lovers who knew each other far too well to nee
more.

And then she took a long, deep breath and whatever had bee
between us—communication, rapport, sharing, whatever it ha
been—was gone. She stood in silence, face empty of emotio
and there was a wall of frosted steel around the core that I ha
seen and touched, and the woman in the room with me wa
someone I had never met before and never would know.
wondered how long she had been impersonating Maxey, ho
deeply she had buried the original. But it didn't really matter.

"I have bank accounts in the Caribbean and in Switzerland,
she said. "And Sam's plane is at the airport, with the crew

lf-hour call. By this time tomorrow I could be anywhere on
rth.''

True.

"Twenty-four hours," she said. "One full day. For old times'
ke?''

Not much to ask for.

"All right," I said. "Twenty-four hours."

She didn't thank me and I didn't say anything and she moved
ound the suite—into the bedroom and bath, and finally into the
tchen—picking up various things and stuffing them into the
ersized tote she'd been carrying at Holy Joe Gillespie's com-
und the day before. It didn't take much time, and finally she
as standing beside the door.

"No luggage?" I said.

She shook her head. "Nothing I'll need," she said. "Travel-
g light from now on." There was something else, and she
arted to say it but didn't, and turned to the door and opened it
d stepped out into the hallway.

"Preacher . . .'' she said.

I looked at her and waited.

"I love you," she said.

Maybe it was true.

"Good-bye, Maxey," I said.

The moments after the door closed were too long.

She would be going down the corridor to the elevators and I
uld be out there in time to stop her and tell her to come back
d we could work it out, we could work anything out, because
is is not a world of absolutes and people can grow and change
d no one can live a life that is totally logical. It's too cold.
nd too alone.

I stood up, but instead of going to the door I opened the top
awer of the buffet. The Scheherazade thinks of everything;
rds and chips were there in neat array. I took one of the decks
ith the hotel crest on the back and broke the seal and started
ck to the table, but it was no use. I couldn't help going into
e mini-kitchen. And opening the freezer door. And looking
side. And finding what I had expected:

Nothing.

Maxey hadn't packed because she had decided not to leave
day. She would send me instead. The dynamite and blasting
p were gone.

• • •

Once I was back at the table, with the balcony door open, r
hands went on automatic pilot and took over the work of shu
fling the cards and cutting them and shuffling again. Beginni
to deal . . .

My wristwatch was still missing, and the amenities provid
by the hotel did not of course include any form of clock. B
seconds and minutes counted themselves off in my head regar
less of distractions.

The game was five card stud, two handed. Just me and t
presence across the table. Hole cards landed and were covered
once by the first exposed cards.

Both of them aces.

*By now the elevator would have arrived and she would be
her way down . . .*

Rote actions, the repetition of familiar patterns even wh
unproductive, are known as a relatively ineffective way of tryi
to control compulsive behavior. Alcoholics and cigarette smo
ers concentrate on crossword puzzles and take part in athletics
fight their addiction. It seldom works. I dealt the second expos
cards: queen of diamonds for the other hand, eight of clubs f
me. Possible straight bets.

Across the mezzanine and down the escalator . . .

The urge to get out of there, to run after Maxey and stop l
and tell her to come back, was a fire in the blood. There cou
still be time. It didn't have to be this way. We would think
something. But I sat still and moved my hands and gave t
other side of the table the jack of spades and myself the eight
hearts. Low pair bets.

*Out into the VIP garage now, feeling above the grille a
finding the catch and releasing it and raising the hood . . .*

I'd heard the story from Manny Temple years ago: Igniti
bombs had been a kind of occupational hazard in his line
work, but a friend of his had figured out a way to cope w
them. These devices are usually wired to the induction coil a
then grounded, to explode as soon as the car's ignition system
engaged. No danger in planting a bomb as long as the system
off. But if it's left on, the dynamite goes off the moment t
bomber tries to wire up that second contact. The final card
dealt across the table was a ten. I caught a third eight.

Connecting the wire to the coil . . .

• • •

Maxey's suite was directly above the VIP garage and the force of the explosion down below rattled the sliding door to the balcony and the dishes in the kitchen. But my hand was steady. I had already said my good-byes and held the wake, and the funeral had been years ago and I had missed it. I turned my hole card and looked, but it was no surprise because I had been dealing and I had started with the one I would need to complete a full house.

Two aces. And three eights.

That's another thing about cheating at poker: If you're good at it—really good—sometimes you can even cheat yourself.

A BENEDICTION (Concluded)

Amen.

33

WINDING UP DETAILS and touching bases took a while—even poor tame Bill Bowers didn't buy my story about Maxey getting a bomb intended for me because I'd loaned her the key to my car—but Corner Pocket ran a little high-level interference and finally it was done.

We didn't talk again.

Nothing to say.

Two days later I was back in Best Licks, showing Margery the $87,540 Happy Apodaca had saved for me from the first game—and finding out that we didn't need it after all.

"Guy from the IRS phoned," she said. "Told me to forget it. All a mistake. Computer foul-up or something."

Megalomaniac or no, Francis Carrington Shaw was a man of his word.

Wonderful.

I didn't know whether to laugh or cry.

But I had to explain. So I did, all of it, starting with Shaw and not forgetting Danny DiMarco or Manny or Terry McDuff or Happy Apodaca or Sam or the Colonel or Holy Joe or Harry or Big Trouble or Little Trouble or the bomb. Or Maxey.

And when I was done Margery just looked at me.

Her mother was Hopi and her father was Mandingo and the beautiful, imperious face that was their legacy to her never tells anyone anything she doesn't want to tell. In all the time we've known each other, I have never been able to read it.

But I didn't have to.

"You killed her," she said.

"She killed herself, Margery. Trying to wire an ignition bomb to my car."

"She loved you."

"She worked with Goines all the way—until the first time he

315

came off a loser. Killed at least two people, and it didn't mean a
thing. She used her knowledge as a nurse to load the needle Sue
Harriet Gillespie used on Terry McDuff, then rigged a bomb in
Sue Harriet's car to make sure her mouth stayed shut. There may
have been others . . .''

"You loved her."

I didn't reply to that, because I couldn't. I didn't know the
answer then and I still don't and I don't suppose I ever will. I'd
wanted her and needed her and our times together had been good
and maybe that was love or maybe it could have been love. Or
maybe not.

"Margery . . ."

But she was already headed for the door.

"Not now, Preacher," she said, without looking back at me.
"Later. Tomorrow, maybe. But I don't want to talk to you right
now."

She went out and closed the door behind her.

I sat there for a while, wishing she would come back and
wondering if she did what I could say and whether things would
ever be the same between us again. I depended on her. In more
ways than one.

Nariyuki no matsu.

I went into the kitchen and brought out the jug of triple-run
blockader the sheriff of our county had delivered the last time he
came for a visit, and poured three fingers into a glass and
thought about adding an ice cube and sneered at myself and put
the jug back and carried the drink out to the balcony.

The sun was gone and clouds were drifting through the trees
of the pass into the valley, their tops white and dreamlike below
me.

I took a sip of the blockader. But it tasted like the horse had
kidney trouble and I poured it out, over the railing, and stood
there for a long time with the empty glass in my hand watching
the sky and the trees and the clouds below and thinking some
of the darkest, coldest, loneliest thoughts that I own.